DEMON NIGHT

DEMON NIGHT

J. Michael Straczynski

E. P. DUTTON NEW YORK

Published in the United States by E. P. Dutton,
a division of NAL Penguin Inc.,
2 Park Avenue, New York, N.Y. 10016

Published simultaneously in Canada
by Fitzhenry and Whiteside, Limited, Toronto.

Library of Congress Cataloging-in-Publication Data
Straczynski, J. Michael, 1954–
Demon night.
I. Title.
PS3569.T6758D46   1988   813'.54   87-36432
ISBN: 0-525-24646-0

Designed by REM Studio

1 3 5 7 9 10 8 6 4 2

First Edition

For Kathryn . . . for completeness.

Empty-handed I go, and yet the spade is in my hands;
I walk on foot, and yet I am riding on horseback:
When I pass over the bridge,
Lo, the water flows not, but the bridge is flowing.
—ZEN PROVERB

There's little good in sedentary small towns. Mostly indifference spiced with an occasional vapid evil—or worse, a conscious one.

—Stephen King

The conditions of a solitary bird are five:
The first, that it flies to the highest point;
the second, that it does not suffer for company,
*   not even of its own kind;*
the third, that it aims its beak to the skies;
the fourth, that it does not have a definite color;
the fifth, that it sings very softly.

—San Juan de la Cruz

DEMON NIGHT

PROLOGUE

It began as it always did. As it always would.

Back when his last name was Langren, not Matthews.

It was the kind of day when, despite the morning cool, the sun seemed somehow brighter than it should be. The air was clean, the smell of pines almost dizzying. A perfect day, his father had decided, to drive down into town for the few supplies they couldn't mend or make or grow themselves. Following the rains that had ravaged Dredmouth Point, imprisoning everyone behind storm windows and in front of stoves and fireplaces, the break in weather felt almost as good as a vacation.

So they had piled into the mud-spattered Buick station wagon—Eric, his parents Marsh and Claris—and started the long, winding drive down the slope toward town.

In retrospect, it seemed they were no sooner out of sight of the house when the sky went from blue to gray, as if nature had been putting on a pretty face in hopes of drawing them out, and, now that it had done so, quickly abandoned the disguise. Cloud shadows slid across the road, swallowing the old Buick and moving on to engulf the narrow, jagged slope and everything on it in one huge bite.

Eric noted the change only distantly, his attention fixed as usual on his father, navigating the stubborn Buick up furrowed back roads slick with mud and leaves. He was always amazed at his father's ability to sense where the road was firm enough to hold them, steering around leaf-covered potholes in spring and around black ice in winter, the kind of all-but-invisible dangers that could send your car spinning out of control.

There were moments when Eric thought he could almost sense what his father was feeling, share the intuitive knowledge that *that* part of the road was unsafe, but *this* part was okay. It was a game he played sometimes. And sometimes it felt like more than a game.

They were halfway toward town when it began to rain. Gently, at first, then harder. The sound grew to a roar within minutes. Eric wiped his sleeve across the steamed-up window, watching the bloated clouds cutting off the tops of hills and pine trees. The windshield wipers sliced the world in front of them into blurred fragments of gray and brown.

His father sat hunched over the wheel, peering intently into the rain. "Figures," he said, not so much to Claris, or to the boy sitting quietly in the rear seat, as to himself. He allowed a momentary glance to his right. "You see any sign of an ark filled with animals, you be sure to let me know, all right?"

Claris wiped at the windshield with a handkerchief from her purse. "I couldn't see a whole parade of arks go by through this." Despite her efforts, the windshield only became more smeared. "Must be on the outside."

"Don't worry, Mom," Eric said from the rear seat, catching the concern in his mother's voice. "We're almost there."

Marsh smiled. "Eight years old, and calm as a cucumber. Sure you're not eight going on eighty?"

Eric caught his father's glance in the rearview mirror—then lost it as the car suddenly fishtailed to the left, sliding on the muddy incline. Marsh fought the wheel, applying brakes and gas at the same time, easing it ahead until it straightened out. They were paralleling the ridge now, the town proper visible far below. Just a little farther, and they'd be clear of the drop-off and on the last leg of the drive.

But his father was pale, drawn. His fingers opened and closed nervously on the wheel. He looked over at Claris. "I didn't see that one," he said, his voice low, troubled. "I didn't *see it,*" he said again, as if trying to convey something that he either couldn't or wouldn't put into words.

If his mother understood, she gave no sign, just kept watching the road through the rain-covered windshield. "Maybe we can find a spot wide enough to turn around, head back home. We can always try later."

"Yeah, maybe." Whatever concern there had been in his voice was now gone—or under control. "Keep an eye out back there, Eric."

"Yes, Dad," Eric said, and peered down through the window. He could see only fog and trees, a tangle of branches that covered the slope that led down to the lake, now barely visible as a flat grayness that merged with the fog.

Above and to one side, momentarily visible through a break in the fog, he spotted the cave. As always, it brought a shudder. He'd never actually been up there—his father had denied him permission even to go near the place—but he held a secret dread for that great gaping wound in the earth. Maybe it was something he picked up from his father, the way he looked whenever Eric asked about the cave. His cheeks flushed against the cold. What a sissy, he thought. It was a silly fear, and the cave was just a cave. And yet . . .

He was pulled back to the present by the sound of his father's voice. Marsh was barely inching the car along through the rain now, looking from rearview mirror to side mirror to road.

"I don't like this," he said. "I don't like this at all. Something's wrong." Had he seen the cave too, Eric wondered, then stopped the thought. Of course not. His father was a grown man. Grown men weren't afraid of caves.

"Can't we stop for a while, let the storm pass?" Claris asked.

Marsh shook his head. "Some damn fool might come shooting down the road and knock us clear off. Can't stop, can't turn around—"

Above them, the rain pounded on the car roof like some crazed animal trying to get inside.

"Just a little farther," Claris said.

"Yeah," Marsh said, "just a little farther."

Just another few hundred yards, up a short incline, and they'd be off the narrow ridge and onto the main road into town.

There they could stop, or turn back. A little farther. Just around the next bend.

Then: the sound he would never forget. The strangled noise from his mother's throat.

"Marsh!"

Another car barreled toward them, barely holding the narrow road, tires slinging up mud and leaves.

Marsh slammed the horn twice, three times.

Nowhere to turn.

With amazing clarity, Eric saw the face behind the other window, caught in the second before impact: drunk, asleep, or something else. A shadow—

"No!"

The sound of metal rending metal. The car shuddered, veered right. Toward the ridge. Mud shifted and gave way beneath the tires. Then the world spun, end over end over end.

His mother screamed.

Eric slammed into the front seat, felt something crack in his side. The roof buckled. Glass sprayed into the car. Something hit him behind the ear. The world blurred and grew indistinct—

The sound stopped.

The Buick lay on its side. Eric tried to move, but his limbs were slow to respond, and then only with pain that shot up into his skull and made the whole world tilt crazily. He found himself wedged into the gap between the front and rear seats. From the corner of his eye, he could see his mother half in and half out the front window. The glass had worked her like a saw.

"Mom?" he said, and swallowed hard, choking on blood. She said nothing.

Then, from the driver's side, "Eric . . ."

Despite the pain that squeezed his lungs, Eric crawled up over the top of the seat. His father was wedged in on top of the steering wheel. Blood was pouring down over the top of his head where it had broken the windshield. The only sound was an irregular breath, a catch, then a shuddering exhalation.

"Dad? *Dad?*"

His father's eyes glazed, then fixed on him. Eric could see now that the blood on his face was coming from more than the top of his head. It was pouring out of his nose and mouth. In a flash of thought, a hot coal in the middle of his forehead, he knew that his father was all broken up inside, that the steering wheel had punched him like a massive fist, severing arteries and crushing the heart.

Knew beyond all doubt that his father was dying.

"Not . . . fair," his father managed. "Have to—tell you . . ."

"Dad? Please, don't—"

His father tried to speak again, but his tongue refused to obey, only lolled uselessly in his mouth. Eric struggled to move forward, to touch him, but with each move the world kicked slantwise all around him.

Desperately his father uncrooked one shattered finger, and pointed across the lake, toward the other side. His eyes fixed on Eric, pleading for him to understand.

Then he shuddered, and sighed, forcing torn lips to form the last word he would speak, the only benediction he could offer: ". . . watch."

For a long moment, too numb and scared to cry, Eric waited for something more. But his father lay motionless, the wheezing of his lungs silent now, his hand still pointing. Though it hurt to do so, Eric raised his head. For a moment the world spun dizzily around him. He blinked hard, then looked off across the lake, to where a momentary break in the fog revealed the only thing that his father could have been pointing at.

The cave gaped down at him like a black and lipless mouth.

Then it disappeared behind the fog, and Eric felt himself go cold. He trembled, the world graying at the edges around him.

And he heard his father's voice.

He looked over at his father—and found himself staring into the face of something long dead, a horrible thing with patches of yellow flesh clinging to the blackened skull, eye sockets staring vacantly into his own eyes. The voice came from deep inside its throat, echoing up through a lipless, still mouth.

Come home, Eric, it said, over and over. *Come home, come home, come home, comehome . . .*

Eric screamed.

And woke to the sound of glass shattering and wind rushing through his cramped apartment. Woke to the sound of wood creaking in the dark until it snapped. The noise was all around him, deafening. He clamped his hands over his ears, shutting it out, eyes closed tight. *I don't want to deal with this I don't want to see it.*

A moment more, and the sound stopped. He pulled his hands away from his ears, listening in the night. For the moment, it was over.

He reached out, found the bedside lamp, feeling gingerly for shards of broken glass, finding none. This time the carnage had passed it by. He flicked on the light, expecting the worst— and finding it.

"Oh God . . ."

Mirrors were shattered, drawers were pulled out and overturned, clothes lay scattered and torn. The bookshelves he had installed last month were torn down, leaving gaping holes in the wall where the bolts had been yanked out. His black-and-white portable was now a smoking ruin.

No more Carson for you, he thought, and giggled, fighting down the note of hysteria he heard there.

He got up, feeling for his slippers, and stepped carefully around the debris into the next room.

The rest of the apartment was just as bad.

He had done it again. Of that there was no doubt. His head was throbbing the way it always did afterward. Before it had started to get really bad, he had thought—incorrectly—that he could control the impulse. But he had always failed, usually with disastrous consequences.

Now he did not even dare try.

The pain was setting in, just behind his right eye. More evidence that he was responsible. Even asleep.

He stood in the doorway, his head only an inch or two from the top of the frame, and thought, It's out of control. Again.

But that wasn't quite right. It had never been this terrible before. Neither had the dream.

He looked across to what was left of the full-length mirror on the door, and searched the thirty-two-year-old face he saw there for the eight-year-old boy who had gone off the cliff with his father. His hair had been blond then. Now it was thinner and darker. A patch of gray had appeared behind and below his left ear. But the face told it all. Lines in lieu of smooth skin. Shadows under his eyes from lack of sleep.

Not bad-looking, really, he thought. But tired. So damn, bloody tired of running.

Come home, Eric, come home.

That was the part of the dream that had first appeared three months ago. It had been bad that night, too, though not nearly as bad as this. Then, it happened a second time, six weeks ago. Luckily, he'd been alone that night, camping. He had no way of knowing what would have happened if he'd been home, or with someone.

(And yet, even alone, hadn't he thought he heard whispers in the woods, felt that he wasn't alone at all?)

This, though, was the worst yet. The apartment wasn't just damaged—it was now unlivable. Water spilled onto the carpeted living room from broken pipes. The small aquarium he'd bought last month had exploded with such force that bits of glass were actually embedded in the facing wall. The few fish inside were on the floor now. Most had stopped moving.

He would have to leave again. Quickly.

"Why can't you stop?" he asked quietly, speaking to the night. "Why can't you just leave me alone?"

Come home, Eric, come home.

I've tried, he thought. But each time, something had gotten in his way. Each time, it hadn't *felt* right—and wasn't that what his father had told him, so many times, back before he really understood what his father had been trying to say? To listen to his feelings? And the feelings had been borne out. Logistics. Money. Jobs. Relationships. *Something* had always stopped him.

But there wasn't anything stopping him now, was there?

He looked around at the ruined remains of his apartment. Certainly nothing left here to hold him back.

Come home, Eric, come home.

"All right," he said. "All right."

It was time.

Time to go home.

PART ONE

THE POINT

. . . Come, seeling night,
Scarf up the tender eye of pitiful day,
And with thy bloody and invisible hand
Cancel and tear to pieces that great bond
Which keeps me pale! Light thickens, and the crow
Makes wing to the rooky wood;
Good things of day begin to droop and drowse,
Whiles night's black agents to their preys do rouse.

—MACBETH, III, ii

ONE

ERIC

By noon, Eric was forty miles farther north than he had been since leaving Dredmouth Point. He was making good progress, doing what he always did.

He took the way that *felt* right.

When he crossed into Maine, he caught Highway 2 east, past New Sharon and Norridgewock, and over a wide concrete bridge fording the Kennebec River. Then lunch and a fill-up for the thirsty Datsun in Skowhegan, and back onto the highway.

He began to take note of the names of the towns he passed as more than just circles on a map, benchmarks to determine how many miles he'd made that hour. Yarmouth and Bowdoinham, Pittston and Vassalboro. He wondered about the people who lived and worked there, who went to movies and had affairs and complained about the weather. He wondered what the people of Shawmut were like, and how they were different from the residents of Palmyra. . . .

Don't think about what you're doing, just look at the names on the signs and keep driving.

Good advice, he thought, and slowed, getting ready for the next turnoff.

2

After the accident, Aunt Sandra had taken him in, moved him to her house in Minnesota. She had seemed determined to help him get over the trauma. She had formally adopted him, even given him her last name, Matthews—his mother's maiden name—so he would have a real family. At least that was what she had said. But he'd wondered more than once since then if that was the whole truth. She'd never talked much about his father, whom she considered more than a little eccentric, though he could never get her to pin down exactly why, or in what manner. To his aunt, the name Langren would always be associated with tragedy. Better to leave it behind.

He'd grown into a relatively calm youth, though nagged by a sense of frustration and curiosity concerning his father, about whom he could recall very little. He felt a need to *understand,* to ask questions that he knew would go frustratingly unanswered. Other than that, he was reasonably happy. His aunt had been dedicated to making a good home for him. And while the sound of a car backfiring could sometimes cause panic in him, his sleep was sound.

She had never taken him to see his parents' grave. Not since the funeral. In fact, she'd been terribly anxious to get him away from Dredmouth Point altogether.

He always wondered what she'd been so afraid of.

It wasn't until years later, after she was gone and the *feelings* began to awaken in him, that he began to suspect an answer.

But by then it was too late. Whatever answers he could have gotten were buried in yet another grave.

And now the nightmares had come, and with them the destruction that he knew *he* was causing.

What wouldn't you tell me, Aunt Sandra?
And why?
Why?

Eric hit the interchange and angled northeast, leaving the cities behind. By midmorning he had passed Green Lake and Ellsworth Falls, where the highway eased east again. He followed the rocky Maine coastline past farms that grew hay and timothy, corn and alfalfa. Gray and white houses along the road showed cornerboards and shingles weathered by wind and rain. Parapets and widows' walks appeared beside shuttered attic windows that looked out over Bar Harbor and the Mount Desert Narrows. Where earlier the land had been thick with marshes and ponds, here were long stretches of barren rock that led down to the sea. The brisk breeze that whistled in through the open car windows carried with it sharp traces of salt and seaweed.

A parade of tin-reflector names whistled past him: Gouldsboro and Milbridge, Columbia Falls and Jonesboro, with Milton Mountain looming to the north. Then, just after Whitneyville, came the sign that said MACHIAS 2 MI. EAST MACHIAS/JUNCT. 191 6 MI. followed, in short order, by the one for which he had been watching for the last twelve miles. A stenciled sign staked into the ground by an off-ramp that was little more than an access road: DREDMOUTH POINT.

I was born somewhere down that road, he thought. Irrational as it was, he played briefly with the fantasy that he would pull into town and someone would look up, see something familiar in his eyes, some hint of his father in chin or mouth or ears, and say, Welcome home, son! We missed you.

It was a momentary indulgence, and he pushed it away. He would not be recognized. If his name were still Eric Langren, then people might notice. His father had told him that there had been a Langren living in the Point for as long as anyone could remember. But he was Eric Matthews now, and no one knew him.

Which was probably for the best. He might learn more about his family by being a vaguely curious observer than if they knew he was Marsh Langren's son.

He turned off onto the access road, and as soon as he had passed the stand of trees that bordered the highway, he saw for the first time in twenty-five years the thin strip of land that reached into Machias Bay like a bony, pointing finger.

Dredmouth Point.

Or, to those who lived there, simply the Point.

Chuckholes and bumps in the unpaved road took their audible toll on the Datsun's alignment. The road dipped abruptly, then curved past a row of high pines. The bay disappeared quickly as he angled deeper into the heart of the Point. Just short of entering the town proper, though, he took another right, onto an even narrower dirt road that skirted the shoreline.

He wasn't ready. Not yet. It was too soon.

He guided the Datsun past high curtains of goldenrod and pricker bushes until, with a final, slow turn, he caught sight of Machias Bay again. Waves slammed into the shoreline twenty yards past the road, breaking on the long wooden jetty from which (according to the road signs) a ferry departed every two hours for Bucks Harbor.

A gray sea reflecting a gray, overcast sky; black and gray rocks pummeled by darkening waves; and the jetty, gray through the saltwater mist—all of it shadowy, vague, and dreamlike.

Only this time it wasn't a dream. He was home.

3

Eric walked to the end of the jetty and stood with palms flat on the wooden railing, cool and slick with sea spray. He looked deep into the waters below, amazed as always at how the sea never failed to put him at ease. If he stared long enough, he could lose himself in the whitecapped waves that crashed against the pilings with clockwork regularity. Going into town could wait.

For now, it was enough simply to *be.*

"What's she sayin' to you, mister?"

Eric jumped, startled not so much by the voice and the old man standing behind him as by the curious thought hammering at the back of his head: I didn't feel him coming.

"Didn't mean to scare you," the old man said. He was thin, his hands and face weathered into a fine tracery of wrinkles. He sidled up to the railing beside Eric. "The way you were looking at the sea, I was sure she must've been telling you some mighty interesting stories."

Eric followed the old man's gaze. "Sorry. Whatever she's saying, it's beyond me to figure out."

The old man nodded noncommittally and pulled a crumpled pack of cigarettes from his peacoat. He offered one to Eric with the grudging look of someone who'd prefer the offer to be politely refused. It was. He took a cigarette for himself and lit it.

"Too bad. You'll never know what you're missing."

Eric smiled. "Does she talk to you?"

"Oh, sure. Lots of times. The sea talks to everyone—provided you know how to listen. Tells some mighty interesting stories, too."

"Such as?"

The old man winked. "Well, now, I don't think it'd be very gentlemanly to go talking about it to strangers, now would it?"

"No, I suppose not," Eric said, and laughed.

"My point exactly."

After that, they stood quietly for a while, watching the first thin streamers of twilight spreading out over the water. The old man took a long drag on his cigarette. "How soon do you figure on finding a place to stay?"

Eric looked at the old man with growing curiosity. "What makes you think I don't have a place to stay?"

"Common sense. I've never seen you before, and I see just about everybody. You don't have the look of those rich folk who come crawlin' all over the place every summer, so I'm betting you're not staying in any of the cabins across the bay." He snuffed the butt out against the railing and slipped it into his jacket pocket.

"No," he continued, "the way I figure it, you just now got here, you're not rich—not even well off—and you're lookin' for a place to stay that won't cost you your life savings."

"Dead on," Eric said, impressed. "You got all that from just looking at me?"

"That," the old man said, "and the fact that I took the liberty of lookin' inside your car parked out in front. I saw a couple of beat-up looking suitcases and a bunch of other stuff, none of it what I'd call fresh from the Sears catalogue."

"Just a regular Sherlock Holmes, eh?" The old man nodded his acceptance of the compliment. "Of course, it *is* a violation of privacy. I don't know if I should be upset or not."

"Depends on whether or not you want the name of a place where you can get a room cheap."

Eric considered it. "I'm not upset."

"Try Point Cabins. Over on the leeward side of the Point. Ask for Zachariah C. Franklin. I'll be headin' that way myself in a bit, if you want to follow my car. Just got to wait here for the ferry, in case there's any more folks comin' in."

"Is this some kind of public service you provide—meeting tourists at the dock and telling them the cheapest place to stay in town?"

"Something like that," he replied. "So all you have to do is tell the folks at Point Cabins that I sent you, and you'll get a good deal."

"All right, so when I get there, who shall I say sent me?"

"Most folks around here call me Zach."

Eric grinned. "As in Zachariah C. Franklin? As in Point Cabins, Owner Of?"

"Caught me," he said, only a corner of his mouth betraying amusement. He thrust out a hand. "Pleased to meet you."

The ferry arrived fifteen minutes later, empty of passengers.

4

Eric followed Zach's mud-spattered green pickup around the tip of the Point to the western side, which was sheltered from the winds that swept in off the Atlantic at dusk. Point Cabins dotted the shoreline in a dozen tiny places, sprouting up like stubble on a craggy jaw. The wooden cabins had been cut from the surrounding pine and elm trees that grew wherever the ground stood firm enough for roots to take hold.

They stopped beside the two-story house that Zach shared with his wife—the Big House, he called it, in tones meant to be both melodramatic and foreboding—long enough for Zach to point to a small cabin a few hundred feet distant. "Rent's due promptly each Monday, no public drunkenness and no illicit activity permitted—drug-related or otherwise. Meals are served twice a day at the Big House. Stragglers late for breakfast or supper fend for themselves.

"Beyond that, you can do what you want—which, around here, ain't exactly a whole lot." Zach considered this for a moment, then glanced slyly at a figure silhouetted in the lighted window behind him. "Guess it's sorta like being married, eh?"

Eric allowed that it might be.

"Well, dinner's on in about half an hour," Zach said. "I'll tell the missus to set another place."

"No, that's all right. It's awfully short notice—"

Zach waved away his protest. "Nonsense. Lord knows, she'll carry on all right, but you pay her no attention. That's just her way. She'll fuss and crab, but she's always glad to have someone new to talk to."

Eric started toward the cabin. "What about the key?"

"The cabin door's open. You can pick up the key when you come for supper. 'Round here, there's no sense in keeping an empty cabin locked. We've got our share of oddballs, no mistake. But the Point's a safe place to live. It's a nice town. I think you'll like it."

With that, Zach turned and clumped up the wooden stairs that led up to the back porch. For a moment, Eric glimpsed an old-fashioned tile kitchen with a gas stove and a metal sink, over which someone was working. Then the door shut again, and Eric started off along the footpath that led to the cabin.

Shouldering his bags through the narrow door, he stepped inside.

It wasn't much.

A double bed stood with its headboard against the far wall, a nightstand on one side. Along the narrow right wall a dresser and sideboard framed an open closet. A few sticks of furniture—two wingbacked chairs, a coffee table, a larger table, and a footstool—were arranged in a rough circle on the wood floor. A long couch that sagged slightly in the center was hunkered against the near wall, beneath a bay window. Another doorway, presumably leading to the bathroom, was at one end of the cabin, a large fireplace at the other.

No, it wasn't much. But, like most of the places he had lived in the last few years, it was comfortable and reasonably clean. The walls looked solid enough to keep out the wind, and the bed was depressed in all the right places. With a few logs burning in the fireplace, the cabin might almost look friendly.

He threw his duffel bag onto the bed, unzipped it, and pulled out his clothes. Some he deposited in the dresser—in drawers lined with fresh, rose-scented paper—leaving the rest for later. He stripped off his clothes, stepped into the spartan bathroom, and showered quickly.

As he toweled dry, he glanced at the medicine cabinet mirror, and the Tired Man peered out at him.

Christ, he thought, I'm actually here.

He headed out of the bathroom, pulling on a heavy gray sweater and a brown corduroy jacket. If I didn't know better, he thought grimly, heading out the door, I'd almost think I looked normal.

Outside, night had slipped quietly over Dredmouth Point. Most of the other cabins were dark. Their windows stared out over the water like dead eyes—eyes that would remain lifeless until the next season.

And yet, somehow . . .

Perhaps it was a trick of the light, the twilight glimmering off the water, but the cabins seemed almost to glow, like an afterimage, or like a positive photograph overlaid with its own negative. He picked one cabin out, then another, and in each case he felt he knew something about it—the sorts of people who had stayed there, the joys and tragedies that had taken place within its walls.

Like recordings that only he could hear, the deserted cabins still vibrated with the subtle touches and sounds of the departed summer boarders. Over there, in that cabin, an old man had died peacefully, in his sleep. From another, not twenty feet away, he could almost hear the sound of children calling out in the cool night for permission to linger just five more minutes in the enchanted darkness. The shadows that stretched along wall and water, door and tree, resonated with the sounds of life. But they were only echoes, and in time they would fade, grow pale, and finally slide off into silence.

With that thought, the sensation fled, bleeding away like quicksilver.

Eric quickened his pace toward the Big House, troubled almost as much at feeling like an unwilling voyeur as he was by what the shadows seemed to be telling him.

Dredmouth Point was dying.

TWO

LIZ

Despite its ominous name, dinner in the Big House turned out to be altogether pleasant. Zach and his wife, Sarah, held forth at either end of a long table flanked by a handful of boarders in high-backed wooden chairs. A single place setting at Zach's elbow was conspicuously empty.

Sarah Franklin was a jovial, friendly woman of a size just short of grand. She brought in an apparently endless parade of trays from the kitchen, slipping in and out of the conversations that ringed the table, adding little jokes and chiding the diners—Zach in particular—whenever the opportunity arose.

For the most part, Eric simply listened as he ate, trying to keep all the names straight.

Sitting directly across from him was Sam Crawford, professor of anthropology at the University of Maine in Farmington. Reared in the Point, he was, as Zach related with considerable pride, one of the few locals who had ever gone on to college and academic success.

"Usually, once they make good outside," Zach said, "they never come near the place again. Not Sam, though. No common sense."

Seated beside Sam was Father Duncan Kerr, who had been transferred to Dredmouth Point, and the parish of St. Benedict's, ten years ago. Finally, there were Mark and Kathy Orwoll, who kept largely to themselves throughout dinner and left quickly afterward, ending their week's stay at Point Cabins in time to catch the last ferry out.

As Eric had expected, there were the usual questions: What was he doing in the Point? How long did he expect to stay? Had he ever been to these parts before? He answered in terms he hoped were general enough to satisfy without arousing further curiosity: late-season tourist, just passing through, had only been in the Point once before.

Which was considerably easier than: Yes, I was born here, and my father died here, and I'm here to find out who he was and what I am and why I can't sleep at night without something tearing the place up and my name is really Langren but no one's supposed to know that, you don't mind, do you?

Oh. And pass the butter, please.

After dinner, they adjourned to the front room of the Big House for coffee and cake. The room was decorated in an explosion of furniture gathered in bits and pieces over many years. There were old brass lanterns, ships' bells, and a barometer mounted in the wheel of a sailing ship. There were painted seascapes and carved bits of driftwood inset with mother-of-pearl. Dozens of framed photographs filled in the few remaining gaps along the walls and paraded across cabinets like a family reunion in miniature.

"Quite a load of junk, isn't it?" Zach asked, noting Eric's glance.

Eric nodded. "It's very nice. Must've taken you a long time to collect all this."

"All my life. I was raised right here on the Point—not counting the War, of course. When I came home, I came home to stay. Flew in an airplane for the first time since V-E Day when I had to go to Los Angeles for my son's wife's funeral."

Zach glanced over at a portrait in the center of the fireplace mantel, clearly a place of honor. A young man smiled out of the framed photograph alongside a pretty, gentle-looking woman. The young man had Zach's eyes.

"He just married again, last year. It's been awfully hard on him. Me, I could never do it. Being left alone like that, especially at my age, I guess I'd probably just wither up and die."

He stole a mischievous glance at Sarah and whispered, "Besides, if it's all the same to you, I'd rather not spend eternity with *two* wives, thank you very much. One's hard enough for a man to tolerate, even when he's alive and can escape to the pool hall for an hour. But once you're in heaven, there ain't no place to go, is there, Father?"

"I don't think you'll have much to worry about on that score," Sarah cut in, setting down a tray of coffee cake. "Where I'm going, they won't let you in anyway. Even the Lord has some standards."

Father Kerr sipped at his tea, smiling faintly. He was a stout man, just short of heavyset, who worked hard to maintain a stern expression. But the effect was sabotaged by a sense of humor that hovered just behind his eyes, and a voice that, no matter how he worked at it, sounded open and friendly. "You wouldn't have much choice in the matter, Zach. Once you're in, you're in. There's no place else to go—at least, no place you'd care to spend your holidays. Assuming, as Sarah said, that you'd be admitted in the first place, which is problematic at best. And as far as pool halls are concerned, there's no scripture on the issue either way, but if anyone can find a poolroom in heaven, it's you."

"You just watch me," Zach said. He stood and picked up his cup from the coffee table, leaving a wet ring on the polished walnut. "I'm goin' back for something with a head on it—anybody else want one?"

Sam shook his head. "If I'm ever going to make it to your age, I think I'll stick to coffee." His voice was firmer than it had to be.

He drinks too much—no, he *used* to, and he's afraid he'll start again, Eric saw in a flicker of thought.

"Suit yourself," Zach said, and continued on toward the kitchen. "Me, I live by what Sam Clemens said a long time ago: 'If you can't get to seventy by a comfortable road, don't go.' Last chance. Anybody else? Eric?"

"I'll pass."

"Not a real man in the place," Zach grumbled, then disappeared into the kitchen.

Eric sat back in his chair and relaxed, feeling better than he had in a long time. "Is it always like this around here?"

"Most days," Sam said. "You said you'd been here before?"

Eric nodded. "I came here on vacation with my parents, but that was over twenty years ago. I don't remember much of it." It was a lie, but a necessary one. There was always the chance that he might say something that would indicate his familiarity with the Point; better to provide a reason in advance.

"Too bad your timing wasn't a little better," Kerr said. "It's practically the end of the season. The best weather's behind us by at least two weeks, and the few tourists we got this year are pretty much gone." He shook his head. "I can't help but wonder how much longer the Point can survive as a place for tourists. The way things are going, in a few more years it'll turn back into the quiet fishing town it was before anyone even thought much about tourists."

"There's a new real-estate development going up across the bay, over by Buck's Harbor," Sam said. "Some investors got together, bought a hefty chunk of land, and now they're putting in a whole line of fancy hotels, cabins, restaurants, stores, even a multi-cinema—things we can't offer. When they finish up in a few years, we won't be able to compete. Truth to tell, folks around here have been losing business for five years now, and most figure this'll drive the last nail in the coffin."

"Fewer people these days want to get away from it all," Kerr said. "They want to get away from it all *and* bring it all with them. I think most of them are just in love with the idea of going from *here* to *there*, as if that meant something. As if they'd enjoy being alive more if they were living out of suitcases. But it's what's inside that counts." Kerr tapped his chest, over his heart. "If there's nothing worthwhile inside, if there's no private vacation spot in the heart, corny as that sounds, they won't find it anywhere outside."

"Warming up for your Sunday sermon?" Sam asked.

Kerr grinned sheepishly. "Preview of coming attractions. Not that it means much to you, being a heathen and all."

"Now, I thought we agreed we weren't going to get into that tonight. The Big House is neutral ground, remember?"

Before Father Kerr could respond, the front door swung open. A cold evening wind blew across the room, and someone dressed in layer upon layer of clothes bustled past the group too fast for Eric to see who it was.

Zach stepped back into the room just in time to pass the figure en route to the kitchen, barely avoiding a collision. "Just like a damn torpedo," he said, setting a full glass of beer down on the coffee table and settling back into his chair.

A moment later, the latecomer reentered the living room, a cup of steaming coffee in one hand, and in the other a platter bearing several slices of corned beef and two thick slabs of warm squaw bread. "Zach," she said, setting the plate and cup down on her knees, "you are married to a saint. She knew just what I'd need—coffee, food, and a minute standing in front of that wonderful oven. Had it all ready and waiting for me."

"Just don't get used to it," Zach said. "If the missus wants to treat you like you're something special, well, that's her right, I suppose, but as far as I'm concerned, you're just another boarder who can't keep mealtimes straight in her head."

"To which I respond: phooey. We both know she doesn't do anything without your permission, so you can leave the 'crabby innkeeper' act in the closet, where it belongs." She lifted the cup with both hands to warm them, and took a long sip. A shiver raced through her. "God, I may never recover."

"Serves you right for going out on that boat in the first place. I warned you about it, but did you listen? Of course not. And furthermore—"

"And furthermore," she mimicked perfectly, right down to the furrowed brow and downturned lips.

"Furthermore," Zach continued, paying no attention, "the least you could do is to act civilized and say hello to company when you come into a room."

"You have to feel human before you can act civilized, and I'm only now getting to that point." She looked up from her plate, smiled, and nodded demurely to the others. "Good evening, Father Kerr, Sam." She paused, noticing Eric for the first time. "I don't know you," she said, and turned back to Zach. "The least you could do is introduce us. That is, after all, the *civilized* thing to do."

"He's got a tongue, though he hasn't had much chance to use it. Let him introduce himself."

She looked at Eric. "Is it true that you have a tongue? And if so, to whom is it attached?"

"The name's Eric Matthews."

"Pleased to meet you, Eric Matthews. I'm Elizabeth Chasen. Liz is also acceptable. Liz'beth," she said, glancing sourly at Zach, "is not."

"She's a writer," Sam said. "Up here doing a book. A real book, too, not one of these bodice-rippers you see at the supermarket."

"Then that makes this a first for me," Eric said. "Don't think I've ever met a working writer before."

"The way she talks should've tipped you off from the start," Sam said, "the way she used *whom* instead of *who.* Anyone around here found guilty of proper grammar is either a writer, an out-of-towner, or under suspicion on general principles."

"Have you ever sold anything?"

In the middle of taking a bite of squaw bread, Liz rolled her eyes heavenward and sighed. The rest laughed, exchanging looks that indicated a private joke.

"Liz," Kerr said, "how many times now have you been asked that question since you got here?"

"How many people are there in the Point? Sam? You're the town Keeper of the Figures."

"During the summer, maybe thirteen, fourteen hundred. Right now, I'd say between eight-fifty and nine hundred."

"Then you're the nine hundred and first. And to answer your question—yes, I've sold a few things. Articles, mostly, a few historical novels, that sort of thing. And one bodice-ripper, to use Sam's unbiased term. Enough to make a living, anyway. Anything else you'd like to know?"

"That covers it," Eric said. "Sorry if I offended."

"Don't be. I've gotten used to it. When you tell someone you're a plumber or a shoemaker or a brain surgeon, almost no one will ever ask you to prove yourself. But as soon as you say you're a writer, they can't believe you're really *doing* it. Around here, it's even worse. The first thing most folks say is usually, 'Oh, my poor dear—when did you last have anything to eat?' "

"It's her own fault," Zach said. "Women writers are supposed to be frumpy old ladies with blue hair who spend all their time behind a typewriter because if they ever showed their faces in public, somebody'd drive a stake through their hearts. So when it comes to looks, Liz, let's face it—you just don't fit the bill."

Eric decided that on that point Zach was right. Liz had auburn hair that was feathered from ears to shoulders, features that were almost aquiline, green eyes, and tiny laugh lines around the mouth. He suspected she had a good figure—what he could make of it through the layers of clothes.

Zach reached over and tapped Eric's knee. "Make quite a stripper, wouldn't she?"

Liz sighed. "Zach's being irascible again." She addressed herself to Eric, speaking as a teacher might of a particularly difficult child. "You must excuse him. The attacks are coming more and more often these days."

"Though it might be asking for trouble," Eric said, "what's the second most-asked question you get?"

"That's easy. 'What's a writer doing in the Point?' "

"You mean there's a reason beyond annoying Myrna about none of your books being in the town library?" Sam asked.

"There are a *lot* of books that aren't included in Miss Cranston's so-called library," Liz said, then turned her attention back toward Eric. "For the last six months I've been going from one small town to another, gathering research for a new book—*Hidden Places: An Oral History of Maine Villages.* Not the snazziest of titles, but I'm picking up some fascinating material."

"She comes in every day and picks our brains," Sam said. "Just spends hours, talking a little now and then, but listening mostly."

"Sam's been a terrific help. Give him half a chance, and he'll fill you in on all the history of the Point you'll ever want to hear. A lot of it is extremely quotable, parts of it are a little dubious, and some of it even makes a rough sort of sense."

"Thanks bunches," Sam said.

Liz put down her empty cup and stretched back in the chair, finally looking warmed and at least reasonably content. "There," she said. "Now I can die happy."

Kerr tapped out the last tobacco in his pipe, and started another bowl. "How much longer till you're finished? You've got a whole town waiting to see whether or not you're going to write anything they can sue you for."

Liz considered it. "As of yesterday, I had nearly a hundred hours of taped interviews to transcribe and edit. After spending a whole day with Fred Keller on that old boat of his, add another four, four and a half hours of usable material. I may also need a new recorder; there was more salt water on deck than in all of Machias Bay. *If* the recorder and the tapes are all right—and they'd better be—I've still got about a dozen interviews ahead of me. Then I can take a deep breath, crawl back to my apartment, assuming it hasn't burned down in my absence, and try to make sense of it all. Writing, despite what you may have heard, is *work*."

"Damn shame, too." That from Zach. "It's not right for a pretty woman to spend that much time alone, cooped up with a bunch of petrified old farts like us. She should be out on the town, enjoying herself." He looked to Eric. "Any ideas how we can work that out, Mr. Matthews?"

Liz spoke up before Eric could formulate a judicious response. "Mrs. Franklin," she called into the kitchen, "it's time you gave Zach his warm milk and cookies, and sent him up to his room." She shot him a disapproving look. "It's *way* past his bedtime."

2

Liz rummaged through the cluttered backseat of the old Volkswagen, finally struggling the cassette recorder and box of tapes out from under boxes and newspapers and piles of books. With her free hand she unlocked the door to her cabin and stepped inside, kicking the door shut and setting the equipment down on the bed.

She'd considered putting the confrontation between woman and machine off until tomorrow, but it was better to face it now. The thought that the recorder might have been damaged by the salt water had plagued her all night. She'd had the recorder ever since she'd started writing, back in college, and considered it a battle-worn but faithful friend. The thought of losing that friend was almost more than she could stand.

Corned beef and conversation had helped her forget about it for a while. But then Sam and Father Kerr had left, and finally the new boarder—what was his name? Eric? Yes, that was it, Eric Matthews—had gone off for a walk before turning in. At that point, it was either head back for her cabin or trade insults with Zach all night. Which, to quote one of her interviewees, was "sorta like teachin' a chicken to stand on its head. You can work at it all you like, tell yourself you're doing somethin' worthwhile, but when you're done, the only thing you've got is an upside-down chicken."

Though first impressions were always chancy things, Eric struck her as nice enough—but tentative, guarded. Thoughtful. That was the right word, the *mot just* that the writer in her demanded. And not bad-looking, either. He had the kind of eyes that seemed eager to find something, anything to laugh about. Very attentive, and very much *at attention*—the sort of person who looked as if he were standing up even when he was sitting down.

Just the very sort of man her parents would like, she thought, and caught herself frowning. There was no point in letting that prejudice her against someone she'd just met.

She could almost hear them in the back of her mind. *Seems a nice sort of fellow. Does he have a job? Any prospects? Lord knows, you'll need someone to take care of you.*

It was stupid to allow herself to get steamed, and she was determined not to do so. She'd only get wrought up and annoyed, playing all the parts herself, reciting the lines back and forth until she realized the absurdity of acting out the very argument she'd left home five years ago to *avoid*.

Dumb. Just plain wood-dumb.

She looked at the table, where two piles of paper threatened to spill together into a completely unmanageable mess. One pile consisted of her notes on the oral history book, but the other—ah, that was her special pile, where she kept the notes, ideas, and snatches of dialogue for her novel.

Liz caught a glimpse of the title page sticking out of the pile. She always made up her title page long before she began actual work on a project. *The Dangerous Games of Solomon Greene.* A mystery. She was only a few chapters into it, after nearly a full year of squeezing in the work between other projects, but she was proud of it.

So proud of it that once—just once—she made the mistake of mentioning it to her father. He shook his head and sighed his disapproval, as she'd known he would.

"Now look, Lizzie," he said, "I can see maybe how some folks might be interested in the historical stuff, reading about other people and the like. That's just plain curiosity. Can't go too far wrong, relying on people's nosiness. But if you think anybody's going to want to read something you just made up out of your own head . . ." Even before he had said it, she knew what his next words would be.

When was she going to quit all this running around and settle down, find herself a good man? There was nothing wrong with her having a hobby, heavens no. But a hobby didn't fill the bed or put food on the table, did it?

They were the same words he'd spoken when she'd gone off to college. They were the same words he'd spoken when he'd learned she was taking journalism and creative writing classes for reasons other than as an excuse to meet men.

Her mother, of course, had said nothing, but simply looked on helplessly, in that aggravating, passive way of hers.

"He's your father," she would say afterward, as if that explained everything.

Liz never mentioned the novel again. She would go ahead on her own, write the damned thing, and then, when it was a best-seller, well, *then* they'd see.

That, at least, was the theory.

One step at a time, she thought, and dragged herself back to the task at hand. No point in putting it off any longer.

She sat on the bed, put the recorder in her lap, and stripped off the machine's leather cover. Dried bits of seaweed and gritty sea salt were visible in the speaker slats and around the tape lid. Carefully she picked at the encrustations with a fingernail, clearing away as much as she could without scraping the black-and-silver finish. The bits of grit wedged in around the speaker would require a chemical bath before her trusty recorder would ever look the same. But at least the insides were dry, and the tape heads looked okay.

She picked up a tape marked F. KELLER #2, and slipped it into the recorder. A moment later, the gravelly voice of Fred Keller filled the small cabin, bringing with it the distant thrum of the fishing boat and the keening cry of the seagulls that had followed them all day.

The tape picked up in the middle of her interview.

"Well, sure," Keller was saying, "it's part trainin', part experience. Never said it wasn't. Only a damn fool goes off half-cocked, thinking he'll *look* for fish. You *look* for fish and all you'll see is weeds, old tires, and a damn fool looking up at you from the water. Y'have to know where the warm waters run. Y'have to know the deep waters where the fish hide when it's hot, and the shallow waters they play in when the night's cool.

"Reason I do so well is I know all that, and more. Been runnin' nets around Machias Bay since I was twelve. Same for my father, and his father before him. But even knowledge ain't all of it. Why, I seen folks headin' out to the the bay with all kinds of fancy equipment. Sonar, thermometers, enough doodads to open up a Radio Shack—and they come back empty-handed. Why do you think that is, eh? They can find the same places I can, just as easy. But it has to *feel* right, too. Maybe it's something about how the water looks, or just knowing when the fish are likely to move from one depth to another. And maybe it's got somethin' to do with respect. You got to treat the sea like a lady, and I don't mean one of them liberated types, either, no disrespect intended. But you can't just go around throwin' beer cans in her gardens and carrying on—you got to have *respect.*"

Satisfied with the sound quality, Liz lowered the volume a little, letting it play as she took out the rest of the cassettes and began filing them away in a long plastic case. Keller had proved to be a gold mine of colorful stories—just what she needed for chapter two.

She pulled off her sweater and put it on the pile of laundry that was threatening to spill out of its hamper and take over the room. She would have to take care of that sometime soon, she thought as she took a cotton nightgown out of the dresser and spread it out on the bed. Moving quickly to avoid the cold, she pulled her blouse off over her head, then followed with her bra, depositing it on the dresser next to a miniature brass lamp.

As she changed, her attention drifted back to the low murmur of the recorder, from which her own voice droned out at her.

"Is there any place you *haven't* fished?" she heard herself ask.

"No place worth mentioning. I've pulled in pike out of every big lake in Canada, and bass the size of your arm out of the Colorado River." There was a pause, filled in by the call of gulls. "As far as the local product goes, well, I s'pose there's always Indian Lake, over by the caves. That's one place I've never fished, and never intend to. It's too small, for one thing, and for another . . ." Another pause. Again the call of gulls was the only sound in the cabin.

"This may sound funny," Keller continued, "but the fish out by Indian Lake just don't *look* right. If you asked me what it was about 'em that makes 'em different, I couldn't tell you. I mean, they aren't bigger or smaller, or colored different than the fish out of, say, Gardner or Cathance Lake. But there's just somethin' about 'em that's wrong somehow—somethin' in their eyes, the way they hardly fight at all when you hook 'em. You can call me crazy if you want. Lord knows, there's lots of folks 'round here who'd agree with you. But there's no way on God's green earth you'd ever get me to eat a fish out of Indian Lake."

Liz slid out of the grimy pants next, wondering if she should toss them into the hamper or just stand them up in the corner for future generations to find. They were so heavy with grit and salt and the sharp smell of fish that she was sure they'd never be the same again. She frowned. True, they were getting old and worn, but they had once been designer jeans. . . .

The thought fled. Standing in her briefs in the middle of the small cabin, she felt it.

Someone watching her.

She turned quickly, eyes darting toward the large bay window.

Toward the thin break in the curtain.

A flash of movement outside the window.

Right *there!*

"Hey!" Liz yelled. "You get the hell out of—"

Whoever it was, did. She could hear someone running away through the thick brush outside the cabin. She raced to the door, determined to—

She stopped. "Damn!" What was she going to do? Go after whoever it was? In nothing but her panties? *"Damn!"* she yelled again, feeling stupid and helpless. If only she'd seen him—presumably it was a him—even a minute earlier.

She started to turn away from the door, then froze, listening. Someone was walking up the front path, toward the cabin. Possibilities catapulted through her mind, ending with the same question:

What if he'd come back for a closer look—and more?

She glanced around the cabin. No phone.

No clothes.

No time.

She grabbed for her purse, fumbling for a moment before coming up with the canister of CS gas she kept there. The hell with grabbing a robe. There wasn't time, and in the worst of all possible worlds, it wouldn't make a difference anyway.

The footsteps came up to the door and stopped. Silence. Liz slipped the white plastic safety on the canister to one side and held it as she'd been taught. Whoever was on the other side of that door was in for a nasty surprise.

Two knocks at the door. A pause. Then two more.

"Who is it?" she called.

From the other side of the door: "It's me. Eric. I was heading back to my cabin, and heard you shouting." Liz breathed a sigh of relief, recognizing the voice. "Are you okay?"

"Just a sec." Liz slid the safety on the Mace can back into place and stuffed it into the pocket of her robe, which she pulled on as she headed toward the door. She found her hands were trembling, and silently cursed the lapse in her defenses. She almost wished it *was* whoever had been peeking into her cabin tonight. A good taste of Mace would straighten him out. As far as she was concerned, the only thing worse than a peeper was a slug.

She opened the door a crack. A thin draft of cool night air seeped inside. Silhouetted in the doorway, Eric nodded a greeting, but his eyes were focused beyond her, to see if anyone was in the cabin with her. A sharp one, she thought. She allowed herself a moment's satisfaction, noting that he didn't try to look down the front of her robe. At least there were a few Boy Scouts still around.

"Any problems?" Eric asked.

"Not now. Just a Peeping Tom. I don't suppose you happened to see anyone running past you?"

Eric shook his head. "I thought I heard someone running, but whoever it was, they were long gone by the time I got here. When I heard you yell, I figured I'd better check to make sure you were all right. I can still go after him if you want—"

Liz shrugged. "Forget it. He's probably clear on the other side of town by now."

"Do you want me to go on up to the Big House, call the police?"

"Same problem," she said, frustration edging her voice. "By the time our good Constable Crandall got his butt out of bed, dressed, and out here, whoever it was could get married, have three kids, and send them all to college. I'll file a report tomorrow. Have to go into town anyway. Though I have a hunch Crandall's one of those people who thinks a little peeping is about as dangerous as spitting on the sidewalk."

"You want a witness?"

Liz considered it. "I thought you didn't see anything."

"I didn't. But I think I heard someone." He smiled. "And by tomorrow, I'll be sure I did, if it'll help."

"It will," Liz said. "Thanks."

"Any time." With a final good night, he turned and headed back down the path.

Liz watched him go, then shut and locked the door. She found her sewing kit and fastened the curtains together at the top with a safety pin, hoping that this would take care of any remaining gaps.

For tonight, at least, the show was over.

3

Eric headed down toward the beach. At the shoreline he climbed onto a high outcropping of flint rock and sat down. Ten feet below, the water surged in dark whirlpools, while farther out over Machias Bay, the moonlight was caught and broken on the waves rolling in toward shore.

He had to decide what to do, where to start the process of finding—what? His past? Himself? The elusive something that would end the dreams.

First thing tomorrow, he'd go by the local newspaper office. The clipping files should give him a place to start piecing it all together. His family had lived here since the Point was founded; surely there would be clippings.

His family. He had lived so long with other people that the word was at once familiar and alien, like the Point itself. Part of him felt at home here, as if he'd never left.

Or—and the thought's suddenness surprised him—it was as if the Point had been waiting for him all this time. But then, he'd had a lot of strange thoughts lately. Take Liz. He'd been far away from her cabin when he'd felt a sense of *wrongness*, like the feeling he got in school when the teacher was handing back papers and he knew, somehow just *knew*, he'd flunked, even before seeing the red *F* on the page. A sick, sinking feeling in the pit of his stomach.

It was the same feeling that told him he had to check on Liz, just to see if she was okay.

And he'd been right, hadn't he?

He lay back, enjoying the cool ocean scent, the soothing sound of wind and surf. After a moment he felt a strange, sub-cutaneous thrill, a kind of current that pulsed just beneath the surface of his skin. Without thinking about it, he closed his eyes and emptied his mind of anything but the sound of Machias Bay. He could almost see an imagined point of light behind his eyes, and he concentrated until it grew, became distinct, with clearly defined edges. It expanded further, until it consumed his thoughts, surrounding them in a cool glow.

Then, slowly, carefully, he could feel himself reaching out with his thoughts. The sensation was strange, exhilarating. His body tensed, almost vibrating, like a bell resonating out into the night. He imagined his thoughts moving out into the vil-lage, moving cautiously, lingering here, hesitating there, mov-ing out and back and away, sending random images back to the calm center of thought:

A man and a woman making love—furiously, anxiously, before her husband returned.

Children sleeping.

An argument; a lamp being thrown against a wall.

And the distant feather-touch of other people's dreams.

He let out a little cry of delight. What a feeling this was! Such curious ecstasy—as if he could, with but a thought, launch himself into the night and fly. But he didn't move, didn't want to break the spell of whatever it was he was doing, or was being done to him.

He wanted to explore further. He pushed at the night with his thoughts; there was resistance! But that was absurd. This was his dream, his pleasant delusion. Surely he was entitled to a little unopposed happiness in the world of his own dreams! But the resistance did not diminish, no matter how vigorously he struggled against it. His mind drew a compass, pushed north, south, and west. No resistance. But east—something to the east resisted him.

Then it struck him.

To the east lay Indian Lake.

And the caves.

He felt suddenly sick. The sense of terrible wrongness he'd felt earlier returned more strongly this time. He lurched forward, fighting the urge to retch. His thoughts recoiled before—what? He couldn't name it. A shadow that was deeper than the night; a shadow that hovered over Dredmouth Point like a great black bird circling its prey.

Before that unknowable darkness, Eric retreated into wakefulness, barely fighting off the panic that welled up inside him. The sensation of being one with the town disappeared, replaced by a pain that ripped through the back of his head, hammering at the juncture of spine and skull.

He forced open his eyes, found them strangely gummy. He rubbed at them, blinking until the bay went from a blur to a clear view of silver and green moonlit water. The moon was much lower than it had been when he started. He checked his watch. Two hours had elapsed while he could have sworn only minutes had passed.

Slowly he made his way to his feet. His back was cold, stiff. Still blinking, he turned toward the east. Toward the caves. They were too far, too obscured by tree and hill, to be seen from here. But they were there nonetheless.

Watch, his father had said, pointing to those same caves. What had been so important about them that he would use his last breath to try to express it? Of all the things he could have said, why that?

Why had his father's eyes shown fear that day? And more than just the fear of dying, Eric was sure of it.

And why now, so many years later, was *he* afraid?

Eric glanced back over his shoulder at the bay, then started picking his way down the rocks, heading for his cabin. If Zach was right, the sea could tell stories about this place, perhaps even about him.

But just now, Machias Bay wasn't talking.

THREE

THE POINT

It was a little before 4:00 A.M., still dark, as Bud Simmons brought the milk truck to a shuddering halt inside the Ashford Dairy loading dock. The engine cranked for nearly a minute after he shut off the ignition, then finally sputtered and died. Bud shook his head. He'd have to get her tuned up again. Maybe next week, after he made his collections. That would make what—two tune-ups in five months?

He had to face it. The old Ford was dying. A replacement would have to be found, the sooner the better—which would mean around the first of the year. He winced at the prospect of yet another load of monthly payments. Just the thought twisted his stomach and brought the taste of bile to the back of his throat. He forced himself to relax. The last thing he needed now was a repeat performance by his ulcer.

He jerked the truck door open and stepped up onto the loading dock, cold air biting at his ears, and filed the problem away for later. No point in ruining a new day before it had even started. He'd leave that to Beth. She was the expert, after all.

A shrill whistle echoed through the dairy, followed by a heavy rumble as Clement Ashford appeared at the helm of a forklift carrying the day's load. It roared toward Bud like some yellow, two-fanged bat, and he wondered if it was possible to get ticketed for speeding in a dairy.

The forklift rumbled past the rows of stainless-steel milking machines lining either side of the corridor that emptied onto the loading dock, each connected to stalls that held the cows. Bud frowned at the sight, as he always did. Anyone else would have sequestered the cows away from the docks or, better still, put them in a different building altogether. It made working conditions better, and it was a hell of a lot more sanitary. But Clement Ashford wasn't anyone else, and if there was anything Clement knew, it was how to shave expenses.

It was a talent Bud would trade several years of his life for. And why not? He'd sure as hell wasted the *last* five years. What difference would another few make, if he could get Clement's way with money? 'Course, there would still be Beth to contend with, and Lord knew she could go through money faster than the U.S. Treasury could mint it. . . .

"Hey, Bud," Clement called.

Bud forced a smile of greeting and put Beth out of his mind. "Mornin', Clement."

Clement jiggled the worn controls and set the pallet down at Bud's feet, then eased his heavy frame out from behind the wheel and wandered over to the milk truck.

"Pretty good timing," Bud said, a little too cheerily. He didn't like anybody poking around in his truck. "Got the stuff all ready for me."

"Timing, my ass," Clement said. "I could hear you coming five miles back. Sounds like you're drivin' a dinosaur these days. Is that what this is? A Ford Brontosaurus? Didn't know they were still making that model." He laughed too loudly, as always. It was the self-assured laugh of someone who knew he could say just about anything and get away with it.

"I sometimes wonder myself," Bud said. He pulled open the side panel and began loading the racks with cases of milk, cream, buttermilk, cottage cheese, and butter.

"Um-hm," Clement said, and leaned back against the truck, watching as Bud struggled with the heavy racks. He always struck the same stance, one that reminded Bud of a grossly overweight cat sitting in a bay window.

"There's this car salesman I know down by Cutler," Clement said at last. "He's a good man, a friend of my wife's sister—a real close friend, if you get my meaning. Proves there's no accounting for taste in some people." Again, that laugh. Bud smiled thinly as he dropped and carried, dropped and carried.

"Anyway, if I put in a good word for you, he might be able to give you a reasonable price on a new truck. Whaddaya say?"

Bud bit back the immediate reply that came to mind: *And how much of a kickback would you get for telling him how best to stick it to me with the payment plan?* Instead, he rapped his knuckles against the side of the truck, hoping he looked more confident than he felt. "I appreciate the offer, Clement, I truly do. But I think the old gal's got a few good years left in her."

Clement nodded. "Whatever you say, Bud. Just trying to be neighborly. After all, if she breaks down and you can't handle the Point, our customers'll be *in-con-venienced,*" he said, drawing out the word for effect. "You know how I'd hate to make our customers think we can't meet our deliveries. Bad for business." He glanced sideways at Bud with eyes that reminded him of poached eggs. "Don't know what I'd do if that happened."

Bud let the observation sit there. No reply was probably wanted, anyway. The only sound was Bud's heavy breathing as he loaded up the last of the heavy cases.

"I *guess,*" Clement continued at last, "I guess I'd have to get someone else to handle the Point, someone I could depend on to be there when he's supposed to be there. But with this crate . . ." He slapped the side of the truck with one meaty hand. The thud echoed down the corridor. Bud jumped at the sound, looked up to meet the somber gaze of Clement's little eyes.

Just like a fat pig and oh God I'd love to see you squeal just once as the hammer fell, and fell and fell. . . .

"Makes me worry," Clement finished. "I don't like worrying. Life's too short."

"She'll be all right," Bud said, an edge in his voice. "Don't worry about it, okay?"

Clement looked unconvinced. Bud began to suspect that there might be more to this than getting kickbacks on a new truck. Somebody, maybe even somebody from the Point, was sucking up to Clement, trying to muscle in on Bud's route. It wasn't the best route—there was barely enough for a man to make a decent living—but times were tough, and there were a lot of folks who made even less than he did. If somebody was hungry enough to promise Clement better distribution, faster delivery, more customers—someone with a newer truck . . .

"I'll think it over," Bud said.

"You do that."

Bud slid the side panel shut and climbed into the front seat. Clement leaned back against the hood, watching as he turned the key. Bud caught the smug look on Clement's face, and tried to pretend he hadn't.

This time he was lucky. The engine caught and held, though it idled rough. He started to ease the truck back out of the loading dock, then stopped, calling out to Clement over the engine's rumble. "By the way—think I might have some new customers for you in a couple of weeks." It was a lie, but he needed to say *something*. And who knew? In a week or so, maybe he *could* persuade a customer or two to increase their orders. Maybe he *could* add a new name. Maybe.

And maybe he'd end up eating another order of his own inventory to support the lie.

Clement snorted. "I know that route. How do you figure you can add anyone on?"

"Just a feeling I got."

"As far as I'm concerned, feelings don't mean shit."

"I wouldn't be surprised," Bud said under the sound of the engine.

Clement's face jerked upward. "You say something?"

"Nothing."

"And you damn well better keep it that way." With that, Clement climbed onto the forklift and steered it back into the dairy.

Bud eased the truck out of the loading dock and headed back onto the main road, the transmission fighting him as he went from first to second gear.

"Goddamn the whole fucking world," he muttered. It was only 4:10 A.M., and already his day had been officially ruined.

Robert T. Williams—R.T. to his customers—eased down the thirty-five steps to the lobby of the general store. For more than forty years he had walked down those same thirty-five steps at the same time every day—except, of course, for the one morning when Winnie had gone into labor with Joel, their only child. He'd hoped for more, but Winnie had been nearly beyond child-bearing age when she'd had Joel. One miscarriage and a still-birth later convinced them that one would have to be enough. Which reminded him . . .

"Winnie?" he called up the stairs, toward the loft where they'd lived ever since taking over the general store, and where Winifred was clearing up the breakfast dishes. "Haven't we got a birthday coming up sometime soon?"

"Joel Junior," Winnie called back over the clatter of dishes. "He'll be eight a week from Thursday."

"Did I promise to get him anything in particular?"

"Well, he *did* seem inclined toward one of those tabletop video games, but that was, oh, four months ago, I think. Better give Joel or Susie a call, just in case he's changed his mind again."

"Right." He frowned as he headed for the door. The phone call to California would probably cost as much as the toy, and when they finished adding on postage and handling—well, that was what this grandparent business was all about, wasn't it?

He unlocked the door and turned the window sign around so that the red OPEN was visible from outside, and cracked the door a little. A cool, crisp breeze filtered into the store, ruffling what little hair he had left. He took a deep breath, savoring the sweetness of it.

"Gonna be a good day," he said, only partly to Winnie. "A mighty good day."

Across the street from the Dredmouth General Store, Karin Whortle saw the OPEN sign appear in the window at seven-thirty, right on time. Same as usual. You could set your clock by Mr. Williams, she thought as she set out the sign announcing that the Point Inn was also open for business. She waved through the window to Mr. Williams, but couldn't tell whether he'd seen her or not. No matter, she'd made the effort, and as her mother had impressed upon her, that was the important thing. *Nobody, from the Good Lord on down, likes to see a sour face first thing in the morning.*

She glanced the other way down Birch Street, and saw Walter Kriski on his way up the street. She closed the door and hurried back behind the counter, checking her appearance in the long mirror that ran behind the counter—then chided herself silently. Just like a schoolgirl. Yes, Walter had asked her out a few times (she'd said no, of course), and yes, Walter was a widower, and yes, from the talk around town he was friendly enough for a Polack and a newcomer. But that last was unfair; if you hadn't been born in the Point, you didn't stop being a newcomer until you were buried in the town cemetery.

There she went again, she thought, dwelling on it. The cemetery.

Her gaze wandered back to her reflection. Even now, at forty-five, she was far from unattractive. She was perhaps a few pounds overweight, and so what if her hair was going gray, not the silver she'd hoped for? The only lines on her face were laugh lines. There were a lot of good years left in her. Hadn't her mother always said that she'd make a fine catch for some lucky man one of these days?

Not to worry, she thought. Good wine takes time to age to perfection.

Besides, if she wasn't still attractive, how then to explain Walter's attentions? He could cook for himself as well as she could, but that hadn't stopped him from coming in every morning now for two weeks straight, for a breakfast of eggs (over hard), bacon, corned-beef hash, toast, and coffee. He was always the first one in the restaurant, so they could talk without anyone else around.

Behind her, the bell above the door jangled. At the sound, she took a deep breath and decided that maybe she should say yes the next time he asked her out.

She turned, smiled. "Morning, Walt." He took his usual seat along the spotless Formica counter and returned the smile. Not a bad fellow at all.

If only he wasn't a groundskeeper—and at the Cutler cemetery, at that.

4

At 8:00 A.M., Constable Tom Crandall switched on the heater in the tiny office that represented the only intrusion into Dredmouth Point by the forces of law and order. He pulled a Marlboro from his shirt pocket, lit it, and took a deep drag.

Funny how things worked out sometimes.

On most days he wouldn't hear a peep from anyone until nearly ten o'clock. Then there were days when no one called at all, and he could spend the whole day reading the magazines that lay on his desk: *Police Product News, Police Times, Command Magazine,* and *The Trooper.* On a really slow day he might even drag out the magazines he kept in the lower desk drawer— *Penthouse, Playboy*—and, on those too-rare occasions when it ran pictures of big-name actresses, *High Society.* Those were his best days. Quiet. No drunken fights, no treed cats, no noisy neighbor calls, *nothing.*

And then there were days when the whole world decided it would start in on him first thing. Days like today. He'd no sooner gotten off the telephone with Mayor Morgan when that lady writer called in with a Peeping Tom complaint. He'd probably have to investigate it, even though he figured it for nothing more than some kid trying to usher in puberty in a public place. No real harm done.

Still, he resigned himself to asking around, trying to find out whose kids might have been allowed to stay out later than usual. Shouldn't be too difficult to find a peeper in a place as

41

small as the Point—assuming she didn't just imagine the whole thing in the first place.

But that's right—she had a witness, didn't she?

As if that weren't enough, now the mayor was riding his butt about next year's proposed budget. The figures had to be presented to the budget committee at the town meeting next week, and he'd only begun to sketch them out. A lot of other constables worked up budgets requesting things they could never use—tear-gas guns, semiautomatic weapons, and the like—but as far as he was concerned, the simpler and more painless the process, the better. No point in wasting the taxpayers' money for unnecessary equipment.

And, the more he kept the public pocket-picking to a minimum, the more the townsfolk were disposed to keep him on as chief constable—and he'd trade an M-16 for that security any day.

He decided to turn the Peeping Tom complaint over to Ray Price, his deputy. That would free up a little time to work on the budget. If they actually turned up a peeper, then of course he'd step in and take over.

It was a reasonable compromise.

Besides, if Price expected a raise in next year's budget, he'd damn well better start earning his money.

And where the hell *was* Ray, anyway?

5

Father Duncan Kerr walked down the center aisle of St. Benedict's, genuflected before the altar, and turned toward the sacristy. He hesitated before opening the door, nervously anticipating what he might find there, then stepped inside. The cross that normally hung beside the stained-glass window (the Archangel Michael triumphing over Satan) had once again fallen off the wall. As before, it had landed nearly five feet from where, by all rights, it should have. He picked up the heavy crucifix, dusted it off, and returned it to its place over the table upon which his vestments and altar linens were spread.

He stared up at the crucifix for a moment, as if hoping the Christ figure might answer the questions that troubled him.

For three nights in a row it had fallen. No, he corrected himself. Not fallen. Had been hurled across the room. There were no signs of forced entry, and St. Benedict's had been built on a solid rock foundation. He'd used that fact to good advantage in several sermons. But even the most solidly built structures settled over time, sometimes unevenly. That might explain it, he thought, making a mental note to pull out the architectural files for any help they could offer. Still, he'd mention it to Constable Crandall. Perhaps some of the local boys had learned a few new games.

As he stepped back through the door, he dipped his fingers into the small basin of holy water, to cross himself before entering the church. He jerked his hand back, startled.

The night had not been that cold.

Why, then, was the water frozen solid?

He glanced back at the Christ impaled on the wall crucifix, but found no answers there.

6

At 8:15 A.M., Dr. Will Cameron set down the receiver after his first telephone call of the day. Barbara LeMarque was having her rush of dreams again, and could he give her anything to help her sleep? He wrote out a prescription for a mild dose of Valium, enough to see her through. The interludes of dreaming generally started around this time each year, and—fortunately—lasted only a couple of weeks.

The first time she'd come to him about the dreams, he'd been skeptical. Barbara LeMarque had always been a skittish, nervous woman, and yet terribly empathic. Whenever she sat in his waiting room too long with the other patients, she'd grow so sympathetic to their problems that by the time she actually got into the examining room she'd picked up some of their symptoms by emotional osmosis. He'd also treated her for the occasional hysterical complaints that came more frequently with the approach of middle age, but the dreams were always the worst.

He'd read a few articles about people troubled by vivid dreaming. It was a harmless affliction, by most accounts; at worst a nervous disorder that led to dreams so real—and often so frightening—that the person was left exhausted by morning. Barbara seemed bothered almost as much by the fact that she could never quite remember the contents of her dreams as she was by the constant fatigue and nervousness they brought on.

Perhaps it was the need for a little attention that triggered them off. Lord knew, she could use some, living with Gregory. There was something about that man that didn't sit right with Will. Sullen, silent except when he was drunk, always going from one job to another—the man was on a twenty-four-hour-a-day short fuse.

The only thing he knew for certain was that the dreams had started not long after they had moved into the old Langren place, over by Indian Lake.

He finished with the prescription, pulled off his glasses, and looked out through the window of his office, a pleasant, wood-paneled room at the back of his house. It was a relief from the close work. Normally, his eyes were fine until late afternoon. But lately they seemed to grow dry and tired faster. Getting old, he decided. Soon enough, he'd have to go into Machias for another prescription. Perhaps it was time to look into those eye exercises he'd been reading about in the journals.

Tomorrow. He'd look into it tomorrow.

The morning weather report had promised clearer days with cooler temperatures along the coast. He sighed. That would mean an increase in calls from his patients with arthritis, bursitis, and rheumatism. Factor in the usual contagion caused by telephone-line fallout, and he could also count on an increase in calls from the patients on his Placebo Run, those with nothing more wrong with them than old age and a lack of anything better to do with their time than exchange symptoms over the phone. So he would answer their calls, make his stops, hold their hands, listen to their complaints, and, in most cases, leave behind a vial of sugar pills covered with the worst-tasting coating he could find. Everyone knew that medicine was valuable in direct proportion to how vile it tasted going down.

He picked up his bag and the long list of stops slated for today, and started for the door, tucking Barbara LeMarque's prescription in his jacket pocket. Maybe he would stop by and have it filled on the way down to the farm. Save her the trip and lengthy explanations. He knew how Gregory felt about her throwing away money on medicine. She could owe it to him, repay it whenever she could.

He shook his head. Poor Barbara.

He wondered how long it would be before she ended up as one more stop on the Placebo Run.

7

Ruth Miller picked up the four-person party telephone at 9:15 A.M., cupping the mouthpiece and holding the receiver to her ear. She was in luck. Winnie Williams was talking to Judy Markle, Dave Markle's wife. She pressed down harder on the mouthpiece, making sure that not even the sound of her breathing could slip through. With the other hand she reached for a coconut praline, nibbling at it while Winnie went on about her grandson's upcoming birthday.

Honestly, she thought, dismayed, didn't people have anything better to do than babble about birthdays? She shifted in the lounge chair, her bulk causing the wood to make threatening noises that she hoped were inaudible over the telephone line.

Footsteps came up behind her, and Karl Jergen stepped into the living room. "I'm goin' out, Ma," he said. He said it quietly, but there was no softness in his voice. He was a big man, with broad hands and angular features. A shock of unruly black hair ended abruptly just below the collar of his denim shirt and spilled forward onto his forehead. "Ma?"

She shushed him, holding up a finger until she could hang up, moving slowly to avoid a click on the line. "Karl, I've told you not to surprise Mother like that."

"Sorry," he said, without—she suspected—meaning it. There was something about him that made even an apology sound like an insult. At these times, he reminded her too much of her late husband—the same close-set eyes, and a mouth that seemed perpetually curled into a look of contempt.

"I'm goin' out," he repeated.

"I heard you," she said. "Where?"

"No place. Just out."

"You were out awful late last night. You doing anything I should know about?"

"No." He met her stare, held it until she looked away.

"What if somebody calls, asking for you? What if somebody's got a job—"

"Tell 'em I'll be back sooner or later." He grabbed his jacket and stepped out onto the unpaved walk, slamming the door behind him.

Damn old woman, Karl thought. Always messing around in his business, never mind her precious daughter, the one who pissed perfume and walked on water just for kicks. Never mind the slut putting out all over town, the jokes he heard, the sneering. Don't bother even trying to tell her—no, she'd sooner believe that Moses was an ax murderer than think anything wrong of her One and Only.

As for last night—screw it. Let her wonder. Oh, he'd love to see the look on her face if she found out what he'd done. But nobody would know. Nobody would ever know. Serve that goddamn Duane Kincaid right, thinking he was a big deal just because he runs a pharmacy. Thought old Karl wasn't good enough to hang around with his daughter, that he was too old for a high school girl ten years his junior. Even made noises about talking to his mother, then going straight to Tom Crandall if he didn't stay away. Thought he could push him around.

Well, screw you, too, Duane Kincaid. You've got a few new thoughts coming.

He couldn't wait to find out how old Duane took it.

Even now, his cheeks burned at the memory of being told off in front of the pharmacy, in front of everyone. And he'd seen Jessie inside the store with her friends, making fun while her daddy played hotshot. He'd teach them to think twice before insulting decent folks. No, they'd never know it was him, but they would know somebody did it, and that might be just enough to give 'em pause next time.

Besides, *he* would know. And that was what counted.

He squinted into the sunlight, the gnawing thought that had bothered him all night returning again. *Maybe* nobody would ever know it was him. Trouble was, as he'd driven back last night, old Sam Crawford's car had gone by, catching him for just a second in the headlights. Now, there was every chance in the world that Sam hadn't gotten a good look at him. On the other hand, maybe he had. Either way, Karl wasn't too worried.

Sam was smart. Even with all his college-learning, Sam knew the rules; he would know better than to cross him. And if he didn't . . . well, Karl would have to teach him, too.

He turned onto the path that led down from Morton Hill to Walnut Avenue. He'd parked the car by the general store, needing a good walk then as much as now. Glancing back over his shoulder, he found the window where he knew his mother would be sitting with her binoculars, scanning the town with hungry eyes.

As he reached Walnut, he shot Ruth the bird. He was too far away to tell if she saw him or not, but it didn't matter.

He knew.

8

"Again," Cheryl Miller said. She giggled, grinding against the car seat where she lay, half-reclining, skirt hiked up around her waist.

Ray Price raised his hands in mock surrender. "No way. I'm late enough as it is." He glanced at his watch. Cheryl Miller was the best piece of ass in the county—but he *was* late, and he wasn't sure any girl was worth the grief that Tom Crandall would give him if he didn't make it to the station soon.

"You sure?"

"Positive. Playtime's over. C'mon, get your little butt moving." He finished tucking in his shirt and opened the back door of the 1980 Ford Mustang that doubled as a patrol car when the flashing red bubble he kept in the glove compartment was stuck on top.

"You're no fun," she said. "*I'm* playing hooky, why can't you?"

"It's different, that's all. I've got a job to do."

"Playing policeman. Big job, huh?" she said playfully. "I've got it! I'll file a complaint! That'll give you something when the chief asks where you've been." She thought about it, eyes flashing behind lids narrowed against the midmorning sun. "I know. I'll say some guy came along and molested me in the back of his car. I'll say I screamed and screamed, just like this."

She opened her mouth to scream, but Ray clapped a hand

over her mouth. She giggled through his fingers. "Jesus!" Ray said. "Cut the crap! You want to get us both in trouble?"

She shook her head, and he removed his hand. She toyed with the badge hanging over his left pocket. "Don't be such a nerd. There's nobody around. Not even Mom. I think that's funny. Don't you? I mean, there she is, the town busybody, missing one of the biggest scandals around." She laughed again, deep and throaty, running one hand through her blond hair.

"Okay, it's funny. But just barely," Ray said, and nudged Cheryl into the front seat. He walked around to the other side, and climbed in behind the wheel. "You want to see something else funny?" she asked, leaning close to him.

"I don't have time for games," he said, then stopped, looking down the barrel of his service .38. The holster lay empty on the seat beside her, where he'd left it after they'd parked.

"Cheryl—now put that thing down, honey." He didn't move, didn't grab for it. Her finger was on the trigger.

Cheryl laughed. "You got a real problem, Deputy Price. You know what it is?"

Ray shook his head, eyes fixed on the barrel that was pointed at a spot just between his eyes.

She tightened her finger on the trigger. "Your problem is," she said, "you got no sense of humor."

She closed one eye.

"Cheryl—"

"*Bang!*"

It was all too much for her. She dropped the gun and collapsed into a giggling heap against the car door.

Ray realized that he was sweating heavily. "Damn you, Cheryl Ann Miller," he snapped, snatching up the revolver and putting it in the backseat. "That wasn't funny." He gunned the patrol car and sped out onto the road that led into town.

"Like I said, no sense of humor. Besides," she added, looking over at him as if he were some pet she had just acquired from the pound, "what're you going to do? Report me? Just remember, I might have a few things to report myself."

As he drove, teeth clenched, silent, Ray wondered, not for the first time, if this was such a terrific idea. He sometimes thought her whole family was nuts—her, her brother Karl, their mother—hell, everybody knew their father had been crazy as a loon.

But Cheryl was *such* a good piece.

9

Barbara LeMarque went upstairs to the bedroom and shut the door—away from Julie, away from Billy and his early-morning cartoons, away from the radio and the telephone and the requests for breakfast that quickly turned into demands. . . .

She sat on the bed, put her head between her knees, and tried to breathe evenly. In. Out. In. Out. But nothing helped.

She'd thrown up twice last night, the slightest noise was all but unbearable, and a headache was forming just behind her right eye, as though someone were pressing against it. Pressing harder by the second.

She'd had the headaches before, always at this time of the year, but never this bad.

It happened in the fall, and each time it got worse. At times, she was sure her head would burst from the pressure. If she could at least know what was causing it, she'd feel better, could deal with it with something resembling dignity. But the X rays had showed nothing, no tumor, *nothing*. The pain was just *there*, and it made everything around her part of her discomfort.

Outside, Billy clomped up the stairs and started pounding on the door, demanding ice cream when he *knew* it was too early, she *never* gave him ice cream this early. . . .

She wished that Dr. Cameron would hurry.

She needed someone to talk to. Badly. She needed to know that she wasn't going insane.

10

By the time Jay Carmichael got around to opening up Jay's Union 76 Service Station, it was well past ten o'clock, and a line had already formed in front of the pumps. Ace Jackson was leaning on his horn as if it were an air-raid siren. Jay came out and made for the pumps, unlocking them and slipping the nozzle into Ace's station wagon. Two more cars, a Toyota and a Ford, awaited their turns.

As soon as his tank was full, Ace roared off and the Toyota moved up. Judith Carlyle nodded at Jay through the window. "The usual," she said.

He nodded back at her, and started to fill the car with twelve dollars' worth of regular, stealing a glance at her through the rear window. A pretty girl, but awfully shy. She always dressed in long-sleeved, high-necked blouses or long dresses, even in summer. Not that it mattered much, he thought with a furtive smile, remembering nights he'd sat perched in the tree that fronted her bedroom; nights he'd seen her take off all those layers of clothes, lie down on her bed, and run her hands in all the secret places she'd never let anyone else near.

A damn pretty woman. Not as big in the tits as that lady writer over by Zach's, but nice nonetheless.

At that thought he caught himself. You were stupid, he thought. Could've got yourself caught by that guy last night. Stupid and clumsy and overexcited. He'd have to be more careful in the near future. Stay away for a few days, then try again when she lets her guard down.

Strategy was everything when it came to this particular hobby.

He racked the gas nozzle, and went around to the driver's side to collect the twelve dollars. She handed him the bills without glancing up. It pleased him to know that she couldn't possibly know what he was thinking as he pocketed the money and watched her drive off.

Yeah, a real pretty woman. Too bad she's not a natural blonde.

But that would be their little secret, he thought as, still smiling, he went on to the next car.

11

Ginny Kincaid stepped out onto the back porch and shielded her eyes from the sun that was finally burning away the mid-morning fog. "Here, kitty," she called. "Come on, Catt." She always felt a little silly, calling Catt by his generic name, but that was what Duane had named him when the brown-and-rust tabby had first wandered into their kitchen five years before. He had been just a kitten. Though he was still sweet, age had made him as particular about everything from food to where he slept as they were.

The only thing he hadn't objected to over the years was his name.

"The name's Catt," Duane would tell visitors, "with two *t*'s." When asked why the two *t*'s, he'd respond, grinning that infectious grin of his, "Because he stutters."

Ginny stepped off the porch, wiping her hands on her apron. "Here, Catt! Do you want breakfast or not?" No movement in the bushes along her garden, where he liked to sleep away the morning. She was starting to get concerned. Catt hadn't been in all night. But that wasn't entirely unusual; he'd gone out hunting all night before, usually returning with a dead sparrow that she'd have to dump in the garbage. She checked along the fence that ran alongside the house.

Nothing.

She looked up at the rain gutters, in case he'd gotten caught on the roof, as he had last Thanksgiving, when it took Duane and half the police force—such as it was—an hour and a half to get him down.

She shaded her eyes, and glanced up at the weathervane that Duane had installed last summer—

And froze. Her hands flew to her face. "Duane!" she yelled, backpedaling toward the house, eyes wide with horror. *"Duane!"*

Breaking free of the shock, she ran inside, away from the terrible day, and away from the spiked weathervane upon which Catt was impaled, disemboweled.

Behind her, the weathervane swung in the wind, and dead eyes in a mask of brown-and-rust fur turned to stare blindly at the house, from which came the sounds of crying.

The eyes remained impassive.

PART TWO

THE BREACH

But wherefore thou alone? Wherefore with thee
Came not all Hell broke loose?
                    —PARADISE LOST, BOOK IV, 917

FOUR
ERIC

On her way to pick Eric up for the drive into town, Liz decided that she was going to talk about anything and everything but her work. That had been the main source of conversation the previous night, and she didn't believe in one-note symphonies. But after perfunctory greetings and a few dead-end comments about the weather, she felt herself falling back on old standbys. The best compromise seemed talk about the Point. Locally, it was a pretty good icebreaker.

And, it wasn't *exactly* talking about her work.

"The Point was settled back in 1603, two years after the French tried to install a colony up north, along the St. Lawrence River," Liz said as they passed Cambridge Road, which proscribed the edge of the town proper. "The settlers were mostly English, along with a few French who vowed allegiance to the British crown. They were lucky enough to establish good relations with the Algonquin Indians early on."

Eric *hmmm*ed a reply, gazing out at the passing houses as the town slowly closed in around them.

So much for idle chatter, Liz thought, and turned her attention outside as well.

Dredmouth Point was a quiet town, and looked friendly enough, in a noncommittal sort of way. Close-clipped lawns were bordered by splashes of color where flowers struggled to survive in the cooling weather. There were just as many clay paths as concrete sidewalks, but the streets were kept cleaner than any large city could manage. Chimneys, garrets, and attics rose from gray-sided or red-brick houses, their faces framed by ornate keystones and curtained sidelights above and beside the doors. Wrought-iron fences with elaborate scrollwork abutted gates of brick and wood.

Friendly. Quiet. Rural. But intensely private, wary of strangers. Liz fidgeted in her seat. Even now, after having spent so much time here, she almost anticipated the shuttered windows to slam shut at the sight of outsiders; for clouds to blot out the sun, turning Dredmouth Point into night—and nightmare. But nothing happened. Here and there, residents watered lawns, drove cars, talked over fences. . . .

Liz looked at Eric, sitting silent beside her. "I'm boring you, right? History not your thing? Be honest. Just because I've had to live this for the last year doesn't mean you have to."

Eric waved away her comment. "No. Really. It's interesting."

"You're not just being polite?"

Eric smiled. "I've been called a lot of things, but polite isn't one of them."

With a sideways glance, Liz sized up how truthful he was being, came up with a satisfactory equation, and continued. What the hell. It was her car.

"Actually, the Point wasn't much more than a bunch of farms until the township was officially proclaimed around 1749. When the news came, the whole town turned out for a week-long party. Even the Algonquins were allowed to demonstrate their rites of celebration right in the center of town—which was pretty unusual for the times. A fair-sized portion of the local population was convinced that the Indians were the Devil's own. But even they couldn't ruin the party.

"Aside from that, the Point's always been a pretty dull little town. There have been flare-ups now and again—what town doesn't have its skeletons?—but they're more the exception than the rule. One rumor has it that the Point once served as a base for rum smugglers and slavers. Then there were the wars, of course. Some folks from the Point fought on our side in the Revolutionary War. Most of the others were Tories. There were a few witch hunts, but nothing quite so spectacular as the Salem trials, and of course there was the incident with the Algonquins." She frowned at this, her voice trailing off.

"What happened?"

She shrugged. "Nobody's really sure. It was right around the French and Indian Wars, 1755 or thereabouts. Skirmishes with the Indians were popping up everywhere, so the local Algonquins made a peace treaty with the Point, vowing to remain neutral. They were a small tribe, as private in their ways as the settlers—which may explain why they got along—and only distantly related to the other tribes in the area. From what I've read, they wanted to keep their group small, and interact with the other tribes as little as possible. Which is why what happened doesn't make much sense.

"Some say the Indians broke the treaty, allied with the French and the other tribes, and attacked several local families. There were stories of horrible mutilation. Later reports said that the French did all the dirty work, and the Indians took the blame. Whatever the truth, it triggered off a small war hereabouts. The tribe was virtually wiped out. The few remaining survivors scattered. One group was trapped in the hills and shot or starved out. Which is something else that, if you think about it, doesn't make much sense. They could've been halfway across the state by the time they were discovered. But they stayed up there in the caves. Refused to leave, even when they were offered a fair trial."

"Which caves?" Eric asked.

"Indian Caves, of course. Hence the name. Why?"

"Just curious."

2

It was nearly ten when they arrived at the constable's office, and it didn't take Eric long to decide that Crandall was in less than a receptive mood. Liz repeated what she'd told him over the telephone about the Peeping Tom, then dictated it a third time while Crandall filled out his report on an old Underwood typewriter.

He finished, read the statement back, and asked her to

sign it at the bottom, adding her permanent address in New York next to her temporary address at Zach's.

"And what about you?" Crandall asked, turning to Eric. "You're the witness?"

"I saw someone, yes. But I couldn't get a good look. Do you want me to fill out one of these as well?"

Crandall shook his head. "More trouble than it's worth, for the moment. Just got into town the other day, right?"

Eric nodded.

"Figure on staying long?"

"A while. Why?"

"No special reason. Just like to keep tabs on things. Helps discourage the transients." He glanced over his report. "Sure you didn't get a good look at this peeper? Anything that could help us find him?"

"Wish I could help, but all I saw was someone running through the woods outside Liz's cabin."

"Then it could have been anything. A dog, maybe." He looked at Liz. "You said yourself you were exhausted. Think it could've been an animal?"

"No," Liz said. "I know a man when I see him, even when I only see part of his face. I'm a writer; I'm supposed to be observant. That's what people pay me for."

Crandall sighed. "Ma'am, I know just about everybody in town by his first name, and none of 'em are the type to go peepin' in somebody's window. They're all good, God-fearing people. Well, most of 'em, anyway. Now, I'm not saying you didn't see *anything*, so don't get that look on your face. Could've been some kid playing a joke, or somebody who doesn't even live in the Point, who just kept on going. In the first case it's harmless, and in the second, whoever it was is probably long gone by now."

"Which saves you the trouble of looking into it," Eric said. "Admitted, this isn't first-degree homicide, but don't you think it's at least *possible* that one of your God-fearing folks has his own peculiar ideas about what a good time is?"

Crandall's voice was hard. "Sarcasm doesn't do squat for me, mister. You're making a lot of assumptions for somebody who doesn't know what the hell he's talking about."

"Just trying to do my civic duty, Constable."

Crandall threw up his hands. "All right, all right. I give

up." He looked to Liz. "I'll poke around, ask some questions, see what I can come up with. But I can't promise anything."

"That's fine," Liz said. "Thank you."

Crandall escorted them out, watching as they headed across the square to the general store. He regretted the tone he'd taken. Of course she had a legitimate complaint. And on any other day, he would have turned Ray loose on the case, make enough noise to put a scare into whoever was doing the peeping.

But Ray wasn't here, he'd had to take the complaint himself, and he was up to his ears as it was with the mayor.

Then there was that phone call from the Kincaids, not five minutes before Liz had come in.

Christ, he thought. Who would kill somebody's cat?

The back door opened, and Ray strode into the office. "'Morning, Tom."

Crandall wheeled on him. "Where the hell have you been?"

Ray stopped in his tracks. "Ran into a little car trouble."

"Then why didn't you call in? I could've sent someone to get you."

"I didn't think—"

"That's pretty obvious, I'd say." Crandall snatched up his jacket and moved toward the door. "We'll take this up later. Right now I want you to stay put. I've got to run down to Duane Kincaid's place."

"Trouble?"

Crandall jerked a thumb toward the forms on his desk. "It's all in the reports. We've also got a peeper out getting his jollies taking long lingerings at that writer, Liz Chasen. I want you on it as soon as I get back."

"Must've been quite an eyeful," Ray said, grinning broadly.

Crandall caught Ray's expression. "You've got exactly ten seconds to get that look off your face and replace it with the one you had on when you took your oath."

Ray did it in three. "Anything else?" he asked, subdued.

Crandall considered it for a moment. There *was* something, now that he thought about it. That Matthews character had just rolled into town last night, the same night somebody killed Duane's cat. And who knew? Maybe it wasn't just coincidence that he was right outside Chasen's cabin when the peeper was there.

"Yeah, there's something. I want you to do a fast check on the guy who cosigned the peeper complaint. Nothing elaborate, just put his name on the wire, see if there are any outstanding wants or warrants, anything unusual."

"Got it."

"Give a shout if you come up with anything," Crandall called back as he headed for the car parked out front.

3

Liz stopped in front of the general store and pulled a notebook and her recorder out of her bag. "I've got an interview with the owner. You want to sit in?"

"Not this time. I'll just walk around for a while. When should I meet you?"

She checked her watch. "Two hours, over by the park."

"See you then."

They separated, and Eric continued down the narrow sidewalk. It was a picture-postcard kind of town: the barber shop, with its rotating pole (doubtless worth quite a lot to an antique dealer, but here it was, still functioning); a stationer's that also doubled as the town post office; a diner; a fish and tackle store; and a drugstore. Even without looking, Eric was willing to bet that in the drugstore there would be stainless-steel blenders and high metal cups to go with a real soda fountain, just like the places he'd haunted as a kid.

He turned onto Walnut Avenue, looking up and down the street. From what Liz had said, it should be somewhere around here. . . .

Then he spotted it. A squat, crackerbox affair with gold-leaf lettering on the window: the Dredmouth Point Public Library.

Inside, the library was as tiny and understocked as Liz had said. A thin, hawkish-looking woman, her chestnut hair tied into a bun so tight it made him wince, looked up at him as he stepped inside. From Liz's description, this would have to be Myrna Cranston.

"Can I help you?" she asked.

"Just looking," Eric said, scanning the rows of paperbacks and hardcovers. A few magazines were arrayed on a wooden stand next to two chairs and a couch, none of which matched. "What newspapers serve the town?"

"The *North Cutler Journal*. Publishes a weekly supplement for the Point. There's some talk about starting up our own newspaper, but I don't think that will happen for a while yet."

"What about back issues?"

"We have complete copies of the *Journal* going back to 1960. Anything earlier than that, you'll have to go to North Cutler for. We also have some clippings indexed by name and subject that go back quite a bit, but that's pretty catch-as-catch-can, datewise. Were you looking for any day or year in particular?"

Eric answered without hesitation. "November third, nineteen sixty-three."

"All right," Myrna said, rising. "If you'll give me your library card, I can get the material for you."

"I'm sorry—I don't have one."

She picked up a red card from her desk. "Fill this out and give it back to me, along with a driver's license and a social security card. This will let you use the library temporarily, and to check out two books, no more." She handed him the card. "You can sit down over there while you fill it out."

Eric sat and attempted to answer the questions as best he could, surprised at how much information she needed. Finally, he carried the completed card and his license over to her desk. She looked from his picture to his face and back again with, he thought, the undisguised suspicion of a customs agent sure he was trying to smuggle heroin into the country.

"Just one moment," she said, and walked to the back of the library, where she vanished into a side room. He could imagine her consulting a huge computer system back there, looking for felony convictions or allegations of page-crinkling.

Finally, Myrna returned carrying a heavy black binder mottled with dust and dark brown spots—the stigmata of decaying chemicals. She handed Eric the binder. "Please be careful of the pages. They're rather brittle. The *Journal* didn't begin using a decent stabilizer in their printing process until 1970."

Eric went back to his seat, spread the binder out across his lap, turned the page—

And there it was.

Eric Langren, age eight, missing since the car crash that claimed his parents Saturday afternoon, was found early Sunday morning by police from North Cutler and Dredmouth Point after a night-long search.

The search began when witnesses, alerted to the accident by a cloud of smoke, reported finding tiny footprints in the mud leading away from the scene of the crash. Calls to authorities quickly identified the driver and his female passenger as Marsh and Claris Langren, of Dredmouth Point. Police, concluding that the third passenger had been their son, Eric, launched the search in spite of heavy storm conditions, fearful that the youth might be injured or in shock, and might not survive the night alone.

The boy was found shortly before dawn Sunday morning, just inside Indian Caves. Although searchers who discovered the boy described him as "confused and frightened," his physical condition is reportedly fair, with minor injuries compounded by exposure. Police believe that the boy, in shock, possibly looking for help for his injured parents, wandered away and became lost, eventually finding his way to the caves, where he took shelter for the night.

"He did just fine," said Constable Phillip Dejunne, who supervised the search party's efforts throughout the night. "He knew that staying out in the open would be more dangerous than finding some sort of shelter." Dejunne emphasized the boy's courage in trying to find help for his parents, while adding that he was lucky not to have wandered too far into the caves, which are well known locally for their winding passages. "If he'd gone much farther inside, we might have missed him altogether," Dejunne said.

Eric scanned the article again. This was the first time he had read any of the specifics about what had happened that afternoon. Somehow, seeing it in cold type brought the experience back with an immediacy he had not felt in years.

The curious thing was that he had *no* recollection of being found at, in, or near Indian Caves. He could remember the accident, that most vividly. And waking up in the ambulance, being examined, the too-friendly policeman who'd tried to tell him his parents had gone far, far away and wouldn't be coming back. . . .

The caves were at least two miles from the scene of the accident. On the other side of the lake.

He closed his eyes. Trying to remember. Why on earth would he have gone there, of all places? It was—

dark—it was dark and he was alone and he hurt oh god how he hurt and the voices were all around him calling him calling him the glow far inside that flickered inside his eyes but not on the wall so how could he see it and always the voices so soft so friendly calling to him to play and come inside just a little more where it's warm but it's not it's cold and dark and—

His eyes jerked open. He was breathing fast, beginning to hyperventilate. Just like all those times when he would wake from a terrible nightmare, the kind he could never remember afterward, able to recall only the sense of horror and being unable to move, to do anything, to run or cry out. His hands were perspiring, gripping the binder until his knuckles whitened. Gradually he forced them to relax. It was several minutes before they stopped throbbing, and his knees steadied enough for him to rise and return the book to the front desk.

What had happened that day? Why on earth would he have gone up to the caves? And why couldn't he remember?

There *had* to be an answer.

Now, though, even more than before, he couldn't bear the thought of going there, not within view of the caves. Not without knowing more first.

Last night, without knowing why, he had sensed something dark and dangerous there. Before he went near that place, he would know more about it.

Myrna accepted the heavy binder, noting with dismay the dark spots where moist fingers had temporarily stained the cover. She buffed the cover with the back of her hand. "Anything else?"

"Could I see everything you have on the caves, please?"

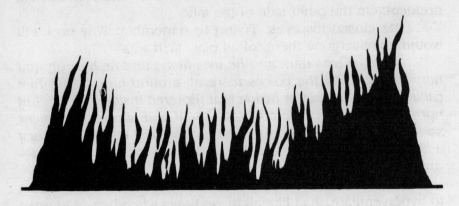

FIVE
WILL

Will Cameron grabbed his black bag out of the backseat, checked that he had Barbara's prescription, shut the car door, and walked up the cobblestone path. The LeMarque house was silent. Normally, the sound of the television—of "Sesame Street" and "The Electric Company," or "One Life to Live"—filtered out through the windows. Barbara was big on the value of the electronic baby-sitter. Barbara's station wagon was still parked in the driveway, so she *had* to be home—unless she and the kids had gone off with Greg in his car.

Only one way to find out, Will decided, and rapped on the screen door and waited. Nothing. He stepped back a pace and looked up to the second-floor windows. "Hello? Anybody home?"

Something moved at one of the windows.

He rapped at the door again. "Barbara?" He pulled open the screen door, found the inner door unlocked, and stuck his head inside. The long hallway was empty, shades drawn at either end, dark except where the light behind him splashed the wooden floor. He stepped inside, leaving the door ajar.

"Barbara?" he called again. "It's Will. Will Cameron."

Nothing. But at least he had announced himself—no point in getting mistaken for a burglar. He continued down the hall. The living room was deserted, the television off. To his left, the kitchen was also empty, a bowl of cereal overturned on the table, milk and Cocoa Puffs spilling down over the edge.

When he reached the staircase at the end of the hall, he paused. He didn't know how long he'd been hearing it, but now he was aware for the first time of the sound of whimpering. He backed off the first step and went around to the storage space below the stairs. The whimpering came from deep inside the gap. He knelt down, looked inside.

Billy LeMarque huddled against the far wall, cradling his four-year-old sister. It was from her that the whimpering came. Billy looked dry-eyed at Will, his seven-year-old face drained, frightened. "Mom," he whispered. "Upstairs."

"It'll be okay, Billy," Will said. "Just wait there. I'll be back in a second."

"It was our fault," Billy said. "But it was an accident. Tell Mom we didn't mean it. We were just trying to help. We didn't mean to make a mess." His lower lip was quivering. "Tell her not to be mad, please?"

Will nodded, patted Billy on the shoulder, and started back up the staircase. What had happened to scare Billy so terribly? He was always such a happy kid, and as far as he knew, Barbara had never laid a finger on him.

The second floor was silent. He headed away from the stairs, passing the kids' bedroom first. Sheets, pillows, and mattresses were thrown all around the room. Shattered toys littered the floor. Frowning, he continued down the hall toward the master bedroom. Something was seriously wrong; he didn't need to see the damage to know that. There was a tension in the air, a sense of something waiting to happen. He'd felt it as soon as he'd walked through the front door, and now it was almost tangible. He hesitated at the door to the master bedroom. He licked his lips, found them dry. No sound came from inside.

Gently he knocked on the door. "Barbara?" He spoke in a whisper, but it seemed like a shout in the silent hall. He tried the knob, found it unlocked. A low moan came from inside the bedroom. Will inched the door open. The bedroom was a shambles; hampers overturned, drawers pulled out, curtains pulled down from the windows. With a final push, he opened the door all the way and stepped inside.

Something. There. In the corner.

Barbara was huddled in a fetal position in a corner of the bedroom, rocking back and forth, her hands clamped over her ears, moaning—a low, rhythmic, tuneless hum that filled the room with a sound like moth wings beating against a killing jar.

"Barbara?" He started toward her. She was dressed only in her robe, cinched tight around her, the collar turned up and shrouding her face. As he drew closer, it occurred to him that her actions reminded him of the way a child covers its ears and hums to try to block out what someone is trying to say.

But there was no one else in the room.

He knelt down beside her. She seemed oblivious to his presence. Rocking. Humming. Blocking out the world. "Barbara? It's me. It's Will." Slowly he reached out and touched her arm.

Barbara screamed. Her head jerked up at his touch, her eyes wide with terror, seeing not him but something else. "No! *No!*"

She rolled from his grasp and scrabbled across the floor, batting at the empty air. Will followed on his knees, fending off the blows that rained ineffectively on his shoulders. Her hands were everywhere at once, like two pale birds battering themselves against him.

He managed to snare one of her hands, then the other, holding them tight. Barbara screamed, struggled in his grasp. He pulled her closer, forcing her to face him. "Barbara! Look at me! It's Will. Will Cameron! You called me, remember? I'm here to help you."

He kept talking, saying every soothing thing he could think of, trying to fight his way through her hysteria. Even if he'd wanted to slap her, he didn't dare let go of one of her arms long enough to try. Finally she seemed to tire, and after a few minutes her eyes found him through the haze, focused. "Will?" It was barely a whisper. Her face twisted with pain and tears, and she collapsed into his arms, sobs wracking her body.

"Oh God, Will, oh God," she managed. "The kids . . . I didn't hurt them, please God don't let me hurt them—"

"They're fine. A little scared, but fine. You're the one we've got to worry about right now."

"Thank God they're all right," she said. She buried her head in his chest. "I couldn't take it anymore, Will. They kept calling me. All night. Can't sleep. I could hear them—they knew my name, Will. How did they know my name?"

"They're your kids, Barbara, they—"

She shook her head frantically. Pounded the floor. "No! Not them! It *wasn't* the kids! I checked! I—Will, they were calling me. Don't you understand? They were—God—how did they know my name, Will? How?"

"Who was calling you?"

She looked at him, her eyes desperate. "I don't know. I just—please, Will—help me! Don't leave me. Don't let me hurt the kids. Please, God . . ."

"Don't you worry, I'm not going anywhere. I'm right here."

He held her tight, waiting for the sobs to end, adding what little strength he had to her own. He tightened his grip, determined, despite the ache in his muscles, that he would go on holding her forever, if that was what it took.

"It'll be okay," he murmured over and over, soothing her, "everything's going to be all right."

SIX

SAM

Clutching his crudely drawn map, Sam Crawford made his way back to the main chamber at the cave mouth, passing from shadow to light—not that it helped much. The air that swept through Indian Caves was cold, damp, and altogether uncomfortable, with the oppressive, heavy scent of dirt and stone. The chill seeped painfully into his joints. He longed to step out of the caves and warm himself in the meager sunlight that was reflected up from the ridge—but he was too tired even for that.

Instead, he settled heavily onto the folding chair next to the cooler containing his lunch. He tried to work up some enthusiasm at the prospect, but he still wasn't hungry. This place could kill anybody's appetite, he decided, then shook his head. No, it wasn't the cave that was doing it. A cave is just a hole in the ground. It had nothing to do with what he was feeling.

He was finally coming to the realization that he was a fool. And an ass. An old man chasing shadows.

Ten years. Ten years since the first dig he'd led at the caves had produced a sensation. Who'd have figured a couple of wet-behind-the-ears Anthro 1 students would stumble—more or less literally—across a batch of Indian relics in a place everybody had spelunked clean years ago? But there they had been, in a previously unexplored passage, not even on any of the maps: bits of pottery, drawings sketched on animal hide, arrowheads and tools. Oh, but it had been fun! The news reports, the interviews, the publication in journals both popular and obscure, and the tenure at the university. Yes, he thought, splendid indeed.

With the discovery, they'd been able to declare Indian Caves as an official dig, get it preserved against tourists and residents alike. There'd been some resistance from the town council, of course; they didn't want a flock of long-haired college types running around the Point, digging up who-knew-who's bones. But eventually they gave in, as he knew they would, especially when the university approved the research grant, with a stipend approved for the town council in exchange for all the inconvenience.

As it turned out, all their efforts on and off over a period of five years—with two extensions from a college board growing increasingly impatient for some result that would justify the expense—had turned up little else new or interesting. They had hoped—vainly, he knew, even then—that the caves had once been part of a colony of Algonquins, and that further digging might unearth a whole generation's worth of artifacts. But that did not seem to be the case, and finally the money ran out with the board's patience.

For the next few years, while the caves were still closed to casual tourists, there had been a few more attempts to further explore the caves—all of them spotty, poorly financed, and of questionable scientific value. Sam still cringed at the memory of the psychic who'd tried several times to locate a supposed treasure that she'd seen in a dream.

There had been other unstable types who had trudged the narrow path up to the caves, claiming to hear the voice of God or Martians, looking for salvation or a sign of the imminent apocalypse. After a while, the local folks had just stopped giving directions to anybody who looked as if he wasn't quite all there. That had pretty much put an end to the whole business.

There's something about this place that attracts oddballs, he decided, and wondered if that was why *he* was still here.

He looked down at the hand-drawn map resting on the

cooler beside him—a photocopied sheet representing (collectively) ten years of spelunking, and still the map was incomplete, covering only the maze of passages that extended down to the first level. Beyond that, the passages were so narrow, so winding, so prone to sudden dead ends and merges and drop-offs, that surveying any farther was risky even for a well-equipped party.

Soon enough, the caves would be reopened to tourists. With the decreasing numbers of out-of-towners coming around each year, the Point could use a good tourist attraction, and he knew this was just what they had in mind. The place would end up crawling with spelunkers, more than ever before, and some folks with more guts than brains would try the lower levels in spite of the warnings. Then it would only be a matter of time before someone stumbled across something that'd make all the papers. . . .

No. Those were *his* caves. If there was something to be found here, he would find it.

He looked around the cave mouth, his heart still beating fast from the last round of exploration, an old man running around in the dirt. Looking to reclaim past triumphs.

Fat chance.

So.

So why the hell was he still here, prowling rock-bottomed passages he'd walked dozens of times before? He rubbed his hands together for warmth. The skin was smooth, dusty, almost sandpapered by constant contact with the passage walls as he looked for imperfections, unnatural lines, anything out of the ordinary.

Why?

Because, he thought as he slipped off the lid of the cooler, part of him was *sure* they hadn't found everything! Yes, it was illogical. But the nagging feeling that they'd missed something kept drawing him back to the caves year after year, refusing to go away even in the face of relentless logic.

There was something here, he thought. And he was determined to find it.

But *after* lunch. As he liked to point out every so often, he might be eccentric, but he wasn't crazy.

He reached into the cooler and brought out his bag lunch and several bottles of orange juice. Rye bread, ham, a dill pickle . . . his stomach growled in anticipation.

Then the smell hit him.

"God*damn!*" He held the sandwich at arm's length, covering his nose and mouth with his other hand. The bread was powdery and blackened, and what little he could bring himself to see of the meat and cheese was covered with a thick, viscous layer of mottled white and green mold.

But he'd made the sandwich fresh that very morning; he'd picked up the sliced ham just yesterday.

"How the hell—" he said, and jumped just a little at the sound of his own voice.

It was then that he realized the cave was no longer entirely silent. The sound might have been there for a while, but it only now impinged upon his thoughts—a scraping from deep within, echoing faintly from the nearest passage. It was, he thought, the sound of rock scraping against rock.

The first concern that sprang to mind was a cave-in. But the sound was too steady, too restrained. He put his hand to the wall, feeling for the vibrations that would signal a major shift. The wall was quiet. He stood in the cave mouth, caught between the instincts of fight and flight, the impulse to stay or to run, the spoiled sandwich all but forgotten.

Another moment, and the sound increased in pitch as well as volume, as if a huge rock were caught inside a massive vise being screwed steadily tighter. The sound rose higher, until it reached a point where it sounded as if the rocks themselves were shrieking. Sam backpedaled toward the cave mouth, got ready to run, in case it *was* a cave-in.

Then, abruptly, the sound stopped. Sam hesitated, half in and half out of the cave. He strained to hear anything else, but the caves were silent again. No rocks fell, no cracks appeared. There was no sign of further disturbance. Cautiously he picked up the map and the Coleman lantern and edged into the main passage.

He held the lantern out in front of him, the light throwing stark shadows that chased one another down the long, rocky passage. It looked undamaged. He hesitated, then stepped forward, continuing down the passage. Just a little more.

This is crazy, he thought distantly, as if in a dream. But he crept forward anyway, every vestige of common sense crying out to him to go back. This was unreasonably dangerous. And yet it felt strangely safe. The passage was the same; the passage was somehow different; and all the while he continued

71

ahead, turning one corner, then another. He moved as if drawn by some long-dormant instinct, a sense that there was something important just around the next corner.

But there was nothing around that corner, or the one following. By degrees, his cautious nature began to assert itself again, especially as he neared the end of the first level. To go on any farther would be madness. Therefore he would not go any farther. He continued on. Turned a long, slow corner. A few more steps, no more, and that would be it.

He stopped, determined now to go back. He knew this passage, had checked it more times than he cared to think about. There was nothing here. He *knew* that.

So much for instinct.

He was about to turn back when a glimmer of light caught his attention. He squinted ahead, to where the glow of the lantern was caught and thrown back by a fine line along the near wall. He stepped forward, running his hand along the line. He hadn't noticed this before. He pressed gently.

The wall moved.

A section of the passage wall swung freely away from him. He stepped back, ready to run if the wall started to give. Nothing happened. He gently pressed at the wall again, and it swung back farther. Sam's hands trembled against the cold stone, inspecting every line, his mind almost afraid to confront the realization of what he had found. He blinked hard. It remained. A door.

A *door!*

Slowly he edged into the doorway. He cast the glow from the lantern up, tracing the door's edge. Where once it had seamlessly joined the roof of the passage, now there was a gap of several inches. The door had been cut from the surrounding stone, then made to fit back in perfectly, the edge weaving slightly with the natural patterns. No wonder they had missed it!

Sam's mind raced. The noise he'd heard must have been the stone door settling, the motion perhaps triggered off by a slight tremor somewhere else in the cave. When that happened, the weights that operated the door must have shifted, and the entrance became visible.

He edged farther into the open space beyond the door, his emotions torn. His first instinct was to get someone else in here as fast as possible. But at the same time he wanted, *needed* to know what was on the other side of the door that someone had worked so hard to conceal.

And he wanted to know *now*.

He squeezed ahead the last few inches, then held the lantern high. The light revealed a high, circular cavern marked on all sides by dark recesses where the light was swallowed into shadows, indicating the possibility of a whole network of previously unknown passages extending off in all directions. He stepped forward, his feet leaving tracks in dust that had lain undisturbed for—how long? One hundred years? Two? If the Algonquins had built this passage, then it might not have been opened since the French and Indian Wars.

He swung the lantern in a long, slow arc, letting the glow linger here and there, finding only the darkness of the many passages. But at one opening the light returned, bouncing off something just inside. Which meant that it might not be a passage, but perhaps a shallow alcove. Best to explore it later, he thought. Remember the buddy system.

Nevertheless, he stepped forward.

No, he thought, but the impulse had no effect. More than before, he felt drawn toward whatever lay just beyond the glow of his lantern. His feet moved ahead as if of their own volition, as they did in nightmares, when he would try to escape but find himself paralyzed, unable to do anything but continue with the dream.

Halfway across the cavern, he was near enough to distinguish colors within the alcove. A few steps more, and he was there. His breath came in excited shudders as he held out the lantern.

"Ah!" he cried. The sound came involuntarily at the sight of the drawings. They were by far the most elaborate cave drawings he had seen. Preserved deep within the cave, away from light and air, they were as brilliant as when they had first been drawn.

Some were fairly standard renderings of antelopes and bears, pictorials of the hunt, designed to bring good fortune to the hunters. But there were others: detailed drawings of Indians, and beside them, additional drawings of each figure, identical except for the coloration. The duplicates were sketched in black, the edges indistinct, as if the artist had been trying to intimate a living shadow, a representation of the spirits of the deceased. There were scenes of pitched battle, of faces hanging above firepits. But the drawing that caught and held Sam's attention, that forced him to breathe deeply in a futile attempt to steady his nerves, was the centerpiece.

His first thought was: Jung was right. There had to be a collective unconscious. At a rough guess, the drawings before him had to date back to a time before the first settlements, and yet there it was: *Quadricornutus serpens.* The four-horned serpent. Identical to drawings he'd seen by sixteenth-century alchemists. Symbol of Mercury, known to the ancient Greeks as *drakon.*

The Dragon.

Christian translation: the Devil.

And there was more. The drawings that ringed the centerpiece were similar to the gargoyles atop the cornices of European cathedrals. There were some small instances where the images did not correspond exactly, but they were trivial, a matter of interpretation. The basic images were there, although the specifics of line and shape had clearly been influenced by the naturalistic beliefs of the Indians rather than by the strict dogma of the Christians.

All of them sketched onto these walls hundreds of years *before* explorers had ever set foot in the New World.

He repressed a shiver of excitement. This wasn't the right time for reveling in the anticipation of what this find would do to the fields of anthropology and psychology. The first order of business would be to get photographs of the drawings as quickly as possible. Now that they had been exposed to the air, they would begin fading fast. He cursed himself for not having his time-exposure camera along: The one time I need it, it's home.

Afterward, once he'd developed the pictures, he'd bring in others to help document the drawings, come up with an approximate date of origin, and write up the findings. Then he would submit the results, sit back, and watch the explosion.

He pulled his thoughts back to the present, and discovered that for several minutes he had been staring into the eye of the painted *serpens.* Simultaneously, and with vivid clarity, he became acutely aware of where he was—and the realization brought with it an unaccountable sense of panic. He was suddenly aware of being deep underground, of the closeness of the stale air—air that had not been breathed for hundreds of years. He backed away, glancing nervously at the *serpens,* as though expecting it to strike from its painted stance.

Claustrophobia—something he hadn't felt in years of digging through caves and caverns—swept over him in gut-wrenching waves. Bile bit at the back of his throat; nausea built. He turned away, fighting for breath. Before him lay the newly discovered passages, each leading off in a different direction, deeper into the darkness, down and down. They loomed large in his mind, as if he were standing on the ledge of a tall building and looking straight down, the edge crumbling beneath him. Fear rose in his throat; he felt the need to run, to be anywhere but *here*. And yet—and yet the tunnels beckoned, their darkness inviting, as if soft voices murmured deep within, too faint to be heard on any but a subconscious level.

No, he thought, backing out of the room, trying to find the door and trying not to be sick. It would be cooler down there, in the comforting darkness, just take a single step, just like rolling downhill. . . .

He found the edge of the door, started around it—and almost against his will his gaze returned to the *serpens*, pinned against the far wall by the thin stream of light. Caught by the light just *so*, it seemed almost to be looking right at him, through him.

With a final lunge, he staggered back into the passage. Instantly the sense of nausea and panic diminished. He started to retrace his steps. Though he knew by heart every turn needed to get out of the caves, he checked the map again. He was in a tricky part of the caves, and if the panic hit again—

No. He couldn't trust himself. Not yet.

He walked faster, the lantern making an all-but-useless smear of light on the cave floor in front of him, barely showing him where to put one foot in front of the other. Left. Left. Right. Then another right. One more turn lay ahead. He tried to think only about walking. The air inside was becoming truly oppressive. It pressed in on him from all sides, seemed almost to hold him back, to stand between him and the way out. He cursed himself for his weakness and walked faster.

Ten more steps and he'd be out. Eight.

He imagined he heard footsteps behind him, knew it was just the echo of his own footfalls, but hurried nonetheless. Six. Four.

Faster.

Right—and out. Around the long curve of the cave came the glow of the noon sun. He switched off the lamp, breathed deeply, and shook his head at his foolishness. He hadn't had a moment of panic like that since he'd started digging around in caves, twenty years ago. He felt ashamed at the idea of it, privately glad that there had been no one around to see.

He crossed to the cave mouth, noticing just how sweet the air smelled. From here he could see nearly all of the Point, clear to the high pines along the shore. Just beyond the treetops he could make out whitecaps rolling in off Machias Bay. It was a familiar sight, and the imagined terrors of the darkness were lessened by that familiarity.

With a shrug he threw off the last of the uneasiness, attributing it to his momentary, if rather embarrassing, failure of nerve. He now turned his attention to his immediate needs, foremost among them getting his camera equipment from home and setting up here as quickly as possible. An infrared or low-level strobe would be necessary. He didn't dare risk the glare of a standard flash; it would only hasten the fading of the drawings. The thought of returning alone filled him with a momentary but quickly suppressed twinge of concern. There wasn't time to wait for someone to come down from the university. If he was going to get the pictures before the air diminished the colors, he'd have to do so on his own.

He glanced behind him, first at the passage, then, as his gaze caught it, at the sandwich that lay all but forgotten on the ground. Insects crawled in and around the blackened slices. His stomach turned at the sight.

Not hungry anyway, he thought, and stepped onto the narrow path that would take him back to the main road, and his car, far below.

2

Fifteen minutes later, Sam reached his green 1968 Buick LeSabre. He had barely unlocked the door when he heard the rumble of another car, and turned to see Constable Tom Crandall's black-and-white come up over the top of the hill. It came to a stop on the other side of the road.

Crandall stepped out and crossed the road. "Morning, Sam."

Sam nodded. "How's it going, Tom?"

Crandall shrugged. "Not great. You still puttering around up there?" He jerked a thumb toward the cave.

"Just a hobby," Sam said.

"Yeah, well, there's hobbies and there's hobbies. I don't want to have to go looking for you if you get lost in there."

"Thanks for the advice, Dad. Mind if I borrow the car tonight?"

"Okay. Point taken."

"Good." Sam noted the tension on Tom's face. "Something wrong?"

Tom nodded. "Ever have one of those days when a lot of little things kept going—not wrong, exactly, just weird?"

"Every day. Really got you hopping, eh?"

"Believe it. Damn phone's been ringing all day with one thing or another—most of them piddly little complaints—and I just got word over the radio that something's going on with Barbara LeMarque."

"Is she all right?" Sam barely knew Barbara, just enough to say hello to on the street, but she had always seemed friendly enough.

"As far as I know, yeah. And on top of that we've got peepers and vandals and kids stealing newspapers off front lawns, and some sick character killing Duane Kincaid's cat." He shook his head. "Just one thing after another."

Sam turned thoughtful. "What you said about Duane's cat—when did it happen?"

"Jeez, I don't know. Sometime between eleven last night and seven this morning is as close as they can put it. I just came from there. Poor cat just got the insides cut out of him. Takes a real sicko, if you ask me."

Sam frowned. Last night he'd seen Karl Jergen running to his car just down the road from Duane's place. It had seemed curious enough at the time, but he hadn't attributed too much to it. Figured Karl might be having car trouble. Then again, Karl was always getting involved in something, very little of it good, and the timing was about right.

He considered mentioning it, but it wasn't considered a good idea around town to mess with Karl, who had a long memory and a nasty temper. And there was so much to do right now. He *needed* that camera, fast, which left little time to waste on someone like Karl.

"Well," Sam said at last, "if I hear anything, I'll let you know. Anything else?"

"No, I guess that covers it. Just passing through, wanted to see how *you* were doing. One less thing to worry about. See you around."

"Later," Sam said.

And hesitated. Damn it, he owed Tom. He'd helped Sam out more than once, with everything from permits to traffic tickets. The least he could do was return the favor.

He rolled down the window. "Hey, Tom?"

"Yeah?"

"You may want to talk to Karl Jergen. I'm not saying he did anything—but I did see him out around Duane's place late last night. Might be nothing, but you never know. Just don't mention my name, okay?"

"No problem. At least it's a place to start. And even if he didn't do it, he might've seen the guy who did, or saw somebody who saw somebody else. Just one big crapshoot." He gunned the engine. "Thanks for the tip, Sam."

The black-and-white sped off down the road, scattering leaves on both sides, a trail of brown and red and gold that whirled up and away, falling back onto the road in slow arcs.

Sam waited until Tom had driven out of sight, then headed in the opposite direction, toward town, hoping he had done the right thing.

SEVEN

LIZ

It was nearly one o'clock when Liz stepped out of the general store. R.T. was quite a talker, but their discussion had left her more interested in what he *didn't* say than what he did. It was pretty clear that he knew more about what was going on in town than even the constable—knew the kinds of things people talked about when they gathered inside his store on cool days to shake their heads and whisper, or when they sat out on the front porch when the days were warm, remembering events that hadn't been recorded in any of the local papers. R.T. was trusted, and for good reason: he was remarkably tight-lipped. He was an expert at the maddening game of letting you know he knew something, but without *saying* he knew it, or giving more than tantalizing hints about what it was in the first place.

She'd accused him of being a most uncooperative interviewee, but he'd just smiled and denied knowing what she was talking about.

"I mean, sure, you've got a town, and folks who've lived here going back four generations, so there's bound to've been feuds and intermarryings and more than our share of bad blood and worse tempers—plenty to talk about."

"Except, to listen to you," Liz said, "everything interesting stopped after the Second World War."

"No, just with all due respect, I can't see what that has to do with your book, ma'am. If I understand you, you're looking into the past. The present isn't important."

"It's important to the whole picture. This is about the *life* of small towns—past, present, future. After all, isn't a town the way it is because of what happened in the past?"

"If you're talking about who's been mayor and why, what laws got passed, and the way most folks 'round here have managed to keep out your ethnics, then I guess you've got a point." He polished the base of a brass lamp, smiling quietly to himself. "But the rest . . .

"Look. For the sake of argument, say I was to tell you what I've heard. And mind you, not everything I've heard is true. But let's say it's even half true. What if I told you that the guy down the street's an alcoholic? That the man who owns the store next door beats his wife when he gets drunk? Or that so-and-so's wife is playing around with so-and-so's husband? What good will that do you? None at all, that I can see.

"Sure, there's gossip. And scandal. But there hasn't been a serious crime in this town, not a murder or a rape or anything like that for—well, for as long as I can remember. I think sometimes there's something that watches over the Point. Keeps the rest of the world outside, where it belongs."

With that, the tiny bell over the door had chimed a customer, and R.T. had headed off, the interview effectively over.

Outside the store, Liz shaded her eyes, looked across the street, and found Eric sitting inside the white gazebo in the shade of a war memorial—a statue of a Revolutionary War soldier looking east, toward the sea, the bronze plaque at his feet bearing the words ETERNAL VIGILANCE IS THE PRICE OF FREEDOM.

Even from here, Eric seemed intent on something he was reading. And yet he surprised her by looking up at her as she crossed the street, long before he could have heard her approach. He smiled a greeting, then briefly returned his attention to whatever he was reading. She only caught a flicker of it, but there was something in his face that troubled her, as if the smile had been erected exclusively for her benefit. Sitting there all alone, enveloped by the gazebo, there was something about him that reminded her of a young boy she'd seen once—lost, frightened but trying not to show it, and trying even harder to find his way home. Strangely, she felt an irrational longing to go over to him, put an arm around him, and tell him that it was all going to be okay.

Whatever it was.

As she stepped up onto the gazebo, Eric smiled at her again, pausing only to fold up the papers he'd been studying and stick them in his jacket pocket. She glimpsed columns of white print on black paper, the sort of photocopies produced by the library's ancient copier.

"Find anything interesting to read?"

"Nothing worth mentioning," Eric said, stuffing his hands into his pockets. Once again the image of the young boy came back, and she could almost see him scuffing his toe in the dirt, caught in the act of stealing an apple from a street vendor. "How'd the interview go?"

She shrugged. "Nothing worth mentioning."

If he caught the sarcasm, he gave no indication, but only patted the gazebo's railing. "Haven't seen one of these in years."

"They still use it, too. The mayor gives his inauguration speech here, the Fourth of July picnics always end up with a fireworks display right overhead, and twice a month they have band concerts."

"It's like walking into the past."

"Or like the past walking into the present."

"Makes you wonder what it would've been like to grow up here, in one place, not moving all the time. . . ." His voice trailed off.

She joined him by the railing. "It is pretty around here, isn't it?"

He said nothing, but stared across the town square to the church of St. Benedict, the biggest building in the Point. Though two blocks away, the Gothic structure dominated the town's center. It was a sober, almost severe place.

"Impressive," Eric said.

Liz nodded. "And about half as old as the town itself. It's supposed to have quite a history."

"Oh?"

"Just rumors, really old stories, but I'd love to try to verify some of them. They say the place was built with some pretty odd sources of income, but I haven't been able to get anything specific. I wouldn't be surprised if most of the stories were made up just to bring in the tourists."

"Spoken like a true skeptic," said a voice from behind them. They turned as Father Kerr climbed up the steps.

"I thought eavesdropping was reserved for the confessional, Father," Liz said.

"Well, since you don't come to confession, perhaps it was the Lord trying to compensate." He grinned. "Actually, I was running a few errands when I saw you, and thought I'd invite the two of you to dinner tonight. I may even invite Sam along, in case I get dull. Assuming we can get him anywhere *near* a church."

"Sounds fine," Eric said.

"You're on. When should we stop by?" Liz asked.

"Six-thirty. I'll see you then." With a cordial nod, he started away. "Oh, and Elizabeth?"

"Yes?"

"Since you mentioned it, for you I'll keep the confessional available twenty-four hours a day."

"I'll try not to waste it, Father—so any mortal sins I commit between now and dinner are exclusively your fault."

Kerr shook his head with mock resignation and crossed the park, heading toward the church.

"It's at times like this, when I'm dealing with the folks around here—Sam, Zach, Father Kerr, and just about anybody else you want to name—that I'm glad I grew up in New York," Liz said. "I can match 'em smartass remark for smartass remark."

"From what I've seen, I'd say they get a kick out of the way you hold your own."

"Probably. They also get a kick out of matchmaking. Or didn't you catch the subtext there?"

"Caught it. But I can think of worse excuses to have dinner with you."

Liz gauged her response, opted for flippancy. Truth was, it seemed like a nice idea to her, too. "C'mon," she said, "we'd better get you out of the hot sun."

"I feel fine."

"One of the most dangerous signs. Don't you read the papers?"

As they stepped down from the gazebo, Eric casually took her arm. "It's a long time until dinner. What do you say to some lunch?"

"You're buying?"

"Sure."

"Then lead on." As they headed for the diner, Liz found herself feeling generally pleased with the world, despite the unsatisfying interview and the overcast afternoon. She wasn't going to get her hopes up, but for as long as she was here, and he was here . . .

After all, she'd been working on her book for the better part of a year. No reason why she couldn't mix a lot of business with a little pleasure.

Or a little business with a lot of pleasure.

EIGHT

THE POINT

The old milk truck rumbled to a halt in front of the Royal Flush Tavern shortly before four o'clock. A little early, even for Bud Simmons. Nonetheless, Ace Jackson automatically set up a glass and a bottle of Heineken so they were ready by the time Bud eased onto the red barstool.

Ace nodded a greeting. "How's it going?"

Bud shrugged and filled the glass, watching the head rise. He took a long swallow, then sat staring at the suds.

Must be a real heartbreaker, Ace thought, without much sympathy. Bud always did wear his heart on his sleeve.

A second long swallow emptied the glass, and Bud signaled for another round. Still silent. Wouldn't last. Bud was that kind of drunk; a few more beers, and he'd spill his guts all over the place. That was the kind of drunk Ace had no patience with. If something's bothering you, then by God get it out and over with, don't wait for the booze to give you the nerve and an excuse for the next day.

Still, Bud was a regular—and you didn't run a business by getting your clientele pissed off at you. "So how's Beth?" Ace asked, not really expecting an answer.

Bud played with a water ring on the bar top. "How the hell should I know?"

"Well, I just figured—"

"She was fine when I left, okay? But that was then. This is now."

Real profound, Ace thought.

Bud glared at him. "Any other questions?"

"Not a one," Ace said, and went around the bar to start setting up chairs for later tonight. And screw you too, he thought.

For the next half hour, Ace went back behind the bar only long enough to dispense another bottle of Heineken. He made no further attempts at conversation. No one else entered the tavern to break the thick silence.

Finally, Bud slid a dollar tip across the bar, stood, and headed back across the tavern toward the door. "Thanks," he muttered, and stalked out to the beat-up milk truck parked just down the street. Ace watched through the bay window, past the neon sign that spelled out Coors in red neon, as Bud stood in front of the truck, looking as if he were thinking hard about something. After a moment he slid into the front seat, and tried to start the engine. The only reward for his efforts was a grinding and a clanking that could be heard clear up to Walnut Street.

No wonder Bud was upset, Ace thought. Sounded like a broken piston, no doubt about it. Nothing else to do but take the old truck out and have it shot, maybe sell it for scrap. It sure as hell wasn't ever going anyplace. As if in confirmation, the sound stopped and Bud climbed out of the truck, slammed the door behind him, and started walking down the street toward town. There was no bus service in the Point, so unless he could pick up a lift from someone, Bud would have a long walk ahead of him.

Ace went back to getting the bar ready for the after-work regulars.

He'd sure hate to be home when Bud got there.

He had a hunch that ol' Bud and his lady were going to have a long, hard night. But better Beth than him—and at that, he smiled.

Hey, Beth, he thought, this Bud's for you!

Karin Whortle rang up the mayor's bill: one Reuben, easy on the sauerkraut; cole slaw, fries, coffee, and a slice of pie. She wondered if this wasn't the exact same meal George Morgan ordered every time he stopped by the diner—which was only when he was getting ready to run for office again. Lord knew, his wife could cook up a storm, Karin thought. But a man in his position sometimes had to be seen in places he wasn't usually seen in, so that when he campaigned in earnest, nobody would think anything about seeing good old George glad-handing everyone and anyone in sight.

Then again, she considered, he just might be hungry and want a quick bite before heading home. No reason for her to be cynical all the time.

She held out his change, but he pulled away, palms raised. "Karin," he said, "you're the finest waitress in all the Point. Keep it."

She looked down at the three-dollar tip on a six-fifty bill, smiled, and slipped the money into her apron. "Thanks," she said.

George was *definitely* getting ready to run for office.

Perhaps, she thought, there was something to be said after all for a healthy sense of cynicism.

Exuding practiced joviality, George headed toward the door, pausing here and there to clap several diners on the shoulder. Then, with a wave to someone at the back of the room and a glance at his watch—didn't busy mayors with pressing schedules always check their watches?—he bustled into the fading afternoon.

"Looks like Good King George is on the move again."

Karin turned at the voice and found Walter Kriski leaning on the counter, smiling at her. She noticed what a pleasant smile he had. It was something she was noticing a lot lately.

"By the way," he said, handing over his check, "I was wondering if you had any plans for Friday night. *Fantasia* is playing up in Cutler. So if you're interested—"

Karin busied herself for a moment by ringing up his bill

while her mind flickered over one response and then another. He was a nice enough man, certainly persistent enough to make her think he was at least somewhat serious.

The process of deliberation seemed longer than it was, and by the time she'd counted out his change and handed it back, she had her answer ready. "Sure," she said. Four letters, one word. Some response, given all the work she'd put into it. But it was the content, not the quantity of the words that mattered.

Walter seemed to positively glow at her agreement—at the same time looking so genuinely surprised that Karin had to stifle a laugh.

"Six o'clock, then? We can have dinner out. Let someone wait on you for a change. See you then," he said, and headed for the door.

For the rest of her shift, Karin played out one scenario after another, most of them ending in a name change, from Karin Whortle to K. Kriski, and Karin Kriski. It sounded funny, she had to admit. But that was one of the dangers of getting involved, wasn't it? If the relationship went anywhere, maybe she should think about keeping her own name. Because, frankly, she thought, Karin Kriski sounded like a kid's cereal.

3

It was a quarter after four when Constable Tom Crandall drove back into town and noticed Karl Jergen walking in the general direction of Veteran's Hill. He killed the engine half a block from the station and climbed out of the car, heading in Karl's direction. The Kincaids hadn't been much help in trying to figure out who had tortured and killed their cat, but Karl's name had come up more than once in the course of the conversation. Seems he'd been told to get lost after one too many unwanted phone calls to Jessie, Duane's oldest. Hardly seemed reason enough to do something as sick as kill a cat, but Sam *had* placed him in the area at roughly the right time.

He stepped up onto the curb. "Hey, Karl. How's it going?"

Karl stopped, shrugged. "Fine."

"Haven't talked to you in a while. Anything new?"

"No. Sorry."

Tom thrust his hands into his jacket pockets. "Wish I could say the same. Been a lot of excitement the last day or so. You probably heard about what happened over to the Kincaid's place last night."

"You mean the cat? Don't think there's anyone over by R.T.'s that hasn't. Ray couldn't talk about anything else."

Tom made a mental note to give Ray hell for shooting off his mouth again. "I don't suppose you'd like to tell me where you were last night."

He looked for the slightest flicker of emotion on Karl's face, and found none. "Home."

Just like a big, ugly statue, Tom thought.

"Can anyone verify that?"

"Yeah," Karl said. "Why?"

"Well, let's just say I have reason to believe you were wandering around last night, maybe even near the Kincaids' place."

"Then you believe wrong," Karl said. "I was home. Okay?" There was a note in his voice that said that the conversation was over. "If you've heard something to the contrary, then somebody's either crazy or feeding you lies. Anything else?"

"No, not now."

"Good." Karl stepped around the constable and continued on his way, not looking back.

Frowning, Tom headed toward the station. Normally he'd be inclined to think that anyone who acted like Karl had something to hide; trouble was, Karl *always* acted like somebody just stuck a beehive up his ass.

One thing was sure, though. He trusted Sam. And if Sam said Karl was out that night, then Karl *was* out that night, and if Karl said otherwise, he was lying.

Tom pushed open the door and found Ray sitting at the desk, talking on the telephone. He raised an index finger to signal Tom that he'd just be a minute. Finally he hung up and tapped the sheet of paper in front of him. "Got it."

"Got what?" Tom still intended to give Ray hell, but that could wait for whatever the deputy had to say.

"Got all the stuff I could on that Eric Matthews. The guy's a full-time transient. Nobody on the wire has anything on him that covers more than a year. Seems he left a trail of bad news from one end of the country to the other—nothing anyone could pin on him, but he was questioned more times than an only daughter five hours late for curfew."

Tom frowned. Until now, Karl was suspect number one. But if this Matthews fellow was a troublemaker . . .

"Any wants or warrants?"

"No. A couple of the sheriffs I talked to said they'd like to ask him a question or two sometime, but as long as he stayed out of their town, that was good enough for them."

"Then that's as far as we can go, for now. Can't pick someone up just for being a drifter. If he's staying over at Zach's place, that means he's got money, and *that* means we can't pick him up for being a transient. And as for being a trouble-maker, hell, if we went around locking up everyone who was a troublemaker, we'd empty half the town inside of an hour.

"Which doesn't mean we have to ignore him, either," Tom continued. "We've got every reason to keep an eye on him until he drifts off somewhere else. Maybe nothing'll happen. Maybe he's just had a string of bad luck. And maybe we should make sure he doesn't try to have any bad luck while he's here."

At that, Ray smiled. "Understood." He started toward the back room for some coffee. "I think we can handle that."

"Good," Tom called into the room. "Then maybe you could help out with this other troublemaker I heard about. Real pain-in-the-ass deputy constable who keeps shooting his mouth off about investigations in progress."

The silence that filled the station for the next few minutes before Ray finally worked up enough nerve to step back out again was the only time Tom could remember Ray being quiet for that long.

On reflection, he decided he liked it.

4

It was four-thirty when Fred Keller pulled in his net. His prac-ticed fingers found all the familiar places along the weave, keeping the loops from tangling as they piled up in concentric circles on the deck of the small boat. To the east, the horizon was darkening, and a cold wind ushered in the feel of imminent night. Time enough for one last run, and that would have to do it for the day.

Keller leaned against the gunwale, feeding the net line to the winch, testing it for tension. The line felt disappointingly slack. In a few more minutes, the rest of the net was drawn into a tight circle behind the boat. Where normally there would be the thrashing of fish trying to escape, there was only stillness and the rippling tracery of the net. For the third time that day, the net was empty.

Keller sat down heavily in the fighting chair. It just didn't make any sense. By all rights, the fish should be running on top, as they always did when it got cool. But the first net had shown that they weren't on top. So he'd tried lowering the skirts of the net—and still nothing. He'd even pulled out the spinning rods and set them along the cockpit, each baited for a different depth, to check for nibbles. And still there had been nothing—not a bite, not a nibble. *Nothing.*

He walked over to the cockpit freezer and pulled out a beer. On any other day, he would've caught *something* in the net—a blue, a mackerel, even a flounder. He'd been fishing all his life, and he'd only had luck like this twice before, both times when he'd made the mistake of putting out in the face of a storm. Fish weren't as stupid as most folks thought; they knew when a storm was coming, and sought the deepest water to hide in until it was all over.

He scanned the horizon. A few clouds, yes, but otherwise the sky was clear. No storm anywhere in sight. Which eliminated that theory.

Deciding that sitting here wasn't going to get him any closer to a full net, Keller put down the beer and fired up the engines. Perhaps he'd have better luck on the leeward side of the Point.

At least it was worth trying.

5

Karl Jergen slipped into the house and climbed the stairs to his room. He changed to a warmer checked shirt and a peacoat, and started out again, hoping to make it to the door without interference. He wasn't in the mood.

As he might have expected, Ruth was waiting for him in the front hall, binoculars in hand. "I saw you talking to the police. Are you in trouble again?"

"No," Karl said, pushing past her.

She spun on him, grabbed him by the arm, and stuck her face in front of his own. He wanted to smash it. "Oh, sure—he just stopped to chat, right? I'm warning you, Karl, if you're into something—"

Karl plucked her hand off his arm, squeezing it until he could see the look of pain on her face. "Don't you ever, *ever* touch me."

She twisted in his grip. "Stop it! You're hurting me!"

"You gonna touch me again like that?"

"No, all right, no," she said, and retreated across the hall. "Bastard!" she spat. "I'm your *mother!* Show some respect, damn you! Go on—get the hell out. I don't care. Goddamn son of a bitch!"

Karl looked down at her, feeling nothing but disgust. For a moment he pictured her with her damn telephone cord knotted tightly around her neck.

As if sensing this, she drew back further. "Go on," she repeated, fear this time edging into her voice, "get out!"

So Karl got out, hearing her lock and double-bolt the door behind him. No matter, he thought. There were plenty of ways into the house, even if she did dare try to keep him out. But he wouldn't be back for a while in any event, not until she was asleep, which was just fine by him.

Rage rose inside him. Everybody was trying to jam him up. First Kincaid, then the constable, and now his mother, though that was hardly new. But Sam . . . he'd have to teach Sam a lesson now, would have to demonstrate just how bad an idea it was to mess with him. It must've been Sam who'd placed him out by the Kincaids' place last night.

Well, Sam would change his mind real fast about what and who he'd seen. And Karl knew just how to do it. Like most everybody else, he knew Sam was up to something, up by Indian Lake. All he'd have to do was drive around the lake until he found Sam's car, track him down from there, and then—

Then what?

He considered the question as he climbed into the old Chevy station wagon. Didn't matter.

He'd think of something.

NINE

ERIC

Eric closed and locked the door to his cabin, grateful for the few minutes of solitude before Liz would pick him up for dinner. He needed to be alone for a while, to think.

He spread out the clippings he'd found at the library, the events of the day running through his head. Crandall was going to be a problem if Eric hoped to retain his anonymity. The constable struck him as the sort who made it a point to know everything he could about folks—visitors especially. The strength of Crandall's personality had been almost palpable. Which meant that Eric would have to watch his step, and pray things didn't get out of control again before he finished what he came here to do.

Out of control. It hardly conveyed the reality of his situation. He thought of his demolished apartment, of the string of demolished apartments and trailers he had left behind all over the country, and imagined the destruction happening here. The thought frightened him. Though no one had been hurt yet, the outbursts were getting worse. Last night had been quiet. As usual, the force was dormant for a while following a major attack. But how long would it remain dormant this time? He wondered if being back here, where it all started, would make it worse, or better. Would the interludes of normalcy last longer, or pass more quickly?

What were you trying to tell me, Dad? he wondered. What are you *doing* to me?

Or was it all done long ago?

Come home, Eric, come home.

"Well, I'm here," he said, looking over the papers on the table. "So tell me what I'm supposed to do."

The room remained quiet. Even the echoes in his head faded quickly into silence.

Fine. I'll figure it out myself.

He flattened the crinkly white-on-black photocopies against the tabletop. The stories spread out before him spanned nearly eighty years of the Point's history—specifically, that part of its history that included the caves. As he examined them, he again felt a sense of familiarity, as if he'd known what they contained even before finding the clips.

Either that, or he'd *seen* them. In his mind, or his sleep.

The first clipping was dated June 12, 1962:

MISSING GIRL FOUND

A fourteen-year-old girl, missing since early Tuesday morning, was found today, wandering near Indian Lake. Authorities say that the girl, who disappeared during a field trip from Cutler High School, was sexually molested. There are no current leads as to the identity of her assailant, although police have put together a composite picture of the man, and are looking for a green van with Maine license plates. . . .

Another clipping was dated September 28, 1973:

UNEMPLOYED TIN MINER, 49, KILLS SELF

Robert Jergen, a longtime resident of Dredmouth Point, was found in Indian Caves last night, after an all-night search turned up his car parked near Indian Lake. Jergen, unemployed since the closing of the Henderson Paper Mill in North Cutler last year, was described by authorities as depressed over finances and the recent death of his oldest son in Vietnam, and was reportedly upset over a family argument. Jergen was noted for frequent barroom fights, and had been picked up on several occasions for unruly behavior. Found near the body was a brief note, the contents of which have not yet been released, and the double-barreled shotgun that it is believed he used in the suicide.

Jergen, 49, is survived by his wife, Ruth, his son Karl, and a daughter, Cheryl.

January 3, 1967:

SEARCH PARTY ABANDONS EFFORTS

Attempts by state and local police to locate a boy, 11, missing since Wednesday, have been called off in the face of subzero temperatures and heavy snow that have made tracking impossible. The boy was reported to have gone skating on Indian Lake without his parents' permission, and is presumed to have been caught in a snowstorm and disoriented. Attempts to search Indian Caves, where the boy may have taken refuge, have proved unsuccessful in light of the poor conditions and the unmapped, winding passages within the caves. Constable John Daniels issued a statement indicating that the search would be resumed as soon as conditions permitted, though forecasts for the next 24 hours do not indicate any easing of the storm. Asked what the boy's chances were of surviving the storm until the search could be resumed, the constable offered no comment.

August 19, 1979:

VIETNAM VET KILLS WIFE, SELF

Dredmouth Point was rocked today by one of the most vicious crimes in its history, as a Vietnam veteran camping in the Indian Lake area took his wife hostage and, after a day-long series of negotiations with local police, abruptly shot and killed his wife and then himself.

The couple, whose names are being withheld pending notification of next of kin, were reportedly exploring Indian Caves when, according to retiring Constable Richard Markham, "he went berserk." Complaining of hearing voices and experiencing other hallucinations, the alleged killer refused to allow his wife to leave, and accused police who arrived soon afterward of being in league with the voices. Asked if Delayed Stress Syndrome, which seemingly affects a number of Vietnam veterans, could be involved, Markham commented that he was "not ruling out anything at this time." Further details on the murder-suicide are expected pending a further investigation and inquest.

Eric switched on the table lamp. The room was getting darker as evening grew on. Altogether, there were nearly a dozen accounts, and those from only a perfunctory examination. Judging by what he could gather from references in the more recent articles, there had been even more incidents, stretching back across the history of the Point. A pattern was beginning to emerge. Most of the incidents took place during a storm (it had been dark that day, as his father drove off toward town, the afternoon sun suddenly eclipsed by clouds, gray and menacing . . .), and since the caves were the only shelter for several miles, they were therefore a virtual magnet for those in distress.

The rest of the incidents seemed to involve persons of a violent or unpredictable disposition. The caves seemed to bring out those traits—which made sense, in a way. If the person was unbalanced to start with, being underground could only exacerbate the problem.

Damn it, Eric thought, there has to be something more to all this. His father had warned him specifically about the caves. That much he remembered. He must have had a reason. And now that Eric had examined their history, he began to see that the warning had not been quite so inexplicable.

But now more than ever he was determined not to go up there until he was ready. Maybe Liz could help him to—

Liz! He glanced at his watch and cursed. Nearly five-thirty. He had only a few minutes before Liz would come by for him, just enough time to change.

He trotted toward the bathroom, stripping off his shirt as he went. As he splashed water on his face, he did a quick mental inventory, and decided to wear the brown pants and jacket, and a sweater-vest over his white shirt. The nights were getting cooler, fast.

Toweling off, he stepped out of the bathroom—and stopped dead in the doorway.

On the bed, which had been empty when he'd left the room, were his brown pants and jacket, sweater-vest, and white shirt, spread out in orderly fashion.

Eric felt his knees go wobbly. "Jesus . . ."

It was happening again, all right. He'd hoped for at least a week. But he wasn't going to be that lucky. The pattern was starting up quickly. First, things start moving around on their own; next, mirrors start exploding, the walls start whispering, everything violent and uncontrollable and—

Wait a minute, he thought. Stop.

He looked more carefully at the clothes on the bed. Not thrown, not scattered. Laid out in precise order, as if arranged by a butler. Just the way he always laid out his clothes.

The pattern had changed!

This was new. He'd always assumed that his thoughts influenced whatever it was—the power—and that he was in some way responsible. Even so, there'd never before been so precise a control over outside objects, even when he'd tried, consciously, to control the impulse.

He hadn't been trying now. Had, in fact, been entirely unaware that he was doing it.

Assuming, of course, that it *was* him doing it.

"Damn," he muttered, and began to dress.

TEN

WILL

Nomth Cutler Memorial Hospital wasn't much bigger than a modest clinic, but it was the only facility near enough to the Point to be of any use to Will. The first step was to isolate Barbara LeMarque from the rest of the patients, then institute a series of tests that would be practically impossible to run in his home office. He'd need a full workup—blood levels, hormones, everything. It would mean canceling the day's Placebo Run, but he was sure his regular patients would understand—and they hardly needed him anyway. Barbara was a different matter.

Will headed down the narrow corridor past the examining rooms labeled OB/GYN, SURGICAL, PEDIATRICS, and PODIATRY, past the pharmacy and a heavier door marked RADIOLOGY. The overhead fluorescents cast too-bright rectangles of light onto the carpeted floor and pastel-colored walls. Arrows painted bright blue, green, and red pointed the way toward different sections. All very quiet, efficient, modern.

Will sniffed his dissatisfaction. A hospital should look like a hospital, not a college arts department. He turned a corner, coming out into the cheerful-looking waiting room, where Gregory LeMarque stood smoking a cigarette.

"I came as soon as I could," Gregory said. "I was out making a pickup in Bangor. Gone since before dawn. When I got home and found your note . . ." He ran a hand through his hair, looking distracted. "How is she, Will?" he asked. "It's those damn dreams again, isn't it?"

"We don't know. It's possible that something stressful—dreams, whatever—triggered off her episode."

"What do you mean, 'episode'? You're saying she had a nervous breakdown?"

Will spread his palms. "That's what we don't know—what we'd like to try and find out. Could be nothing more than a momentary lapse into irrational behavior. If so, if it's just stress and nothing physiological, then she should be okay—with some counseling. We have to find out what pushed her this far. We can't just write it all off to dreams. Dreams like hers are usually a symptom of something deeper, something—"

"But she's okay now, right?"

"For the moment, yes, she seems fine, though a little shaken up."

"And the kids?"

"They're on the second floor, in pediatrics. They've got a special waiting room up there for kids." A place filled with enough pastels to induce the DTs in a teetotaler, he thought, but didn't say it. "They're taking it well enough. And Barbara had the good sense to keep far away from them during her episode."

"All this trouble," Gregory muttered. "Shit. Just shit."

Will stopped, sizing him up for a moment. "Greg, how you and Barbara get along, that's none of my business—unless it has something to do with all this. If so, that's something you'll have to deal with in time. But right now I suggest you leave your attitude outside. Barbara's going to need as much support and understanding as you can give her. She's been through a rough time. We can treat her chemically, with antipsychotics, but you can be the best medicine she could possibly have right now. Got that?"

Gregory met his eyes. "Can I see her now?"

Will started back the way he'd come. "This way," he said, unlocking the doors to the isolation wing.

"Is this the mental ward?"

"Isolation wing. Not the same thing. We use it whenever we want to keep one patient away from the rest. That includes everything from people with communicable diseases to—"

"To the crazy?"

Will looked at him hard. "Barbara is not crazy. Let's get that straight right now. She's a hell of a lot saner than most folks around here, and that includes some of the doctors."

They paused in front of the door to Barbara's room. Will didn't need Gregory causing more problems for her, but didn't see any way to justify keeping him out. Some folks just have a hard time coping with spouses who start acting irrationally. After a while, they either deal with it or they don't. Gregory would just have to deal with it.

Will pulled open the door. "Right in here."

Inside, lit only by an overhead lamp, Barbara lay quiet, her eyes closed. For a moment, Will thought she might be asleep. But at the sound of the door her eyes fluttered open and found them. Her face softened. "Oh, Greg . . ."

Gregory stepped around to her side of the bed. "Right here, honey." He smiled, but his voice was curiously flat. "How are you?"

"Okay," she said, returning the smile. It looked a little thin, Will decided. "I think I can head home now that you're here, can't I, Will?"

"I'd prefer you to stay overnight, just so we can keep you under observation for a little longer, make sure you're back to your usual difficult self."

Barbara sighed. "I guess we can get my mom to come by the house for a few days, can't we, Greg?"

"Is this necessary?" Gregory asked.

"Not technically, no. I can't force her to stay. But as her physician I would recommend—"

Gregory cut in. "Then she's coming home. Her place is at home, with her family, not here. Right, Barb?"

She looked uncertain, but took his hand, squeezed it. "Sure."

Will frowned. "Then I insist she come back tomorrow for a follow-up. There are still a few tests we'd like to run."

"No. I won't have any wife of mine being treated like a crazy woman."

"Greg!" Barbara said. "He's just trying to—"

"I know what he's trying to do," Gregory snapped. "And I know what you're trying to do. Just looking for a little attention. All I've been hearing from you for weeks now is these dreams, and now this—"

"I've been worried, that's all. Upset."

"Upset? About *what?* Jesus. You stay home, you watch TV all fucking day—what the hell do *you* have to worry about?"

Barbara smoothed out the sheets over her chest again and again, compulsively. Her eyes were moist. "Greg," she said, slowly, "I—I need help. I realize that now. It's those dreams—"

"I don't want to hear another word about your goddamn dreams! I'm fed up with—"

"Okay, that's enough," Will said. He took Gregory's elbow a little harder than he'd intended, and pulled him to one side. "You're not going to help matters by blowing up. I know this is hard. It's hard for everyone, and that includes Barbara. Why don't you just—"

"Why don't *you* just mind your own business, Will? You're as much to blame as she is, listening to all this stuff."

"I said that's *enough.*" Will lowered his voice. "Since I figure you're under a lot of pressure, I'm willing to forget everything you just said. I don't think it was really you talking. But one more word out of you like that, and I'm going to take *whoever's* mouthing off outside. I may be twice your age, but I'm a doctor—meaning I know fifteen places to hurt you without even trying. Are we clear on that?"

Gregory returned his stare, then glanced away. "Okay," he said, "I'm sorry. It's just been kind of a shock, you know?" He turned to Barbara. "You ready to go home?"

She glanced at Will, as if seeking permission, then nodded. "Just give me a few minutes."

"Sure thing," Gregory said.

They stepped outside to wait. Will crossed to the nurse's station and took out his pen. "I'll make an appointment for her now."

"Can't we do this later? Tomorrow? I'll have to check in with work, see when I can get free."

"Just be sure she gets here. Until we know what triggered the episode, there's no telling what can set her off again. I'd like to have the staff run some neurological tests, then maybe we can sit down later on and—"

"I said we'll take care of it, all right?"

Will bit back a reply as Barbara stepped out of her room. He smiled as warmly as he could. She looked better than she had when she'd checked in, but she was still pretty unsteady. "How do I look?" she said.

"Ready to enter the Miss Universe contest," Will said.

Barbara smiled faintly. "Thanks, but I don't think I'm quite up to any contests yet." She took his hand, held it awkwardly, as a child might. "Thanks again—for everything."

"You just take care of yourself."

"I will."

Gregory took her arm. "C'mon, the car's right around back."

With that, he steered Barbara away. Will caught one last glimpse of her smiling back at him as they turned a corner, and then she was gone. There was something familiar about the look on her face, he thought.

It was only after he had driven halfway back to Dredmouth Point that he realized what her expression had reminded him of—the way Will Junior had looked on his first day of kindergarten: scared, uncertain, but trying desperately to be brave.

Will frowned. He was going to call the hospital tomorrow afternoon, and if Barbara hadn't been checked in by five o'cloock, by God, there'd be hell to pay.

ELEVEN

KERR

Father Duncan Kerr sat behind his desk in the rectory, awaiting the bad news.

Repairmen, he thought. The Egyptians had it easy—all they had to worry about were flies, frogs, and the rest. If the Lord had been truly angry, he would have sent a repairman. He glanced up toward Providence, hoping for intervention but finding only wooden beams. An observation Sam would appreciate, he thought.

On most days, Kerr loved his parish, small as it was. The church and rectory were rock-solid, constructed back when craftsmen knew how to build structures that were intended to last right up until the Second Coming. Everything that wasn't built from brick and mortar was made of solid, handcrafted wood—dowels through and through, not a nail to be found. The backs of the pews had that worn, warm feeling that only came with the rubbing of countless hands over long decades of Sundays.

Yes, pride was a sin, since it was through pride that Lucifer himself fell from grace and brought evil into the world—but on most days Kerr couldn't quite resist a momentary flash of pride in the perfection of craft that had long ago been worked into the very stones of St. Benedict's.

On days like this, however, he would settle for anything even remotely contemporary, most specifically the kitchen, which had been installed in the 1940s, and only modestly upgraded in the late fifties. And there was the matter of the temperature inside the church, which was too hot in the summer, and frigid in the winter. From October through March, no matter that all the doors and windows were closed, there always seemed to be a breeze blowing in from somewhere. The front doors—

But he wouldn't think about that one just now. Stay with the kitchen. One crisis at a time.

Whatever could be taking the repairman so long? The problem couldn't be *that* bad.

Could it?

He decided to think about other things.

None of which were terribly exciting. The day-to-day life of St. Benedict's was punctuated more by calls from the Rotary Club and canned-food drives than by youth intervention or crisis counseling.

While there was much to be said for a sedate existence, at times he longed for something different. He had originally requested assignment in an urban location, but his superiors had felt that his temperament was better suited to a parish in a small town. He was in no position to disagree. But when he heard the same pattern of confessions repeated endlessly— lustful dreams, petty theft, and missed services—he wondered what it would be like to run a parish in the inner city, where the sins, and the necessity of redemption, were far greater.

It was not that he found no pleasure in his current assignment. He was not possessed of a radical need to change social systems or lobby for laws or write books. It was just that, from time to time, the idea of doing something important was extraordinarily appealing.

He realized that he was falling prey to a common American malady: ennui in the absence of immediate gratification. Was there anything wrong, though, with wanting to feel you were playing an important part in something bigger than yourself?

Probably, he thought, and consigned the idea to his little black box of inappropriate fantasies.

Right now I'd just settle for a stove that works, he decided, standing and pulling on the heavy sweater he kept behind the chair just as Mrs. Graham stepped into the study. Noting her somber expression, he steeled himself for the worst. "Well?"

"The repairman just left," she said. "He wasn't terribly happy about making a call during his dinnertime, but once he got a look at the stove, he got that look of smug satisfaction he wears every time he pays us a visit. Look into his eyes, and you can see him planning an early retirement, a 'round-the-world vacation, and college for his children." She looked as though she had been personally insulted. She was a tall woman, thin, with wide round glasses; her gray hair had been tinted once too often.

Kerr sighed. He'd grown quite familiar with the expression she described, but there was nothing he could do about it. The Bishop preferred to let the money dribble in, replacing the facilities in bits and pieces, than lay out the funds needed for a complete renovation. But no matter. St. Benedict's would outlast even this Bishop, and the next, until finally someone would see the wisdom of refurbishment. "So what's the verdict?"

"He replaced the thermostat, but that's no help to the pot roast, which looks like it's been fire-bombed, and it's a little late to go defrosting another."

"What do we have on hand?"

Kerr could see her running through the mental menu of available food—an inventory that she kept accurate up to the least carrot stick. "Bits and pieces of this and that, some of yesterday's beef—"

"Leftovers," said Kerr.

"Stew," said Mrs. Graham.

"Then stew it is. Do the best you can; I'm sure it'll be more than sufficient."

"I'll try," she said, and turned sharply on her heel—a move that Kerr had always thought looked just a little too military. Just short of the door, however, she stopped.

"Something I can do for you, Mrs. Graham?"

She looked back over her shoulder. "I hate to bother you with this, but frankly I'm at my wits' end with those kids."

"Which kids?"

"I don't know, exactly. I haven't seen them, but I've heard them. When you were a boy, Father, did you ever throw stones onto a roof and watch them roll back down again?"

Kerr, smiling, allowed that he had.

"Well, I think we've got some kids who've been doing that to the church. Started last night, then again this morning. I keep hearing stones rolling down the roof. I even saw a few of them, and they were good-sized rocks, Father, maybe an inch across. I tried to find the little vandals, but for the life of me I couldn't figure out where they were hiding. Now, I know it's just the way kids are, but I'm afraid they'll clog up the rain gutter or, worse still, break a window."

"All right, Mrs. Graham. I'll give the constable a call first thing in the morning."

"Thank you, Father." She headed out into the hall. "And if you should catch the little joys, I'd appreciate five minutes alone with them."

Kerr smiled. Five minutes with Mrs. Graham could do more toward rehabilitating a lost soul than prison.

TWELVE

BARBARA

"Honey? You okay?"

Gregory LeMarque, barely visible in silhouette against the window, nodded but said nothing. Ever since they had come back from the hospital, he had shut himself away in the darkened bedroom.

Resigned to his continued silence, Barbara left the door open just a crack in case he called her, and padded quietly downstairs. At first she'd thought the silence was her fault, that Gregory was having a hard time accepting what had happened. But now she was beginning to wonder.

The coldness was hardly something new.

Ever since they'd taken this house, Gregory had gradually withdrawn from her. His actions tonight, here and at the hospital, weren't so much new as simply more obvious.

She hadn't even wanted to take this house. The price had been excellent, but there had just been something about it—something she couldn't put her finger on. Sometimes she would wake up in the middle of the night, feeling that there was something terribly wrong, that there was something she had failed to do, that she wasn't alone in the room. It was silly, of course, but hard to shake nonetheless. Maybe it was their distance from town that did it, or their nearness to the caves.

The caves. She'd never cared much for that place, had never been inside herself, and certainly would not permit the kids to go hiking up there with their friends, no matter how they pleaded. It wasn't safe. It even *looked* creepy. And, of course, she'd had the wonderful luck that their bedroom window faced right out onto the lake, and the caves. They were often the first thing she'd see in the morning.

Sometimes she'd wake up to see Gregory just lying there, staring off into the distance, staring at the caves. Once, late at night, she'd awakened to see him watching the caves again, and for several minutes she was sure he didn't blink. Next morning, of course, he denied even having been awake.

After a while, she started closing the curtains at night. But lately she'd been waking in the morning to find the curtains pulled open again.

It was ironic; here she was, more in need of his support than ever before, and where was he? Sitting by himself in the dark, staring out into the night as if he were expecting some friends to show up any minute.

Well, fine, she thought. When he's ready to talk, I'll talk.

When she reached the bottom of the staircase, she checked the living room. Billy sat flipping glumly through comics he'd read and reread, while Julie played listlessly with her doll. Have to face them sooner or later, she thought.

Billy looked up from his comic at the sound of her approach. "Is Dad coming down for dinner?"

"Not yet, dear. I think Daddy just needs some time to himself. He'll be down soon enough."

"Can we watch television now?" Julie asked.

Barbara considered it. The television would provide at least the semblance of normal life, but somehow she couldn't bear the thought of loud commercials, chase scenes, and comedies with annoying laugh tracks. Laughter seemed inappropriate just now. There was a strange tension in the house, as if they were all waiting for something to happen—though, Lord knew, they'd been through enough for one day.

"I don't think so, Julie," Barbara said. "But I'll tell you what—if you'll wait just a little longer, I'll let you stay up half an hour later, and watch whatever you want. Deal?"

Julie mulled it over for a second. "Deal!"

"Fair enough," Barbara said, and planted a tiny kiss on Julie's head. She began to collect some of the toys that had been scattered around the room as Billy came up alongside her.

"Mom? Are you going to be okay now?"

"I think so. At least, I hope so."

"And you're not mad at us anymore?"

This is the worst part of it, she thought. God, I never meant to hurt you, Billy.

"I was never mad at you. Either of you. Mommy just—had a bad day, that's all."

Billy smiled—a small, tender smile that Barbara thought would break her heart. "Okay," he said, and went back to his comics.

Barbara continued to the bathroom, where she opened the packet of pills Will had given her and, on schedule, took another of the antipsychotics. She tried not to think about Billy's question, but found it impossible.

Was Mommy going to be okay? she wondered.

She wondered in particular how she was going to get through another night with the fear of having another dream like the one last night. The fear was like something cold and coiled in her stomach, ready to claw its way out. If the dreams did come again, she'd have to deal with them better this time. She would have to be strong, because, as matters stood now, she knew she couldn't count on Gregory for support.

Was Mommy going to be okay? She hoped so. But as she looked up toward the bedroom at the top of the stairs, *their* bedroom, still dark and silent, she wondered if the question now was—would *Daddy* be okay?

And what was he watching for, out there past the bedroom window?

THIRTEEN

SAM

Not long after sundown, Sam Crawford returned to the caves with his low-intensity lights, camera, and tripod, full of renewed excitement. The panic and unexpected claustrophobia of the afternoon were, if not forgotten, at least set aside.

Now, less than an hour later, Sam wanted nothing more than to get *out* of Indian Caves.

Setting up the camera had proven a massive effort. His concentration wavered constantly; he kept looking around, unable to shake the irrational sense of being watched. As he loaded up the highly sensitive film, his fingers felt numb, unpracticed. He felt as he had back in college, whenever he knew a professor was looking over his shoulder as he worked out some obscure equation.

But there was no one watching him now. He was being foolish. Nonetheless, as he adjusted the viewfinder, he continued to avoid the eyes of the black and green *serpens* painted on the opposite wall.

Next thing, I'll be leaving the light on in the closet at night, he thought.

And chuckled at his own silliness.

And the sound was swallowed by the darkness.

And he continued to avoid the *serpens.*

He wondered if the sensations he was experiencing were caused by something in this part of the caves, rather than by a sudden lapse into irrationality. If, as he suspected from the drawings, this had been a center for ancient Indian rites, then perhaps a mix of trace chemicals from herbs burned long ago had been sealed in the airtight chamber. Combined with the staleness of the air, might they not have some impact on the human nervous system?

Probably not, but at least it gave him something to think about that wasn't black and green with slitted eyes.

Finally the equipment was set up. He switched on the battery that powered the low-wattage bulbs, and set the camera for automatic time-lapse photographs at the most sensitive exposure level possible. Atop the tripod, a tiny motor kicked in with a slight meshing of gears that sounded amazingly loud in the chamber. The camera would automatically shift five degrees between shots until all of the wall had been photographed.

There was nothing else to do now but come back and pick up the film in the morning. He stepped carefully back into the main passage, which was lit by flashlights he had set along the floor at regular intervals. He allowed a sigh of relief, then headed back toward the cave mouth, scooping up the flashlights as he went.

Once he had the film developed in the university lab, he suspected there would be no problem persuading the mayor and the commission to prolong the caves' protected status.

He slipped on his jacket, feeling infinitely relieved to be leaving the caves. It was only now, his mind no longer preoccupied, that he realized he hadn't eaten since his abortive lunch. At the thought, he wondered if perhaps the fumes and chemicals that had affected him had also spoiled his food.

At the thought of food, his stomach growled. Thank goodness Kerr and Mrs. Graham put on some of the best dinners in all the Point. He looked forward to the occasion with a sense of enthusiasm bordering on the grand. He regretted that he could not tell them what he had found. Not yet, not until he had it confirmed. But verification would come soon enough.

Tonight he would celebrate.

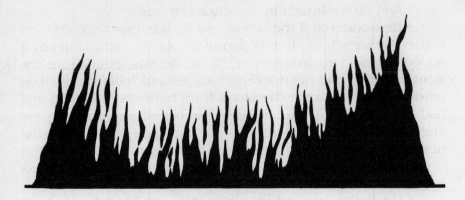

FOURTEEN

ERIC

"You're awfully quiet," Liz said. Outside, beyond the windshield, the headlights stabbed out, briefly pinning firs and pines against the darkness before they vanished again. "You do realize that Father Kerr is going to expect us to be witty and urbane."

Eric pulled his attention back inside the car. The darker it got outside, the more he felt that something was wrong. "Sorry," he said. "Just thinking. When we get there, I'll be so witty and urbane you could scream."

"Ah. Well, then, how about a little of that charm for the chauffeur?"

"I offered—" Eric began, then jumped as the car scraped the branches of a pine tree that was so close to his window that he was sure he could reach out and carve his initials in the trunk. "Is that why you wanted to drive, so you could treat a newcomer to a case of cardiac arrest?"

"Just trying to get your attention."

"*That* you got the first time I saw you."

"Flatterer."

"When my life's at stake, I'm capable of anything, no matter how disagreeable."

Liz glanced over at him through narrowed eyes that would have been better served by tracking the road, he thought. "How do you feel about walking the rest of the way into town?"

"Too late," Eric said. "We're here."

At night, lit by floodlamps, St. Benedict's was even more impressive than it appeared by day. A tall cross thrust up into the sky, illuminated by colored lights. Just below it, a stained-glass wheel window with elaborate tracery was lit from inside. A row of narrow, lozenged windows bordered the wheel, revealing stained-glass renderings of Jesus and Mary. They looked down at the town, their faces severe and drawn. Below, a pair of high oak doors led into the church. Off to one side, a flagstone footpath led around to the rectory in back.

On their way in from the car, Eric paused on the footpath, resting one hand against the side of the church. The wall felt strangely warm to his touch, seemed almost to vibrate. Here, he thought, was a place of power. He traced his fingertips along the brickwork, and a sudden cold seeped into his fingers as he touched another part of the wall, a bitter cold that came from more than the night. Cold, and images. Sensations, vague and yet—

Yes, he thought. Something bad had happened here.

Or was *going* to happen here.

But what?

"You coming or not?"Liz called.

Eric rubbed his fingers together where the numbness lingered, and hurried to catch up.

Kerr met them just inside the rectory, which was smaller but no less ornate than the rest of the church. He greeted them warmly, then ushered them down the long wooden hall into the study.

Liz gestured toward the main body of the church. "It's even more beautiful up close than from down the street."

"We like it."

"Pretty elaborate church for a town this small, isn't it?" Eric asked.

"Yes, well, the man who designed it—a Reverend Milcraft—had spent a lot of time traveling in Europe. He decided that if cathedrals were good enough for Germany and England, they were good enough for Dredmouth Point."

"But the cost—"

"I've heard that wasn't a problem," Liz said, shooting a glance in Kerr's direction.

Kerr sighed. "I know the stories. Supposedly, Milcraft's fund-raising techniques were—well, *unorthodox* is a good word. Yes, he was aggressive. If you want to start up a church with the kind of grand ambitions he had, you have to be at least a little aggressive. Which probably put off a lot of the people living here.

"He was supposedly cold, a loner in a tight-knit village. More than a little secretive. And that may be true. But I'm inclined to think that the stories spring mainly from jealousy and local snobbery. After all, what he wanted to create was a little different from the traditional steepled church. As far as I know, no one has ever proven that the funds came from questionable sources. And even if they did, I can't see what difference it makes. Historically speaking, some of the greatest cathedrals in the world were built with money taken through wars of conquest— but they're still works of art, and tools of God. Because a tree has its roots in rocky ground doesn't mean that it will not bear fruit. This church is the heart of Dredmouth Point, and it's a good heart."

"I'm sure it is," Eric said, taking in the heavily paneled walls and good, sturdy cabinets. It was a fine place, no mistake. But from what he'd read and felt since his arrival, he suspected that the real heart of the Point was not here, but somewhere else. And still there was that nagging sense of wrongness somewhere. . . .

There was a knock at the door, and Mrs. Graham entered. Tagging along just behind was Sam Crawford. "Our last guest has arrived," she said, "late as usual."

"That's why God gave us patience," Kerr said, taking Sam's jacket.

Sam chuckled. "Duncan, I'm in such a good mood tonight, I'll let that pass unchallenged. In fact, I'm so content with the world that if you want, I'll even call you Father—just for tonight, mind you."

Kerr waved away the offer. "Thanks, Sam, but at your age I'd rather not put such a strain on your heart."

"Suit yourself," Sam said. "So when do we eat? I'm starved."

"Ten minutes," Mrs. Graham said.

"Ten minutes it is, then," Kerr said. "Will that be sufficient?"

"It'll do," Sam said. "I'd ask if you have some wine, but in a Catholic church you never know where—or who—it's been."

Noting Eric's alarmed expression, Sam smiled. "Don't worry. If I give Duncan a hard time, it's because we're friends. I only make fun of people I like—which is why I'm not going to make fun of him anymore."

Eric laughed along with everyone else, even though his look of concern had little to do with Sam's sense of humor. Something about Sam's presence felt *different,* somehow. He struggled to verbalize the sensation. But all he could come up with was the feeling that Sam had been at or near a place of considerable power. He seemed to Eric like a phosphorescent watch dial that had just been exposed to a bright light. The more he gnawed at the thought, the closer he came to the conclusion that he had sensed this kind of power before. It was—

Sam's been to the caves, he's been inside, there in the darkness that waits there he's been inside inside—

The realization slammed into him with the same gut-sick sensation he had experienced the night he'd let his thoughts wander toward the caves. There could be no doubt. He *knew* it.

Sam had been to the caves.

No. More than that.

He had been *inside,* Eric thought, fighting a sudden sense of vertigo.

Inside . . .

FIFTEEN

KARL

Karl Jergen navigated the last stretch of narrow rock leading up to Indian Caves. He entered the cave mouth, sweeping the open chamber with a flashlight. So this was where Sam had been spending all his time! All sorts of goodies littered the ground—a dozen flashlights, a cooler, boxes of film, some open, some still closed. He snorted his dismay at the sight of a moldy sandwich. Some big-shot university professor. Didn't even bother to clean up his mess; just let it sit there until the maggots got it.

He was beginning to wonder if maybe Sam wasn't quite as bright as most folks seemed to think. With little enough effort, he'd followed Sam up here and stuck around until after he had left, all without being noticed. Which was just as well. He didn't want to be disturbed in his search for something he could use to hurt the professor. For Sam's sake, he hoped he found it.

Otherwise, he might have to resort to a more direct form of retribution.

Karl stepped further into the cave, and felt suddenly cold. He thrust his hands into the pockets of his peacoat, feeling uneasy—and knowing the reason why. During the climb up here, he had tried to keep the thought suppressed, just as he had tried over the years, but now it bubbled up at him, clawing for attention.

This was where it had all happened.

This was where his father had killed himself.

He looked at the dark cave walls, swinging the flashlight in a slow arc. *This was the last thing my old man saw before he pulled the trigger.*

Rage rose up within him, as it always did. Rage at the company that had fired his father; at the others who didn't think he was worth teaching another trade; at his mother, that cow, who two months after the suicide married some jerk who took what he could and ran; at his sister, for taking the jerk's name rather than keeping the name of a man who had killed himself, because the old name made her *unpopular* all of a sudden. Well, the Jergen name was good enough for Karl. And one of these days, he'd show all of them—his so-called family, the town, people like Kincaid and Crawford who thought they were so damned better than everybody else. He'd show them *all!*

Starting now.

He examined the stuff on the floor more closely. Something wasn't quite right. He'd watched Sam lugging all kinds of equipment up here, but none of it was anywhere in sight. And since he knew that none of it had been hauled back to the car, then all that expensive equipment, along with whatever Sam needed it for, had to be farther inside.

That way, he thought, aiming the beam from his flashlight into the main tunnel that led deep into the hill.

For the first time that night, Karl felt uncertain. He'd heard about folks getting lost in the caves. Even trained explorers were supposed to have a hard time with it. Still, if Sam could find his way in and out of the passages, then there had to be a way for him to do the same. He searched the ground with the flashlight . . . and smiled. A long groove—recent, by the look of it—was traced in the dirt, evidently marking where Sam had dragged something into the caves.

It was a thin trail, but good enough for Karl. Snatching up several of the flashlights to mark the way, he stepped into the main passage. A few feet in, he propped up the first flashlight so that it shone ahead of him into the first intersecting passages. Ahead, the groove turned sharply left, then vanished around a corner.

He continued down the narrow passage, deposited another flashlight at the corner, then turned right and moved on, walking slowly, sweeping the walls and floor with the beam of his flashlight. So far—nothing. He scowled. There had to be something around here, for Sam to spend so much time and effort.

Have to keep going it's not much farther I can feel it.

He wished he would find whatever he had to find, and get the hell out of here. The cold air was getting more oppressive with every step, and he constantly had to fight down the memories of his father that kept swimming up to the surface. *It killed him, it could kill me—like father, like son, right?*

He caught himself. *That was a long time ago.*

With every step, he began to wonder if this was such a hot idea after all. There had to be a better way to get back at Sam—but this one had just felt so right at the time, so natural. It had occurred to him as easily as if it had been whispered into his ear. Now the reality of the situation bore down on him. *Okay, just a few more steps and I'm outta here, and—*

He stopped. A few feet ahead, the right passage wall opened out into another section. Indeed, it wasn't a wall so much as a door. There was a small chamber just beyond, dimly lit by a pair of lamps set up on either side of a camera. He swept the room with the flashlight, and found darkened entrances to other tunnels spiderwebbing out from the chamber. Bolder now, he strode into the chamber, depositing his final flashlight just outside the doorway so that it shone inside.

Bingo!

He walked toward the wall drawings that faced the camera. So this was what Sam was so interested in—paintings by a bunch of long-dead Indians. He let his gaze pass over them. Just snakes, he thought, plus a few things he didn't recognize, a bunch of Indians—and a big, winged snake right smack in the middle. He snorted. A snake with wings! His lips curved into a harsh smile, but he found he was having a harder time retaining that smugness, the longer he looked at the snake. There was something about the eyes, the way the light caught them, made them look deeper than they really were. There was something different about them, something interesting—almost familiar. The more he tried to focus on the eyes, the more his own eyes burned. It was as if the eyes weren't really painted on at all, but were instead two gray-black pools of smoke that drifted in front of the drawing. He leaned forward to touch it—

Click!

Karl jumped back, startled. Next came a *whirr,* and he realized that the sound was coming from the camera, which had snapped one picture, advanced the film, and gone on to the next one, rotating slightly on the tripod. He felt a rush of embarrassment at his own fear, and was glad there had been no one to see him.

Then it hit him: *I'm on film.* He crossed to the camera, found the latch, and popped the back. He stripped the film out, exposing it to the light.

Not anymore, he thought.

He could probably sell the camera somewhere. That would set Sam back a few dollars. But it wasn't enough. A camera could be replaced. He wanted to *hurt* Sam.

And there was one sure way to do that.

He unscrewed the camera from the tripod and set it down on the ground, then picked the tripod up and closed its legs, hefting it like a baseball bat. He stepped back to the cave drawings across the chamber and looked into the eyes of the serpent.

"Fuck you, too," Karl said, and swung. The tripod smashed into the drawing, throwing up splinters of rock and dust. The impact made a satisfying clang. He felt immediately better. This was something he could understand. He swung the club again, smashing at the leering serpent face. The eyes lingered, undamaged, mocking him.

He smashed it again. And again.

The impact stung his hands, but he kept swinging, again and again. He felt *big.* He was *doing* something, by God!

Take *that,* Sam!

Smash!

Figured this'd make you, didn't you, Sam?

Smash!

Eyes. Staring.

Smash!

He laughed. The snake's face was cracked now. Not so tough after all! One more swing should do it.

He brought the tripod up over his head.

The lights died. Darkness swooped into the cavern like a living thing.

Karl stepped back, the swing unfinished, and stumbled over the dead lamps. He cursed as he fell, hitting the ground hard in a tangle of power cords. He scrambled frantically to one knee.

Then: *Wait a minute, how can it be* completely *dark? What about the flashlight—*

He strained in the dark for the slightest glimmer of light. Nothing.

Impossible. How could it have gone out too?

He remained in a half-crouch, afraid to move, letting his eyes adjust to the darkness. Even if the flashlight at the entrance was out, the ones farther down the passage should at least be partly visible. He opened his eyes wider, until they stung with the effort.

Nothing.

He tried to remember the way he had come in, but the fall had turned him around, left him unsure where the main passage was in relation to his position. He could *feel* the tunnels around him. Any of them might be the right one. And any of the rest would just lead him deeper into the maze of interconnecting passages. After that—

He swallowed, fought the panic rising in his throat. He wanted to bolt, but didn't dare. He could only crouch in the dark, feeling the walls close in.

Damn it, though, he had to do *something*. He couldn't sit here all night. Sam would return soon enough—and wouldn't he look the prime fool, sitting here, waiting to be caught because he was too afraid of the dark to find his way out?

Like hell, he thought, and began to crawl forward. All of the flashlights couldn't have gone out at once—could they?

No, he thought frantically, and continued forward. If any of the flashlights nearby were still working, there would have to be some light spilling down this way. He'd just keep moving, circling the perimeter of the chamber, until he saw some light.

After a few minutes he began to notice a difference in the darkness in one of the passages. Not so much a light as a curious absence of dark, like a retinal flash that lingers in the eyes after the flashbulb has popped. He thought he could almost see it better with his eyes closed, but that was ridiculous.

Fanning his hands out in front of him, searching the ground for further obstacles, he veered right, crawling faster now.

He moved into the passage, its walls no more visible than the chamber behind him, despite the beckoning glow. He couldn't be sure whether it was the same tunnel he'd come in through or not. But the light had to signal a way out. *Had* to.

A little farther on, he stood unsteadily, feeling his way along one wall. He came to a Y in the passage, where yet another passage intersected this one. The first passage he'd come through had led him around a corner—but had there also been another passage there? He couldn't recall. He looked down both passages, one dark, the other dimly etched with the strange light.

He followed the light.

Several minutes passed, and yet he seemed no closer to the source of the light. Worse still, the passage was getting narrower.

He cursed in the darkness, his voice catching. *Oh Christ,* he thought. *Christ, Christ, Christchristchrist.* The closeness was stifling. His throat felt constricted, as though someone were closing a fist on it. His heart was pounding. He had to get *out!* Couldn't breathe!

But which way? Back toward the chamber, try again, or forward? He froze, unable now to remember which way he'd taken when he turned the corner. He was aware of dust falling from the roof of the passage. *Which way?* He bit down on his lip, and stepped forward again.

Following the light. It was the only hope he had.

With each step, the passage narrowed further. Soon he felt both walls brushing his arms. Yet the light seemed to be getting stronger now. Then he felt it—a breeze! His heart jumped. Where there was wind, there had to be an opening! He pressed ahead, worried now only that the walls might press in too closely to let him reach the exit.

Running, stumbling, he squeezed through the passage. Closer now. Almost there. The passage widened. Karl smiled, stepped forward . . . and found nothing there.

He fell forward, clawing at empty air, nothing to grab on to in the half-second before his momentum carried him over the edge, and down into the hole.

Several feet down he struck the sloping walls of the pit, bounced and slid downward, bashing elbows and knees. Rocks and grit sprayed into his eyes, his mouth. He tried to yell, but only a wheeze came out, the wind knocked out of him. He fell down and down until he slammed into the bottom of the hole. The impact brought a new blackness that danced behind his eyes.

For a moment he could only lie still, fighting for breath. Small rocks and debris clattered down upon him, as if to taunt him. His breath finally returned in deep, heaving gasps. God, he wanted out! He would never do anything to anyone else again, as long as he lived, if only he could please, just please get the hell out of here!

"Help," he cried to the darkness, "somebody . . . anybody."

But there was no one to hear.

With slow, painful movements he worked his way to his feet, afraid with each movement that he would discover a broken arm or leg, knowing that if he did, he would never get out. But his limbs seemed intact, though he could feel blood from cuts along his arms and legs seeping down his skin and into his clothes. He tried to summon up the strength to keep moving, and for a moment he failed.

Finally, fighting the blackness behind his eyes that threatened to return with every exertion, he took one step forward, then another. He moved straight ahead, feeling his way along as the chamber narrowed, funneling into yet another passage. Now the light he had been following had all but disappeared. He stumbled blindly ahead, arms outstretched. Abruptly, the passage turned. He followed it, and came out into a room. Though he could not see, he could tell from the way his footfalls echoed that it was slightly larger than the other chamber. He peered into the darkness, and saw, once again, the light. It was brighter now, just off to his left.

His spirits rising, he stepped toward the light, which glimmered off the walls at strange angles, as if it were being reflected in from somewhere else. And yes, now he could see it—there was a corner just ahead, dimly visible, around which the faint light was coming. Perhaps he'd doubled back another way.

He closed the distance. Fifteen feet. Ten. He reached the entrance to the light's source and stepped through.

Inside, a fine mist rose from tiny fissures in the floor of the cavern, diffusing the light. He blinked hard, trying to focus.

At the opposite end was what seemed to be a solid wall of mist, roiling thick and milky against the far wall. He moved forward.

There was something about that wall. . . .

He stopped.

No. He *was* stopped. Frozen. He had not intended to stop, but he did, just five feet from the wall. His arms fell at his sides, numb. He tried to back away, but could not move. He could only rock slightly in place, frantic, as though gripped by invisible hands that squeezed his chest. He stared straight ahead, toward the wall, toward the thick mist—and realized that there was no wall behind it.

Nonetheless, there was motion behind the mist.

Something approaching.

He tried to move, tried to scream, but, as if in a dream, couldn't. He could only watch, helpless, as the shape—vague, distant—grew nearer through the mist. It stopped just short, as if hesitating on the other side of the mist, unable to come all the way through. But he could see it. A form—angular, dark, changing and shifting with each second. Only one feature remained the same: the eyes. They pinned him against the darkness like a needle through a butterfly. Cold eyes, impossibly deep, that latched on to his soul through his own eyes and clawed their way down inside, filling him.

Karl's last thought as the darkness rushed in on him was that he had seen those eyes before.

Back in the chamber.

Then, as if permitting him a moment of mercy, the eyes allowed him to scream.

Just once.

SIXTEEN

LIZ

It was curious, Liz thought as she picked at her stew. Ever since Sam's arrival, there had been a subtle change in Eric. So far, she seemed to be the only one to have noticed it. Father Kerr, sitting to her right, was listening to Sam with a look of long-suffering patience, and of course Sam, sitting across from her, was wrapped up in his point-by-point assault on all things religious.

Not that she could really blame either of them. They were less familiar with Eric than she was. And he wasn't actually *doing* anything out of the ordinary. It was just the *way* he wasn't doing anything—an observation that would probably make sense to no one but herself.

It was a collection of little things. The way he had gotten progressively quieter as dinner had gone on, and the odd expression on his face whenever he was looking at Sam. Once, she'd managed to catch his gaze right after he'd been looking at Sam, and for that flicker of an instant she'd felt as though something inside him had reached out and hooked right into her soul. Then, as quickly as it had come, the sensation passed. He turned his attention back to his dinner, and when he looked at her again, there was nothing at all unusual in his gaze.

Afterward, she tried without success to catch him unawares again, to get another glimpse of the strange depths she'd sensed. Either he was being more guarded—had he sensed her interest?—or the experience had been entirely in her imagination.

And all the time, as he listened to the conversation, there was his curious expression. There was something naggingly familiar about it. It was an hour before she finally remembered where she'd seen the like of it before.

It was a long time ago. She had been on vacation from junior high school and visiting her uncle's ranch in upstate New York. She'd taken along her cat, Mowser, thinking he might enjoy a few weeks on a farm after a life spent entirely in the city. Overall, the cat had adapted quickly to his new surroundings. Then, one afternoon, Mowser found his way into the pen where her uncle kept his prize possessions: a pair of peacocks. Mowser knew what a bird was; he'd hunted more than his share of pigeons at home. But as Mowser had stood in one corner of the pen, watching the peacocks, which were easily three times his height, she could see that he didn't know *what* to make of them. Finally, as though reaching some inner decision, he went into his hunting crouch, and began stalking the birds. For a moment she feared that she would have to rescue him before the birds pecked him to death. But at the edge of the fence, just as he was set to pounce, he looked up. One of the peacocks looked down. Their eyes met. It was almost as if the peacock were saying, *Go ahead, want to make something of it?*

Without changing his hunting posture, Mowser turned around and stalked out of the peacock pen, never to return.

The look on Mowser's face as he'd studied the peacocks marked the first time she had ever seen a cat actually looking confused. And *that* was exactly the expression that was stamped on Eric's face during dinner. Confusion, and somewhere deep inside, the hunting instinct fighting for control.

But who was there to hunt?

She tried to puzzle it out, only to be brought sharply back into the ongoing debate as Sam slapped his hand down on the table in apparent triumph.

"Then you admit it," Sam said, jabbing a finger in Kerr's direction.

"I admit only that there are certain passages in the Bible that don't lend themselves to easy understanding. He communicates His word in ways that are eternal. Some things may not make sense right now, but perhaps in a few years, when we know more, they will. This also applies to any seeming contradictions."

"*Seeming* contradictions!"

"Science does not always explain—"

"I'm not talking about how the Bible contradicts science, Duncan, though that's bad enough all by itself. I'm looking at the internal inconsistencies as well. On the one hand, you've got Jacob saying, 'I have seen God face to face, and my life is preserved.' "

"Genesis 32:30," Kerr said.

"And yet there's John 1:18: 'No man hath seen God at any time.' You say that God is all-powerful, but in Judges 1:19, He can't drive out the inhabitants of the valley because they have chariots of iron."

"For someone who says he's an atheist," Liz said, "you seem to know the Bible awfully well. Isn't that something of a contradiction in itself?"

Sam shrugged. "Know thy enemy."

"Religion is no one's enemy," Kerr said.

"Really? Then I suppose all those folks behind the Inquisition and the Crusades were just funnin' everyone."

"Ancient history," Kerr sighed. "If you can't do better than that—"

"You mean like the trouble in Ireland, people in the Middle East hacking one another's hands off for stealing bread, books being banned right here in this country, that sort of thing? And I'll be honest with you, Kerr—for all the talk of Christians being persecuted and discriminated against, there's no way you'll see a professed atheist *ever* elected to high office."

"Very true," Kerr said, "which proves once again that it's an ill wind that blows no one good."

Sam looked over at Eric and winked. "He'd make a wonderful fascist, don't you think?"

Kerr ignored the dig. "You'll find a few bad apples in any organization. That doesn't invalidate the belief itself. You have to look at the spirit of the religion, not the actions of a few of its followers."

"Which is rather difficult, you must admit."

"That's what faith is all about. But there's nothing wrong

with asking questions. All paths lead to God eventually. Remember what happened to Saul."

"Threats will get you nowhere," Sam said, and even Kerr had to laugh.

There was a well-timed lull as Mrs. Graham brought in a tray filled with dishes of rice pudding. Then Sam sat forward, his expression serious. "One more thing, all right?" he asked. "Then I'll be quiet, I promise."

Kerr's eyes rolled skyward. "If—and only if—our guests aren't getting bored."

"Not at all," Liz said.

"Agreed," said Eric.

Kerr looked at them with despairing eyes. "Traitors," he said, then turned back to Sam. "Proceed."

"All right. Let me start with an assumption. The basic tenet of Christianity is that Christ let himself be killed so that the world could be saved, correct?"

"Correct."

"That is, saved from hell?"

"Yes."

"Meaning, saved from the Devil?"

Kerr sighed. "Is there a point buried in all of this somewhere?"

"I'm getting to it. According to Christian theology, there's a God, there's a Devil, and there's an ongoing battle between them to see how many souls they can rack up, right? But the thing is, it's an uneven match. The Devil's frighteningly powerful—he'll do anything to get his soul quota. And people have no defense against him."

"Objection," Kerr said. "That's why we have the Bible, so that we can learn how to avoid Satan's traps."

"Exactly!" Sam slapped his palm on the table again. "So now I ask you this: What about the Indians?"

Kerr frowned. "All right, Sam, I'll bite. What about them?"

"What about *their* immortal souls? There were Indians all over North and Central America long before missionaries bearing the Good News ever got here."

"The Bible tells us that those who have not yet heard the Gospels are judged according to their works. Obviously they can't be damned if they've never had access to the Word of God."

"I'm not talking about how they're *judged*. I'm talking about *protection*. I'm talking about the little game going on between God and the Devil. Practically speaking, the Devil doesn't care if someone's heard about God. All the better that he hasn't. Now, we know from Job that the Devil walks all over the earth, so a quick jump over to the Americas is nothing to him. Christianity also teaches us that Satan has the power to manifest himself physically, to possess people, tempt them, deceive them, influence their behavior.

"So I go back to my original question: What about the Indians? Look—let's say that Satan came over to the Americas a thousand years ago. What if he manifested himself physically before a primitive people who had absolutely no way of knowing who or what he was. He could tell them anything he wanted, with no one to contradict him. He could perform seeming miracles, make himself a god—or a destroyer. How could they ever hope to stand up against him? God's never put a leash on the Devil's activities—why didn't he just move into the Americas and take over?"

Kerr considered this for a moment, and Liz wondered how he was going to work his way out of this one. At the other end of the table, Eric was staring hard at Sam. With *that look* again. For just a moment, she had the curious idea that Eric was trying not to look *at* Sam as much as *into* him; almost as though, if he could look at Sam just *so*, he could see past all the exteriors to—what?

"What you're pursuing, of course," Kerr said at last, "is the very line of thought that led to the formation of Mormonism—that Christ appeared to the Indians after leaving Israel, and brought them the Gospels."

"No, I'm not assuming that at all. I don't buy Joseph Smith any more than I do mainstream Christianity. I'm just asking you a simple question: How could God turn Satan loose on the Indians, who would have no idea how to defend themselves? Don't you see the implications? Look—with no one to oppose him, Satan could have had a field day. Imagine what kind of damage he could do to a culture unaware of his existence. If he's truly the embodiment of evil . . . Duncan, the mind reels. So when explorers reached the Americas, by all rights they should have found either utter devastation or an entire continent of Devil-worshipers.

"But they didn't. They found ordinary people. Civilizations, cultures, language, art. Why, Duncan? Or, more to the point, *how?* If they were able to survive that long without the aid of Christianity, then logic leads us to one of three conclusions: first, that the Devil has a sense of fairness that prevents him from picking on the spiritually uninitiated; second, that they were somehow able to defend themselves without the need of Christian doctrine, which would imply that there are powers around other than the Christian God. To the average Christian, the first two would be patently unacceptable. Which leaves only the third possibility: that there was never any danger because the Devil doesn't exist in the first place.

"I'll take it one step further. What if we could prove that the symbol of the Devil was known to the Indians prior to the first missionaries arriving here from the Old World? What then to make of the fact that the Indians got along just fine in the absence of Christianity? Wouldn't that tend to reinforce the idea that Satan is not a real being, but rather a kind of universal archetype? That he is nothing more than a symbol for darkness dredged up from the collective unconscious? And if we follow that train of logic, doesn't that also call into question the very existence of God as well?"

"Can I butt in for just a moment?" Eric asked. He had sat quietly for so long that the sound of his voice startled everyone. "Maybe I'm misreading you, but I get the feeling that you're not being rhetorical. Do you have something concrete in mind—an answer to go along with all your questions?"

Sam paused before answering, abruptly subdued. "No, nothing specific. Not yet, anyway. Just working on some theories, most of which would probably be of no interest to you. Indian lore is a hobby of mine."

"Hobby?" Kerr said, and looked at Eric. "He may be too modest to admit it, but Sam's our resident celebrity. Made quite a name for himself when he led a successful dig at Indian Caves a while back."

"Find anything interesting?" Eric asked.

As if grateful for the change in topic, Sam started in on his story. Liz had heard it before—Sam had been one of the first she'd interviewed in the Point—but she listened again anyway. It was curious that Sam would so willingly let the subject be changed just when he had Kerr against the theological ropes.

"We found a few relics," Sam was saying, "the usual batch of arrowheads and pottery. But it was the *mix* of things that was most interesting. Most of the artifacts went back only a couple hundred years, to about the period of the French and Indian Wars. But among them we also found relics that went back six, seven hundred years.

"The clear implication was that the caves had been used for some religious purpose. The Algonquins, like most Indians, never cared much about owning things. The world belonged to the world, they belonged to themselves, and it seemed a pretty equitable arrangement all around. A father might hand down his favorite bow, or some other tool, to his son, but not much else. As a rule, the only items regularly handed down across generations were those with some religious significance. So finding a mix like that was a pretty clear tip-off.

"The curious thing is that some of the pictographs on the pottery indicated that several large battles had been fought in, around, or for the caves. Which is singularly uncommon. The Indians regarded their holy places as sacred. No fighting allowed, no trespassing. Quite a little mystery."

"I suppose we'll never know the full story," Kerr said.

"You never know," Sam said, smiling. "You never do know."

2

It was after ten o'clock when Liz and Eric left the rectory. The rest of the evening had gone well. The debate forgotten, they had exchanged stories and personal histories. True to form, Eric's stories had been the vaguest, though he had finally begun to warm up by the end of the evening.

She looped her arm in his as they walked toward her car. "You're a little shy around new people, aren't you?"

He smiled. "A little. Mainly, though, I was just interested in what Sam had to say."

Liz nodded. Good-looking, shy, a good listener, she thought. She'd always found shyness to be an endearing quality. "Sam talks a lot, that's for sure. Which can be as much negative as positive. Sometimes I think he's spent too much time teaching, and not nearly enough listening. He certainly got your interest with all that talk about the caves, though." It came out less a statement than a question.

Eric said nothing. After a moment she wondered if he'd even heard her. Then, a few feet from the car, he stopped. "You want to walk for a bit?"

"Sure."

He headed down the street that led into the heart of town, now quiet except for occasional strollers. Her arm slipped back into his. He started slowly. "I like you. You're fun. Which makes things more difficult the more I see you. So, if it's okay with you, I'd like to tell you a few things—if you'll promise not to repeat them."

"It's okay with me. But what makes you think you can trust me?"

He smiled. "Just a feeling," he said. "So the truth is—I'm not exactly a stranger here. I was born in the Point, about five miles from here."

As they walked, he filled in the gaps. Parents deceased, years spent living with relatives, drifting from town to town when he got older, trying to figure out who and what he was, lost and without direction. It was a feeling she could sympathize with, having sought for so long to establish her own identity.

She guessed from some of the pauses, the backing and filling, that there were some things he wasn't telling her, but that was all right, too. The subjects he seemed to skirt most were the accident that killed his parents, the terrified escape, and the rescue up in the caves—of which he remembered little. Small wonder he looked haunted, driven, so much of the time.

After a while he grew quiet again, and they started back. On the other side of the street, the diner was closing up, the last two customers wandering out to disappear in the darkness. "So why come back now, after all this time?" she asked.

"Long story," he said, and his smile was a little sad. "Mainly, I guess I wanted to see the place that would've been my hometown, my real home, if the accident hadn't happened. But I wanted to deal with it quietly, without a lot of attention, just put it all behind me. That's why I haven't told anyone else. I just want to see the town on my own terms, then head out."

Again, she sensed that he was holding something back, but decided not to pursue it. "What about the caves?"

131

"What about them?"

"Are you planning on going up there before you leave? Might jog loose a few memories."

"I was thinking about it," Eric said as they reached the car. "Right now, though, I figure I'll just hang around for a while, soak up the atmosphere. Then, maybe on the way out—"

Liz stopped suddenly, the keys in her hand. "Damn!" she said. "The tea cake."

"Oh." Mrs. Graham had been so apologetic about the stew that she had insisted they take back some of her homemade tea cake. Leaving it behind would surely offend her.

"Be right back," Eric said, and raced back down the darkened flagstone path that led to the rectory. He turned a corner, and the rectory door opened before he could knock. Mrs. Graham stood framed in the doorway, the tea cake boxed and ready for pickup.

Doesn't miss a trick, Eric thought.

He took the package. "Thanks again for dinner," he said.

"My pleasure," Mrs. Graham said, then leaned forward conspiratorially. "Not that it's any of my business, but I think she likes you."

Then, with a wink and a smile, she closed the door.

Eric stood on the step, grinning.

Nope, not a single trick.

Then he started back again, jogging toward the street, and—

In the bushes—the dark—hiding—THERE!

The thought slammed into his brain with such force that he almost stumbled. Then:

A gun—he's got a gun!

He walked faster. Fifteen feet to the end of the path and the sidewalk. Up ahead, Liz was already in the car, waiting. He ran now.

Suddenly: "Okay, hold it right there!"

Eric froze. A shadow separated from the darkness and stepped toward him. Deputy Constable Ray Price stepped forward, shining a flashlight in Eric's eyes. "Just keep still—keep your hands where I can see them."

"Something I can do for you?" Eric asked.

"You just mind your manners," Ray said. "What's in the bag?"

"Tea cake," Eric said.

"Then you won't mind if I check. We've got this policy about drifters running around in the middle of the night."

Liz came up from the street.

"He's with me, it's ten o'clock, we've both got business being here—unless the Constitution's been changed—and that *is* a tea cake. Any other questions?"

"Just keeping tabs on things," Ray said. "Like I was telling your friend here, we don't mind drifters, we just like to keep an eye on 'em, make sure there's no trouble. Especially someone with his kind of background."

"What's that crack supposed to mean?" Eric said.

"Nothing. Just my way of saying we did a little check on you, that's all. Common sense says nobody drifts as much as you do unless he's got something chasing him."

"Give it a rest, Ray," Liz said. "Somebody wants to see the country, that's his business. I haven't exactly led a sedentary life myself."

"I wouldn't talk. You're not exactly a normal case yourself," Ray said.

All right, Eric decided, that's it. "Look. You've done your job. Rousted the out-of-towners. Now what say you just push off, okay? If we need you, we'll call you."

His gaze locked with Ray's. Without meaning to, he dipped into the thoughts behind the eyes, felt a sarcastic reply swimming up inside the deputy constable. He thought, hard, *Go away and leave me alone—*

And suddenly Eric felt something deep inside himself tremble, hesitate a fraction of a second, then leap out, forcing itself out not through his eyes but through his *face*. His cheek muscles twitched. Everything grayed for an instant.

At the same instant, there was a blankness behind Ray's eyes. His jaw went slack, just for a second, almost too quick to notice if you weren't looking for it. Then the look was gone again.

It was only a moment, a slight pause in the conversation. But it changed everything.

Ray's mouth closed, then opened again. He looked away. "Yeah, well," he said, "guess I'd better push off now." He passed Liz. "If you need anything, you'll call."

"Well, I'll be," Liz said, watching as Ray disappeared down the street. "I've never seen him take orders from anybody except Crandall and the mayor."

"Yeah," Eric mumbled, his thoughts elsewhere, working furiously. *It was like I reached out, grabbed his will, and—and squeezed it!*

"Just a natural-born leader of men, right?" Liz teased.

"Uh-huh," Eric said. His voice sounded distant to his own ears. "Sure."

But that's never happened before I just squeezed him what the hell's going on I could feel it like a new muscle—

"Come on, General Patton," Liz said, taking his arm. "We better leave before Ray changes his mind and cites us both for breathing too loud after seven o'clock."

Eric allowed himself to be walked to the car.

Whatever had been going on inside him these last few days—whatever had been *growing* there in his head—was accelerating.

The question was—why?

SEVENTEEN

JIM

Jim Stevens blew into his hands to keep them warm. He jumped from foot to foot, clapping hands against his jacket. It was just too goddamn, chicken-scratching cold. He looked down the long road for any sign of an oncoming car, though at this stage he'd take two clowns on a unicycle; it was just that goddamn *cold*.

He pulled his jacket closer around him, wishing he had never left the freeway. The guy in the Ford pickup—Gary, was that his name?—had said he was only going to get off the interstate long enough to drop off a few packages. Jim had considered getting out right there, thanking Gary Whatsisname for the ride, and picking up another one. But he hadn't. He should've known better. But he didn't. That's when good old Whatsisname decided he'd driven enough for one day, got himself a room, and told good old Jim, Jim who had kept him company for the last hundred and twenty miles, to go screw himself. Just tough luck, ol' buddy. You're on your own from here.

"Damn," Jim muttered, and kept moving.

He walked along the side of the road, leaves kicked up by the wind dancing around his feet. Now he'd never make it to

Portland by morning. No way in hell. And there went the tickets to the Bowie concert, there went one whole day and night of nonstop partying, and there went Linda, who'd probably find somebody else to party with. But he'd come too far to turn back now. He had to keep going until he got to the freeway, and then hope for the best.

The road behind him glimmered briefly as two headlights sliced through the darkness. He turned, faced into the light, and stuck his thumb out.

C'mon, can't you see it's too damn cold out here for anybody to be walking for his health?

A '79 Buick Skylark roared past, continued another twenty yards, then stopped. Jim grinned and raced up to the side door.

David Bowie, here I come!

He grabbed for the handle. It didn't budge. Locked.

He had just enough time to catch a glimpse of the driver, who shot him the bird before flooring the gas pedal. The Skylark sped away, horn blasting.

Jim ran after the car a few paces then stopped, out of breath. "Asshole!" he shouted.

The red taillights of the Skylark leered back at him like the eyes of a terribly self-satisfied demon, then disappeared into the night. He watched them vanish, then thrust his hands back into his pockets and trudged on.

What else was there to do?

For the next ten minutes, not a single car passed him on the road. The cold bit at his cheeks. Was a David Bowie concert *really* worth all this?

Hell, yes, he thought, and continued walking.

A moment later he heard the whine of another car. He turned, stuck out his thumb, and gave the driver a big smile, one of his hundred-watt specials. All-purpose, all-weather, good come rain or shine, man, woman, or animal. Stop, you sucker, stop!

The van topped the little hill, rumbled past—then pulled off onto the shoulder. Jim ran up alongside, pulled at the handle. This time the door was unlocked.

"Hey, thanks a lot, man," Jim said, climbing into the van. "You really saved my ass. Going toward the freeway?"

The driver nodded. He was only dimly visible in the dull

green glow of the dashboard. He was a large man, heavy, with eyes too close together for Jim's taste.

"Great," Jim said. "I'm heading to Portland, myself."

"Me too," the driver said, and eased the van off the shoulder and back onto the road. Never even looked over at his new passenger. The trusting kind, Jim decided. Or maybe he had a lot on his mind. Either way, Jim was back on the road again, and that was all that mattered.

"So," Jim said after a minute, "you live around here?"

"Sort of."

Definitely not the talkative type, Jim decided. Still, no harm in trying to be friendly. Portland was a long drive. "The name's Jim. Jim Stevens."

The driver spoke softly, watching the road. "Karl Jergen."

"Good to meet you, Karl," Jim said. Silence. "Yeah, like I said—real glad you picked me up. Got two tickets for the Bowie concert waiting for me in Portland, and man, I'd hate to waste 'em. You a Bowie fan?"

Nothing.

Probably one of those folks who didn't talk much when they were driving, Jim decided. Rather than risk annoying him, Jim sat back, relaxed, and watched the road go by, looking for the freeway on-ramp.

After several minutes, spent going down one bumpy road after another, he snuck a look at his watch. He hadn't been *that* far off the freeway, had he? Unless they were taking the long way around—but that didn't make much sense.

"Should be almost to the freeway," he said.

"Almost."

Jim tried not to let his paranoia start bubbling up. He'd just lost track of how far he'd come, that's all. Easy enough to do in this type of country.

Another few minutes passed.

Almost there, Jim thought, just before it happened. Just a little farther.

He should've seen it coming. He was too smart not to see it. But he hadn't. All he saw was everything happening at once and everything happening in slow motion: Karl reaching down by his right foot, real casual-like, and coming up in a sweep with a baseball bat, or half a pool cue, or a big stick, or whatever it was, nothing mattered except that it was long and hard and Karl swung it around fast, not taking his eyes off the road as the club slammed into Jim's face right above the bridge of his nose—

Then the world kicked slantwise, and was gone.

EIGHTEEN
LIZ

"It reminds me a little of my own place," Liz said as Eric held open the door to his cabin. "What an amazing co-incidence."

She slipped off her coat and set it on a high-backed chair beside the table. Except for a few details—a square table rather than a round one, and a different pattern of fabric on the chairs—Eric's cabin was, in fact, virtually identical to her own.

Eric closed the door behind them. "Can I get you anything? There's some tea, coffee, even a couple of beers, if I remember right."

"Tea's fine."

"Coming right up."

Liz walked around the cabin, which was unmarked by anything resembling personal decoration. True, Eric had only been here a little while, but she always made it a point to es-tablish her territory immediately, scattering pictures, books, and clothes everywhichway. It was a marker, a way of saying *I live here*—a rationalization that was, according to her mother, an excuse for inbred untidiness.

Her mother would have loved this place, she thought. It

was tidy to the point of being spartan. Nowhere was there anything that might provide an insight into its occupant—just a couple of suitcases and a knapsack beside the bed (all closed tight), a razor and a tube of toothpaste (squeezed from the bottom up) on the sink in the open bathroom. A few papers were scattered on the main table—which meant there might be hope for him yet. But that hope seemed dashed by the bed—a bed so carefully made that she was willing to bet she could bounce a quarter off the blanket. If, as her mother said, you can tell a lot about people from the way they keep their rooms, then Eric either didn't exist, was scrupulously neat, or was prepared for a fast exit.

She shifted a few of the papers on the table, and recognized the newspaper photocopies from her own early research into the Point. The white-on-black clippings seemed to concern Indian Caves, which at least corroborated what he had told her earlier. Not that she'd really doubted him. He had one of those faces she'd found easy to trust—friendly eyes, a laugh that wasn't raucous—more than that, though, he seemed one of the few really sensitive people she'd met in a while. He *listened* when you spoke to him. And the way he moved—sometimes it seemed almost as if, when he walked, he was listening to some distant music that she couldn't quite hear.

Liz frowned. *Love's Fair Musician,* a romance novel by Elizabeth Chasen. Grow up, she thought. She was moving pretty fast for knowing someone for twenty-four hours. He was pleasant enough in an odd sort of way, but that didn't mean much over the long haul. Anybody could be pleasant for twenty-four hours. It was after twenty-four *years* that you discovered you'd married the Phantom of the Opera. She smiled at her own practicality. A pragmatic viewpoint didn't significantly alter her plans for the evening, but it was always better go to into these things with one's eyes wide open.

"Milk and sugar?" Eric called from the alcove, startling her. She replaced the papers.

"Milk and sugar is fine. Just a touch."

Eric emerged from the alcove carrying two cups. By turns he had been somber or smiling for most of the trip back from town. Nothing wild, no mood swings, just a sense that he was mulling over something that could be positive or negative, depending on how he looked at it. She decided that she liked him best when he smiled, like now. It made his cheeks dimple funnily.

Love's Fair Dimpler?

Oh, piss off!

She took the cup and sat in the wingbacked chair beside the table as Eric turned his attention to the fireplace. Soon the first waves of heat began to spread, throwing a warm flush across her face and hands.

"I love a good fire," she said. "When I was a girl, I used to sit by the fire in my uncle's house, toasting marshmallows and tossing in little bits of paper. I'd let the fire catch them and whirl them away into little spots of light that lasted just a second, and then vanished. I used to make up stories about where they went."

Eric sat on the floor beside her chair. He grinned. "When I was living in a commune in San Diego—this was a long time ago, when I was first out running around the country—the house had a huge fireplace, one that makes this one look like a match. We'd get it going strong, and sit around on the carpet, and pretty soon, nobody would say anything, just look into the fireplace, seeing—well, whatever it is people see when they look deep into a fire."

He turned slightly to look at her, and found her smiling. "Did I say something funny?"

"I was just thinking—barring the biography, that's the longest speech I've heard from you since you got here. I was starting to wonder if you had some obscure religious belief against putting more than ten words into the air at the same time."

"I guess I'm just one of those people who never learned how to make small talk," he said. "I talk when I have something to say."

"Well, that's a start," Liz said. "What else do you do?"

"I move around a lot, mostly," he said, a little quieter now. "The deputy was right about that much. There's so much country out there to see, you could never cover it all in seven lifetimes. But I try anyway. I've pulled in bonito off San Francisco, cut trees, worked in restaurants and hardware stores in the Midwest, driven rigs from Philadelphia to Los Angeles, hiked through Canada—a little of everything, really."

"I envy you. I've only been as far west as Connecticut. Sort of a disadvantage to a writer, I guess, whereas you've got the perfect background. Hemingway would approve."

"It's not nearly as poetic as it sounds," Eric said, and there was something in his voice that said he preferred not to think about it. "Besides, I thought it wasn't as important where a writer comes from as what he comes up with."

Liz shrugged. "Depends on your philosophy about what makes good writing. A lot of writers think you should only write what you know. But if that were true, then no one could write a mystery or a thriller, since most writers haven't actually killed anyone."

"Which camp do you belong to?"

"I guess I fall somewhere between the two camps. I'm up here because I think it *is* important to get a real feeling for a place before you can write about it. Because the one thing you can't get from research is the way someone looks when he's telling you what happened next door. It's the personal side of the story that interests me most, how history affects people, places, that sort of thing."

"Didn't you say you'd written some novels?"

"Historicals. Not exactly what I want to write." She stared into the fire. Could she afford to finish the story?

Why not? she thought.

"But now, finally, I'm working on something I really believe in. A *real* novel. *The Dangerous Games of Solomon Greene.* A mystery. I kind of like it. I keep working on it in bits and pieces, and I really think it could be a success. This is going to sound funny, but now that I'm really doing something I want, the thing I worry about most is that something'll happen to me before I can finish it. Sounds pretty morbid, doesn't it?"

"So why aren't you working on it full time?"

"Maybe because I'm not quite so sure of myself as I like to think."

"I could tell."

"Oh?"

"I've never seen anyone who began her sentences with more 'I guess's' and 'I think's' than you. Nothing wrong with it. We all do it, but in your case, I sense it's because you think it sounds funny to say those kinds of things out loud. 'Yes, this is a good piece of work.' 'Yes, this is what I want to do.' As if you didn't take it entirely seriously, though it's obvious that you do."

Liz nodded. Training, she thought. You hear other people treating your work lightly, like a hobby, it sinks in after a while. She recognized her father's attitudes in her own voice, and hated herself for it.

She smiled. "I didn't know you were a part-time psychologist."

"Sorry," he said. "I just think you've got a lot to offer, and you shouldn't put yourself down."

"Understood." It hadn't been intended as a put-down. If anything, she was pleased. He was the first man she'd known who'd made the effort to see even that much about her.

She returned her attention to the fire, feeling warm and comfortable. Now and again, one of them would say something quiet and inconsequential, then watch the fire again.

"Interesting," she said at last.

"What?"

"You. Drifter, traveling psychologist, rescuer of young women in the cross-hairs of Peeping Toms, terror of deputy constables everywhere. What do you do in your spare time?"

Eric made a great effort of seeming to think about it, the smile returning to his face. "I give the best back-rubs west of the Mississippi."

"I see you've taken your own advice about not hiding your light under a bushel," Liz said. "But as someone who's never been west of the Mississippi, I'm afraid I'll have to ask for some evidence to support this outlandish claim. So what's the going rate for one of these wonder-rubs?"

"Free of charge. Accept it as my thanks for all the help you've given so far."

"So far? You mean there's more to come?"

"Always," he said, and began kneading the muscles in her shoulders. He *did* seem to have a gift for this sort of thing. "There's a catch to just about everything, you know."

"And what might that be?"

She could hear a smile in his voice. "We'll work something out."

"I'll bet," Liz said, then surrendered to the fingers that moved up and down her spine. She closed her eyes, letting her head laze to one side as he probed and stroked, working his way down and across. His hands seemed extraordinarily warm. A healing touch.

"Careful," she said, quietly. "I get too relaxed, and you can forget about anything else this evening."

A deep chuckle. "And just what makes you think that anything else is going to happen?"

"I don't know. It just sort of popped into my head."

Then, strangely, for just a moment, he seemed to hesitate. "Really?" he asked, his voice suddenly serious.

"No," she said. "I guess I've been playing with the idea ever since you showed up at the Big House." She caught herself. "That was another 'I guess,' wasn't it?"

"Forgiven," he said. Even without looking back at him, she could sense his—relief? Pleasure? "I just wanted to make sure I wasn't having an undue influence on you."

"For a back-rub? I don't come that cheap."

"Never thought you did."

At this, she glanced over her shoulder at him. He leaned forward, kissed her shoulder, her neck, and, after what seemed a tantalizingly long time, her lips.

And she found something else she liked. He kissed with complete attention, the same sense of *being there* that he seemed to give to everything he did.

It was, she decided, very nice.

NINETEEN
KARL

The cave was cold, though he hardly noticed. Karl's mind was turned in on itself, caught in a loop. He was like a drunk repeating over and over the procedure for opening a front door and heading upstairs to where a warm bed waited. But there was no warm bed here. So why—

(clear the slab the slab hurry)

Yes, of course. That.

He set down the bag he'd hauled from the van, and walked to the stone slab that jutted out from the far wall. The stone was gray, with tiny white lines, rough-hewn but worn down by time. There was a body on it. Not the new one—

(don't think about it)

—but old. So old that the moist air of the cave had worked its way into the decayed bones and restored moss where there had been flesh, fungus where there had been hair and eyes and ears. Eye sockets filled with insects stared up over his shoulders. Karl raised his eyes just a little, to trace their stare to the wall that wasn't really a wall. Walls were solid. Some part of him that was still left knew that. Walls were made solid. This wasn't. The solid part slid into a confusion of angles and smoke and a light that wasn't really a light at all, because he saw it more in his head than with his eyes. The whole thing shimmered like a heat devil on a hot road. He looked away quickly. It hurt to stare at it for too long.

The *old* body was tied to the slab by vines that had long ago rotted to husks. Only barely conscious of what he was doing, he pushed the body off the slab.

(the other—hurry—)

Yes. The other. The *new* body.

The hitchhiker—had his name really been Jim, or was that just another part of the dream?—lay a few feet away, unconscious but breathing shallowly. In addition to the gash on the side of his head, his arms and face had been scraped during the long descent into the caves. The body had been limp, hard to manage in the narrow passages. At first Karl wondered if they would mind, if that would spoil things, but now he knew that it didn't matter, that nothing would matter soon.

And a pinprick of thought flared up from deep inside. *Why would nothing—*

And the pain struck again, drilling into his skull like a rat burrowing into his brain through his eyes, teeth tearing at the soft, gray tissue.

(don't ask questions, don't think, just—)

—do. The pain cleared a little. The thought retreated back to wherever it had come from. He blinked to clear his eyes. Through the blur he found the hitchhiker. Jim. Jim who was going to the Bowie concert, whatever that had to do with what the voices behind the wall had in mind. Karl grabbed the younger man's arms and dragged him across the cavern to the now-empty slab. Blood from the head gash seeped over his sleeves. He arranged the body on the stone, then turned back to the bag, pulled out several lengths of rope, and looped them over the slab and around the body. He cinched the knots tight, making sure the arms were pinned tight at either side, palms up.

The hitchhiker moaned, fighting his way back toward consciousness.

(faster faster fasterfasterfaster)

The last loop went over the feet. Karl yanked the knot tight, not risking a glance over his shoulder at the strange wall, where things flickered and danced just beyond, just behind. When he was finished, he stepped back into a corner and waited for more instructions.

And watched. Watched as the body on the slab stirred again, and finally the eyes fluttered open. The hitchhiker moaned softly, tried to look around, and moaned again with the effort. Moving more slowly now, he let his head roll to one side, and found Karl. From the expression on the hitchhiker's face, Karl knew that memory was catching up with him, filling in all the blanks.

"Hey, come on, what're you—where am I—" He struggled weakly against the ropes, looking confused, as if he couldn't quite accept what was happening. Jim—that was his name, wasn't it? Jim? Karl couldn't put enough thoughts into a straight line to find an answer, and somehow it seemed important that he know. "Let me go," Jim was saying now. "I never did anything to you. Come on." He was trying to keep his voice reasonable, modulated, appealing to the rational. But Karl was not rational. Was, in fact, barely there at all.

And the things behind the wall were less rational still.

"Look, what do you want from me? Money? I can—I can call my dad. He's got lots of money. He'll give you anything you want. I won't tell anyone if you'll just let me go, okay?"

Karl said nothing. Only watched, and waited. For instructions.

Knowing they were watching.

"Come on!" Now fear was obvious in the hitcher's eyes. He struggled against the rope that held him tight against the stone slab. "God damn you!" he screamed, and that small corner of Karl that was still at least partly himself agreed. Yes, most likely, God *would* damn him. He had done some bad things in his time, some very bad things, and he was proud of them, but this—this was different.

God damn him indeed.

And the pain began again, tearing at his brain, pushing thoughts and directions down through his eyes into his brain, snarling as it encountered the thought he had held there a fraction of a second ago. Without deciding to do it, he trudged to the bag, and took out the fishing knife he'd put there next to—

(don't think about it don't think about it)

—and now he was holding the knife by its wooden handle, his hand opening and closing, opening and closing. The blade was as long as his hand, the lower edge smooth, sharp, the upper edge serrated but just as sharp. He looked down at the stainless-steel teeth. He'd used that edge to scale fish once upon a time, so long ago.

The hitchhiker twisted around, trying to see where he was. "Hey, what're—" Then he *did* see. "Oh God," he whispered, and then began screaming.

That was good, Karl thought from far away. They'll like that.

He advanced, knife in hand, serrated edge down.

He stood above the hitchhiker, who twisted helplessly on the slab, tears in his eyes. "Please . . ."

The knife arced down. The hitchhiker screamed. The blade tore a long, jagged gash down his forearm, from elbow to wrist, following the blue tracery of veins, opening each of them with careful detours. Blood surged out thickly. Karl turned the knife and cut across the open wound, careful not to nick the rope, as methodically as if he were cleaning fish. The blood flowed more quickly from the inverted cross. Fast, but not too fast. There had to be time for what was to come.

Karl moved to the center of the cavern, above and behind the slab, no longer hearing the screams that echoed off the stone walls. He knelt and opened his mouth, and words formed: words he had never heard before; words that didn't seem to fit in the human mouth; words that hurt him to shape. But still he continued, as the hitchhiker's blood collected in a depression at the base of the slab. There was a pounding in his ears, a sound like the beating of huge fists on the walls all around him. There was the sibilant whisper of voices that weren't voices as he knew them; voices from the other side of the wall that echoed the words he spoke. The pale light behind the wall grew, shifted into every color in the spectrum, shimmering, fragile, *bending.*

Then he stopped. Abruptly. One last sentence remained unspoken on his lips. Just one more—

(not yet, almost)

He looked down at the hitchhiker, who was now barely conscious. His skin was gray, lips turning blue as his blood ebbed away. Karl could somehow feel the hitchhiker's heartbeat, hear his pulse, sense his breathing. Slower now. Irregular. But not ready. Not yet. It had to be right. It had to be the one moment when Jim was on the thin line, not dead, not quite alive, trapped—

The hitchhiker shuddered.

(NOW!)

The final words were ripped from Karl's throat. A wind roared through the cavern. The light behind the wall burst free and flooded the cavern, a burning flash that seared his eyes as they struggled to fix on a color he knew, finding none. The hair stood on his arms, sizzling with the heat. And with it all, there was a sense that something terrible, something impossibly old, had entered the cavern.

Karl forced his eyes open, focusing past the burning and the pain to the non-light that fractured into a frenzy of angles and colors as it hit the walls. Nothing looked the same. Not the cave, not his clothes, not the hitchhiker, frozen in that final shudder, in the middle of a heartbeat not quite finished, a breath not quite exhaled—

(dead but not dead, alive but not alive, caught, the foothold)

The colors pulsated against his skin like a thing alive. And there were other things that waited, still behind the wall, moving like oil, so close, so far away, not quite through, still *there* and not *here*.

One last thing to do.

Karl pulled off his coat and shirt, fighting to move against the cloying, thick air, fighting the feeling that he was somehow falling, falling. . . . He tried not to look at the hitchhiker's eyes, failed, and glimpsed the terrible awareness there.

He knows.

Karl bent down, reaching into the bag and pulling out the pistol he had put beside the knife. The pistol he had gone target-shooting with, had used on squirrels and rabbits and to put deer out of their misery. Not the gun his father had used to kill himself in these very same caves, but it might as well have been.

That would have been nice, he thought as he raised the pistol and pressed the cold barrel against his own bare chest. He tried to summon up the willpower to do something, anything other than what he was supposed to do. With painful slowness he opened his cracked, dry lips.

"No," he managed, barely.

They allowed that much.

Then, forcefully, irresistibly, inevitably, came their reply.

(yes)

He pulled the trigger, slow and steady, as he'd been taught.

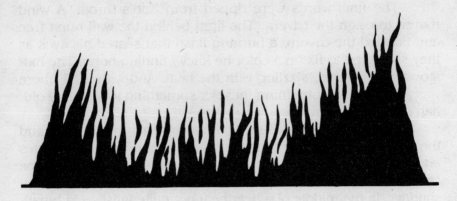

TWENTY
THE POINT

Zachariah Franklin rocked slowly on the porch of the Big House. This was the time of evening he liked best. Late, but not too late. Quiet, but not too quiet. The porch glider creaked with his motion. It would snow soon now, he thought. Maybe even in the next few days. He liked the snow. Always had.

The screen door behind him opened. "I thought I'd find you out here."

So much for the quiet, Zach thought.

"Look at you," Sarah said, reaching across his open sweater. "The least you could do is button up. I won't have you getting pneumonia on me."

He lightly batted away her hands. "Leave me be. I like the cold. You don't have to do for me all the time."

"You usually don't mind."

"Well, that was then. This is now. Don't much feel like taking from you. Just mad, I guess." He caught her look, shook his head. "No, not at you. Me. Just a damn fool, that's all."

"All forgotten," she said, and sat beside him.

He *hmph*ed a reply. The argument they'd had not half an

hour ago seemed strange to him now. He couldn't even remember what they had been fighting about. All he could remember was feeling suddenly closed in, trapped in this house—
the house they'd shared for thirty pretty good years. But tonight
every sound seemed amplified just enough to drive him to distraction. "I guess all that rattling of dishes just got to me."

"It happens. No more need be said."

They sat quietly for a while. Curiously, it was at times like
this that he felt closest to Sarah—after doing something foolish, stupid, blaming her for one thing or another, as if he were
doing her a favor by being around, then finally realizing, as he
always did, that damn near anybody else would have tossed
him out a long time ago. She meant so much to him, particularly now, with the kids long gone and only showing up once
every few Christmases.

He decided that he really ought to tell her that more
often.

"You about ready to go in?" she asked finally.

"Yeah, I think so." Zach pulled himself back from his
thoughts, then gestured in the direction of their newest guest.
"By the way, did you see—"

"I saw, and I'm not saying a word about it. Neither should
you. Where a person chooses to spend the night is his or her
own business."

"Said right from the start that all she needed was a good
man to get her head all straightened out," he said with a wink.
"Did wonders for you, didn't it?"

"Yes, Zach," she sighed, but he saw the little flicker of a
smile on her face, caught and held by the moonlight. How pretty
she still was.

Something else he should tell her.

Without asking, she again reached across his sweater,
and this time he did not interfere as she buttoned it. "There.
That's better. Now, are you coming in or not?"

"Why should I, now that you've got me all buttoned up
and warm out here?"

"Zach . . ."

"All right, all right." He stood up slowly, deciding that it
might be good to get warmed up about now anyway. The cold
was starting to seep into his joints. In the light from the door,
he could read the lines etched in Sarah's face as he would a
familiar book. Over the years he had been responsible for many

of them. "I sometimes think you're a damned fool to keep me around."

"And you're probably right," she said.

He was still searching for a reply when the screen door clattered, and she was back inside again. He watched her through the wire mesh as she picked up the last of the dishes and put them into the sink filled with warm water. At once he was filled with an overwhelming awareness of how precious she was to him. That thought seemed to come more often these days. Now, more strongly than before, there was the terrible, consuming fear of losing her, of not wanting to be alone.

He shook his head. *Just being a foolish old man,* he thought, and stepped inside the house.

2

Bud Simmons didn't care where he drove, as long as it was away from *her.* He sped the Ford around a bend in the road, daring anyone or anything to get in his way. He chewed his lip, the anger still raging within him. He should've known that he'd get about as much moral support from Beth as a child murderer would from a mother of five.

"Well?" she'd said when he told her the milk truck had gone on to another, presumably better life. "What are you going to do about it?"

"I don't know."

"Can't you get another one?" She had stood in the middle of the living room, her voice shrill, her eyes condemning him for the hard times she knew would now be coming.

"Sure, we can get another—if you don't mind not eating for a year or two."

"Then get it fixed."

"I can't! It'd cost more to fix the damn thing than it's worth. And even if I *did* bring it in, let it sit a few days, that doesn't do me a whole lot of good right now, does it? I've got to have something for tomorrow, or Clement'll give the route to somebody else."

"God, Bud, I *told* you to take that thing in more often. If you'd just listened to me—"

"We couldn't afford it."

"Well, we can afford it a lot less right now. That's you—penny wise and pound foolish." Then she'd given him her martyred look. "So now what am I supposed to do?" she asked, as if he had been deliberately doing this just to make her life difficult. At that moment he could easily have slammed her into a wall.

The more he thought about it, the more he felt like doing just that very thing, too.

"Why don't you go fuck yourself?" he snapped, and rushed out of the house. He'd driven off with no clear goal in mind other than getting as far away as possible.

Now he swerved around another bend, then turned down an access road, heading for the lake. The car bounced over chuckholes, its headlights scissoring through the darkness, only a little better than useless, but enough to guide him through the trees. After a minute he came out into a clearing a few hundred yards from the lake, where he stopped and killed the engine.

He watched the still surface of the lake for a while, then crossed his arms on the steering wheel and lay his head on them. "Damn," he said, feeling nearly ready to cry.

What *were* they going to do? He'd thought about borrowing a truck from someone, but no one in the Point had the proper equipment to keep everything in cold storage. He could just see Clement's piggy face smiling as he gave the milk route to "someone who could handle it." He could get unemployment compensation, but that wouldn't amount to much. And there would be Beth beside him the whole time, with that injured look on her face. . . .

He started at the sound of a twig snapping.

Karl Jergen stood not twenty feet away, just visible in the moonlight. Grinning.

Karl approached the car.

Great, Bud thought. Last thing I need now is to put up with him, too. He rolled down his window. He'd find out what Karl wanted, then get out, find someplace private if it took him all night.

Karl was closer now, moving fast. He still hadn't said anything, just kept grinning in a way that bothered Bud. Wasn't so much a smile as a rictus. And something about him just looked wrong somehow.

'Course, he thought, swallowing a chuckle, that was pretty much the way Karl looked most of the time.

"Hey, Karl," Bud said. Then he saw the thick red-brown smear on his chest, the wad of dried blood. "What the hell—"

The smile became a snarl as Karl grabbed Bud by the neck, and yanked him out through the open window. Held him up over his head, shook him, then threw him down, like a vicious dog with a rag doll. Bud landed facedown in the dirt, the air knocked out of him, his back twisted in the fall. Lights danced behind his eyes.

He tried to get to his feet—and in an instant Karl crossed the distance between them, coming fast. Impossibly fast, and then Karl's steel-toed boot slammed into his ribcage. Bud flew back, landed in the dirt again. He felt bone grinding against bone. Pain shot through his chest like a hot iron.

Couldn't breathe.

Couldn't move.

Then another kick found his head, and something went soft behind his right ear. He tried to scream but wasn't sure if he succeeded. He couldn't breathe, the only sound was the rushing of blood in his ears, just nothing, and still not a word from Karl, advancing again, silent, silent, not giving him a chance to recover.

Why? Bud thought through the pain.

Then Karl was on him. Wrapped hard, cold, thick hands around his throat, and squeezed. Bud struggled, beating at the arms that held him, and the arms were not flesh but stone, cast around his neck. His lungs strained frantically, but the fingers were there, pressing down, pinching like steel clamps. Bud felt himself falling. He looked up at Karl—and the face wasn't Karl's anymore. It was something else, something terrible. Its eyes burned into his soul.

Empty. Hungry.

He wheezed, gasped, fell further into darkness. This is it, he thought.

Then, abruptly, he wasn't alone—something was burrowing into his face, his chest, pushing him out of his body.

Something.

Something that wanted *in*.

3

Jay Carmichael was sure his heart would stop. He crouched low outside George Morgan's window, and wondered if it was really possible to die of excitement. Lord knew, the risk alone was enough to give him a heart attack. After all, this was *Mayor* George Morgan's rear window he was peeking into! But the reward was worth the risk. Funny thing was, this place hadn't even been on his mind when he'd left the house. He'd been heading for Judith Carlyle's place, moving through the woods, and he'd seen the window shade open just an inch. More than enough for his purposes. He'd approached, knowing the risk, but still curious. One quick peek and he would be gone.

But he had been wrong.

The mayor was out, and Carol—*the mayor's* wife, *can you believe it?*—was alone in the bedroom. She'd just come in, and as he watched, she stripped off the flower-print dress, the silk slip beneath, and the lacy underthings, until she stood naked in the room. A shower was running in the bathroom, the door open. She was an attractive woman, far younger than George had any right to. On other days, he'd watched her when she'd come into the gas station, admiring those breasts, the way her ass moved when she walked back to her car.

He found himself actually trembling with excitement. She was all by herself, on display just for him.

He edged closer to the window. No one home, he thought. I could just go in and take her. He imagined coming out of nowhere behind her, startling her; imagined himself sliding between those thighs, the look of surprise that would change to acceptance for a real man, not some limp politician.

He leaned forward. He could see it in his mind's eye. It would be so simple. He peered up at the window latch. Unlocked.

So simple.

He froze as he reached for the window frame.

What the hell am I doing?

He jumped back from the window as if it were red-hot. Panic squeezed his heart at the thought of what he had been considering. Not fantasizing. Not playing. Actually *considering*. He'd never gone that far before. It was sick. This—*this* was a hobby, but that . . . *that* was sick.

The mayor's *wife*, for chrissakes!

He backed away, no longer interested in staying for the rest of the show. Once he was far enough away not to be heard, he turned and ran, not slowing until he reached his car, parked just off the road, where it couldn't be seen unless you looked for it. He got in and drove off as fast as he could, not feeling safe or clean again until he reached his front door and stepped inside. Then he could only stand against the door, breathless, wondering:

What the hell is *wrong* with me?

4

R.T. Williams woke for the third time in two hours. He glanced at the digital clock he'd gotten two Christmases ago. 1:35. Beside him, Winnie slept soundly. More than slept. Snored. He propped himself up on one elbow and looked at her.

How could she do this to him? How could she lie there, snoring callously—and maybe, who knew, *deliberately*—depriving him of his sleep? He wasn't a young man anymore! He needed his sleep just like everyone else. The more he thought about it, the angrier he got, until he was ready to push her off the bed. Waking her was too simple, too good for her. Besides, she'd just roll over and go back to sleep again—and back to snoring.

Knowing only that the more he sat there listening to her, the angrier he was going to get, he eased out of bed, found his slippers on the hardwood floor, and stood up. Behind him, Winnie stirred.

"Dear? Are you okay?"

"Just damn fine."

She rolled over. "What got into you?"

"Nothing. It's you that something got into, and it's probably waking half the neighborhood." He stalked out of the bedroom and headed down the hall staircase. Let her chew on that one for a while, he thought. Let *her* lose some sleep for a change.

Serve her right.

5

Judith Carlyle sat with the lights out, blankets pulled up around her knees like a tent, a flashlight beside the bed. This time she would find out if she was right. Twice before, she'd thought she'd heard someone outside her window at night, but she hadn't been sure. She hadn't exactly *seen* anyone. . . .

And yet she knew. She could feel it.

So tonight she'd taken every precaution. The downstairs doors and windows were locked. The phone was not two feet away. If there was someone out there, she'd catch him with the flashlight, and report it to the constable.

She shuddered in the cool night, and drew the flannel nightgown closer around her. The idea of someone spying on her was too distressing to think about for very long, which was probably why she'd been so slow to countenance the possibility until now. She'd tried at first to convince herself that she was just being paranoid. It wouldn't be the first time. Ever since Kent had passed away the year before, she'd grown intimately familiar with every noise that the house made at night, fearing that each uncategorized sound signaled an intruder. But each time she had investigated, she had found that it was only the wind, or the house settling, or—

A sound came from the yard below. Footsteps.

Judith grabbed for the flashlight. The metal was cold in her hand, yet somehow reassuring. Quietly she slipped off the covers and slid out of bed, crouching beneath the window frame. She crept forward, feeling her way along the wall until she came to the window.

She waited.

Another sound. Closer.

Now! she thought, and jerked upright, clicking on the flashlight as she threw open the window. The light lanced through the night, spotlighting the figure that stood in the middle of the yard below. She was right! There *was* someone!

And she recognized him immediately.

"I see you, Karl Jergen," she shouted, confident now, as if knowing the peeper's name gave her some atavistic power over him. "Now you get the hell out of my yard before I call the police!"

He said nothing, his face unreadable from her vantage point upstairs.

He advanced on the house.

"Oh Christ," she said. She ran to the telephone, picked up the receiver, began to dial the number she knew by heart.

No dial tone.

Impossible! The line came directly down from the pole to the roof. There was no way it could have been cut from below.

Then, abruptly, the line was no longer silent. From the earpiece came the scream of lunatic laughter. Far away at first, now closer.

She clicked the receiver, frantic at not knowing where Karl was. She hadn't heard glass breaking, but still . . . "Hello?" she said into the phone. The laughter took no notice. "Who's there? This is an emergency, please clear the line!"

The laughter grew louder. Now there was not just one voice, but a chorus.

She slammed the receiver down, ran to the dresser, and pulled open the top drawer. Kent's .38 revolver shone dully in the moonlight. He'd taught her how to use it not long before he died, and she always kept it loaded. Now she grabbed it, slipped off the safety, and fled back toward the far wall. She faced the door, the only entrance into the room. He'd have to come in that way if he was going to come at all. She listened, straining in the darkness for the slightest sound.

Where was he?

She edged closer to the open window to try to see what was happening below, knowing that this at least was safe. There was a drop of twenty feet to the ground below, no trellis, nothing to climb up. If she could get a glimpse of him, she'd feel better. She glanced down, saw only the empty yard. *Where?*

Then something came between the window and the moonlight. A cloud? she thought.

Karl hung suspended in the air just above her window, grinning.

Judith screamed and fired, half running, half falling back

across the room. She fled to the door, away from the huge form that hovered impossibly in the night air. Then suddenly he was inside the room. She turned. Too late to run. She brought the gun up, held it in both hands. He stepped toward her, seeming not even to notice the revolver pointed at his heart.

"Get back!" she cried, and fired twice. The revolver bucked in her hands.

No effect.

She spun toward the door, then his hands—cold and hard—were on her, turning her around, ripping the gun from her grasp, that face, that terrible face, closer, and from somewhere nearby the howl of lunatic laughter.

Then the coldness was on her, and the laughter was inside her head.

6

Sam gave up on the idea of sleep. He couldn't get his mind off the caves, off the paintings, off what this find would mean to his career. He thought about how Duncan would react, how the dean at the university would take it after having written off the site, how the townspeople and the press would respond. His mind was caught in a parade of thoughts that dovetailed one into another like a serpent swallowing its own tail—

You're doing it again.

He frowned. One way or another, his thoughts kept returning to the serpent in the cave drawing. He had to fight off the impulse to go to the cave right now, retrieve the camera, develop the film, and head off toward the university. Instant gratification.

Patience, he thought, and reminded himself that any cave was going to be more dangerous at night than during the day. This one in particular. He forced his eyes closed. First thing in the morning, though. . . .

7

Beth Simmons awoke at the sound of the front door opening. Well, he's finally decided to come back, she thought. On the nightstand, the clock showed 1:45 in glowing green numerals. She turned under the covers so that her back was to the bedroom door. If Bud wanted to apologize for his behavior, let him come to her. She was damned if she was going to so much as sit up. The man certainly didn't seem capable of doing much else right—keeping a simple thing like a milk route, sticking out an argument—why not see how good he was at apologizing?

The bedroom door opened.

Beth closed her eyes. *Let the bastard think he woke me up, that I wasn't sitting up waiting for him.*

She could barely hear him approach—amazing, how quietly he could walk when he tried—until she could tell he was standing beside the bed. Nearly a full minute passed, and still Bud said nothing. Beth sighed inwardly at the thought that he was probably too much of a coward even to wake her up so he could apologize for being a jerk. She rolled over, her eyes squinting open just a bit, enough to prompt him. She stared up at his silhouette.

Strange, she thought. His neck was twisted at such an odd angle. She reached over, switched on the bedside lamp. In the instant before he fell upon her, his hands gripping her throat like steel claws, there was no time to scream. There was time only to wonder at the dead face, and the dead eyes that gazed into her own.

Eyes that weren't Bud's anymore.

8

Father Duncan Kerr sat in the study that opened onto his bedroom, a copy of Carl Jung's *Man and His Symbols* open in his lap. Sam had lent him the book weeks ago, suggesting that it might shed some light on his comparisons between Christian theology and Indian lore.

He began by scanning a paragraph that Sam had underlined.

"In the obscure tribe of North American Winnebago Indians, the Trickster is a figure whose physical appetites dominate his behavior; he has the mentality of an infant. Lacking any purpose beyond the gratification of his primary needs, he is cruel, cynical and unfeeling."

The Trickster. In Christian theology, Satan was always described as the Great Deceiver. Hardly startling, but a decent enough parallel, Kerr conceded.

He skipped ahead to another underlined segment: "The next figure is Hare. He, like Trickster (whose animal traits are often represented among American Indians as a coyote), also first appears in animal form. The Winnebago believe that, in giving them their famous Medicine Rite, he became their savior as well as their culture hero. This myth was so powerful that the members of the Peyote Rite were reluctant to give up Hare when Christianity began to penetrate the tribe. He became merged with the figure of Christ, and some of them argued that they had no need of Christ since they already had Hare."

Perhaps that was what Sam had been referring to. If so, then he had deliberately left out half of the spiritual equation. Yes, it was possible that the Indians had legends that corresponded to Satan long before missionaries arrived. But they had a Christ legend as well. But Sam would probably just interpret this as further proof of the tendency by different cultures to come up with similar god-legends—and that Christianity was just one more such legend.

The Bible said that God revealed Himself to the heathen through the forces of nature itself, and thus was His Word made manifest every day. Might God also have made Himself known to the Indians in forms they might be best equipped to understand? And if so, did that mean that the worship of Hare had been sufficient to protect them from the forces of Satan?

His gaze settled onto a line on the facing page: "The Winnebago, like the Iroquois and a few Algonquin tribes, probably ate human flesh as a totemic ritual that could tame their individualistic and destructive impulses."

No, Kerr thought firmly. God would never permit cannibalism within any branch of His church, no matter how many times removed from what Kerr understood as Christianity.

He set the book down on the side table. That was enough for one night. He still had to make his final rounds before retiring. Leaving the study, he started at the front doors and made his way back from there, checking locks and making sure all the windows were latched shut against the wind outside.

He moved up the aisle toward the baptistery, checked the empty chapel, then paused to kneel at the chancel rail before trying the sacristy. This time he would make doubly sure that no one had access to the church. If morning found the cross in the sacristy back on the floor again, then he would know that the church was settling improperly. In that event, he was resigned to dragging out the blueprints and hiring someone to do a thorough check of the foundation.

As he stood at the chancel rail, he was startled at the sound of a knock from the front doors. Who on earth could be there at this time of night?

Another knock sounded, this one so loud it reverberated throughout the church. It would take a massive fist, swung with considerable strength, to make such a noise. Perhaps someone in great need.

He started toward the doors, but with each step he felt a heaviness settling over his heart. The knocks were coming now at regular intervals. The pounding was slow, deliberate, not the sound of someone in distress. There was something in the sound that troubled him. The way it echoed, perhaps. The force required for each blow.

"Who's there?" he called.

No response. Just the slow, steady pounding on the door.

"I said, who's there?"

Still nothing.

Stranded midway across the nave, unwilling to go forward, not yet ready to make a retreat, he scolded himself for his reticence. This was a house of God. A church was open to anyone, at any time of day. He was not about to betray the responsibilities of his holy office simply because of—

Because of what? Because he didn't know the identity of whoever was knocking on the door? Well, there was one solution to that, wasn't there?

He crossed the rest of the nave and paused in front of the doors, his resolve weakening with the proximity. "Who's there?" he called again, with no response. In the gap between door and floor he saw the shadow of someone moving on the other side, pacing back and forth. He watched it sliding back and forth, a black stain against the thin line of light that spilled in from the lamps outside. He felt a strange dread as he watched that shadow swaying from side to side.

Pushing aside his reluctance, Kerr reached down and grasped the brass handle. Strange, how cold it was. At the precise instant that another knock sounded, he unlocked and pulled open the door. There was a clatter as something tumbled in through the opening, falling from where the shadow had been only a second earlier.

Kerr jumped out of its way, then looked down, mystified, at the object in front of him. He peered out the door, but saw no one, which was impossible. He had opened the door just as it was struck; no one could have raced away fast enough to avoid being seen. And yet there was no one here.

The only thing here was the crucifix from the sacristy, now lying faceup on the floor, the crucified Christ staring blindly at the high ceiling.

9

Billy LeMarque couldn't bring himself to go to sleep. Not the way things were now. Several hours ago, his mother had come into the room he shared with his sister, Julie, and tucked them in. But then, instead of leaving, she had wrapped herself up in a blanket, sat down in the big corner chair, and gone to sleep. Now she was talking in her sleep. Had been for several minutes. He watched, fascinated, as she twitched, mumbled something he couldn't hear, then suddenly sat upright in the chair, as if searching for someone else in the room.

"Oh my God," she whispered. She ran to the window and looked out. Billy wondered what she was looking at; there wasn't much to see out there but the lake, and the caves. "Oh God," she said again, and suddenly turned to him. "Billy?"

"Yeah, Mom?"

"We've got to get up, dear, come on." She helped him

up out of bed, then went to wake up Julie. Billy felt strange, as if he were moving through a bowl of Jell-O.

Billy sat up on the edge of the bed, rubbing his eyes. She never let him get up this late. "Mom?"

"Ssh, not so loud. We've got to go. We've got to get away from here."

"Where're we going?"

She struggled with Julie, who looked even sleepier than he was. "Away. Now. Before it's too late." She kept glancing over her shoulder at his window, the one that looked out over the lake, as if expecting something to come smashing in at her. The look in her eyes was wild. He had never seen his mother look so frightened before.

"Mom? I'm scared."

"I'm scared too, honey, but you've got to hurry. Something—something's happened," she said. "I don't know what, exactly, but I had a dream—oh God, so real—and something—something's very wrong, something in the—" She didn't finish the sentence, but froze, listening. The only sound was his father walking around downstairs. "Be very quiet, Billy," she said. "Don't move for just a minute. Mommy's got to make a call, Mommy's got to get help."

"What about Dad?"

But her only response was a worried look at the window. Moving quietly, she slipped out into the hall. Billy pulled on his shirt, listening as she dialed the phone. There was a second of silence, then he heard his father calling up from downstairs, heard his mother abruptly hang up the phone.

"Nothing," she said in response to whatever his father had said.

He heard his father climbing the stairs. He couldn't make out the words, but his voice sounded different. Billy shivered. Julie looked over at him through eyes barely open.

Suddenly his mother cried out. "Oh my God! Gregory, where did you—put that thing down!"

Something else from his father—low, menacing. The sound of it made Julie whine. Billy put a finger to his lips, shushed her.

"Greg, please—we've got to get out of here. Think! Think for yourself. You don't know what you're doing. Please, just—just let the children go. Do what you want to me, but the kids, Greg, please!"

"Mommeee," Julie cried. "He's gonna hurt Mommy."

"Ssh! No, he's not," Billy said, unsure.

"Oh God, please!" his mother cried. *"No!"*

A sound. A metallic click.

"Run, Billy!" she screamed from outside. "Get out!"

A blast rocked the house. Julie screamed. An instant later, the door burst open. His father stood in the doorway, eyes wide. Billy saw past him into the hall; blood was sprayed over the wall.

Gregory LeMarque pumped the shotgun barrel, brought it up to his shoulder, pointed it at Billy. Julie screamed.

"Daddy!" Billy cried.

His father pulled the trigger.

10

Thirty seconds ago, Will Cameron had grabbed the telephone on the third ring, and pulled it across the bed, finally finding his face.

"Hello," he managed.

There was a sound on the other end of the line—it sounded like a female voice, but he couldn't be sure. Then, abruptly, it was gone.

"Hello?" he said again, still only half-awake. But the line was dead, filled a moment later by the dial tone. He reached across the bed to rack the receiver.

Probably kids fooling around with the telephone, he decided, and rolled over onto his side to hunt the sleep that lingered on the other side of his eyes. Just kids.

And yet . . . what if it had been something important? What if she—if it *was* a she; he'd only caught a trace of the voice—had been cut off?

Then she would call back.

He exhaled slowly, letting his mind seek out the rhythms of sleep.

Damn kids.

11

Fred Keller started awake, glanced at his watch, and cursed. The steady rocking of the boat had lulled him to sleep. That, and the two six-packs of Anchor Steam beer. What the hell, he thought—the day was pretty much a waste anyway, why not screw up the night, too?

He made his way out of the pilot's cabin and onto the deck of the cockpit. The air was damp; a low fog lay over the water toward the horizon. Except for his running lights, the bay was dark. Of course, he thought. Who else would be fool enough to be out on the water at this time of night?

What a day, he thought. On his last run, he'd come up no better than on the preceding two. The nets had been consistently empty, and the lobster traps had yielded only two undersized crabs.

What a day.

He bent down to raise anchor, looked down into the water—and stopped at the sight of a school of fish darting past, just beneath the surface. It looked like a living wave shimmering in the refracted moonlight. There were mackerel and bluefish, every kind of fish he'd ever seen. They shone through the water like an immense sheet of foil, extending away into the distance on either side. They were all moving in the same direction—away from the Point, out toward the open sea.

Then, as quickly as they had appeared, they were gone. He ran to the starboard side of the boat, just in time to get a last glimpse before they disappeared altogether. He could only stand there, openmouthed. All day he hadn't caught so much as a dozen fish altogether, and now this! He couldn't help but feel a curious apprehension at the sight. He'd learned the hard way that there was a reason for nature's patterns. When you saw seagulls flocking far into shore, you could be sure a big storm was coming on.

What could it mean when all the fish in the bay suddenly headed out to sea?

Nobody at the Point was ever going to believe this, he thought, and wished that he'd had the good sense to drop a single net overboard. Still, he couldn't bring himself to feel too bad. Had he not awakened when he did, he never would have seen it at all. In a way, he felt as if he had been privy to some secret that only the sea knew.

He shook off the inertia and headed into the cabin, firing up the engine. No, he thought as he turned the boat toward the Point, no one was ever going to believe this one.

In fifteen minutes he was within sight of the dock. He was surprised to see someone standing there. A woman, as near as he could tell. She looked almost as if she was . . . yes, she was definitely waving at him. And dressed only in a flannel nightgown! It looked a little like Judith Carlyle, but from this distance it was hard to be sure.

Keller cut the engine and jumped onto the dock, securing the boat line in one practiced move. She approached him, not speaking, not apparently in any trouble, not even shivering, even though she was barefoot on the cold, wet dock.

He wondered what she wanted.

PART THREE

DEMON NIGHT

. . . What may this mean,
That thou, dead corse, again, in complete steel,
Revisit'st thus the glimpses of the moon,
Making night hideous; and we fools of nature
So horridly to shake our disposition
With thoughts beyond the reaches of our souls?

—HAMLET I, iv

FAUSTUS: *Tell me, where is the place that men call
hell? . . .*
MEPHISTOPHILIS: *. . . Hell hath no limits, nor is circum-
scribed
In one self place; but where we are is hell,
And where hell is, there must we ever be.
And, to be short, when the world dissolves,
And every creature shall be purified,
All places shall be hell that is not heaven.*
FAUSTUS: *I think hell's a fable.*
MEPHISTOPHILIS: *Aye, think so still, till experience
change thy mind.*

—Christopher Marlowe, DR. FAUSTUS II, i

TWENTY-ONE
THE LeMARQUE HOUSE

He was running but it didn't help. The darkness was closing in. And in the dark: eyes. He ran faster now, but his feet were numb with cold. He ran across a wide, open field, afraid to stop, afraid to look behind him, knowing the darkness would be there, swooping down at him like some huge black bird. He felt its eyes on him, burning. It knows I'm here! *And now the fear came again, stronger, a copper taste in the back of his throat. He ran harder—and suddenly he was falling—*

(cold, so cold)

—and there were ropes all around him, and he couldn't get free. Everything was suddenly slow, except for the darkness, the terrible darkness that screamed down at him from a slate-gray sky. His lungs worked like bellows, but he couldn't scream, for the darkness had found him. It pushed into his mouth and rammed down into his throat, choking him—

Eric started awake, his heart racing painfully. He forced himself to breathe deeply. *It's all right, all right. Just a nightmare, that's all.*

He was right, though. It was starting again. More quickly than before.

He rolled over, tried to burrow into the pillow; his legs spasmed with the movement. "Jesus," he moaned, and rubbed at the inflamed calf muscles. He recognized the pain from his days on the high school cross-country team. Then he thought again of the dream, and his heart began jackhammering against his ribs again. Where was I running? Where was I—

(. . . so cold, god it's so cold why doesn't someone come someone please help me . . .)

Eric pushed himself up onto his elbows. The voice sounded close. But there was no one else in the cabin.

No one?

He glanced across to where Liz had been sleeping, saw only a note folded onto the pillow. He opened it.

> *Eric—places to go and people to see. Alas, people around here take that stuff about the early bird quite seriously. Didn't want to wake you, though. You're cute when you're rumpled. Will be in touch later.*
>
> *Liz*

Eric slid his legs over the edge of the bed. The pain was receding now, reduced to a dull throbbing. If Liz wasn't here, who had spoken? He was positive he had heard someone— heard or felt, as if the speaker had a direct line to his brain. The voice had about it the sound of someone in great distress. Someone very cold.

He closed his eyes again and concentrated on locating the voice, but it was gone now. There was only a faint echo in his mind where the voice had been, a sense of urgency that slipped across the convolutions of his brain like a shadow that was even now retreating into oblivion.

He rubbed at his eyes. The nightmare, followed by the unsettling sense of contact, made for a rotten cap to the previous night. It had been a long time since he dared share his bed with anyone. Last night, though, had been different. He'd felt good about Liz, and he'd wanted her. But he was also afraid. He had to be sure that she was interested in him of her own will. At rare, isolated times in the past, he had found he could be highly persuasive when he wanted. He sometimes wondered whether his talent (if he could call it that) was responsible, but he had never given it much thought. Perhaps he didn't want to know.

But last night the contact with Ray Price had been so strong, so undeniable, that further doubt was now impossible. He'd paid for the effort with a headache that finally faded after about an hour, leaving in its wake a sense of nervous elation. If he could influence someone so easily, what else could he do if he truly set his mind to the task? Especially now. His suspicion that his talents would escalate when he returned here, where it had all started, was turning out to be well founded. He found the prospect at once exciting and terrifying.

He stood and stretched, shivering slightly in the cold of the cabin. Pulling on a robe, he went to the window and parted the curtain just enough to peer outside.

Something had happened while he was asleep.

The curving shoreline, beneath the gray, cloudy sky, looked the same as it had last night, dotted here and there with houses that looked out over Machias Bay. Everything was the same—and yet not the same. He had to fight to focus his eyes, as if a negative image were superimposed over everything. After a few moments he finally managed to repress the secondary image, though if he moved his eyes too quickly he could still detect the change, like a retinal flash behind his eyes.

His stomach lurched, felt sick at the silent, undeniable realization: something had happened to the Point.

His mind rebelled at the idea that something could happen that was so massive that the land itself would reflect the change. And yet the picture that his eyes presented to him was all but undeniable evidence that just such an event had taken place. Now there were two versions of the Point struggling for supremacy: one dark, one light.

And the feeling it created in him was the same he had experienced his first night in the Point, when he had sent his thoughts out over the town, only to be driven back by the caves.

"Damn," he muttered. He was a fool. He had been treating this expedition as if he were a tourist visiting his own past. But he'd been deceiving himself, avoiding the real confrontation.

He had been found in the caves.

His father had told him to watch the caves—and he had left. Now he was back, and still avoiding them. Still as afraid as he'd been long ago.

He *was* a fool. And he had waited long enough.

He glanced at his watch on the dresser top. Eight o'clock. Still early. First order of business—a fast shower.

Then he had an appointment to keep at Indian Caves.

2

At 8:15, Sam Crawford pulled an English muffin from the toaster. Since he was in a rush, he decided to let it cool a little on the counter while he finished dressing, than eat it as he drove to the caves. The alarm had gone off as usual two hours ago, but instead of getting up he had turned it off and gone back to sleep—something he used to do only on the mornings after a long drinking bout. Trouble was, he took great pride in the fact that he hadn't touched more than an occasional beer for nearly a year now. And yet he had felt definitely hung over. He was tired, unfocused; his brain felt stuffed with cotton. Probably a reaction to the excitement of the previous day's discovery, he decided.

Just a little longer. He'd retrieve the camera from the hidden chamber in the caves and then drive straight on to the university.

He could barely wait to see their faces when he showed them his latest find.

3

Dr. Will Cameron checked his calendar, and was relieved to find that this was a light day: the usual rounds, house calls, none of them requiring him to be anywhere at a specific time. He didn't feel up to keeping strict hours today. Didn't feel like doing much of anything, frankly. But that was his retirement voice talking, and he listened to that voice even less than he'd listened to his wife.

He pulled out his appointment book and transferred the necessary information. *Friday: Betsy Goodall, house call, check on tonsils. Pharmacy, pick up fresh supply of tetracycline. High blood pressure checks: R.T., Francine Alwood, Zach. Call Cutler Hospital, verify Barbara LeMarque.* He paused before slipping the book into his vest pocket. It might not hurt to give Greg LeMarque a quick call, just to make sure he didn't conveniently forget about Barbara's appointment. And Will was curious to know if Barbara had had any more of those dreams.

For God's sake, man; you're not the woman's father, he thought. Then he remembered Greg's behavior the day before, and the tone of voice he'd taken with Barbara. No, he wasn't Barbara's father; he was her physician, and as far as he was concerned, that was the next best thing.

He picked up the telephone and dialed. It took a while to make the connection, and when it did, the ringing sounded odd, as if he were calling cross country. He waited, counting rings.

No answer.

Will checked his watch. Eight-thirty. This time of day, *someone* had to be home. Perhaps they'd already gone to the clinic for the follow-ups. He racked the phone, then dialed the clinic. The receptionist confirmed that the doctor he'd recommended for the follow-ups wouldn't be in until one o'clock. He thanked her, hung up, and tried the LeMarque house again. Still no answer.

He drummed his fingers on the desktop. There was every chance in the world that he was being overconcerned. He had no real reason to suspect that anything untoward had happened, but Barbara *was* in a sensitive condition, and Greg was being less than sympathetic. Hardly the best environment for her. He found his thoughts returning to the scene he'd found yesterday at the house, the kids hiding, Barbara in a panic upstairs. . . .

The hell with it. He grabbed his wallet and car keys, and headed for the door. He'd stop by on the way to see Betsy Goodall. It meant taking the long way around, but at least it would put his mind at ease.

4

"Too early for you, eh?" Thaddeus Smith yelled over the racket of the mail truck's engine.

Liz shook her head. "Just thinking." Truth was, she would have given nearly anything for ten minutes' sleep. Unlike sensible postmen elsewhere, Thaddeus started his rounds promptly at six, and if she wanted to tag along to get his perspective on the Point, she had to abide by his routine. It had been pleasant enough so far—Thaddeus knew everyone on his route by first name, and he made enough introductions to ease the way for further interviews—but it was all she could do to keep her eyes open. When the truck wasn't hitting chuckholes, something it did too frequently to be accidental, she suspected, it chugged along with a relaxing rhythm that lulled her into a dreamy half-sleep. She almost regretted not getting to sleep earlier last night, but the distraction had been well worth it. Even now, she smiled a little. It had been as nice as she'd hoped for. Eric was surprisingly strong, but there was a gentleness in him; she'd never felt quite as safe as she did while in his arms.

"Well, would you look at that," Thaddeus said, pointing at the docks along the shore.

She squinted into the distance, toward the lake. "I don't see anything."

"Farther out. There."

She followed his pointing finger until she saw, just barely, the silhouette of the ferry gliding away through the early-morning mist. "The ferry. So?"

"So the ferry's supposed to be on the way in, not out." He shrugged. "Henry'll catch hell for being late, that's for sure. Folks need to get to work. Well, most folks, writers excepted."

Several replies came immediately to mind, but she bit them back. For now. I'm going to devote an entire chapter to you, she decided as they hit another chuckhole. *Killer Postman Ravages Village.*

He cast a last glance back at the ferry. "Yep, looks like nearly everybody's running behind schedule today. Everybody except Thaddeus Smith, that is," he added with a wink at Liz.

It was going to be a long morning.

5

"Goddammit, Ray! That's the second day straight."

Ray stopped halfway into the constable's office. He'd expected a little trouble coming in late, but the intensity of Tom's reaction surprised him. "It's just fifteen minutes." The clock on the wall across from him read 8:45.

"That's not the point. You were late yesterday, and now today. I don't care if it's fifteen minutes or five minutes! It's a question of attitude, and I don't think yours fits in this office. If you can't start coming in on time, then maybe you ought to think about some other line of work. Got that?"

Ray grunted. He wasn't in any mood to take this from Tom, but when it sounded as if his job was on the line, he wasn't going to argue.

"Good. Now you've got some backlogged reports to finish. I suggest you get to them."

Ray pulled off his jacket and set it on the coat rack by the door before taking his usual position behind his desk. Tom leafed through the papers in front of him with a vengeance, his jaw set. Man's bucking for an early ulcer, Ray thought, which was curious. Tom was usually the most self-controlled cop he'd ever seen. Something had to be eating at him. Not that that was any excuse. After all, Ray had problems to contend with, too. His cheeks still burned every time he thought about that drifter staring him down last night out by St. Benedict's. Well, he'd set that score to rights next time they crossed paths.

The telephone rang; Tom grabbed it. "Yeah? Yeah, George, I'm working on it," he said in the tone of voice he reserved for the mayor. "Look, I told you I'd have it for the meeting, and I'll have it. But you can bet your ass I'm not gonna have it if you keep riding me about it." He listened for a moment. "Then I suggest you get yourself an accountant, not a police officer, because I've got better things to do with my time than push papers. I've got to—" He stopped, took a long breath. "Okay, sorry I snapped. Look, George, I promise—as soon as I get the budget together, you'll be the first to see it. Yeah. Okay. 'Bye."

Tom hung up. "Ray," he said, shaking his head, "you ever

get the feeling the whole damn town, myself included, ought to think about switching to a decaffeinated coffee?"

Ray allowed a small laugh. The Tom he knew was back. Now he could only hope that the rest of the day didn't go as badly as it had begun.

6

Eric navigated the narrow road that led to the caves. Each time he caught sight of that gaping dark mouth, he shuddered in spite of himself.

What he couldn't figure was his reaction to some of the houses he passed. He noted the names on the mailboxes of two of them. On one plain white box the name SIMMONS was stenciled in black block letters. On another, just down the road, J. CARLYLE appeared in carefully calligraphed print on a box shaped to resemble a hollow log. He could connect nothing unpleasant with those names, but there was something about them and the houses themselves that troubled him—a sudden intensity in the negative image that kept flashing behind his eyes. Far from wanting to stop and investigate, he felt an overwhelming desire to get as far as possible from those strange houses with their blankly staring front windows.

He gunned the engine, unable to shake a growing sense of urgency.

7

Sam reached the entrance to the caves shortly after eight-thirty. He paused just long enough to catch his breath, then stepped through into the darkness beyond—

And a wave of panic slammed into his brain. It struck like a white-hot hammer blow between the eyes. He staggered backward and cried out, hands raised to stop the next blow— but it struck again, and this time he fell.

They were all around him. Everywhere. Things that moved

in the shadows ahead of him. Things without faces, things without eyes, but looking at him, right at *him.* They moved, and where they walked the stones screamed. They were coming at him through the walls, he could feel it. Felt the walls moving, buckling, felt the walls crumbling under dark fists beating, beating, the walls—

The walls?

Collapsing.

Cave-in?

Cave-in!

He scrabbled to his feet, tried to run, but now there were things crawling up his legs—insects, long and brown, mandibles quivering—and just as suddenly there were maggots chewing at his eyes, his mouth, looking for a way in. . . .

"No!" Sam screamed, smashing at the things, but they were everywhere, no way out except to back away on hands and knees, back away toward the cave mouth, toward the narrow path, feeling for the way out, feeling for the path. Oh God, just let me find it, let me out of here!

Then suddenly he was falling, the sky wheeling above him, the ground coming up fast. Every detail was frozen in his mind: the clouds, the ground below, the rocks, someone climbing out of a car and looking up at him as he fell, someone he thought was familiar. But before he could complete the thought he slammed into the first rocky outcropping and everything went gray, then dark, and then the world was gone.

8

At 9:15, Will Cameron pulled up in front of the LeMarque house. The LeMarques' station wagon was parked in the driveway. The house was silent. Nothing moved on the road. Will didn't like the silence that came from the house, remembering what he'd found the last time it had been this quiet.

Just being foolish, he thought. Bag in hand, he headed across the front yard toward the porch. They'd probably just slept in after all the trauma of the previous day. As it was, he fully expected to catch hell from Gregory. Which was all the more reason to turn around and head out, maybe call later.

He reached the house, pulled open the screen door, and knocked twice. A minute passed without response. He knocked again, harder this time. Still nothing. Not again, he thought, pained. Reluctantly, he tried the door.

Unlocked.

He pushed open the door. "Barbara? Greg? Anybody home?"

Silence.

A strange but familiar smell wafted through the open door, and in an instant he was back in Korea, where as a medic he had come across the bodies of a half-dozen men missing for several days.

Oh Christ, he thought, and felt his knees go weak beneath him. Oh God, please don't let it be.

The first floor was deserted. He approached the stairwell, grasped the railing for support, and slowly climbed the steps. Five feet from the top of the stairs, he saw a hand draped over the top step. A woman's hand. More slowly now, he crossed the remaining distance, his eyes sweeping the long upper hallway for the slightest movement. The only indication that anything was wrong was the body of Barbara LeMarque. She lay crumpled on the carpeting, her left hand twisted under her, half of her face blown away. A single eye remained intact, staring up at him accusingly. *Why weren't you here when we needed you*?

Will leaned on the railing to support himself, bile biting at his throat. There was no point in checking her vital signs; she had been dead for several hours at the very least.

Then: *The kids!*

He stepped around her legs and continued down the hall, toward the children's room at the far end. The door was slightly ajar. And on either side of the door—blood. There was more blood on the wall and on the folding ladder that led up to the closed trapdoor of the attic.

Careful not to touch the doorknob (fingerprints, said the small part of his mind that was still rational), he pushed past the bedroom door just enough to see inside. A moan escaped his lips at the sight of Billy and his sister, half-dressed, side by side on the same blood-spattered bed. Julie's face was buried in Billy's arms, perhaps seeking shelter there before the gun had been turned on her as well.

Will staggered away, only to be faced again with Barbara's lifeless body and its single, sad eye. *Was that your call*

---

last night, Barbara? Were you trying to contact me, to get help? Did you know what would happen? But from the still blue lips, no answer came.

"The bastard," he said, aloud. "Lousy goddamn bastard." In the back of his mind, he knew that neither Gregory LeMarque nor the killer had yet been accounted for, could still be somewhere in the house. Could even be the same person.

Get out of the house! The rational voice within him was screaming at him now. *He's still here, he's got to be here, so for Chrissakes get out!*

No. Not yet.

Fists clenched until they hurt, he located the hall phone, found it still working. He would leave—after he got word to Tom to get here as fast as possible.

9

The crucifix from the sacristy wall was propped against the back of the couch in Duncan Kerr's study. Kerr continued to study it from behind his desk. He had spent the better part of the night staring at it, until finally he had retired to a fitful sleep. An hour ago, he had barely touched breakfast before wandering back here, to his office, to the crucifix, to the questions that were looming before him.

He was a logical man, he prided himself on that. And yes, he believed in God. Without question. But as for the supernatural, well, that was a different matter altogether, wasn't it? In his experience, practitioners of the so-called dark arts were neither more nor less dangerous than radicals of any stripe. Left to their own devices, they were generally peaceable.

There was also a Satan, the Bible was quite clear on that point. But privately he had always believed that Satan was more metaphor than supernatural being. The concept of a horned devil looking over everyone's shoulder was a difficult one to accept. Even the Church, going back as far as the twelfth century, had regarded most cases of spiritual or supernatural manifestation as symptomatic of a psychological disturbance.

But there was that word again: *most.*

True, the roster of Church rituals included rites of exorcism. True, they had been used on occasion. But like many priests, he believed that they were often more therapeutic than spiritual. If a person believed in possession, and believed that a certain rite would cure him, then whatever the real cause, the rite *would* work.

Kerr believed that the world, like the Trinity itself, consisted of three parts, God, man, and evil, and that more times than not, it was man who was his own worst enemy.

Or was he being hypocritical? While it had lately become fashionable to believe in God, it was less so to believe in devils. Even the evangelicals were now spending more time decrying Democrats than devils. Was that, then, the reason behind his reluctance to face what seemed so evident—a disinclination toward being unfashionable?

He stared at the crucifix. No matter how he approached the question, the answers continued to point in directions he didn't feel comfortable pursuing. He was a logical man, but the facts did not allow for logical choices.

One: The sacristy doors had been locked last night. He had the only key, and the windows had not been disturbed. Nothing else from the room was missing. And yet the crucifix, which weighed just under twenty pounds, had been moved to a different room.

Two: After locking the sacristy doors, he had made his rounds in the nave, just down the hall. He had been in constant line of sight of the doors. It would have been impossible for anyone to slip by him, let alone carrying a twenty-pound cross.

Three: There was no way for anyone to knock on the doors of the church and run away at the exact second that Kerr opened them without being seen. The front of the church extended away from the doors by forty feet on either side, and was well lit.

Four: There had been other things. The crucifix falling— no, being thrown—to the floor on preceding nights when the sacristy door had been locked; frequent and unexplainable breakdowns in equipment; and lately there had been an oppressive feeling in the church that he'd never felt before. It was even getting Mrs. Graham down.

Five: For two nights now, he'd found the holy water in the sacristy frozen solid, whereas a dish of ordinary water in an adjoining room had remained liquid.

He toyed with several sheets of blank paper on his desk, unsure how to proceed. He had never come across anything quite like this before. There was always the possibility of consulting with the Bishop, but he preferred to hold that in reserve. In the meantime, he would continue to pursue a logical solution. He would go over the church blueprints, in case there was some point of entry into the church that he had overlooked. There might yet turn out to be some perfectly mundane explanation that he had overlooked.

His gaze returned to the massive crucifix, where Christ was staring at him from shadowed eyes.

Then again, maybe not.

10

Tom Crandall sped up Old Lake Road, the car's siren splitting the morning air. He could scarcely believe what had happened. If it had been anyone but Will making the call . . .

Poor Barbara, and those kids. He worried about how the news would affect the town. This sort of thing just didn't happen in the Point. New York or Chicago, maybe. But not here. Not while he was constable. And now there was Will to worry about. As soon as he got the call, he'd told Will to get the hell out of that house; there was no telling when or if the killer might come back.

The killer. Whoever it was. He'd find out, though, that much was certain. His lips thinned as he guided the car through a sharp S-turn where the road worked its way around Indian Lake.

Then, suddenly: *Someone on the road!*

Tom slammed on the brakes; the car shuddered to a stop a few feet from the two figures. The first was the drifter, Eric Something-or-other. The other was Sam Crawford, unconscious on the ground beside Eric. They had emerged from a stand of trees just as he'd turned the corner. Another second later and he might have hit them.

He jumped out of the car and raced over toward where Sam lay.

"What happened?" Tom knelt over Sam, checked the eyes. Dilated. Sam's face and hands were covered with scratches and marks that were already purpling with broken capillaries, and Tom didn't like the way Sam's arm hung at a sharp angle.

"He fell," Eric said. "He came running out of the caves and went right over the edge. Slid most of the way down; lucky for him it wasn't a straight fall, or I don't think he'd be alive right now."

"We have to get him to a doctor. C'mon, give me a hand." They picked up Sam as gently as they could, and eased him into the backseat of the police car. As he closed the door, Tom noticed the scratches on Eric's face and arms, scratches that could have been caused by dragging Sam's body through the undergrowth. On the other hand . . .

"Better come with me," Tom said. "I'll need you to file a report."

"But my car—"

"I'll send someone around to pick it up later."

Reluctantly, Eric climbed in, the car speeding off even before he closed the door.

Tom snatched up the radio microphone. "Ray, this is Tom. The coroner on his way to the LeMarque place yet?"

The radio squawked noisily. "Ten-four."

"Well, better have an ambulance meet us there, too. Sam's been hurt."

A second's pause as Ray took this in. "Jesus—how bad?"

"Bad enough. I'll check in when I get to the LeMarque place." He hung up the microphone. "Thank God Will's there; at least that much good has come out of this."

"Something's happened," Eric said.

Tom tightened his grasp on the wheel. The way Eric said it was more statement than question. For some reason he couldn't put his finger on, that bothered him. "Yeah, something's happened. You'll find out what soon enough. As my dad used to say, we're hellbent for trouble, and trouble's meeting us halfway there."

11

On the other side of the Point, Thaddeus Smith reached into the back of his truck and grabbed the mail for this stop. Nothing much, just a few letters, a church circular, and a *People* magazine renewal notice. The mailbox outside the house read SIMMONS.

"Bud Simmons—the milkman," Thaddeus explained as Liz jotted down the information. "His wife, Beth, she grew up around here too, just like Mrs. Dunkle."

"Milkman . . . might be a nice bit of local color. Could you introduce me?"

"He's probably out on his rounds, but I can check, if you like."

She smiled. "That'd be nice, thank you."

Thaddeus headed toward the Simmons' front door. He stepped onto the porch, raised his hand to knock, and hesitated, suddenly feeling acutely uncomfortable. The house was silent, the shades drawn. Looked like nobody was home. And yet he couldn't shake the feeling that he was being watched.

He looked back toward Liz, smiled faintly, and knocked. Very lightly. Hearing no response, he started to turn away, but stopped, listening. He could swear he heard something moving inside.

"Hello? Mrs. Simmons? Mail call." He tried to sound cheerful, but the sound of his voice seemed to vanish even before it hit the wooden siding.

From inside: "Leave it." The voice was low, but definitely Beth's. Still, something in it sent a shiver through him.

"Is Bud around? Got somebody wants to meet him."

"No." Again, the odd timbre to her voice.

"You okay, Beth? Anything I can do?"

"No." More insistent this time.

"All right, I'll just leave the mail in the box." When nothing more came, he shrugged and headed away down the walk. He reached the box, dropped the mail inside, then climbed into the truck.

The writer-lady was fast asleep.

Typical, he decided, and drove off.

12

Tom Crandall pulled up in front of the LeMarque house. Will had been sitting on the porch, but at the sight of the patrol car, he'd come on the run to meet them.

"Got somebody here needs your help," Tom said, opening the rear door.

Will started as he recognized Sam, and set to work immediately. "Where did you find him?"

Tom quickly filled him in on the details, then cocked his head toward the house. "Anything been disturbed?"

"Nothing. How about an ambulance?"

"Should be here in a few minutes. Meantime, I'd better check out the family. Nobody's come out since you've been here?"

"Nobody in that house is likely to go anywhere. You go on; at least here I can do some good."

Tom started toward the house, then noticed Eric tagging along behind him. "You'd better stay outside. This is police business. Besides, Will might need help."

"Looks like he's got things well in hand," Eric said. The intensity of his expression made Tom uncomfortable. "I don't think you should go in there alone."

Tom broke the stranger's gaze. As much as he hated to admit it, Eric had a point. There were at least three dead bodies in there, no clue as to where Greg or the murderer might be, and he didn't much like the idea of going in without someone to cover his back. "Consider yourself temporarily deputized," he said. "But you're to keep your hands where I can see them, don't touch anything, and if something moves that shouldn't, just get the hell out of my way, all right?"

When no reply came, Tom glanced back at Eric to discover him staring up at the house with a look of shock, as if he'd just now recognized it. "You hear me?" Tom said.

Eric focused on him. "I hear you. It's your call."

Tom stepped up onto the porch, pulling open the screen door from the top rather than further smear any fingerprints on the knob. The stench struck him instantly. Though Will had described the location of the bodies, he checked the rooms on the lower level anyway, just to be sure. Finding them deserted, he started up the stairs, Eric walking silently behind him.

The scene at the top of the stairs was as bad as Will had said. He checked the kids' bedroom, and felt his gorge rise. Christ, he thought. He turned in the doorway, saw Eric standing thoughtfully over the body of Barbara LeMarque, as if considering something the dead woman had just told him.

His face somber, Eric let his gaze shift away from the body and linger briefly on Tom—who felt a strange, chill depth in those eyes—before shifting to the back of the hall, where a folding ladder led up to the attic. "He's up there," Eric said.

"Who is?"

"The killer."

"How do you know?"

Eric shrugged. "I just know, that's all."

Tom filed the remark away for future reference. It was a curious thing to say, though it was certainly a reasonable inference from the bloodstains on the ladder. And it made sense to check out the whole place before assuming it was safe.

He grasped the bottom rung of the ladder and pulled. The spring that held it in place must have been old, because suddenly it dropped to the floor with a bang and a clatter. Tom jumped, cursing under his breath. But Eric was lost in thought, looking at the bloodied wall, his head cocked at an angle, as if listening to something.

There's something not quite right about that fellow, Tom decided. He'd seen many reactions to death while he was in the army, but nothing like this.

Tom steadied the ladder and began to climb. He reached the trapdoor and pushed. It gave slightly. It wasn't locked, but weighed down with something. He pushed harder, and the weight rolled off the other side. The way clear now, Tom eased the door open, his other hand never leaving the butt of his revolver. The view from the trapdoor revealed nothing; the attic looked deserted. Boxes and broken toys were heaped together into unidentifiable piles on the three sides before him. The long room was musty with the pungent smell of dust, insulation, and old wood. His head just past the edge now, he looked behind and around the other side of the trapdoor.

He started at the sight, nearly losing his balance.

On the other side of the door, a body lay crumpled on

the floor. Tom recognized the clothes as the type Greg usually wore. A few inches away from his right hand, a shotgun lay next to a box of shells. Tom leaned forward, trying to make out the face in the dim light that filtered into the attic through an open window. It was definitely Greg. He recognized the face—despite the lack of a throat. As near as he could tell, Greg must have stuck the muzzle of the shotgun under his chin, angled it up slightly, and pulled the trigger.

Or else someone had done it for him.

The barrel of the shotgun, Tom now noticed, was covered with blood. Now standing fully inside the attic, he moved from the body to the window, which looked out upon Indian Lake and, beyond it, the caves.

Eric had known. Or had guessed. Either way, he was right. Or did it just look right? It was pretty damned convenient that Greg had fallen on the door; it would be difficult for anyone to leave and position Greg on the inside of the door well enough to block it off.

Unless he went out through the window.

Tom looked out. It was a straight drop. But not far to the left, probably within jumping distance, was one edge of the second-floor roof. It was possible to jump it, if you were agile enough.

There were only two alternatives: murder, or murder-suicide. The latter seemed remarkably convenient. About as convenient as Eric just happening to be standing around when Sam had his accident . . . *if* it was an accident.

It smelled funny. All of it. The way Eric had reacted to the sight of the house. There had been surprise in his eyes, and definite shock. Why? There was the way he had stared at Barbara's body. His strange calm. And then it hit him. Eric hadn't just said that there was *someone* upstairs—he'd specifically said *the killer.*

Awfully coincidental. Too much so.

Tom started back toward the trapdoor as the sound of an approaching ambulance broke the morning calm.

13

Eric crossed the LeMarque living room. He leaned against the front window, seeking light, air, support—anything that was not part of the atmosphere inside. But no air seemed to penetrate the wire screen, as if the world outside were unwilling to enter the house.

His house. It had taken him a moment to recognize it, but as soon as he'd gotten a good look, he'd been certain. This was the house where he had spent the first eight years of his life.

No, he thought, that wasn't quite right. The structure, the paint, the silhouette—those were the same as his house, yes. But it was different now. Changed.

There was a sickness in the house, a darkness that had seeped into the walls. Was this a part of it all, he wondered? Was this the key? Had whatever changed the Point come here—looking for him? His father? His family? And found not them, but another family altogether?

Until this morning he'd assumed that whatever was wrong with the Point was confined to the cave. But now he began to wonder if the trouble might be with the Point itself.

14

Ray climbed out of his car just as the ambulances sped away from the LeMarque house. Trouble. Nothing but trouble.

He found Tom standing on the porch, watching as the coroner's assistant took photographs of everything in sight. A thin yellow plastic strip had already been stretched across the base of the porch steps, announcing POLICE INVESTIGATION—DO NOT ENTER. So far, the number of people gathered farther down the road amounted to only a few, and Ray doubted that they would want to get any closer.

He came up alongside Tom, who nodded grimly in his

direction as a body, covered with a green sheet, was wheeled out of the house on a stretcher. The stranger, Eric, stood a few feet away, looking out at the woods beside the house, his back to them.

"I don't remember calling in for a backup," Tom said.

Ray shrugged. "Figured you might need a hand. Nothing much to do at the station anyway. I made all the calls, the mayor's putting together a statement—so I figured—"

Tom waved away the rest of the explanation. "Yeah, I know. Maybe you did the right thing after all."

"Something up?"

"Maybe. Just stick close," Tom said, as Eric approached. Ray was surprised at how pale the stranger was.

"Are we done?"

"For the moment, yes," Tom said.

"Good. Look, I know you're up to your ears with this, but if you or someone else here could give me a lift back to my car—"

"Not going anywhere special, are you?" Tom asked, his voice low. Ray's pulse quickened. Something was definitely up.

Maybe the drifter caught the inflection, because he seemed to stiffen. "No. I've just got some errands to take care of. Any objections?"

"I'm afraid so, Mr. Matthews. In the last couple of hours you've been on the scene when one of our residents was hurt, and now here, and both times you seemed to know more than you were telling. Certainly more than you should know about what happened in there."

"It was a murder-suicide," Eric said.

"Probably. And there's probably a good explanation for why you were in the wrong place at the wrong time, and how you happened to know stuff you couldn't have any way to know. But until I have those answers, I need to know where you are at all times—and there's only one way I can do that."

Eric's face darkened. "There's no need. I had nothing to do with this." His voice was low, intense, as if concentrating on every word. Straining.

Ray found himself agreeing. *Of course he had nothing to do with it. You can just look at him and tell that.*

Tom let the silence hang for a second. "That may be, Mr. Matthews, but I'm going to have to hold you for questioning.

After that, if the coroner turns in a verdict of suicide, well, you're free to go about your business."

Eric sighed in resignation—

And at that instant, Ray glanced up sharply, almost as if released from a brief waking dream. Of course Tom was right. What had he been thinking?

"Please turn around and put your hands behind your back," Tom said, pulling the handcuffs out from their belt clasp. Eric hesitated briefly, as if searching Tom's face for some trace of doubt, then reluctantly complied. The handcuffs snapped shut.

They led him down the steps from the porch, and the few onlookers pointed toward them. Ray knew what they would be thinking: *There he is; that must be him.*

The murderer.

TWENTY-TWO

ST. BENEDICT'S

Father Kerr stood under the basement's only light-bulb and studied the faded blueprints. The basement was not his favorite part of the church, but as the part of the building he frequented least, it was as sensible a place as any to begin going over the drawings. The dirt floor was slightly moist, as always, giving the basement a perpetually musty smell that had defied every attempt he and his predecessors had made to correct it.

The basement was one of the building's many structural eccentricities. The church was always drafty; the doors never seemed to close quite properly, and there was a constant dampness to everything below the floor level. The problem, as he saw it, was twofold. The first was the building itself. One of the oldest structures in the Point, it was long overdue for renovation. But the problem was further complicated by the church's oversized construction. It was simply too big to heat efficiently—something that had presumably never occurred to its founder, pastor Edgar Milcraft. Milcraft was one of the favorite characters in local history—eccentric, colorful, possessed of a vision for a great church that he would build someday.

His vision had been met by some with scorn and derision, but still he had persisted in his work, and somehow succeeded in getting the funds he needed to complete the Church of the Everlasting in style. Local gossip at the time said that it was conscience money paid by some of the rum smugglers who plied their trade in Machias Bay during the late eighteenth and early nineteenth centuries. But gossip was usually just that, and Kerr had learned long ago that most such tales had dubious origins at best.

Whatever the source, once he had secured the needed funds, Milcraft's plans took on a grander scale. Some said that Milcraft sincerely wanted to build a church in the classical tradition, modeled after the great cathedrals of Europe. Others, though, saw it as Milcraft's attempt to rub his success in the face of the community that had mocked him—many of whom he now employed in his effort.

Finally the construction was completed. But the controversy did not end there. For many years the structure was considered an act of architectural presumption—in short, an eyesore—and there had been at least one failed attempt to burn it down. But its very eccentricity drew visitors, and though the town founders would probably be scandalized at the thought, it eventually became an official historic landmark, and a frequent attraction for tourists. Milcraft would have found the situation amusing, Kerr thought.

But the question foremost in Kerr's mind right now was whether or not Milcraft had followed through on his imitation of the great cathedrals to the extent of including hidden rooms or passages. To that end, he was determined to check every inch of the church, from the bottom up, until he was satisfied that there was nothing untoward anywhere within it. Once he had ruled out the possibility of hidden passages through which an intruder might have been traveling—and Milcraft was just unusual enough to have included them in his design—he could move on to other prospects.

Assuming, of course, that he did not go blind from squinting first. Or as mad as Milcraft had gone in his last years. "Mad as Milcraft" was a local expression that had become popular toward the end of his life. After a few prosperous years, the church had suddenly gone downhill fast. Some said Milcraft had abruptly lost heart concerning the enterprise, or lost his faith.

Following Milcraft's death not long afterward, the church sat empty for years before the first parish priest, on orders from the bishop to locate a suitable spot for a Catholic church, chanced upon it and won the bishop's grudging approval. That it still stood was a testament to Milcraft's vision.

Kerr brought the blueprints close to the bare bulb, trying to make out the dimensions of the basement. As near as he could tell, it was supposed to be thirty feet long by twenty feet wide. The basement didn't look that long, but in the dim light it was hard to be sure. He wished that Milcraft had put in a few windows along the top of the basement, but the walls were solid. And the piles of old clothes, decorations, folding chairs, and boxes left over from past rummage sales made an accurate estimation even more difficult.

He measured off the width of the basement. Twenty feet. That checked with the blueprints. Next he checked its length. Twenty-five feet.

Kerr frowned. The blueprints indicated thirty feet. Kerr worked his way through the clutter until he was at the middle of the far wall. The bricks *did* look a little different here, he thought, now that he examined them closely. With a screwdriver, he began rapping on the brick wall at intervals of six inches. After a few feet, the rapping produced a pronounced echo, as if there were a chamber or crawl space behind the wall. He dug at the mortar with the blade of the screwdriver. The surface of the old mortar crumbled slightly, held firm for a moment, then gave way altogether. The screwdriver plunged in to the hilt. He moved the handle back and forth; it swung easily, encountering no resistance on the other side.

Kerr withdrew the screwdriver, then moved it farther along the line of mortar and slipped the blade back in again, jiggling the handle up and down until the brick began to slip toward him, the mortar crumbling into powder. With a fine spray of dust and powder, the brick came out. He peered inside, but the single bulb behind him could not penetrate the darkness beyond the false wall.

Kerr went back for a flashlight, realizing that he had been right, at least in part. There was more to the church than the blueprints indicated. Even if it brought him no closer to determining how the sacristy had been violated, it renewed his overall confidence. If there was this one discrepancy in the blueprints, who knew how many others there might be? The church might be riddled with hidden rooms and chambers; given Milcraft's eccentric nature, Kerr thought it altogether possible.

He shone the flashlight into the opening, revealing a gap behind the wall that corresponded to the discrepancy in the blueprints. Beyond that, he couldn't make out any details in the narrow glow of the beam.

Well, he thought, I've come this far. . . .

Kerr applied the screwdriver to the mortar surrounding the rest of the bricks. Now that one had been removed, the rest came loose easily. Within five minutes he had cleared away an opening some three feet in diameter. Now he could clearly make out a series of narrow steps leading up into a stairwell built behind the wall. Picking up the flashlight, he stepped cautiously into the opening. A long-dead mouse lay in one corner, but otherwise the stairwell was empty.

Kerr tested the first step, found it solid, and walked slowly up, checking each successive step before putting his full weight on it. At what would be the second floor—which would put it just behind and above the baptistery, he thought—the stairway ended abruptly in an L that opened into a small room, windowless and pitch black. Kerr swept the floor and walls with the glow of the flashlight, revealing a hand-hewn table, several standing crates, a severely straight, high-backed chair, and two china cups on the table, now filled with dust and the discarded knitting of spiderwebs. Three casks were lined up against the far wall—the south wall of the church, Kerr decided. There was a shapeless pile beside the casks, shadows within shadows pinned by the light. Kerr crouched down for a better look, and found it to be a sheet of thick canvas, laid over something bulky beneath. With thumb and forefinger he lifted up the sheet.

Kerr gasped. A mummified body lay partially uncovered beneath the canvas. Its clothes were rotting away in places, but were clearly old in their design. Kerr guessed at the early nineteenth century.

Milcraft? he wondered, and immediately rejected the idea. Milcraft had died in 1860 and had been buried in North Cutler. He could see no overt signs of violence to the body, but that did little to ease the discomfort he was feeling—discomfort that grew from one question after another racing through his mind. If it was death by natural causes, then why the attempt at concealment—the sheet, the false wall erected to seal up the room, creating a hidden crypt in the very body of the church? And if it was death at the hands of another, then why not remove the body altogether?

Kerr inspected the room more carefully now. He went first to the table, then systematically checked the open crates and the cask. In the second cask he found a cloth-wrapped book. Careful not to damage the brittle pages, he eased it open just enough to peek inside. It was a journal of sorts, but only the first twenty pages bore entries, written in a hand too small to be read with the flashlight.

Careful not to brush the dusty volume against his shirt, he glanced back at the mummified body, murmured a prayer for the dead, and headed for the stairs. His immediate impulse was to call the constable, but he paused at the thought of scandal, of how the community and the Bishop would react to the thought that babies had been baptized, and communion given, inches from a makeshift crypt. Though the scandal would be less if the body had come to be there through natural causes, rather than anything sinister.

Perhaps, he thought as he stepped back into the basement, perhaps the book will provide the information. If so, he would be able to minimize the scandal by stating right up front the reason for the body's presence. There was no way that he could conceal this from the authorities, nor did he intend to. But there was no immediate hurry; after being concealed for over a hundred years, the body could wait another few days while he worked out the solution. It wasn't going anywhere.

He piled up chairs and boxes to obscure the opening in the false wall. Satisfied that the entrance could not be seen, he started for the stairs just as Mrs. Graham appeared at the top of the steps.

"Were you down there all the time?" she asked.

"Yes." It was, more or less, the truth.

Mrs. Graham shook her head. "I'm surprised you didn't hear me calling you. It's Mr. Crawford. There's been an accident."

Kerr felt his heart skip a beat. "What happened? How badly is he hurt?"

"The police didn't say; they just said the constable told them to tell you that he was being taken to the hospital in Cutler."

"All right," Kerr said, "I'll be on my way as soon as I change clothes. And cancel my appointments for the rest of the day. You may as well take the day off yourself."

"Consider it done," she said. "But if you need me for anything, I'll either be home or over by Judy Carlyle's place. I hear the poor woman's under the weather, so I thought I'd stop by, cheer her up a bit."

"All right," Kerr said, climbing up from the basement, carrying the journal with him. Poor Sam! he thought, shaking his head. I wonder what he's gotten himself into this time?

TWENTY-THREE

THE SIMMONS HOUSE

Ruth Miller paced back and forth in the living room, annoyed with her son. Karl hadn't come in until nearly dawn— or at least that's what she assumed. All she knew for certain was that she'd been sleeping fitfully, disturbed by confused dreams she could only dimly remember, when, at nearly five o'clock in the morning, she'd heard the door to his room shut. After that, she hadn't heard a peep from him. He hadn't come out of his room since then, not even for breakfast.

Probably out drinking, she decided. Just like his father. Stay out all night, sleep all day, good for absolutely nothing. How was he going to support her in her old age (which, of course, was still a ways off) and Cheryl until she finally got married and moved out? What did he expect of her, anyway? Maid service and breakfast in bed?

Like hell, she thought.

"Mom?"

Ruth turned at the sound. Cheryl came into the living room from the kitchen, brushing her hair back so that it feathered around the ears. "What is it, honey?"

"I'm going out for a while. Be back in a couple of hours."

Ruth frowned. "I thought you weren't feeling well." Cheryl had complained of a stomachache earlier that had left her not up to going to school.

"I wasn't. But now I'm better. Besides, I could use the air."

"Is it too late for you to go on to school, finish the rest of the day?"

"No way! It's already past noon; what's the point? Besides, it's Friday—you wouldn't want me to ruin a perfectly good Friday, would you?" She pouted, trying to look cutely innocent. It was the same look she'd used to get away with little infractions for as long as Ruth could remember.

"Well, all right, I suppose. But you'll be back in time for dinner?"

"Promise," Cheryl said, already halfway toward the bathroom. A few more strokes of the hair, a little makeup, and she'd be on her way. She was an attractive girl, a *good* girl. Ruth looked up at the second-floor bedroom door. Too bad certain *others* couldn't be like her.

Her mind made up, she moved up the stairs to Karl's bedroom door, determined to give him one last talking-to. If that didn't take, well, she would just wash her hands of him. He was almost thirty, and if he wanted to become a good-for-nothing like his father, so be it. She wasn't going to waste any further time or breath on him. Besides, all this distraction was keeping her from her hobby, the conversations that murmured back and forth on her party line.

She paused before the door—and abruptly found the idea of knocking repugnant. She was being silly. She didn't think Karl could have a girl in there with him—God knew he was as ugly as a bullfrog and as likely to get a woman interested in him as a horse could tapdance—but nonetheless she felt a curious reluctance to touch the door.

Oh, don't be an old woman, she thought. Pushing aside her reservations, she knocked on the door, starting at how loud it sounded. No reply. Well, she wasn't about to be ignored. She could wait as long as he could.

When it became apparent that the door wasn't going to open, she rapped again, harder.

"I know you're in there, Karl, so there's no sense pretending you're not. Now come out here—I want to talk to you."

For a moment there was no answer, just a rustle of

movement behind the door. Then: "Leave me alone. I warn you once; I will not warn you again."

Ruth stepped back as if she'd been slapped. The voice was strange, but still Karl's. What shocked her was the tone he had taken. He was *warning* her, was he! Well, just who did he think he was talking to, anyway? She grabbed the doorknob and turned. Locked.

Locked! How dare he lock her out of a room in her own house?

"Karl, you open this door right now, you hear me? Right this instant!"

She listened again, waiting for any sign that he was coming to unlock the door. If not, she would just have to go and get the key she kept beside the—

The lock clicked. She had not actually *heard* him come to the door, but—the bolt moved back. That was all, though. Apparently he wanted her to come inside; he wasn't coming out. Well, fine, she thought, and pushed open the door.

She stopped barely past the threshold. The air in the bedroom was thick and musty, as if the windows had been tightly shut. It was dark. The shades were drawn, and boards had been placed in the windows to keep out the light. It could be night within that room.

She looked through the gloom for Karl, and finally found him—barely—standing in a far corner. He was hardly noticeable, just a dark stain against the faded wallpaper. How could he have gotten all the way over there so fast, after just unlocking the door? And so quietly? She stepped forward, the floorboards creaking beneath her weight. "Karl?"

"*Shut the door!*" It was a direct command, an order given in the tone of someone used to giving them, and used to having them obeyed. She instinctively reached for the door—then caught herself. He could take that high-and-mighty attitude of his and stick it. Nobody ordered her around in her own house!

Nonetheless, Ruth's hand reached behind her and, seemingly of its own accord, closed the door. As soon as the bolt clicked into its slot, the room was swallowed in an even greater darkness. The room felt hot, the air close, as if she were suddenly somewhere far underground. "Karl?" she said again. She couldn't see him now; she was aware only of a vague sense of movement within the darkened room. She felt as if she had been left alone with a large, stalking animal. For a fleeting moment she even thought she saw a pair of slitted eyes throwing back the all-but-nonexistent light.

Then it came. She didn't hear it immediately, perhaps startled as much by the sinister softness of the voice as the fact that—though it was clearly impossible—it seemed to be coming from the ceiling just above her head. It was one word:

Punish.

A hand slapped her, hard; slammed her back against the door. Her right cheek burned from the impact, and it took her a moment to realize that it had been her own hand that had slapped her. She held the hand out in front of her, looking at it as if it belonged to a stranger. Then, suddenly, it balled into a fist and slammed into her face. Lights danced behind her eyes. Through the door she could hear the sound of the downstairs door opening, of Cheryl heading out. She wanted to scream for help, but the world beyond this room was no longer relevant. At this moment, the only thing that existed was this room, and whatever moved within it.

Punish, the voice murmured again, as soft as the sound of moth's wings. This time the hand remained still, but inside her, something twisted. She gasped and dropped to one knee, struggling for breath. It felt as if a hand had reached into her stomach and begun tearing at it. Pain lanced into every organ, hammering at her heart, her lungs, her head. The room rocked beneath her, and she fell to the floor, fighting for breath.

Somewhere in the room, far away, something laughed. Ruth felt her heart beating hard in her chest, knew that any second now it would burst, and that would be the end of the pain, and for that at least she would be grateful. But before that could happen, the pain slackened. In the dizzy, dark silence that followed, she sensed that her fate was being debated with cold, remorseless logic. Finally, as if a decision had been made that she might yet be of some temporary value, the pain subsided entirely.

Stand, the voice commanded.

Ruth struggled to her feet, supporting herself against the wall. Another second's silence, then:

Forget.

And the pain came again, this time knifing in through her eyes and into her brain, chewing at her like a rat on something not yet dead. She gasped, her hands flying to her face to bat at the clawing darkness. The struggle was brief, and then she straightened. Where once there had been pain, there was now only a distant throbbing, a numbness that reached down through her cheeks and settled in over her head like a blanket of snow. Calmly she turned, sought for the doorknob, found it, and stepped back into the hall. She closed the door and paused only momentarily before heading down the steps and into the front room, where she took her usual seat by the window.

She did not take up the telephone, but only stared at it without moving, as if it were something alien but interesting that had suddenly materialized out of the air. Perhaps it would ring. If it did, she would say that Karl and she had been up all night together, that they had been working on the family's finances, and that Karl was asleep and not to be disturbed.

In time her gaze strayed from the telephone, and she dared a glance at the stairs. Yes, she would let him sleep. He needed his rest.

2

Thaddeus Smith pulled into the Union 76 station at the edge of town, one of the last stops on his mail route. "Right on time," he said. Thaddeus took particular pride in making sure that all of the mail was delivered before one o'clock every day of the week, come rain or shine. Liz, seated beside him, knew this because he had taken every opportunity to remind her of it. Just in front of them, Jay Carmichael finished talking with someone in an old Chevy, then approached them as the driver sped off.

Jay stuck his head in through the window on Liz's side. "Hey, didja hear?"

"Hear what?" Thaddeus said. Liz noted from the sound of his voice that he didn't take to Jay any better than she did. There was just something about the man that set her teeth on edge. "Somebody up and die or something?"

It was meant as a joke, but Jay's head bobbed up and down with excitement. "You got it! Not just died, though. Killed! All four of 'em." He began to recount the stories he had heard from nearly half a dozen customers as word had spread.

Thaddeus's face was pale by the time Jay finished. "Un-believable," he said. "It's the kind of thing you never think can happen here. New York, maybe, but here . . ."

"When did it happen?" Liz asked. The LeMarque house had been among their first stops. It had been dark and silent, but at that time of the morning she hadn't thought much of it. The idea that the LeMarques might have been lying inside, dead, as Thaddeus slipped the mail into their box, sent a shudder through her.

"From what I hear," Jay said, "the police figure it must've happened sometime during the night, maybe early this morn-ing."

"Jesus." Liz closed her eyes. When she opened them, she found Jay eyeing her openly. She could swear he was enjoying this.

"They got any leads?" Thaddeus asked.

Jay shrugged. "A couple of folks who know people who work in the hospital in Cutler said it was Greg LeMarque who did it, some kind of murder-suicide. But they aren't sure." He gestured in the direction of the car that had just pulled out. "Just heard from one of the neighbors who was there when it happened that Tom arrested somebody on suspicion."

"Somebody from here in town?" Thaddeus asked, un-willing to admit the possibility that someone in the Point, someone he knew, could have been responsible.

"Naw. I heard it's some stranger, new in town. Eric some-thing."

Liz felt as if her stomach had turned to stone. "Eric Mat-thews?"

"Yeah, I think that was it. The police've got him locked up nice and tight. You know him?"

She turned away, ignoring the question. "Thaddeus, can you drop me off at my car? I know you've got the rest of your route to finish, but it'll only take a minute, and it's important."

"Sure thing," he said, and handed Jay his mail before starting up the engine. "This'll be the first time I haven't made my schedule," he continued, "but I guess there's a first time for everything. God knows, this is the first time anything like this has happened in the Point. I just pray it doesn't ever happen again."

Liz could see the muscles working beneath his lined

cheeks. "Those poor kids," he said, clearly outraged beyond anything he could begin to convey. "I hope they hang that lousy son of a bitch."

3

Will closed his medical bag just as Father Kerr stuck his head into the room where Sam Crawford lay without moving, attached to an array of tubes and electrodes that monitored his condition.

"How is he?" Kerr asked.

"Not here," Will said softly, and moved past Kerr into the hall.

Kerr waited until the door had swung shut, closing off the view to Sam's room. "Well?"

"He's not good, but he could be a hell of a lot worse. As far as we can tell, there's been no internal damage, no critical drop in blood pressure, no hemorrhaging in the blood vessels or main organs. He's got a fractured humerus—left arm, so at least he can write—two fractured ribs, massive bruises along the upper torso; the list goes on. Mainly a lot of lesser evils. By and large, he's intact. All the vital signs are solid."

"I believe I hear a *but* coming."

Will looked at the polished floor. "He's been unconscious ever since they found him. There aren't any significant lesions along the head, so if we're lucky that means no brain damage, but it doesn't rule out the possibility of concussion. At this point, I'm not calling it coma. There's every chance that it's just a psychological reaction to the injuries, the mind shutting down while the body heals itself, escaping the pain. But if he doesn't come out of it in twenty-four hours, I'm going to arrange for a CAT scan."

"Any idea what happened?"

"Tom and that fellow they picked up say he fell off the path just outside the caves, and so far I haven't seen anything to disprove that. But that's just a preliminary opinion; there'll be others poking around until we get a medical consensus. Ditto on the autopsies; I hear the county coroner's due within the hour. We were lucky enough to get him on an otherwise slow day." He found it hard to make even a lame joke. He couldn't put Barbara's face out of his mind.

Was that you last night, Barbara? Would you still be alive if I'd just answered the goddamn phone a few seconds earlier?

"I heard about the LeMarques," Kerr said quietly. "An orderly in the emergency room mentioned it when I came in."

"Last rites?"

"They were Protestant. I understand that the hospital has reached some family members in New Hampshire; they're arranging for transportation of the bodies, all the rest. I heard that you were the one who found them."

"Yeah," Will said. "And too late, damn it." He rubbed at his eyes. They were tired, and had seen too much lately.

"Do you want to talk about it?"

"Not now, not yet. Maybe later. Give me a few years."

"Do you think he could have done it?"

"You mean that Eric fellow?" Will shrugged. "Who knows? I only met him for a few minutes, outside the LeMarque house. He was acting pretty strange, I can confirm that much at least. Then again, what with finding Sam, being deputized, and getting volunteered to go into a house with a dead family, I can't see how I can fault him for acting a bit odd. So I just don't know."

"I had him over to dinner last night," Kerr said. "And Liz, and Sam. I kept noticing the way he kept watching Sam, as if he were studying him somehow. Still, he seemed a nice enough fellow. Quiet. Intelligent. But, these days, I guess that doesn't mean much, does it? I mean, isn't that what they always say about killers—'He was a nice guy, quiet, the last person you'd suspect'? But on the other hand—"

"It's true what they say about you, isn't it?"

"What's that?"

" 'Go not to Father Kerr for advice, for he shall tell you both yes and no.' " He forced a smile, but it felt tired, as if it might very well drop right off his face. He checked his watch. "Got to run. I'm meeting the coroner in half an hour. He wants me to sit in on the autopsies. Figures I might be able to add something since I was first on the spot, saw how the bodies were laid out, that sort of thing."

Kerr nodded toward Sam's room. "Is it all right if I go in, sit with him for a while?"

"I suppose so. Might even do some good, if we're dealing

with a psychological problem rather than a physiological one. A familiar voice can sometimes draw someone out of a condition like his."

"All right," Kerr said. "Anything I should know?"

"Just don't go fooling with his IV, don't get him into a baseball game, and no hospital jokes. Beyond that, you're on your own," Will said, then turned and headed down the hospital corridor. Kerr took a moment to compose himself, then stepped through the door into Sam's room.

4

It was well after one o'clock when Liz entered the Dredmouth Point police station. Tom sat behind a desk, filling out reports, while at the next desk, Ray was on the telephone. They looked up as the door slammed shut.

"I understand you've got Eric Matthews here," she said. "I'd like to see about getting him released." A glance passed between the two policemen; Liz suspected that her request had been more or less expected. Good, she thought. It'll make this a little faster.

"I'm sorry, but we're holding him for twenty-four hours on suspicion of murder, and suspicion of assault."

"On what grounds?"

"Mostly circumstantial evidence. So far, he hasn't been formally charged with anything."

"Can't you release him into my custody?"

"Sorry. He said you'd be coming by, and suggested the same thing, but there's no way I'm turning him loose until I get the final word from the coroner's office."

"Did Eric tell you why he thought I would be coming here?"

"No, only that you would, and for us to let him know when you got here."

Ray chuckled. "You'd think he was staying at the Hilton or something, and we were the next best thing to room service."

She ignored the comment. "Look, I know for a fact that he didn't do anything."

"Oh?" Tom said.

"I was with him last night. If he needs an alibi, I'm it."

Tom made a brief entry in a notebook. "Not to be personal, but were you with him all night?"

"Most of it, yes."

"Until what time?"

"Why?"

"Just answer the question, please."

"Until four, maybe four-thirty this morning."

"And after that?"

"I was with the postman, going along on his rounds."

Tom put down the pencil. "Well, now, that's where we run into a problem. The bodies we found hadn't been dead very long. Rough estimate is they were killed somewhere between one in the morning and five. We're still waiting for the coroner to give us a better estimate. If the killings took place before four o'clock, then you've got a case. But if they happened after four, then you can't be sure he wasn't anywhere in the area, can you?"

Liz shrugged in agreement.

"And he was found with Sam at about ten o'clock, when you were on your rounds. So, once again, he might have had the opportunity."

"But that doesn't make any sense. Why would he do anything to hurt Sam? They'd barely even met."

"That's true. We don't have anything on motive—yet. And it may have been an accident, just like he says. But the only person who can confirm that is Sam, and we won't know his side of the story until he wakes up."

A few feet away, Ray hung up the phone, an excited look on his face. "Got something," he said, crossing to Tom's desk. "Check it out. I'd say we've got a connection."

Tom read the slip of paper. "We had the main computer up in Bangor run a check on your friend," he said. "Did you know his name was originally Eric Langren?"

"What does that have to do with anything?"

"Just that the house where the killings took place used to belong to his family. Last son of the Langren family comes back to town years later, doesn't tell anyone who he is, finds someone living in the house he remembers as his own. Next thing you know, there's a family dead there. I'd say that was reason to keep tabs on him, wouldn't you?"

Liz looked away, her image of herself as rescuer crumbling behind her eyes. "Has he called for a lawyer?"

"Not yet." This from Ray. "Said he wanted to talk to you first."

"All right," Liz said. "Can I see him for a minute?"

Standing stiffly, Tom took the keys from his desk drawer and motioned for her to follow. "You'll have to leave that here," he said, pointing to her purse. She set it on the desk as he unlocked the door to the jail proper. They moved past the door into a long hallway flanked on either side by identical cells, all unoccupied—except the single cell at the end of the hall.

Eric moved toward the bars as they approached. He looked tired, perhaps even a little embarrassed, but not confused or angry. Controlled. His hands dangled outside the bars. It was the same gesture she'd seen when she'd written a feature story about prison conditions—but that had been a million years ago. How quickly they fall into the habit of seeking out those eight inches of freedom, she thought.

They stopped in front of the cell. "I'll be right down the hall if you need anything," Tom said. "You've got five minutes." He moved away.

Liz smiled faintly. "Hi."

"Hi." Eric returned the smile, a little wanly. "See what happens when you leave early?"

"I'm sorry," she said, "but I had this appointment with Thaddeus, and there was so much to do—"

"Don't worry about it," he said. "It's no one's fault, really. Just a mistake. A tragic mistake." His face darkened. "I just hope it doesn't get any more tragic."

"What do you mean?"

Eric sighed. "I'm not sure. But there's something up. All I know is that I've got to get out of here as fast as possible. I don't think twenty-four hours will make a big difference, but I can't be sure."

Liz searched his face. He was deeply worried, that much was certain. But he was innocent; surely the coroner's report would prove that.

"Is there anything I can do?" she asked.

"I wish there were." He leaned closer to her. "How's Sam? If you can get to him, talk to him—"

"No good. He's still unconscious. Did you see what happened to him?"

"Only in part. He was coming out of the caves and he fell. Not so much fell, actually, as jumped, like he was being chased by something." He frowned. "Liz, I've got to know what he was doing up there. Keep an eye on him, if you can. Make sure he's okay. Then, as soon as he comes to, you've got to find out *exactly* what he was doing in the caves. Anything he might remember would help. This is important, Liz. Can you do it?"

"I suppose so. But why all the details? The main thing is that he can testify that you had nothing to do with the accident—"

"You'll just have to trust me, Liz. I wish I could explain, but I don't entirely understand it myself. There are too many pieces missing. I only know that what happened to Sam has something to do with the killings. If you can do this one thing for me, I can take care of myself on this end. All right?"

Liz smiled bravely. "You've got it, masked man."

Eric returned the smile. "One thing's for sure—this'll make one hell of a chapter for your book."

Then, from behind her, "Time's up."

5

Karin Whortle sat at the counter, searching for the words she needed. R.T. had come over from the general store to fill her in on the latest news—and still she couldn't believe it. She'd known Barbara LeMarque only a little, Greg not at all. It was an oversight she'd intended to correct. That was the irony of it. She'd been *sure* there would be time for it. There was always time, she'd thought.

She'd been wrong.

Funny how people lived each day as if they were immortal, as if they had all the time in the world. It was a mistake she'd made in other ways, she realized now. Imagining that there was plenty of time to find just the right man, who met all the criteria she had established long ago. Well, she hadn't found him. And now, more than anything else, she realized that while there might not be time enough to find the right man, there was time enough to find someone who cared.

Through the window she noticed more and more folks going into the general store. R.T. followed her gaze. "More bad news, or more folks lookin' for bad news," he said. As usual, the store had become a center for the grapevine, for any news that bore even the slightest whiff of truth, and some that didn't. Conversely, the diner had been emptier than Karin could ever remember it. Folks were either staying home in shock, or were at work, or were over in the general store.

If business didn't pick up soon, she'd be over there herself, waiting and listening.

R.T. finished his cup of coffee and stood up, slipping fifty cents onto the counter.

"On the house," Karin said. "And thanks for the latest."

"No problem," R.T. said, but left the change anyway. "Well, back into the fray, eh?"

"And if anything develops with Sam—"

"You'll be the first to know," R.T. said from the door. "After the rest of the whole civilized world, that is," he said, then headed toward the crowded store.

Karin pocketed the fifty cents and was about to pick up the cup when the telephone rang. She picked up the receiver. "Point Inn."

She recognized the voice on the other end. Walter Kriski. "You heard?"

"I don't think there's anyone in town that hasn't."

"Yeah, well, I was just thinking," he said, "that with everything that's going on, maybe we should put off the movie until tomorrow night, if that's okay with you. Besides, I've got some work here to take care of, probably keep me a little late."

Makes sense, she thought, he works at the cemetery, so— She couldn't finish the thought. "Not the LeMarques—"

"No, no," he said quickly. "They're being sent out of state for the burial. Family or something. That's how I heard about it, a call about helping with the transportation."

Karin relaxed. The news itself was bad enough, but to think that Walter—the man she was about to go out with—was groundskeeper at the cemetery where they would be buried was almost too much. Then she caught herself. She was thinking like a choosy immortal again. His job was every bit as honorable as hers.

"You still there?" Walter asked.

"Right here. Tomorrow night's fine. Same time?"

"Same time. See you then. 'Bye."

Karin started to hang up the receiver, then stopped, listening to the dial tone. It sounded—funny, somehow. Hollow. The way it sounded when someone was listening in on the extension. But there was no extension.

"Hello?" she said. Nothing. Only the hollow tone, and a curious hissing that seemed to undulate softly. She thought of a snake, and pushed the image away. A bad connection, that's all, she thought.

6

Father Kerr sat beside Sam's bed, trying to think of other things to say after filling the silence for nearly an hour. "I guess you were wrong about me," he said. "Looks like I'm not quite the bag of wind you thought."

Sam lay still on the clean hospital bed, his eyes shut, face swollen above a bruised neck and shoulder. Theirs was, Kerr had to admit, a curious but satisfying friendship. As two of the Point's more prominent citizens, they had met many times over at dinners and at town meetings. Sam had reacted to the new priest with sarcasms intended, Kerr realized, more to test than to deride. Instead of reacting with dogma, as Sam had no doubt expected, he decided to meet logic with logic. He sensed in Sam a good man in search of the truth, and Kerr had no quarrel with a genuinely curious man, for, in the end, all truths led to God.

"Did I tell you that I've been reading that book you loaned me—*Man and His Symbols*?" No reply. "Rather interesting, all things considered. I've been working over what you said at dinner, too, and laying in a pretty considerable store of ammunition for our next talk. Maybe then you'll learn better than to throw the Devil at a Christian who's willing to read your heathen books."

Kerr felt himself run out of words, his thoughts wandering. What had he been talking about? Where was he going? It was so hard to keep his thoughts in a straight line; so much had happened. The killings, Sam, the strange incidents in the church, the discovery of the hidden room, the body and the book—so very much to deal with at one time.

No, he decided. All the rest could wait. Sam needed him. Sam, who had never needed the Church in all his life. Right now, that was the important thing—the only important thing, in fact.

Reaching out his hand in a gesture of friendship that he hoped would penetrate the wall of trauma, Kerr was surprised to find the pallid arm cold, terribly cold. He checked both hands, found them frigid. It wasn't right; Sam's hands shouldn't be that cold.

He pushed the button over Sam's bed. A moment later, a nurse appeared at the door. "Yes, Father?"

"I hate to bother you, but could you please take his temperature?"

"His temperature was checked just fifteen minutes ago."

"I know, but he seems awfully cold—I just want to be sure he isn't going into shock."

The nurse pressed an electronic thermometer into Sam's mouth. "A degree or two higher than normal, but well within tolerance," she announced a moment later.

"Higher, you say?"

The nurse nodded.

"But he's so cold. See for yourself."

She felt along Sam's arm down to his hands. "He feels fine, Father. A little warm, but fine. Will there be anything else?"

"Thank you, no," Kerr said. The nurse padded quietly out of the room. When she was gone, he took Sam's hand. It felt as cold as ice.

Impossible.

And yet the readings had been normal. Why should Sam's temperature seem normal to everyone and everything but him?

He searched Sam's face for an answer, but this time Sam didn't have anything to say.

Kerr held the hand more firmly, trying futilely to warm it.

7

Ray set down the telephone, careful not to let his anger show. Fortunately, Tom was on a call of his own, too busy to notice what had just happened. He'd *told* Cheryl never to call here; there was always the chance she'd get Tom.

But then, Cheryl was crazy. He'd known *that* a long time ago. He couldn't blame her for wanting the latest information on the killings, that part was fairly normal. Hell, the phone had been ringing all morning. But while picking up the latest, she'd said she still wanted to get together for a little—for a *little*. On a day like this. With all hell breaking loose. Fact was, she'd actually sounded excited by the prospect of sneaking off to the woods for a quick one while all this was going on.

Crazy, he thought. Absolutely stir-fried crazy.

"We've got a problem," Tom said, hanging up the phone.

Ray winced. *Another* one? "What's up?"

Tom indicated the phone. "That was Clement Ashford, over at the dairy. Called in madder'n hell, but a little worried, too. He said Bud Simmons didn't come in for his pickup this morning. Hasn't heard from him all day, and when he called the Simmons place, there was no answer. When word got to him about the LeMarques, well, he called here."

"You think it needs checking out?"

"On any other day, I'd say no. Today, I'm saying yes. I just tried calling Bud, and there's still no answer. So why don't you make a quick run over there, just check out the place?"

"On my way," Ray said, heading for the door. He decided that it was probably a nothing call, but at least it got him outside for a while. He went to the parking lot, where Eric Matthews's car had been deposited after being towed from near Indian Lake. No telling what they might find inside it if Matthews was charged. As he unlocked the police car, he momentarily returned to what Cheryl had said. He *would* be out of the office for a while, and she didn't live far from there—

He stopped the thought before it could be completed. No way, he thought. Christ! I must be getting as crazy as she is.

Eric paced the cramped cell, unable to keep from watching the clock. Two o'clock. With every passing moment, the sense of urgency became greater, the need to get *out* of here. The murders and Sam's "accident" were connected somehow, he was sure of it, and the longer they kept him locked up, the longer it would take him to figure out what that connection was, and how to deal with it. He was sure it all tied in with what had happened to him inside the caves, with the forces that had driven him here at exactly this moment in time, and his own peculiar talents.

Feelings. Hunches. Sudden flashes of intuition. But all of it unpredictable. Uncontrollable. As a kid he had found it useful for guessing the correct answers on tests. As an adult it had been less than useless in Las Vegas. If anything, it had steered him wrong with unnatural consistency.

But that had all started to change once he'd returned to the Point, hadn't it?

The ability to influence the deputy last night, that was new, wasn't it? And he had instinctively known how to do it. At the LeMarque house, he had tried again, and again had felt the deputy wavering under his influence. But again his talents had shown themselves to be inconsistent. The constable had been a dead end. All he'd earned from the effort was a splitting headache.

There was always the possibility that the constable was simply more strong-willed, that it would still work, but might require more time and concentration. For that reason, when he'd sensed that one of them was leaving, he'd hoped it would be Tom. Ray alone would have presented an opening, a button to push.

No such luck.

He looked down at the lock on the cell door, and suddenly wondered if the increase of his talents extended to inanimate objects. He remembered the suit of clothes that had arranged itself on his bed. Had he done that without knowing it? Had he subconsciously *willed* them there?

Eric gripped the cell door, felt the cold, rough metal against his palms, and concentrated on the lock. He closed his eyes and tried to picture the internal mechanism. He imagined himself moving past the keyhole, the plug, around the latch assembly to the frame plate, finally coming to the bolt. He thought about the bolt, tried to picture it sliding back. His brow furrowed. Sweat trickled down between his shoulder blades.

Harder. Harder.

Something whizzed past his head.

Eric pushed himself away from the door just as his aluminum cup went flying out between the bars, followed a moment later by the food tray and the toothbrush they'd assigned him; everything loose in the cell was shooting out like shrapnel, flying through the cell bars and slamming against the far wall.

The pain struck at once. He was only dimly aware of the door opening, of Tom coming into the corridor, yelling something about good behavior. Eric barely heard it. This headache was even worse than the last. It hammered relentlessly behind his right eye.

When he opened his eyes again, Tom was gone. Ten minutes had gone by.

He'd failed—but not entirely. He'd made something happen. That was the important thing. Maybe he was misdirecting his thoughts. Had he really been concentrating on the lock, or had he been thinking more about just getting *out*? Perhaps this new talent responded more to his desire than to his tactics.

If that was the case, then again it was a mixed blessing.

And one more mixed blessing was not at all what he needed at the moment.

9

Ray parked in front of the Simmons house. After seeing what had happened up at the LeMarque house, he was far from thrilled at the prospect of poking around somebody else's house.

Well, he thought, at least the odds were good that this one was just a false alarm. As he walked toward the house, he checked the mailbox. The few letters and circulars he found there were as yet untouched, and they had certainly been there for a couple of hours at least. Nobody slept that late, Ray decided soberly—unless they weren't home in the first place.

He stopped in front of the door and leaned toward it, listening. The house was quiet. He stepped back a pace and rapped twice on the door. The sound echoed within the house, but the door remained closed. He tried the doorknob. It didn't move. Stepping down off the porch, he walked across the leaf-littered lawn to the two front windows. He found them locked, the shades drawn tight. Not only drawn, but actually pushed flat, as though something heavy had been shoved up against them.

Ray circled around to the rear of the house. The two windows that looked out on the backyard were also closed off. The back door was locked. Ray wandered toward the lawn chairs, scanning the dark upper windows and wondering what his next step should be. There was no immediate reason to suspect a crime, and equally little justification for anything as drastic as breaking in a door or a window.

While he didn't relish the idea of returning to Tom without an explanation, he was damned if he was going to give anyone grounds to sue him for destruction of private property, not without strict orders to that effect, at any rate. He decided to radio Tom for instructions; if Tom called him back to the office, well, that was one solution, and if he gave the go-ahead for a break-in, then anybody with complaints could take them to Tom.

Who says indecision is no decision at all? With a last look around, he started toward the front of the house.

Suddenly, from behind him: a sound, as of a bolt being thrown.

Ray stopped, looked at the rear door and the surrounding woods, searching for the source of the sound. It *might* have been the door. But why would whoever was inside be playing mute with him?

Unless they were hurt, unable to call out.

"Hello?" Ray called, stepping back toward the rear porch. "Anybody home?" He climbed up onto the porch, tried the doorknob again. It was stiff, but this time it turned in his hand. He opened the door, almost expecting to see Bud waiting for him with a beer. But the room—a storeroom, from the looks of it, filled with coats and old boxes—was deserted.

He stepped up to the connecting door. "Bud? Mrs. Simmons? Anybody t'home?"

He walked through the storeroom and into the den. It was dark here, too—awfully dark. Boxes and boards had been piled up in front of the windows to keep out the light. He hesitated for a moment, letting his eyes adjust to the dimness. He could distinguish only vague shapes—something that might be a couch, a television set, a pair of large chairs. The air was thick inside the silent room; it seemed to catch in his throat as it went into his lungs. His lips were dry.

Ray edged into the living room, trying not to bang into anything sharp. He was amazed at how dark it was. Even with stuff shoved into the openings of the windows and doors, some light should have filtered in. But the only source of illumination was the faint afternoon light from the door behind him. He tried a lamp, but either the bulb was burned out or the power was out.

Several feet into the room, he stopped, determined to go no farther without a flashlight. There was one in the car, he remembered, and cursed himself for not having brought it with him. But then, how was he to know he'd need it in the middle of the afternoon?

He turned to leave, but the motion was confined to his neck and chest. His legs refused to follow his lead, as though he'd been shot with Novocain from the waist down.

Then, for the first time, he sensed that he was not alone in the room.

He started at a noise to his right—the sound of something moving in the far doorway that led into the bedroom. It seemed to slide more than walk across the floor. Instinctively he started to reach for his service revolver, but again his body refused to cooperate. His hands were cold, numb, barely able to close, let alone rise the eighteen inches to the butt of his gun.

And now something else moved to his left. His head whirled, but all he caught was a glimpse of something man-sized, shifting against the dark outline of a chair.

"Who's there?" he tried to say, but his tongue cleaved dryly to the roof of his mouth.

Slowly the door behind him, his only source of light, slid shut.

He strained to see into the sudden night, trying to catch a glimpse of anything, anyone. But the nothingness that surrounded him was absolute. He thought briefly of the times he'd been out on his father's boat, on nights when the stars and the moon were hidden by clouds, and the night seemed to go on forever.

A noise. To his right.

Something—two somethings, as near as he could tell—moved in the false night. They slid closer, circling him. He thought briefly that something brushed his leg, but the numbness made certainty impossible. Beneath the numbness, a scream was building deep in his chest, fighting for release, finding none. There was only the dark, whoever or whatever moved in that dark, and the sound. The new sound that wasn't really a sound at all, a kind of pressure, a buzzing in the back of his head, like the murmuring of bees, and his brain was the hive.

He thought he must be going mad from the fear and the numbness that were edging their way into his thoughts, because he imagined that the bees were discussing him, that some wanted to sting him, to watch him wither and die, while others disagreed—others who noted that since he was alone and could go places where they couldn't, not yet, he might be useful. The stingers relented. They would have their time with him later.

Then the murmuring bees that crawled beneath his skull joined in their intent, their wings pulsing. They turned their attention to the soft, yielding tissue beneath them. Their mandibles dug into the gray substance, pushing aside the folds and thrusting themselves deep, deep into his brain.

Then, at last, they found what they were looking for.

And they fed.

TWENTY-FOUR

CUTLER

Will shifted the overhead light so that it shone more directly into the cavity Dr. Morrison was making in Gregory LeMarque's head. The previous three autopsies had gone quickly; there was no question about the cause of death: shotgun blast at close range, massive trauma to the head and chest area, death almost instantaneous. Time of death, between 3:00 and 5:00 A.M. It was with this final examination that the county coroner was having difficulty. The preliminary lab report verified the presence of powder marks on his hands, proving beyond doubt that Gregory had fired the shotgun at least once. But there was no way of telling exactly how many more times he had fired the gun, which was what they needed to know to determine whether he had killed all three of the victims himself.

Failing that, there was only one question remaining to be answered: Who, and what, had killed Gregory LeMarque?

"There—you see?" the coroner said. His manner was detached, the result of years of poking into corpses, many of them in far worse shape than these. He pulled apart the folds of the brain, just above and to the dorsal side of the hippocampus. "You recognize the area?"

Will examined the region, wishing he had taken refresher courses in physiological psychology; as a GP he took pride in knowing a little about everything—and now he found himself coming up short. Still, he was determined to go down fighting. "Midbrain, around the amygdaloid complex?"

Morrison smiled. "Excellent. You're familiar, then, with the work of Kluver and Bucy?"

"A little." The truth, of course, was that he wasn't, but he was in no mood for a lecture on psychophysiology.

Morrison probed deeper into the tissue, indicating the landmarks with the detachment of a bus-tour guide. "Cortico-medial division—close, but not what we want—here, the baso-lateral region. . . . I take a particular interest in this region, especially when dealing with a suspected killer. It's the area that most psychophysiologists agree can be stimulated to in-duce aggressive behavior. Ninety-nine times out of a hundred, I find nothing out of the ordinary. But every so often—" He poked at the tissue. "Notice, please."

Will leaned in for a closer look. The tissue beneath Mor-rison's probe was swollen, distended; the blood vessels were shot through with tiny lesions that had discolored the sur-rounding tissue. "It's not a tumor," Will said.

"Not exactly, no. But it's curious, isn't it? A condition such as this, in the basolateral amygdaloid nucleus, could lead to a stimulation of the surrounding tissue, resulting in highly ag-gressive behavior."

"Temporary insanity."

"Essentially, yes. Organic, though, not functional."

"What do you think caused it?"

"Hard to say. It's possible that it began as a congenital disorder. You were his physician; did he ever mention any pro-longed headaches?"

"Not that I can recall."

"Then it was not a chronic disorder, but acute—at least in its final stages. That's what I find strange; the rate of deteri-oration must have been extreme, yet there's no evidence of damage to the surrounding tissue. It looks perfectly healthy. It's as if somehow tremendous pressure had been placed only on this one area of the brain."

"If he was in pain, he never said a word about it. So it must have hit late, and then metastasized with incredible speed.

The curious thing is that his wife, Barbara, came to me on several occasions complaining of seasonal headaches."

"Really? Ah, well, too bad there was so little brain tissue left in the cavity to examine. I don't think there's any connection, but it would have been interesting, anyway."

Will shuddered at the offhandedness of the remark. The fact that the observation came from a brother physician did not diminish his reaction. He wanted nothing more than to go home and take a bath.

"In any event," Morrison continued, "as you say, this abnormality opens up the possibility that when and if he committed the murders, he may well have been insane."

"Why do you say *if*?"

"Notice, again, the blood surrounding the tissue. You see how it spread quickly throughout the region? The lesion seems to have ruptured. In such a critical area, that would almost surely be fatal. The conditions would be much the same as a cerebral hemorrhage. Thus far, the appearance of the body would seem to imply murder-suicide. And it's possible that the affected area burst as he was pulling the trigger. Perhaps that's why he finally turned the gun on himself: to eradicate the pain, which must have been immense, to say the least. But to be sure, we have to trace the flow and density of dried blood in the region.

"Because it's entirely possible, given what I'm looking at here, that he died before he could pull the trigger. If that's the case, then we're left with one logical conclusion: that he was dead when the murders were committed. If so, then someone else committed the murders, and then shot him after he was already dead in order to make it look like a suicide."

"But the powder marks—"

"Possibly a red herring. If the victim was dead, it would not be difficult to position the shotgun in his hands, since rigor mortis would not have set in by then, and pull the trigger. The result, an apparent suicide, with powder marks on 'the killer's' hands and clothes."

Will gave a low whistle. "It's going to be a difficult one to call, isn't it?"

Morrison shrugged good-humoredly. "Not if we move swiftly. We must trace the blood flow before the traces deteriorate further. If we can determine that the blood dried first in the area surrounding the aberration, moving outward into the rest of the brain, then he died of natural causes before the trigger was pulled; if the blood dried elsewhere in the brain first, caused by external forces rather than a hemorrhage, then he died of unnatural causes—a gunshot wound. Which would mean that he probably killed himself, just as it appeared." He considered it. "It shouldn't take more than another hour or so to do the trace. I suggest you give your constable a call, get him here for a preliminary briefing."

"Anything else I should tell him?"

"Only that at this moment the odds are about even that he has a murderer or an innocent man in his jail, and that the only man who can break the deadlock"—he indicated Gregory LeMarque—"is being a rather reluctant witness."

2

Behind him, Tom heard the rear door of the police station open. Good, he thought. For once, Ray's right on time.

"Ray?" he called. It was almost three-thirty.

The door to the back room opened slightly. "Yeah?"

Tom grabbed his jacket. "Just got a call from Will. Said they might have some preliminary news on the killings."

There was no response. Usually, Ray's curiosity was boundless, but maybe this day had been enough to sour even his interest. "He wants me to come down for a meeting with the coroner. I need you to stay here and keep an eye on things, so don't go anywhere without telling me. If anything comes up at the hospital, I'll let you know, okay?"

"Fine."

"Be back in about an hour," Tom said, and headed out into the parking lot. He hoped there would finally be some definitive word. The sooner he got this whole matter over with, the better he'd feel.

3

Eric felt more than saw Tom leave—which meant that Ray had returned. He allowed himself a moment of relief. Despite the residual throbbing in his temples, he was sure he could deal with Ray. All Eric needed now was to get him into the cellblock.

Careful, he thought, can't afford to get overconfident at this stage. He braced himself for the effort, then leaned against the bars.

"Hey!" he shouted. "Hey! Listen! I'm ready to confess now." If anything could get Ray in here, it would be the prospect of nailing down a confession singlehandedly. "Hey!"

A pause, and then the door opened. Eric sat on the cell cot, trying to look as nonthreatening as possible. He could hear Ray's footsteps getting closer. Eric closed his eyes, concentrated, hoped he would have enough—*whatever* it was—to get Ray to open the cell door.

Ray stopped in front of the cell. The first thing Eric noticed was that he was still wearing his gun. That was strange, he thought; weren't all police required to leave behind their guns when entering a cell block?

Then he saw the eyes. Not Ray's eyes. The ones hovering over Ray's left shoulder.

They were barely visible, shifting in and out of the range of Eric's enhanced senses. They were shifting, vague, there and not-there: the eyes of a serpent, a goat, a coyote; not human, but sentient. They finally focused on him, and in that instant he knew. He saw the way they widened at the sight of him, and he *knew*.

They recognized him!

Ray's face showed no emotion. His own eyes were dead, turned inward upon themselves. "They knew you would come," he said, flatly. Moving very deliberately, he removed the revolver from its holster and leveled it at Eric.

"No!" Eric shouted.

The eyes—slitted pools of fire-rimmed gold, narrow and shimmering, focused on his own—

Concentrate!

—hard and hot and hateful, do it now, they were saying, do it now—

The gun!

—the trigger being pulled back—

No!

Eric screamed.

And the room erupted into a whirlwind.

Blankets, food, everything went flying through the air, caught up in the tornado. Eric's head vibrated with the rhythms of the wind, but he kept *pushing* with his thoughts, whipping the wind. The eyes behind Ray drew back before the onslaught. Ray stepped back, confused.

One chance.

Eric braced himself against the wall, closed his eyes, and concentrated, reaching deeper into himself than he had ever dared. It had to be now.

Now!

Metal shrieked, ripped. A blast that Eric heard more in his mind than in his ears threw him to the cell floor. The pressure was terrible. He thought his head would explode. Razor-sharp pieces of metal sliced past his ears. Still he pushed, only distantly aware of what he was doing, as if watching it happen from somewhere outside. He flung the storm at the door, at Ray and at the thing behind Ray, his heart ready to burst from the effort.

There was another scream, this time from outside the cell. It rose higher and higher into the spectrum, a keening wail that clawed its way into his ears.

Then, suddenly, the noise subsided. Eric forced his eyes open, suppressing the pain that ripped through his skull, and focused on the spot where the cell door had been a minute earlier. It now lay against the far wall, its hinges sheared off. There was an indentation at least two inches deep where the door had been driven into the opposite wall.

Ray had been thrown to the floor.

He wasn't moving.

Just like the apartment, Eric thought dazedly. But he had never been awake before to see it happen.

Eric stood unsteadily, and stumbled toward the open door, fighting to keep the floor from tipping away beneath him. He bent down beside Ray. There was a deep cut on the deputy constable's forehead, and there were scratches on his face and hands. His uniform was sliced in several places, blood seeping into the gaps in the cloth. But he was still breathing, and the wounds appeared superficial. He would come around sooner or later.

Most important, though—the eyes were gone. For the moment.

Eric hadn't wanted to hurt Ray, and didn't want to abandon him now; what he'd done was not entirely of his own volition. It had been something inside him. Something that had uncoiled, lashed out, then vanished once it was no longer needed.

As for now, he had to get out of here. Trouble was, he had no way of knowing how much of the noise he had heard was in his mind, and how much had actually been audible through the walls of the police station. He could be discovered at any moment, and he doubted anyone would believe his story. Looking at the damage he had somehow wrought, he could barely believe it himself.

More than discovery, he feared the return of those eyes. There was a power in them, and a frightening hunger.

He ran down the cellblock hall, and peered out through the front window. Either no one had heard, or no one had thought to investigate. He decided it was probably the former. Quickly he searched Tom's desk for the envelope containing his belongings, found it, and went to the door. The street on this side was quiet; just a few people were out. Most of the shops had already closed up.

Trying to look inconspicuous, he walked across the parking lot to the Datsun, which had been impounded in the parking lot. With a silent thanks for the constable's efficiency, he started the car, and guided the Datsun onto the road that would take him out of town.

Heading north, he wanted nothing more than to keep going—up to Canada, down to New York, anywhere, as long as it was far from here. On another day he might have done just that—run, as he always had before.

But the eyes had changed all that.

From the instant he saw them, he knew he couldn't run anymore. Knew that wherever he went, they would find him.

They had recognized him!

And they had used Ray to try to get him. They were getting braver, risking exposure to get him. He began to suspect that whatever was wrong with the Point would not long remain confined there.

Question was, how did they know about him?

And exactly who, or what, were *they*?

He was sure Sam held the key. Yesterday he'd sensed that the professor had been hiding something about the caves—and now, today, everything in the Point had changed.

Sam would know something about this. So that would have to be his first stop. It was Eric's best hope, short of a confrontation with whatever was in the caves, which he was not prepared for—not now, not yet, not after what he'd seen. Damn it, he thought, Sam *had* to know something.

He intended to find out what.

4

Alone in her cabin, Liz hung up the telephone. Nothing new from Cutler. The nurse had been helpful, even friendly enough, but there was simply nothing new to pass along. Sam was still unconscious.

She stared at her hands, intertwined in her lap. She felt so damned helpless; there was nothing she could do except sit here and dial the telephone. The other option—to go up to Cutler on her own and wait there for Sam to come around—was unthinkable. She didn't dare leave, not when there was a chance that Eric would need her as soon as word came that he was innocent.

And it would come. It was just a matter of time.

Typical. She could hear her father's voice, weary with I-told-you-so's. *Leave it to you to pick a real winner this time. No judgment in men at all.*

Just like Mom, she thought, and glanced up at a knock on the cabin door. Sarah Franklin stood outside, holding a tray of still-warm food covered by a checkered cloth. The sky visible beyond her was going from overcast to dappled purple. It would be dark soon, Liz thought.

"You didn't come by for supper," Sarah said, "so I thought you might like a tray. It's just meat loaf, a little mashed potatoes, and corn, but I thought it might help."

"Thank you, Mrs. Franklin," Liz said, taking the tray, "though I suppose Zach'll throw a fit when he hears one of the boarders is getting room service."

"Oh, I imagine. But I learned a long time ago that the best way to deal with Zach is to listen to what his eyes are saying, not his mouth. His mouth gets him in trouble every time." She wiped her hands on her apron, and hesitated, as if there was something else she wanted to say.

"I just wanted you to know that I think he's innocent, too," Sarah said at last. "It'll work out all right. Even Zach says so; says he knew the first time he saw Mr. Matthews that he was a good sort, not the kind to do—" Her voice trailed off. "Anyway, we're both behind you, and if there's anything we can do . . ."

Liz smiled, genuinely touched. For all the efforts the local folks made to hide it, a heart the size of Manhattan beat in most of them. "I'll remember. Thanks. I'll try to stop by later, when there's some news."

"All right," Sarah said. "Enjoy the dinner."

"I will," she said, and waved good-bye as best she could around the tray.

"By the way," Sarah called back, "I wanted to ask you if you were having any trouble with the telephone lines."

"Not that I can think of. Why?"

"I don't know—it's just that the dial tone's been sounding funny all day. Probably just my imagination," she said, and continued on up to the Big House.

Liz nudged the cabin door shut with her foot, then went to the coffee table and set the tray down. Curious, she picked up the telephone and held it to her ear. Just a normal dial tone. Still, the more she listened to it, the more she thought it *did* sound a little strange, sort of hollow and cluttered at the same time, as if there were dozens of voices all trying to talk at once, but far away, indistinct, almost unnoticeable unless you listened.

"Hello?" she said, pressing the receiver against her ear, straining to hear through the hissing sound that came back.

No, that can't be right, she thought, and hung up the phone. As Mrs. Franklin had said, imagination. White noise was a lot like a Rorschach test—you heard what you listened for.

Putting it out of her thoughts, she began unwrapping her dinner, positive that she couldn't really have heard someone calling her name.

Eric slipped into Cutler Memorial Hospital through a side entrance. He was in luck; the hall was empty except for an elderly
woman who hobbled toward the room marked GERONTOLOGICAL
COUNSELING. He walked calmly past her and down the hall, trying
to look as if he belonged there. At an intersecting corridor he
slowed as he approached the admissions desk. Two women sat
behind the desk, filling out and filing pink-and-blue forms.

Eric hung back. He was reasonably confident that he could
influence one but not both of them; and neither of them looked
as if she were going anywhere soon. He couldn't risk approaching them directly. If his absence was discovered and reported
soon, one of them might remember a man fitting his description asking about Sam. But he had to find out where they were
keeping him.

He glanced across the hall and noticed a pair of telephone booths just out of their line of sight.

Why not? he thought, and slid into the booth, pulling the
creaky glass doors shut behind him. He looked up the telephone number for the hospital, and dialed. Behind him, one of
the two women picked up the phone.

"Cutler Memorial." Eric heard her through the door of the
phone booth about as well as he could through the phone.

"I understand you have a patient who was checked in late
this morning," he said, "a Sam Crawford."

"That's right, but I'm afraid Mr. Crawford isn't up to taking any calls just now."

"I understand. I just wanted to send some flowers. What
room is he in?"

"Room 233."

"Thank you," Eric said, and hung up. He stepped out and
headed for the elevator, hoping not to be challenged.

Then, from behind him: "Sir?"

Eric turned, smiled. "Yes?"

It was the same woman who had answered the phone.
"Visiting hours are up in another ten minutes."

"This won't take long; just forgot my book."

"Okay," the receptionist said, and returned to her forms. Eric entered the elevator and pressed the button for the second floor. As he waited for the doors to close, he heard her say, "That was another call on Crawford."

"Sure is popular," the other nurse said. "Guess that woman must've called five times by now."

Eric smiled as the elevator doors whispered shut. Good old Liz!

The bed in room 233 was empty.

Great, just great, Eric thought, dismayed. But at least no one else was in the room. He started inside—and jumped at the sound of voices coming around the corner at the other end of the hall. Tom and the doctor. Will.

"Damn," Eric muttered. No place to hide—except the first place they'd think to look, if they thought to look at all: under the bed. There was just enough room beneath. He'd barely scrabbled under when the door opened again and they entered, accompanied by an orderly wheeling a stretcher.

". . . not exactly conclusive," Tom was saying. The stretcher came to a halt beside the bed.

"No, and though we still have some more tests to run, neither Morrison nor I expect them to indicate anything more than what we've come up with so far. Oh, there'll be an inquest, of course, but that's just a formality. At this point, it looks like a clear case of murder-suicide. Greg died from the gunshot wound, not the growth in his brain tissue—not that it made much difference to Greg, I suppose; he was going to die either way, but I'd say it'll make a considerable difference to your prisoner."

"Very considerable," Tom said.

"Does that mean you're going to call and have him released?"

"Not yet," Tom said. "I'll wait until I get back. There are a few more questions I'd like answered about Sam's accident before I turn him loose. Besides, I promised Matthews I'd buy him a steak if it turned out we hauled him in unjustly, and I intend to get my money's worth out of his visit."

"Might owe him more than that," Will said. "From the sound of it, if he hadn't arrived when he had, Sam might not even be alive right now."

"Yeah, but it's still a hell of a coincidence. He never did give me a good reason why he was there in the first place."

The springs creaked as Sam was transferred from the stretcher to the bed. "Everybody's rooting for you, Sam. Even that priest you've been baiting for the last couple of years."

"Where is the Father?" Tom asked.

"Sent him home," Will said. "He was exhausted. He'd been talking to Sam all day, though so far it doesn't seem to have done much good. Maybe tomorrow." He stood. "Tell you one thing, I've never had a day I so much wanted to see the end of."

"Amen to that."

They walked toward the door. "By the way," Will said, "any chance of hitching a ride back with you? All this got me so rattled, I rode in on the ambulance with Sam, and left my car behind at the LeMarque place."

"No problem," Tom said. "Just let me finish up some paperwork downstairs, and I'll be ready to go. Half an hour all right with you?"

"No problem," Will said, and sighed. "People live and die, governments rise and fall, empires are born and topple, but the paperwork goes on forever, eh, Tom?"

The constable's reply was cut off by the closing of the door. When the sound of their footsteps had moved out of earshot, Eric slid out from under the bed.

Great, he thought. Now they know I'm innocent, but when the constable gets back there and sees what I did to his station, he's going to have some very serious questions.

As he leaned on the bed to stand, his hand grazed Sam's arm—

(serpent it was a serpent and it looked at me in the cave and it was dark so dark and the walls were falling and I had to get out had to get out)

—and jerked back.

What the hell? Eric thought.

He held his hand over Sam's arm, and could feel the thoughts coming off the bare flesh like electricity. The contact had been sudden, startling. Almost as startling as the feel of the flesh itself. Sam's arm was unnaturally cold.

Eric sat down next to Sam's still form. Bruises that had only been vague swellings this morning were now angry red and purple. His cheeks looked sunken, his face drawn in tight upon itself.

Well, I'm here; now what am I supposed to do? he wondered, knowing the answer even before he completed the question. He had already done it briefly, by accident. Now he had to finish it.

But he wasn't looking forward to it.

Bracing himself this time, he took Sam's hand, squeezing gently. He closed his eyes, and wondered how long it would t—

(. . . serpens . . .)

Eric arched back from the intensity of the image, but maintained contact, forcing his eyes to remain closed. He concentrated, pushing deeper, catching fragments, images.

(. . . the cave . . . dark . . . passages . . . had the Indians known? . . . the serpens, staring . . . panic . . . get away . . . everywhere, the serpens . . . it knows . . . not just a symbol . . . run . . . it sees everything . . . passages down, away, the hidden room . . . cold . . . picking away at my mind . . . the other . . . get away from the cave . . . they're everywhere . . . got to get out . . . jump . . . jump . . . the ground coming up . . .)

"No!" Eric's eyes snapped open. He backed away, letting go of Sam's hand. Instantly, he lost contact. He touched the bed, struggling to regain his sense of place, the certainty that he was *here,* not in the cave.

It had been only a flash, a moment out of time, but he had caught the sense of what had happened. Sam had found a hidden chamber in the caves, explored it, and at some point, something inside, the *serpens,* had frightened him into leaping out of the cave mouth. That was the gist of it, anyway. There were parts he didn't get, parts that didn't make sense, something about a camera and a sandwich, but put together with what had happened in the last twenty-four hours, it was enough to start him in the right direction.

Sam had set something loose inside the cave, that much was definite, something—or several things—that had been dormant for a long time. It was the only conclusion that made any sense.

Had that been what he had encountered when he'd wandered into the caves, all those years ago? And had that been the same thing he'd seen in the police station?

He wasn't sure. He needed time to think. He needed to go someplace where *they* wouldn't come looking for him until he was ready. Someplace—

He stopped. The answer came instinctively, in the way he recognized as feeling *right.* It was the last place anyone would think to start searching for him.

North Cutler Cemetery.

His father's grave.

6

Father Kerr turned another page in Reverend Milcraft's journal, growing more uneasy as he read the entries written in Milcraft's close, precise hand. He adjusted the desk lamp in his study until he could make out the words.

> *10 June 1868—Another disagreement between Carlton, Monroe, and myself. I do not wish them further to desecrate the Lord's house, and yet I fear that my role in this may yet be revealed, and if that should transpire—no, I shall not dwell on that here. I have been given a mission by God Almighty, to serve Him and to erect a temple suited to His Glory, and this I have done. I shall not allow the Demon Doubt to sully this achievement. Let them use the physical place that only we know of; for does not the Bible say to render unto Caesar that which is Caesar's? It is not that which goeth into a man that defiles him, says Christ, but that which cometh out from the soul. What goes into this house shall not affect the good works that will emerge. And yet, I cannot help but wonder—*

The entry ended there. Kerr turned to the next page.

> *18 June 1868. Blast Carlton for a fool! One of the casks he left in the room was not properly seasoned, and split during the night. Had I not come across it on returning this morning to retrieve the dishes we used the previous night, I do not doubt but that the stench of rum would have seeped into the wood. A fine time I would have had explaining that to my parishioners, few as they may be. Blast Carlton! I care not what he does with his rum, or where he gets it, or to whom he delivers*

it. Rum is for the heathen. But I will not have this place smelling like a distillery! Bad enough that Carlton and Monroe have continued to quarrel about their shares. Greed I can tolerate; but incompetence is another matter altogether.

Another page.

24 June 1868. I fear that there may yet be blood trouble between Carlton and Monroe. They argue incessantly over their shares, and last night Monroe allowed himself to slip into a drunkenness so profound that he began to jest with his fellows about this Church's "true spirit—or spirits." Such loose talk will compromise us all. He is but fortunate that he did not so blaspheme this Church in my presence, or I swear by the presence of God Himself that I would have laid him flat. Would that God could deliver me of this hellish arrangement! I rue the circumstances that compelled me to make partners of these men. Had there been any other source of money for the building of this Church, had the people not been so resistant, then I would not have had to turn to smugglers, nor let them use this place to store their vile goods. Who indeed would think to look in a place of worship for the Devil's brew? Ah, they were crafty, and the village stupid. Well, whatever befalls them will be their own doing, the fruit of their own stupidity.

Kerr closed his eyes. The stories were true, then. But not quite accurate. It was indeed from rum smugglers that Milcraft had found the money to build his church, but it was not conscience money. They had used the church to hide the rum casks while working out their deliveries, and as a hedge against search by the authorities. It was a terrible partnership, as Milcraft himself had slowly discovered.

He skipped to the last entry.

7 July 1868. God have mercy on me! I am lost, undone. I have defiled the Church of God Everlasting, and I am surely damned. Will even Christ Himself find forgiveness for me, after what has taken place? It happened last night, shortly before another shipment of rum was to be left in the room. Carlton and Monroe argued again, this time more violently than before. I feared that they would come to blows, and in my foolishness, I tried to intercede. I would not have violence in this place. Fool that I was! As I drew Monroe aside, and tried to calm him, Carlton took him from behind with a knife. Monroe cried out once, and then fell, unmoving, to the floor. I persuaded Carlton to leave quickly—as if he needed much persuasion at that point!—and said that we would have to decide what to do as soon as calm heads could deal with the incident. We left, locking the room behind us.

This morning, I returned to the room, still uncertain what I should do. What did I find but—God help me to write the words—Monroe had not been dead, as we had thought, but only gravely wounded. When I opened the door, I found Monroe beside it, splinters beneath his fingernails from where he had clawed at the door, trying to reach the lock. With help, he might have lived. So now, for having abandoned him, I am as guilty of the crime of murder as Carlton, who has disappeared. I do not expect that he will turn up here again. He has left me to attend to the body. And so I shall! Although the Church must go on, the good work must continue, I am undone. There is no hiding this crime from God's eyes. I shall ask forgiveness, but there can be no forgiveness without penance. So I shall leave the body here, in this room. This House of God shall become his sepulchre, this journal his eulogy. I cannot confess this crime to any man, so this shall be my confession to the years, that those finding it may pray for my salvation. I shall now seal the room and brick up the stairs which lead to this room. If any find this book, pray find some pity for me, though such I clearly do not deserve. O God of Israel, take this offering as my penance, my desire to do justice where none can be done. As long as this Church stands, I shall be reminded of this crime, and I will pray for forgiveness.

Kerr set down the journal. Horrible, he thought. No wonder Milcraft had gone mad later on; the constant reminder of what he had done, the way he had defiled the church that had been his reason for living, must have been too much for him.

Kerr wondered if there might be some connection between his discovery of the body and Milcraft's journal and the events of recent days. Three times the sacristy crucifix had moved, and once it had appeared outside the church. Perhaps it was Christ's way of finally bringing the crime to light. Had he been deliberately led to the secret in order to finally cleanse this, His house? It would explain much.

Either way, this was a situation that he could not resolve alone. The Bishop would have to be consulted. Unlike Milcraft, he had someone to turn to. The wall clock read 5:15. It would be dark within the hour, far too late to track down the Bishop on a Friday. He would call tomorrow and leave a discreetly worded message; perhaps by Monday they would have the chance to meet and work out a plan of action.

He ran his hand along the worn binding of Milcraft's journal. Poor, tormented soul. He would light a candle for Milcraft tonight, and offer up a prayer for him. Perhaps he would even hear it, and find some peace.

God knew, he deserved some.

7

Alone in the police station, Ray Price opened his eyes. His forehead hurt, and there was blood on his face. But this was of no importance. He had also failed in his mission, but that was no longer important, either; it was too late for anyone to interfere now. All was lost. All was won. He knew, distantly, that this would now mean his own death, but the word seemed meaningless. Nothing mattered. There was just the calm, the darkening afternoon, and his purpose.

Then he felt the murmur of bees moving again in his brain, and he was no longer alone.

8

Eric found a low spot in the fence that ran around the North Cutler Cemetery, and leaped inside. It was too late for visitors; no one would come upon him for a while.

The grave wasn't difficult to find. It had a simple marker, just a headstone with name, family, dates of birth and death. And just below that, two words: *Sorely missed.* Nothing else.

What else was there to say, after all?

After all these years, after all this waiting, Eric had finally made it back. After all the years of grief and struggle, the silence of the cemetery was almost anticlimactic.

Strange, he thought, in this place of death, to feel that he had finally come home.

He crouched beside the grave. Touched the cold stone.

"I'm here," he said quietly.

Eric sat down beside the grave and ran his hand along the ground that had long since settled level with the surrounding grass. He frowned. Something wasn't right.

Then he knew what it was. He still wasn't close enough. His father couldn't hear him.

He lay facedown on the grass above the grave, in very much the same position as the body below, looking down instead of up. He turned his head, pressed his ear to the ground.

Listening.

And suddenly the darkness from below reached out and embraced him, pulled him screaming, into the ground that swallowed him up, dragging him down farther until the wood cracked below him and he looked into the empty sockets of his nightmares, the skinless face, the empty skull.

The face of his father.

It smiled at him. *Welcome home,* it said.

And the world in Eric's mind exploded.

TWENTY-FIVE

LANGREN

In the distance, a point of light.

Rushing forward, like a train coming down a long tunnel. Coming fast. Roaring in the night.

And the light struck.

And the voice spoke.

It spoke in the voice of his father, the voice of his mother, the voice that had come to him in dreams and times of trouble, a voice of dry leaves and wind and gold and compassion.

He strained against the darkness to hear the words.

The words.

The caves have always been a place of power. Long before white men came to this country, the power was there.

And the danger was there.

The Indians knew the story. They repeated it from generation to generation. The story told of how, long ago, Day and Night fought a great battle for domination over the world of men. Their struggle stretched across land and ocean. Their blows leveled mountains and their heels tore great valleys in the earth, until Night, wounded, fled to this place.

The story said that the caves were formed when Night

burrowed into the ground in its attempt to escape. But Day followed Night into the caves, and there they wrestled. Their struggle was fierce, terrible. The sun and stars fell from the sky, and still they fought, Day against Night, their efforts threatening to destroy the foundations of the world. Finally, exhausted, they could fight no more. Unable to gain power one over the other, they divided control over the earth. When Night ruled, Day would go to its lodge over the far hills; and when Day ruled, Night would retreat deep into the earth.

But Night was jealous, the story said, because while Day ruled supreme over the earth, Night was forced to share his kingdom with the moon and the stars. So Night conspired again to seize the earth. Craftier now, Night sought out allies who would fight alongside him. Spirits from deep within the earth and beyond the earth, allies who cared nothing for the earth until Night tempted them. With their help, a door was created between this world and the world of spirit. It was created at the place of power, where Day and Night had fought. Through this door the allies would come like thieves to destroy Day. Then, together with Night, they would command the earth.

The story also said that Day saw what was happening, and appeared to the tribe that lived in these hills, the tribe that had watched the battle between Day and Night. To them was given the keeping of the caves. They were made guardians of the house of Night, watching the caves as an eagle watches for the hunter seeking its young.

But to watch was not enough, for Night was strong and could deceive. So one among them was selected to be given the power to stop Night. The power to see, the power to move. The power was passed on from father to son. Each would teach his successor how to use the power, how to control it so that it would not control the one who possessed it. The power would let the chosen one see through the deceits of Night, and wrestle with Night in Day's absence. The only thing forbidden to the chosen one was to attempt to destroy Night. For there must always be a balance. As the seasons merge into one, and death follows life, Night must always follow Day.

And they must always be at war.

So went the story.

The story continued to be told until the coming of the white men. When they first arrived, some of the Indians thought they had been sent by Day—for was not their flesh as bright as the sun?

They welcomed the white men, and shared with the strangers from across the great water all that they could. But the secret of the caves they held back. Not even their brother Algonquin tribes knew of the caves, and what they contained.

Most of the white men were hostile or indifferent. A few made gestures of friendship. One of these was Nathaniel Langren. He, among all those who moved in to the finger of land that would one day be called the Point, sought out the Indians, learned their language, and partook of their ceremonies. His son, Joshua Langren, was also welcomed into their rites.

Not long before Nathaniel Langren died, the Indians told him of the caves, and of the war between Day and Night. Nathaniel told Joshua, and for the first time the secret left the tribe. But it was in safekeeping, and went no further.

Which was to the good, for evil times were coming.

War was in the wind. War between the French and the English, using the Indians as their soldiers. Many of the Algonquins refused to fight, and established peace treaties with the white men.

They opposed the will of other tribes, who wanted to drive back the white men. Their duty was to preserve Day from Night, to stand as guardians of the caves, not to take one side or another of a war between men. Later they would realize that in their isolation, in their obligation to a higher duty, they had grown arrogant, lazy. They failed to see in this war the signs that foretold their doom.

They had forgotten the cunning of Night.

For Night is as the coyote. It is sly, it wears down its prey and will wait for the unguarded moment to strike; it does not face the light, and does not show its own face when it may work in disguise, or find others who will do the killing so that it may dine on the carrion. As it had sought out allies in the darkness beyond our world, so too it sought to create allies among their neighbors.

Night whispered in the ears of braves, told them that in the caves was a place of great power, that with the correct words and signs, a vast spirit army could be released to do their bidding. The braves entered the caves and sought out that power, intending to turn it against the white men.

By the time their intent was known, they had penetrated deep into the place of power, where not even the chosen one would go without fear for his life. There they found the heart of the caves. There Night's allies whispered to them, poisoned their hearts, and tricked them into opening the door.

When that door was opened, they died.

And did not die.

The spirits of Night, the dark allies that lurked deep in the earth, became one with them. They did this by first injuring the body almost unto death. But death is not allowed. At the moment of weakness, when the soul flutters between life and death, they slip through the door and force out their victims' spirits so that they can enter into their bodies, and take their place.

This was the fate of the braves who dared the heart of the caves. Their spirits were driven out, sent to wander forever in dry lands. And a handful of Night's allies were free to do its work.

But the transition to this world requires great strength, and afterward the spirit of an ally is weak, its power limited. Only by great effort can it leave the caves in its new body, seek out another victim, and attack, opening the way for another ally to be freed. After that it must rest.

For a time after coming through the door, an ally cannot go out in the face of Day, its enemy. The sun destroys it, as do fire and the separation of head and body. But the longer the door remains open, and the more spirits that emerge into this world, the stronger they become, and the more their true natures emerge. They can change shapes, can come as wolves in the night, or as birds. They can bend the wills of weak men to do their bidding.

Their presence alone in this world has a profound effect. It strengthens that which is cruelest in the human spirit, and which might otherwise lie dormant. If misdeeds have been committed in secret, their presence resonates with the new darkness, and refuses to be concealed any longer. They reach out and embrace Night.

Once free, the allies of Night move swiftly, and their numbers grow at a fearsome rate. Two become four become eight. The more that emerge, the darker the sky becomes, causing even the strongest heart to falter. Should they finally triumph, all places would become Night.

That was Night's plan. Once its allies had been freed, they began the assault. They attacked the white men first, for they would not know what was upon them, and would be helpless before the agents of Night. And Night was correct. When the attacks began, the white men assumed that their neighbors had joined in the war against them.

The tribe knew their time was short. In the time it took the white men to organize, they sought out the allies of Night and moved swiftly against them. An ally must be destroyed within three days of its release, or its power becomes too great to overcome. In time, it can even survive once the door has been shut.

The chosen one led the battle against the allies of Night, and the stories said that it was fierce and terrible, full of fury and blood and fire. All who could be captured were assembled in one place, and burned.

Even that, though, was not the end of it.

It was still necessary to destroy the heart of the cave, for as long as the heart survived, more allies could attempt to re-open the door to the spirit world.

So it was that, after destroying the allies, the chosen one returned to the caves and destroyed the heart. But now danger came from another direction.

The white men knew nothing of the caves; they saw only that Indians had attacked them and burned their homes. They did not know, and would not understand, that those who had been destroyed were no longer human.

Exhausted from their war against the freed spirits, they were easy prey to attack by the villagers.

Many died. Others were driven out. Mortally wounded, the chosen one made his way to the home of Joshua Langren. He knew that the Indians would now be driven off the land, that there would be no one left to watch over the caves, to make sure that Night did not profit by its actions.

He had to pass on the power to someone who would accept the responsibility, who would stay in the Point, generation after generation, passing on the power, training his son, and his son's son, to use the power well and wisely.

Joshua Langren accepted the duty.

Accepted the power.

And the curse that went with it.

Since that day, the firstborn son of the Langren family has always remained in the Point. Watching, and waiting.

In the years that followed, Night tried its trickery again and again. The caves lured travelers inside, and if their minds or wills were sufficiently fragile, the allies deep within the earth struggled to influence them. Some died, or killed themselves. Some went mad. And some fell under the influence of the allies.

And it was always a Langren who stopped them.

His father's voice changed, grew somber.

Until my death.

I fell prey to the same mistake the first guardians had made. I grew careless. Overconfident. The caves had been dormant for so long, I began to think that Night had given up the war.

And in that moment of carelessness, Night reached out and struck me down.

He had hoped to strike us all down, and leave no one to challenge him.

But you survived, Eric. Though I left you before I could tell you of the mission ahead, before I could teach you to use the power, before I could explain so much. I was taken away, and you were left to fend for yourself. Left to try to understand feelings that could not be understood, moments of intuition and foresight that could not be explained away.

For that above all I am sorry.

Though not as sorry as I am for that which is still ahead of you.

To kill me and your mother took great effort. After that, the allies of Night needed to rest and gather their strength for their next assault. It took years for their strength to come back after so monumental an effort.

When they started again, I had no choice but to call you.

You had to come back, and finish what I could not.

You have it within you to destroy the door forever, to seal up this portal and free yourself from the duty that has been imposed on our family.

You have it within you to do great good beyond this place.

You may also die.

I can give you little to use in the struggle that is to come. I can give you only the gift of understanding. With this, the power within you will come to full bloom.

It will be swift.

It will hurt you.

Forgive me, my son.

TWENTY-SIX

THE POINT

Myrna Cranston left the Dredmouth Point Library shortly after 6:30 P.M. It was her ritual on Fridays to go over the roster of books that were overdue and prepare the little pink cards that she would drop in the mail the next day. Unlike some librarians, who allowed a grace period before sending out notices, Myrna had never been one to put off until next week what should be done immediately. Lateness indicated an irresponsible attitude toward public property, and she felt it was her obligation as a public citizen to point this out.

She was proud to know that every Monday morning, mailboxes all over the Point were marked by the presence of Myrna Cranston's little pink cards. They were just the right shade to be seen from a distance, informing those who passed that here lived a man or woman of dubious moral character. "The scarlet letter," some called it. Myrna had heard the description, and paid it no attention.

Besides, they weren't scarlet. They were pink.

The cards were stacked neatly beside her as she drove down Lakefront Road, gripping the wheel at exactly ten and two o'clock as she'd been taught long ago. The Volkswagen Rabbit's headlights threw pale circles of light on the road ahead, the same road she had driven twice a day, five days a week, for twelve years. Though she knew every inch of it, she never allowed her mind to stray from the task of driving. Fifteen minutes to town, and fifteen minutes back, every inch of asphalt observed and logged and—

Man on the road!

She slammed on the brakes, barely avoiding the figure that had suddenly appeared in her lane. The Rabbit skidded off the blacktop and onto the shoulder, skidding to a stop between two pines just large enough to include the car.

Myrna's hands were moist; all the muscles in her arms were trembling. She knew it was sheer luck that had saved her from a collision. She took a moment to compose herself before going back and giving whoever it was the worst hell she could think of. She looked into the rearview mirror—

And saw no one.

She turned around in her seat, peered back through the rear window. The road was only dimly visible, lit by a single streetlamp strung between wires well down the road, but she could tell, even from here, that there was no one standing in the road.

But there *had* been! She was sure of it.

A sudden sense of horror crawled up her stomach. What if she'd hit him? Everything had happened so fast—

Oh God! she thought.

Frantically, she unfastened her seat belt and climbed out of the Rabbit, the wind sending some of the pink cards tumbling over the edge of the seat. She picked her way through the root-tangled ground to the road. It was empty.

No, not quite. She squinted into the darkness, past the streetlamp. Was that someone, there, leaning against the tree? She took a step closer. Yes! It looked like a man, but in the dark she couldn't be sure. "Hello? Are you okay?" she said.

She reached the tree, and again found no one there—as if the man had just melted away. Had it been her imagination? She looked back the way she came. A woman stood silhouetted against the distant lamp. There was a glimmer of blue-gray light against blond hair. This time she recognized the figure. Not a man, but a woman.

"Beth? Beth Simmons!"

Myrna started toward her. Beth stood without moving in

the middle of the road. Her features were indistinct against the light behind her. It seemed to Myrna that Beth was looking not so much toward her as *past* her. She glanced back, following Beth's gaze.

A man stood where she had been not a minute earlier. Now he was moving. Coming toward them.

Bud? The silhouette was right, but—

Myrna slowed, then stopped in the middle of the road, now only half a dozen paces away from either of them. Bud didn't look right. He stepped closer, and then she saw it.

His face.

"Ohmygod," she whispered. His face was disfigured, torn in places. She gasped. She *had* hit him! But what was he doing walking around if—

Then she saw that he *wasn't* walking. He seemed to glide along the road, moving slowly toward her—toward her and—

Beth?

Myrna turned in time to see Beth's face—swollen, purple, looking almost ready to burst—hovering overhead, then swooping down at her, soundless but for a hiss that seemed to come from everywhere. . . .

2

Moving quietly, Jay Carmichael climbed the tree that looked in on Judith Carlyle's bedroom. She hadn't shown up for work today at the drugstore. Bill Dumar, who ran the place, said he'd called her, and she'd begged off, saying she was sick. Sounded like hell, Jack had said. If that was so, Jay thought, then she would probably be in the bedroom—and that would give him all the opportunity he'd ever want.

The tree was an easy climb, full of branches at convenient angles, about as difficult as a stepladder. He sat in the perch that afforded the best view of the bedroom, the tree bark already slightly worn from his previous sittings. The shade of the surrounding leaves would prevent anyone from seeing him, even this close to the house.

But, ah, the things he had seen! The window, not more than fifteen feet distant, had brought him some sights he'd not soon forget. Tonight, though, the window was disappointingly dark. He'd noticed that the rooms below were dark, too, but since her car was in the drive, he'd assumed that she was probably watching TV in the darkened bedroom. He sat quietly, letting his eyes adjust to the dimness inside the window, hoping to catch a glimpse of her before giving up. After a while, his impulse was to climb down and go home for the night. But there was no proof yet that she wasn't home. He would wait a little while longer.

After a few minutes, a car pulled into the drive. Jay recognized the lone driver as Mrs. Graham, from St. Benedict's. He knew that she and Judith were friends, and smiled at the fortuitous timing. This would confirm whether or not Judith really was at home, and whether his time might best be spent elsewhere—perhaps checking out that lady writer again. He grinned as he considered the many options he had. Just like a goddamn Chinese menu, he thought.

Mrs. Graham knocked on the front door. No lights came on, but Judith must have said something, because Mrs. Graham opened the door and stepped inside. For a minute, it was as if the house had swallowed her whole—no sound, no movement, no light. Then one light went on downstairs, in the kitchen. Another went on by the staircase. He could trace Mrs. Graham's movements by the lights that switched on, then off.

Finally the bedroom light came on. He could clearly see Mrs. Graham standing in the open bedroom doorway, and though he could not hear her through the closed window, he could pretty much guess what she was saying. *Judy? Judy, dear, are you there?* Mrs. Graham moved forward, as if hearing something in response—

When suddenly, something flashed across the window, springing from where it had been hiding—something fast and lethal. It leaped on Mrs. Graham, a hand strangling the scream that would be working its way up her throat. They fell on the bed, Mrs. Graham struggling, the thing everywhere at once, slapping, clawing, *biting!* Its head reared up for a final plunge, and in the brief flash of light Jay saw that it was Judith, but changed, her face monstrous. He saw her open her mouth to twice the size it had any right to be and, like a snake he'd once seen swallow a mouse whole, slam that mouth down on Mrs. Graham's face.

Jay shrank back in horror until his spine was pressed

against the tree, trying to escape the sight before him, yet unable to look away. Mrs. Graham was still struggling against the thing that had been Judith Carlyle, but after another moment the thrashing stopped.

Jay turned away, dry-heaving, certain he was going to vomit. Bile bit at his throat. But there wasn't time for that. Not now. Not here. He fought to steady himself. He had to get back to the car, report what he'd seen to the police.

Horrible, he thought. And yet his eye was drawn to the window one final time.

He froze at what he saw.

The light in the bedroom dimmed. No, began to disappear, as if the light were going somewhere else, slipping out between the cracks of the house. In the growing dark he saw Judith sit back, and now he could make out Mrs. Graham's body lying beside her. Then, suddenly, a pool of darkness began to appear around her, an unnatural shroud of utter darkness that was so black it was almost painful to look at.

Something moved in that darkness, like a negative image that flickered briefly, and then was gone.

And Mrs. Graham sat up. Only it wasn't Mrs. Graham anymore. The thing's face was distended, almost canine, the flesh torn. It rose—and was lost to sight as the blackness spread to engulf the entire room.

Jay was barely aware of climbing down the tree, jumping the last few feet to the ground, and running on a twisted ankle to his car. He felt nothing except the need to get away from that terrible place, to get help. He didn't care about explaining how he had seen it. Let the whole world know, he thought, driving at top speed into the center of town; he didn't care anymore.

All the way into town, he seemed to see them in every shadow. Watching him. Ready to pounce from the shadows.

After what seemed like an eternity, he reached the police station. He leaped out and headed for the door, only peripherally aware of how strangely silent the town was, even quieter than usual.

"Tom!" he said, bursting through the door. His voice cracked; he could hear the hysteria that was building inside him. "Tom, goddammit! Where the hell are you?"

A door opened. Deputy Constable Ray Price stepped out into the station from a back room.

"Thank God," Jay said. "You've gotta come, jeez, it's horrible! You didn't see it, she just—oh God, Ray, it's—"

Ray didn't move, only stared at him calmly, even a little distantly, Jay thought, noticing—how strange—an unbandaged gash on his forehead. Moving very deliberately, Ray pulled his revolver from its holster, pointed it at him.

"Oh my God, Ray! Don't! *No!*"

Ray pulled the trigger. Just once.

3

. . . Duane, Jess, and Ginny Kincaid. Roberta Kohl. Edgar Jennings. Cee Trent. Bill, Jackie, and Rosemary Dumar. Dave, Johnny, Susan, and Elaine Markle. Walter Kriski . . .

4

Ace Jackson couldn't figure it. Here it was, a Friday night, and he hadn't had but five customers all night. The last couple to pass through had been Mayor Morgan and his wife, but they'd left as soon as they figured that the place was going to stay pretty much empty. No point in going out to be seen when there was nobody around to see you.

The Royal Flush Tavern was flat-out dead.

No sweat, he thought, and continued to clean glasses. Maybe there was some big to-do in town that he hadn't heard about. Wouldn't be the first time. But then, he had never been big on public get-togethers. Holding forth in his tavern, on his own turf, was about as far as he was willing to go to be sociable.

He set up two more bottles of Irish whiskey against the mirror—and started at the sound of the jukebox switching on behind him.

"Well, all right," he said, smiling as he turned to see who had come in.

He was alone.

Short in the wiring? Ace wondered, as the jukebox played on, sounding unnaturally loud in the empty tavern. Not just loud. Different. Shrill.

It took Ace a moment to realize that the lyrics to the country song were gone.

And in their place—the murmur of many voices, rising and falling—whispering, laughing, screaming, *where now, where to, nowhere, nowhere*—a sound like a thousand fists hammering against the tavern walls, *we are legion,* a hissing, *we know you, oh, we know you. . . .*

Ace backed up toward the mirror—and one after another the bottles arranged behind him started to explode. Broken glass and alcohol struck his face, his clothes. He dove under the drop-board and came out the other side just as the last bottle shattered. As if that were a signal, the mirror itself bent out at the center, bowed impossibly, then burst, showering jagged slivers of glass through the tavern. Ace cried out as a hundred tiny needles lanced into his back, his neck, his legs. Pain raced over his flesh like fire. He crawled toward the door and managed to push through to the outside, away from the darkening room, the flying glass, the voices from the jukebox.

He covered a few more feet before collapsing in the dirt outside, blood trickling down his back, soaking his shirt. A pair of feet approached, stopping inches from his face. He followed the green-clothed legs up to where Fred Keller stood, dressed for fishing, his head hanging at an impossible angle.

Staring at him.

As Keller reached down for him, Ace realized dimly through the pain that the voices that had been coming from the jukebox were now coming from Keller.

5

Tom Crandall steered the police car down the winding road that would take them into the Point. His hands shone green in the glow of the dashboard, where the clock read 7:57. Beside him, Will squinted through the darkness.

The tension in the car was palpable. Once they'd crossed the line of thick woods that shielded the Point from the outside world, the few houses they'd passed had been dark, silent. It was too early for the town to be this dead. Tom couldn't shake an unaccountable sense of wrongness, as if every house he passed were the LeMarque house. It was irrational, he knew. But so much had happened in the last twenty-four hours, it was natural to be a little spooked. Even Will seemed to sense it.

Well, soon enough they'd be at the station. He'd check in with Ray, drop Will off at his car, then go home.

They drove in silence until they reached Walnut Road, where Tom turned down the final few blocks that led to the center of town. It was quiet, more so than usual for a Friday night. Then again, after the news from the LeMarque house, it was possible that most folks weren't quite up to a night on the town.

He pulled up in front of the station. The first order of business was to let that Matthews fellow out. Though the final report on Sam's condition, and the cause of his accident, was still forthcoming, there didn't seem much call to keep the man locked up any longer.

A single light burned through the station window.

"Home at last," Tom said, as much to himself as to Will. With the engine shut off, his voice sounded unnaturally loud in the car.

Will nodded. "Thought I'd never get back. Right now, all I want to do is go home, take a shower, and get about three days' sleep."

"Just give me two minutes to get my stuff," Tom said, and stepped out onto the street. Will joined him on the sidewalk just as the light in the station went out.

All around them, streetlamps went out, one after another, until the entire town center was dark.

"*Now* what?" Tom muttered.

"Power failure."

"Terrific. Last thing I need. Well, there are lamps and batteries in the station. C'mon."

They crossed the sidewalk. A quarter moon hung just above the horizon—just enough to guide them to the station door. Tom opened it, stepped inside. Will followed.

Abruptly, Tom stopped. "Wait a sec," he whispered, and peered into the darkness. Something wasn't right. Ray should have gotten out the lanterns by now, should be doing something, anyway. But nothing moved in the station.

"Something wrong?" Will asked.

"Not sure." Then, louder, "Ray? Ray, you back there?" He edged forward, able to make out only vague outlines in the suffocating darkness.

He nudged something with his toe. Something large, that gave slightly when he kicked it. He bent down, knowing even before he touched it that it would be a body. His hand found clothes, then an arm—cool, but not yet cold—and came back wet.

Will knelt down next to him, taking the victim's wrist. "He's dead."

Tom nodded. "Got a match?"

"Better yet," Will said, and handed over a gold-plated butane lighter.

"Thanks," Tom whispered, and thumbed the striker wheel. He fully expected to see Ray's face in the lighter's pinpoint glow, and was shocked to find the body of Jay Carmichael. A bullet hole had been blown in the center of his forehead. Blood and brain tissue peppered the floor and far wall. Some of it was on Tom's hands.

Who would have shot Jay here, in the station? Jay wasn't armed, as far as he could tell, and Ray wouldn't use deadly force without a reason.

But if Ray hadn't killed him, who had?

And where *was* Ray, damn it?

"We got trouble," Tom said, standing and unholstering his revolver. "I think maybe you better head back outside."

"What makes you think it's any safer out there?"

Tom grunted; Will was right. He edged around the railing to his desk. By the glow of the lighter he pulled out the extra automatic he kept in the top drawer, and handed it to Will.

Gripping the revolver in both hands, Tom checked the storeroom. Nothing. Except for tins of coffee and boxes of stationery supplies, the room was deserted. He checked the opposite door that led out the back way. Locked. On his way out, he pulled a flashlight from a box beside the copy machine and flicked it on. The flashlight remained dark. With one hand he unscrewed the bottom and dropped in two fresh batteries—to no effect; the flashlight stayed dark. With a puzzled glance at Will, he stepped out of the room and headed for the door that led to the cellblock. He'd worry about flashlights later; he couldn't afford the time right now.

The cellblock door was unlocked. Tom nudged the door open with his toe. It swung slowly open, banging against the wall with a noise he thought could be heard clear to Boston. His heart slamming inside his chest, he stepped into the corridor, Will close behind him. Nothing moved—nothing that he could see, anyway. He checked each of the cells as he passed them. Empty. When he came to Matthews's cell, he flicked the cigarette lighter on again.

"Jesus!" The outburst could not be contained. Somehow the cell door had been ripped off its hinges and thrown against—even partly into—the far wall. Bits of bedding, metal, glass, and wood were scattered everywhere. Curiously, Tom couldn't detect any smell of dynamite, and there were no burn marks that he could see—which ruled out conventional explosives.

He brought the flame closer to the floor. There was blood on the concrete, a few drops here, and a small pool over by the wall. Either the person who'd been injured—Ray? Matthews?—had managed to get up on his own and walk out, or had been moved by someone else. But why move one body, back here, and leave another out front for all the world to see?

Nothing made sense. The only thing he knew was that he was alone, with only Will to back him up, and he had a hunch he was going to need help.

"Let's go," he said. They made their way to the front room, where Tom picked up the telephone. He automatically noted the time on his watch for the report: 8:15. The power had been out for just over five minutes—five minutes that seemed like a century.

He held the phone to his ear, and frowned. No dial tone—and yet it didn't sound as if the line had been cut, exactly, but more as though it was hooked up to a speakerphone, with someone listening in at the other end. He pressed the plunger and let go again. Still the same noise.

Was there someone listening? Perhaps the very someone who had killed Jay Carmichael, and done who-knew-what with Ray and the prisoner—unless it had been the prisoner himself? Tom didn't know, and didn't want to take the chance. He replaced the receiver.

"Phone's out," he said, "maybe even tapped, I don't know. Best to try the car radio. We're gonna need all the help we can get."

"I think that would be wise."

Their eyes now slightly more accustomed to the dark, they worked their way around the railing, past Jay's body, and out the front door. The street beyond was still quiet; no one moved that either of them could see.

They made it to the car without interference. Tom switched on the radio. Where usually there was a rush of static, there was only silence. He flicked the power switch off, then on again.

"You're sure it'll work with the car off?" Will asked.

"Of course I'm sure," Tom said, then decided to start the car up anyway.

He turned the key six times. The car remained dead.

"I don't get it," Will said. "There's got to be *some*body around. We could go up the block, see who we can dig up."

"I already thought of that. But until we know what the hell's going on, we don't want to dig up the wrong people. We need to find a phone that works, call for reinforcements. Once the county sheriffs get here, we can go house to house, if we have to."

"Agreed," Will said, and opened the door.

They were halfway out of the car when they heard the scream.

"Stay here!" Tom said, and ran toward the source of the scream.

"Not on your life," Will said, and followed.

Tom turned a corner. Ahead of him, a woman was pinned against a car as someone crouched over her, tearing at her throat. The scream died abruptly.

Tom ran forward. "Freeze! Police!"

The figure ignored him. Even in the poor light, there was no mistake. It was Fred Keller.

What the hell? Tom dived onto Keller—and suddenly he was lifted and thrown backwards through the air. He hit the ground hard and came up in a tuck and roll, grateful even through the pain in his knees that he hadn't felt any bones snap.

Behind him, Keller looked back at his victim as she moaned once more. He took a step toward her. Impossibly, Tom thought he saw a patch of darkness form around Keller's fist. Then, before Keller could get to her, she slumped over, dead. Keller snarled, his head lolling back and forth as if his neck were broken.

"Ruined," the figure muttered, and the sound seemed to come more from in front of his mouth than from inside. Keller turned, angling his body so that his head could take in the two intruders.

He stepped forward.

"Hold it right there!" Tom brought up the gun.

Keller advanced another step.

Tom fired four times. The bullets slammed into Keller's chest, but managed only to drive him back a step toward the car.

Suddenly, shots came from over his shoulder. Will fired round after round at Keller, his aim wild, hitting the car door, the window, the gas tank.

The gas tank!

"Down!" Tom yelled, and the word was lost in the explosion as the Pinto burst into flames. A stream of burning gas hit Keller, and there was a scream such as Tom had never before heard. It rose higher and higher until he thought his ears would burst from it. A wind rushed up through the street, and as Keller dropped, the flame turned bright red, then purple, then a color Tom couldn't quite name.

Keller fell, lay still. The stench of burning flesh filled the street.

Will drew near, unable to take his eyes off the sight before them. "First the LeMarques, now this," he said. His hands were shaking. "I think the whole world's gone mad."

Tom nodded. "You could be right. But we'll decide that later. Right now, we've got to get to a phone."

Halfway down the block they found a phone booth. Tom slipped a quarter into the slot, but instead of a dial tone, there was only the same hollow noise, as of someone listening.

He had to risk it, whoever was there. "Hello? Anyone on the line? We need help."

The noise on the line seemed almost to hiss in his ear. "There is no help," a voice whispered.

"Who's there? Where are you?"

Now a little boy's voice, singsong: "Where is God? God is everywhere." Then, snarling, the first voice: "We are here. With you."

"Who are you?"

"We are legion." Again that hissing, deep and terrible. "If you do not run, we will not give you too much pain. Your friends are here with us. Waiting for you."

"Go to hell," Tom snapped, and hung up.

"What now?" Will asked. His face was pale.

Tom slipped a reloading clip off his belt, and thumbed the new bullets into his revolver. "Search and secure," he said. "But first we've got to get organized. This way."

Heading out of the phone booth, he led the way into an alley. They had to get off the street, had to think, and their position was too exposed. The alley between the bait-and-tackle store and the pharmacy was perfect. No one could come at them without being seen.

He ushered Will ahead, checking to make sure they weren't being followed before following him in.

They reached the far end of the alley. "Okay," Tom said.

But before he could continue, the air seemed to thicken around them. The alley grew darker. Tom fought a sudden dizziness, turning in time to see Will's eyes roll up in his head as he slumped to the ground. Tom managed to grab him an instant before his head would have hit the sidewalk.

"Will!" He was lowering the doctor to the ground when his own world grayed, then plummeted into blackness.

6

At 8:10 P.M., Karin Whortle was locking up the Point Inn when the lights went out. She had been nervous enough, what with most of the stores locked up and deserted, and now this!

She turned the lock and started around the counter to the back exit that led to the parking lot, moving with the sureness that came from working long years at the Inn. She'd said more than once that she could find her way around the place in pitch darkness, and now that she had the chance to prove the claim, there was, typically, no one to see her do it. She hoped the power failure was confined to the center of town; there were only two stoplights between here and home, but driving through a dark intersection always made her nervous. Besides, she had a week's worth of steaks in the freezer at home. Her heart sank at the thought of what a prolonged power failure would do to them.

She found the rear exit, felt for the brass knob, and opened the door, looking out at the deserted parking lot.

No, not deserted. Someone stepped out of the shadows behind the restaurant.

She stood in the doorway and waited until she thought she recognized him. "Walter?"

He moved toward her slowly, saying nothing. Her pleasure at seeing him diminished; even in the dim light, she sensed that there was something wrong with him—his walk, the dark stains that covered his face. He held out his hands.

"Are you not happy to see me, Karin?" His voice was hollow, not his at all. "Am I not pleasing?"

Karin slammed and locked the door. This was crazy! She knew Walter. He was safe. Or had been. But now there was only menace in that voice. She expected to hear him pounding on the door, but there was no sound behind her. In a way, that was almost worse. She grabbed the telephone, dialed.

And from the receiver: "Karin, you disappoint me."

She stared at the telephone, almost as if expecting Walter, or whoever, *what*ever was outside to come crawling in through the holes in the receiver. At the sound of footsteps outside, she slammed the phone down and ran toward the front of the inn, grabbing a butcher knife on the way.

She went to the glass door and looked out—

Into the twisted remains of Walter's face. His eyes were hollow—and she realized to her horror that the sockets were empty, ripped out at the roots, *and yet he was looking at her through the glass!* She backed away, hand flying to her mouth.

"Do you not like my smile?" he said, and thrust one hand through the glass door.

Karin stumbled back into the dining room, turning to see that he was no longer at the front door. She ran to a window—and saw his face there.

The other window, on the opposite side of the inn.

His face.

Impossible, she thought, he couldn't run around the building that fast. No one could. She screamed for help, once, twice, but before the third scream could emerge, the air in the restaurant seemed to congeal around her. Her breath caught in her chest, as if she were breathing dust. She fell to the floor, distantly aware of the sound of breaking glass, and though she could not see him, she could sense the thing that had been

Walter crouching above her, leaning down, and she couldn't move, couldn't move, couldn't cry out, the knife useless in her dead hand and the scream silent, heard only in her mind as she waited, helpless, for what was to come.

7

. . . Ginny, Adam, and Mayor George Morgan. Marie Desveux. Thomas, Mark, and Suzanne Bingham. Zachariah and Sarah Franklin . . .

8

R.T. Williams started awake from his brief nap. It was dark. No light came in through the window of the closed general store. He wondered what had woken him.

Then, from somewhere outside, gunshots. Winnie called him from upstairs.

"Richard!" she screamed.

"Coming! I'm coming!" He made it upstairs to find her still wet from her bath, huddling against the warmth of her robe.

"Over here!" She ran to the window. He followed, as four more shots rang out somewhere in the darkened streets. An instant later there was an explosion. A fireball briefly lit up the night, then disappeared.

"What's happening?"

"I don't know, but we'd better call it in," R.T. said, and reached for the telephone. There was no dial tone. "Dead," he said. "Must have been something to do with the explosion. I'd better go out there, see if I can help."

He turned back to Winnie just in time to see her slump to the carpeted floor, and to notice, dimly, as if from far away, that he was doing the same.

The light in Father Duncan Kerr's study dimmed and then died. He sighed resignedly, and closed Milcraft's journal, which he'd been reading again. It wasn't the first time that a fuse had blown, and he doubted it would be the last. He went to the drawer where he kept supplies against just such an occurrence. He tried the flashlight. Dead. Lighting a candle, he went to the end of the corridor, where a door opened onto the basement stairs. He always kept a box of fresh fuses next to the fuse box. He'd just screw one into the correct socket, and—

He stopped. A pounding noise came from somewhere inside the church. He stood without moving, trying to determine its source, but was unable to pin it down. Putting prudence ahead of daring, he decided to investigate *after* he had restored the lights.

He stepped carefully down the stairs to the basement. The fuse box was at the base of the stairs and to the left. He'd found it enough times in the dark to be an expert by now. Swinging open the metal casing, he held the candle out in front of him, trying to pick out which was the blown fuse. Curiously, none of them looked burned out at all. Perhaps the fault was somewhere else, a short in the wiring. . . .

The pounding started again. This time he could clearly distinguish its source.

It came from the entrance to the hidden room.

Kerr froze. Had someone found the church's secret so soon? If so, who? And how had they gotten inside? He held the candle aloft, peering into the darkness. The debris he had set in front of the entrance was undisturbed. And yet the pounding continued, so loud now that he was sure it could be heard to the end of the block.

Crossing the basement, he nudged aside the boxes and stuck his head into the stairwell. The pounding was even more distinct now. And there was another sound, as of something or someone moving. Yes, someone was definitely walking around in the hidden room.

He had to know who had intruded on this place and what

they had found. Blast them, this was his church! He headed slowly up the narrow steps, pausing only briefly at the step that gave entrance to the room itself. He took a deep breath, then stepped into the room.

The pounding stopped with his entrance.

The room was quiet, unchanged since he had left—except that the withered body was no longer lying covered on the floor, but was now seated at the table, the ancient metal cup in its shriveled left hand, scuff marks in the dust, as if the cup had been pounded there by a customer demanding rum. The body sat with its head resting on its right arm, its face turned toward Kerr so that the light caught and filled the empty sockets. It seemed that they were looking directly at him.

Kerr backed toward the staircase, terror rising in his throat. He wants his rum, Kerr thought wildly, feeling hysteria take root in his heart, but the bar's closed!

He bolted down the stairs, reaching the basement just as the night curled and thickened around him. Almost gratefully, he released the horror of what he had seen and fell into blessed oblivion.

10

. . . Thaddeus Smith. Algernon Drake. Vernon and Nancy Wintz. Ruth and Cheryl Miller . . .

11

At eight o'clock, Liz left her cabin and went to her car. She was tired of sitting in the same place, calling the hospital and being told the same thing, over and over. *Yes, ma'am, Mr. Crawford's condition was improved slightly when we stopped by to check on him at six o'clock, but I'm afraid there's nothing more we can tell you.*

What she needed most just now was a drink.

She'd been to the Royal Flush tavern a few times before.

It was a dive, but it would do. She would be back in time for the next call in to Cutler. Then, tomorrow, the authorities would surely release Eric. Maybe then he would tell her what was going on between him and Sam that was so important.

She had just turned the car onto Edgemont Road when the streetlamps went out. And the headlights. And the engine. She worked the brakes, but the car continued its downhill motion, heading for the trees on the edge of the road. She spun the wheel from side to side, trying to build up traction. The car slowed, but not enough. She looked up in time to see the car rolling toward a huge oak. She covered her face as the car slammed into it.

She shot forward, the wheel slamming painfully against her breasts.

When the lights stopped strobing behind her eyes, she pushed back against the wheel, stunned but alive. Nothing seemed broken.

She had to get out, get help. But the door refused to budge; the impact had been enough to wedge it into place. She tried the passenger door, smiling in relief as it opened.

Darkness and a strange dizziness rushed in upon her.

She collapsed forward onto the seat.

I wonder if anyone will find me, she thought distantly, and then surrendered to the night behind her eyes.

TWENTY-SEVEN

THE CLOSED ROAD

When Eric opened his eyes, pain was the first thing he felt. It started in his head and worked its way down through his muscles and into the cold ground where he lay. And the sky was bright, so bright.

I've been here all night.

He tried to sit up, but a wave of dizziness and nausea slammed into his brain. He let his head fall back, his eyes half-open, adjusting slowly to the bright sunlight that bathed the cemetery.

He wondered what time it was. He knew the answer was important, but parts of his mind hadn't yet awakened sufficiently to supply the reason.

More than anything else, he wanted to sleep. A day, a week, a month—just sleep. But there was a tiny alarm going off in his head, and it wouldn't go away.

What was he doing here?

Numbly, he suspected that, too, was an important question.

Now he began to pull his vagrant, scattered thoughts together. He started by lining them up in a rough chronological order, like a child playing with blocks. It was a difficult process; it would be so much easier to lay still and just be.

A blue jay, perched on a tree limb above him, craned its head to get a better look at this curious stranger. Eric smiled up at it with numb pleasure, marveling at the symmetry of wing and form, and yet unable to find words to express adequately what he was feeling.

As he quietly considered its elegant simplicity, his thoughts began to crystallize, though he would have preferred otherwise. All the artifices of identity, place, and purpose began to return.

They killed him. They killed him because he could stop them and he knew it. And they killed my mother. And they would've killed me, too, if they had the chance.

They might yet.

It was an unsavory thought, so unlike the pleasant one he had been experiencing. He rebelled inwardly against it, not wanting to return to the world in which his name was Eric Matthews whose real name was Eric Langren, and who had been born with an obligation he knew nothing about, had never agreed to.

Have I really been here all night?

He rolled up onto one elbow. To his astonishment, the ache and fatigue passed with the first movement. Logically, after sleeping in the open all night, he should be stiff for hours. But now, with each passing moment, he felt better. Rested. He was deeply and intimately aware of his own heart beating, and the feel of cool, dewy grass on his hands.

For the first time he could remember, he felt completely at peace.

He looked at the headstone, noting each nick and cut in the stone, the coarseness of the engraving.

And from below the headstone—only silence. Not emptiness, not void. But finished, for the moment.

Though Eric's work was just beginning.

It was with that last thought that the events of the previous night at last came back in full detail. Sam. The LeMarque house. The jail. The deputy, and the thing that had been with him. His father . . .

They killed him, didn't they, the things that—

He shot upright, horror reaching into his heart and squeezing.

The things that lived in the caves!

The things that would have come out that night.

And he had slept all night!

Instinctively, he reached into his chest with his thoughts, slowed the frantic beating of his heart.

Twelve hours.

What could those things do in twelve hours?

A lot, he thought, and the fear came again. If only he had been able to follow his instincts and come here yesterday morning. He would have been through all this and back in town by dark, in time to try to stop them.

The Night *was* cunning. And now he was late. He thought of Liz, alone. Strangely, he felt that so far she was all right, but that she wouldn't remain all right very long if he didn't get moving.

He stretched, feeling the muscles in his arms and legs responding with new clarity, and trotted back toward the wall that ringed the cemetery, pausing only to look back at his father's resting place before jumping back over the wall and heading for his car.

2

Demons. Allies of the Night, his father had called them. And perhaps his description was the more accurate, Eric thought as he drove toward Dredmouth Point. He remembered something Sam had said during their dinner with Father Kerr two nights ago: "The Christian points to the stars and remarks on the wondrous imagination of the Christian god—but, Duncan, the stars were there long before your religion arrived to claim them, and will be there long after Christ has joined Thor in the great hall of defunct gods."

Sam was right. There had been great forces in the world long before there were men to name them. Some names were more accurate than others, but none of them had ever quite hit the mark. He doubted that any ever would.

It was all so very clear, almost painfully simple. He found he would drift off, thinking about it, then start awake minutes later, still driving, having automatically separated the parts of his mind needed for thinking and simple action. It was in the same way that his mind had parceled out his new-found knowl-edge, filtering it into his consciousness like drops from an IV bottle.

A breach had been opened between two worlds, and through this breach—somehow—the demons had found a way out. "The heart of the cave" was the key. That was what he had to destroy, to seal the door. But he was still not sure what that heart actually was.

Until then, the demons would continue their attack, maiming right up until the instant before death. Then, at that moment, they would force out the human soul and replace it with another demonic entity. Unless they were stopped, the contagion would spread. Even the land would be affected, until each place where they gained a foothold turned into a little piece of hell.

The very worst thought of all he reserved for last. After three days in this world, a freed demon would be able to sur-vive even in the absence of the gate. Since, as near as he could figure it, the gate must have been opened two nights ago, that gave him exactly one night to stop them.

Somehow.

And somewhere out there was the first one through. That one would be the strongest by now, and the most dangerous.

He tapped his fingers nervously on the steering wheel as he turned onto the road that would lead him into Dredmouth Point. There was no getting around it.

He would have to have help.

3

As soon as he crossed into Dredmouth Point, he could sense the terrible oppressiveness that fouled the air. He drove care-fully, searching the road ahead for—

. . . obstacle, a block in the road, roadblock . . .

He slowed the car to a crawl. Around the next bend, he knew, would come the first glimpse of town, but before that there was something in the way. He pulled off on the side of the road, and climbed out as another car passed him, going toward the Point. He edged into the woods, paralleling the road on foot.

Twenty feet ahead, a police car sat parked at an angle, straddling the road. Ray Price approached the car that had just pulled up. A bandage marked the spot where fragments of the cell door had cut his forehead.

The roadblock could only mean that the creatures were at least partially in control of the town, Eric decided, his heart sickening at the thought. Was he already too late?

"—but I was going to stop by and see my aunt," the driver, a middle-aged woman, was saying.

"I'm sorry, but the road is closed. We've had an accident."

"Well, when will the road be open?"

"Not before tonight. Come back then." Ray's voice was calm, practiced, but his eyes were focused elsewhere, far away, on things only he could see.

Reluctantly she turned the car around. This was the only road that led to the Point through its narrow link with the coast. Eric wondered if the ferry was out of commission also.

He ducked into the thicket as the car passed, going back the way it had come. The roadblock would probably succeed. Not much traffic came into the Point even on a good day, so the disruption wouldn't draw any special attention.

As soon as she was gone, Eric glanced back at Ray.

The shadow-eyes that he had seen hovering over Ray's shoulder last night in the jail were there again, though fainter in the intimidating daylight.

They're controlling him, Eric thought, just as he had briefly influenced Ray. Then he corrected himself. No, not the same. He could feel it from here—whatever they had done to him, it was far worse than what Eric had done.

They touched him, inside, in the soft places; touched him and hurt him and changed him.

They needed someone who could function in the day, until they would be strong enough to do so themselves.

Eric reached the Datsun. Despite the roadblock, he had to get into town. He considered walking, but he suspected that he would soon have need of his car.

Which meant driving right past Ray. Eric had been able to influence him twice before; it might work again. True, he had not been able to affect Ray in the jail, but that had been at night, when the demonic influence was greatest.

Eric started the car and guided it back onto the road. He quickly closed the short distance to the roadblock, where Ray approached, one hand on his revolver. Eric hoped he hadn't yet recognized him.

"Sorry. Road's closed." Ray crouched down toward the sun-flecked window. "I said—" And then he saw the driver.

Now!

Eric reached out with his mind, and *squeezed*, fighting to submerge the recognition, fighting the *thing* in the deputy's mind.

Ray hesitated, his hand still on his revolver.

Eric squeezed harder. He could feel his heart slamming against his chest.

"Let—me—go," Eric managed, the strain of talking almost too much on top of the effort that was going on inside him.

Suddenly, Ray snarled.

"You!" It was the thing now, speaking through him. They were still linked, but tenuously in the strong daylight.

Eric pushed through that link to the other side.

"Sleep," Eric said, not to Ray, but to the thing inside him. The shadow struggled, vibrated into the ultraviolet. He squeezed harder. Stared into the eyes behind Ray's eyes. The thing wavered, surged darkly for an instant, then finally collapsed. Ray staggered like a puppet with its primary strings cut, staying upright only by an act of unconscious will.

"Move aside," Eric said.

Ray obeyed.

"Forget that I was here," Eric said. "Understand?"

Ray's face worked; something inside him was resisting.

Eric spoke through gritted teeth, the effort costing him dearly. "Do—you—understand?"

He squeezed harder, despite the pain that throbbed inside his own head . . . and suddenly felt something give behind Ray's eyes.

Quickly, Eric guided the Datsun around the police car, his breath coming in ragged gasps from the effort. In the rearview mirror he saw Ray take up his position again. When night came, and the shadow-eyes regained their strength, his maneuver would be exposed—but there was much that could be done between now and then.

4

The nearer he came to the town, the more oppressive the drive became. It was as though the light were being filtered far above. What little slipped through turned what should have been bright midmorning into a dusky late afternoon. He felt the hidden darkness tugging at his mind, felt the urge to sleep. He fought it and kept going.

He passed houses that four days ago had greeted him with freshly painted sides and newly mown lawns. Now they looked old; colors seemed tinted with gray around the edges. Clouds loomed over the Point like great stone mountains that in an instant might plummet to the ground.

Even the car seemed to resist him, and soon he was forced to concentrate part of his energies just to keep it going.

He passed more houses the closer he came to town, each marked in ways that he alone could read. The houses *they* occupied were more heavily shadowed, and nothing moved in the surrounding trees; even the birds dared not come too near. In other houses he could sense people still alive, but sleeping under the shadow that oppressed the town. He reached out tentatively with his thoughts and tried to get a sense of how many remained unmolested in the town. . . .

The horror of it choked at his throat. His mind refused to accept what it had detected.

A third? A third of the whole town—gone? It was almost too much to comprehend. That would be three, four hundred people! In two nights! And tonight the demons could easily finish the job.

The immensity of the task ahead staggered him. What could he do against so many? What was he supposed to do, alone, with his limited skills?

But he wouldn't be alone for long. He would find the others. He could already sense them in scattered places around town: Liz, the constable, Will, Father Kerr. He turned at last onto

Walnut Road, into the center of town, sensing more life here. No, he thought, it was not yet too late. But it would not be easy. Or pleasant. Or safe.

Welcome to Dredmouth Point, he thought as he drove. You'll like it so much, you may never leave.

TWENTY-EIGHT

HOUSE TO HOUSE

Eric drove up Edgemont Road. He sensed that Liz was there somewhere, but beyond that, nothing. Finally he narrowed the search to a stretch of road masked by trees, and saw her car protruding from the brush. He climbed out of the Datsun and found her lying spread-eagled across the car seat. Her breathing was shallow, her flesh cool. He took hold of her hand, closed his eyes, and *pushed.* The wall of darkness that had been put up around her mind sensed his presence, and resisted. It was as though he were pressing through a thick layer of black ice, with Liz's face floating dreamily below.

Finally the ice shattered, and her face rose through the stagnant waters, her eyes opened—and found him.

"You're all right," Eric said, helping her sit up. "Don't move too fast; give yourself a minute."

She nodded vaguely, and after a moment her face lost some of its blankness as she worked to remember what had happened. "An accident," she said. "The car went out on me."

"How do you feel?"

"Okay, I guess." She sat up in the driver's seat. "Feels like my whole head's stuffed with cotton."

"We'd better take my car," Eric said, fighting to restrain the sense of urgency clawing up inside his chest. He would have to explain what was happening to each of them. That would take time. And they didn't have much as it was.

She focused on him, and the last of the numbness dissolved behind her eyes. "Wait a minute—you're free! When did you get out?"

"Last night."

"Last night? You mean you didn't—I've been out here *all night!* And you didn't come looking for me until now?"

He opened the car door for her. "It's a long story," he said.

2
___

The center of town was the same as he had left it—silent, dark, dead. It didn't take Liz long to notice it as well.

"Where is everybody?"

"Asleep. Most of them, anyway."

"At this time of day?" They passed the husk of a burned-out car. The remains of two bodies lay on the street beside it. "Oh my God—Eric, what's going on?"

"I'll explain everything in time. But there are some things we've got to do first."

Liz turned to look at the deserted, silent buildings. "Christ," she said quietly, "you'd think they dropped the bomb."

The first thing he had to do was to get Liz to St. Benedict's. He had sensed earlier that Kerr was there, still alive. The church was well fortified, and he hoped that the belief behind it would count for something. They would be safe there, though not for long.

They entered the church, and found the priest facedown in the basement, near the stairs. Crouching over Kerr, his back obscuring Liz's view of what he was doing, Eric repeated the process he had used to revive her. He was learning more about the extent of his abilities; bits and pieces of the instructions he'd been given last night kept surfacing as needed.

The effort, so soon after reviving Liz, turned his head into a dark whirlwind of throbbing pain.

Kerr stirred.

"He's okay," Eric said, then stood, knees weak. "Look after him; I'll be back in a few minutes." He turned away from her questioning look and took the stairs two at a time. He was deeply aware of each passing second. Time was going to be required, first to bring back Tom and Will, and then to recover enough himself to lead them in what had to be done. Already it was well into midmorning. So little time!

Where *were* they?

He raced down Walnut Street, his frustration growing by the moment. He knew Tom and Will were there somewhere, but he'd looked everywhere and found nothing. He tried to concentrate, but it was difficult. Making matters more difficult was the knowledge of *other* presences that slept or hid behind shuttered windows on either side of the street.

Finally, in desperation, he tried an alley that he had checked twice before, and that, from the street, looked like a dead end. There he found Will and Tom in a cul-de-sac behind one of the buildings.

Eric decided to revive Will first. Then he would have the doctor's word that he had voluntarily helped Tom. He hoped that would help allay any of the constable's suspicions about his presence, if there were any.

There were.

"You mind telling me how you got out of that cellblock, and what the hell happened to my deputy?" Tom was still numb from the dark sleep, but his anger helped speed the healing.

"Not here," Eric said. "We don't have much time, and I don't want to have to repeat everything four times—"

"Four?" Will asked.

Eric nodded. "Counting Father Kerr and Liz. They're waiting for us back at the church. It's the only safe place." He turned back to Tom. "I know all this is moving awfully fast, but you've got to trust me. We've got big trouble."

"Yeah, well, after what I saw last night, that doesn't exactly surprise me," Tom said. "What the hell time is it?"

"Ten o'clock," Eric said.

"Jesus!"

"Come on." Eric led them out onto Walnut Street, waiting impatiently as they stared, uncomprehending, at the burned bodies still lying beside the car.

"Christ on a crutch!" Tom said. "You'd think somebody'd

have enough sense to—" He looked around. "Say, where is everybody?"

Eric said nothing, only started walking again. On any other Saturday, shoppers would be out in force, park benches would be filled with old men; but this was not any other day, and Eric could feel the tension grow in the two men as they walked behind him, glancing up uneasily at the houses and stores that lined the road.

They don't know, and yet somewhere, deep inside, a part of them understands. That was the part of them he had to reach.

3

Once they had gathered in Kerr's study, Liz listened with the rest as Eric told his story. Some things he held back—things they would not understand, not yet. They would see for themselves what he was talking about soon enough, but they had to be prepared, or all would be lost.

He finished his story to silence. Even Liz, who had already heard bits and pieces of it, was stunned.

"You're asking us to take a lot on faith," Will said. "You're saying something crawled out of the caves and . . . attacked the town?"

"In a sense," Eric said. "They kill—or at least mortally wound—their victims, and another one takes over the host body."

"Possession?" Kerr asked.

"Close, but with a difference. When someone has been possessed, there's still the human spirit inside. In this case, there's just the outer husk and the inner demon."

Tom stood, paced the room. "I don't know about this," he said. "I'll grant you, *something's* happened—you just have to stick your head out the window to see that—but as for the rest of it . . ."

"It's the truth," Eric said firmly. "Now, we've already lost a third of the town, and the longer we sit around debating this, the greater the risk of losing everything. And not just the Point. Unless we stop it, it'll keep on spreading."

Tom was still resistant. "What about something in the air?

Maybe from a chemical accident?" He looked at Will. "That's possible, isn't it?"

"I suppose so," Will said. "There's a lot we don't know about what the government's up to when it comes to these things. Maybe chemical toxins, resulting in delusions, violent behavior—it makes a lot more sense than anything I've heard so far."

"You have to admit, it does sound more credible," Liz said.

"I'd be inclined to agree with Tom," Kerr said.

"And you'd be just as wrong," Eric replied.

"Well, you four can debate it all you want," Tom said, rising, "but I'm calling in some help—medics, the county sheriffs, anybody I can get my hands on." He reached for the telephone.

"Don't do it," Eric said. "The line's not secure."

"Look, Eric, I gave you a fair hearing. I sat here, listened to what you had to say, and now it's time I did something. Maybe you really believe what you're saying. Maybe those chemicals affected your brain like they did Keller's. And maybe you're even right, though I doubt it. All I know for sure is that, one, something's wrong with the whole town, and two, my job is to report it and get some help."

"For the last time, the phone's not safe. Even if it was, Ray would keep anyone from getting into the Point until it was too late to make a difference."

"What's Ray got to do with this?"

"He's under their influence." Tom met this with a look of shocked disbelief. "And they can hear us over the phone lines. Hell, for all I know, maybe some of them are *in* the phone lines. We pick it up, they'll know exactly where we are. We can't afford that."

Tom wavered. He glanced at Will.

"Last night," Will said, remembering, "when you went to use the phone—"

"Cranks," Tom said, but the confidence in his voice was gone.

"I'll make you a deal," Eric said. "You'll have all the proof you want in a few minutes. Just give me that much of a chance."

He paused, waiting for a disagreement. When none came, he pressed on. "Then it's time we got moving. Past time. We've got maybe seven hours before it gets dark. Right now their abilities are limited, particularly the newer ones—and we have to destroy as many of the hosts as we can."

"You're talking about murder," Will said.

"Not murder. The bodies are technically dead already, and the souls are long dead. You've got to understand that. I know you have doubts. But you haven't seen them yet. Please, I'm not asking you to do anything until you're absolutely sure."

"And how are we supposed to destroy these—hosts you're talking about?" Liz asked.

"By decapitation, fire, and sunlight." He seemed not to notice the horrified look on Liz's face. "We have to move quickly; they're weak now, but still highly dangerous."

"Three hundred hosts in seven hours," Liz said. "That's not possible."

"If we're lucky, we won't have to go after every one of them," Eric said. "It'd be too risky, even if we had the time. There's another way we can go later, but only after the first part of the plan is put into effect."

"And what might that be?" Tom asked.

Eric chewed his lip. "I want to tell you, Tom, but if they got hold of you, they'd find out everything you knew in a second. They can read people, penetrate their thoughts."

"And they can't read you?" Liz asked.

"I don't think so. The odds are lower, in any event. They're not omniscient, and that may be our one advantage."

"If 'they' exist," Tom said. "Okay—I'll give you one chance to convince me, but that's all. If you can't, then we're doing it my way." By way of punctuation, his fingers strayed to the butt of his revolver. "Fair deal?"

"Fair deal," Eric said.

4

As much as he didn't want to believe Eric's explanation, Will found the streets outside chillingly quiet. The town felt completely wrong. Except for his years at medical school, and a brief stint in Korea, he had spent nearly his entire life in the Point, had seen it at its best and at its worst, but never with its life at such a low ebb, so . . . *tired.*

Clearly, they were in the middle of something terrible—
and from the expression on Tom's face, Will knew that the constable was feeling it, too.

"Here." Eric stopped and pointed to the general store.
"Two of the sleepers are in there." He turned to Will. "Would
you like to examine them?"

"Of course," Will said.

They found R.T. and his robe-clad wife on the upper floor.
Will checked their vital signs. "They seem perfectly normal in
every respect," he said, "except that they're completely coma-
tose."

"Have you ever seen the mud wasp?" Eric asked. "She
stings her prey into a coma until she's ready to eat them. Same
principle."

"You revived us, so why can't you wake them too?" Will
said.

"There isn't enough time—or enough of me to go around.
Besides, if we fail, it'll be better for them like this."

"We can't just leave them here," Tom said.

"No choice—unless you want to carry them out on your
backs, past the deputy."

Tom grumbled at this, evidently still reluctant to accept
the possibility that Ray might be involved, even against his will.

"All right," Eric said, heading out. "Time to give the constable his proof."

5
———

Tom stayed at the back of the group, his heart coming up with
conclusions his mind refused to accept. If the whole town was
as bad off as R.T. and his wife—well, what *could* have caused
it? He didn't know much about chemicals, but if the effects had
diminished enough for the four of them to be revived, then the
rest of the town should be getting on its feet about now. Not
only that, but the government would have its people crawling
all over the place. And yet the streets remained quiet, save for
the sound of their footsteps.

They stopped in front of Dave Markle's bait-and-tackle
store. "Davy Jones," they all used to call him.

"Okay," Eric said quietly, "this is how we'll proceed. Liz, you stay out front. Keep an eye out for Ray. I don't know if they'll risk taking him off his post to go chasing after us, but there's always the chance."

He looked to Kerr. "Father, your religion will mean more in the day than in the night, so it falls to you to keep the thing occupied while we try to drive it out or destroy it on the premises. I wish I could be more specific, but we'll have to play it by ear until we come up with a process that works."

He paused, looked at their faces as though searching for something behind their eyes. Finally he nodded, seeming satisfied at whatever he found there. "All right," he said, "let's go."

6

Father Kerr hung back as Eric, in the lead, opened the door to the bait-and-tackle store, allowing the others room to move quickly when it became necessary. Kerr caught himself on the word *when*. Was he, then, already beginning to believe Eric? Church teachings and logic went against it. And yet . . .

There had been times when, deep in prayerful meditation, he had sensed a kind of light. It was the kind of personal epiphany that convinced him there was a superior intelligence that looked after humanity. And now it was as if he had been completely immersed in darkness—and he found it equally convincing.

Was this what hell was like, he wondered. Not fire and brimstone, but a bone-wrenching weariness that weighed so heavily upon the heart that it felt ready to burst under the strain? He began to wonder if there might not be some connection between this and the incidents that had been plaguing St. Benedict's.

But he did not have time to dwell on the question. Will stepped through the doorway just ahead of him. He followed, clutching the crucifix that hung around his neck.

As soon as he stepped inside, he felt the presence of evil even more strongly than he had before. It lingered everywhere in the store, which was so heavily curtained that it seemed a tiny piece of night had gotten stuck inside while everywhere else was daylight. Even Tom and Will sensed it; their faces appeared to age years in an instant.

"Strange," he managed, and the word sounded so thick that it seemed to fall just short of his lips and tumble heavily to the ground.

Tom said nothing. Only Eric seemed to have expected this. His eyes roved the dark shop, searching for—whatever. Kerr let his own gaze follow Eric's, drifting across the racks of hooks and fishing lines, cans of dry bait, wooden crates filled with worms, and tanks of baitfish. His gaze lingered on the tanks a moment while his mind put together what his eyes were seeing.

"Dead," he said. "All the fish are dead." In the bait tanks before them, hundreds of minnows and other fish were floating belly-up.

Tom nudged one of the worm crates with a finger. "The worms, too."

"Nothing can live here for very long," Eric whispered. His attention, though, was fixed on the closed door that led to the storage room at the back of the shop. He turned to Kerr. "Think you're up to reciting the Lord's Prayer?"

Kerr smiled. Of course he was.

"Then do so."

"Our Father, who—" Instantly, his voice cracked. It felt as if the air itself were turning solid within his throat, twisting and aborting the words before they could find release.

"*Say it!*" Eric repeated.

Summoning up his reserves, Kerr tried again. This time the words came, though with difficulty. No sooner had he reached "hallowed be Thy Name" than the storeroom door burst open with an explosion of sound and wind. What little light had slipped into the storefront suddenly seemed to be swallowed up by a greater darkness just beyond that door.

A wind whipped through the store, hurling rods, hooks, and other debris around the room. Kerr noticed that some of it was flying against the wind. Lead fishing weights, some as heavy as a pound, whizzed through the air.

Kerr felt his resolve slipping, his voice stumbling.

"Keep going!" Eric said, standing against the wind.

Kerr forced himself to continue—and suddenly the lead weights gathered into a lethal cloud and flew at them, a hail of dull metal.

"Get down!" Eric shouted.

But Eric didn't duck. He thrust a hand toward the cloud of flying metal, and shouted something Kerr couldn't make out. There was a flash of light, and the weights fell harmlessly to the floor.

"Is that the best you can do?" Eric called out. Kerr realized he was directing his words toward whatever was still hiding inside the storeroom.

In the darkness beyond the far door, something snarled. The sound of it sent a shiver through Kerr's body. It was not a sound that could have come from any human throat. He fought down the fear that was building within him and continued the prayer. ". . . as we forgive those who trespass against us, and lead us not into temptation—"

The snarl became a howling, a shriek of pain and rage.

Something was moving in the storage room.

". . . and deliver us from evil—"

The thing struck.

Kerr had time only to get an impression of something leaping into the room, a thing of raw power that knocked him to the floor and kept going. He heard Tom firing his gun, looked up from the floor to see Eric pulling the—*thing*—off Tom, throwing it back into a corner where it crouched, glaring at them through eyes that even in the near darkness he could see were filled with absolute hate.

For a moment, it seemed a standoff. The thing that had once been Dave Markle swayed slightly, like a serpent looking for a soft place to strike. Kerr noted the twisted, scarred face, and the strangely contorted posture. Added to it now were three bullet holes in its chest. It didn't even seem to notice. The gun was less than a toy to a creature such as this. The thing seemed to hesitate now only because of Eric's presence, though its eyes shifted frequently back to Kerr.

Kerr stood and moved slowly toward Eric. The thing's eyes fixed on him, wary. A low, terrible hissing escaped its lips. Then, abruptly, the sound was no longer just noise, but words.

"We know you," it said, and its voice was like something vast and heavy moving in a cold, dark place. "We . . . *expected* you." It looked at them both, and Kerr wondered which of them it was referring to. Then it stared directly at Kerr. "We have many priests where I come from. All of your popes are with us. Would you like to talk to one of them?"

"Don't listen to it," Eric said, his gaze never leaving the thing. He spoke to it. "Who among you came through first?"

The thing grinned obscenely. "Oh, you don't want to meet him, no," it said. "He is old, the oldest of us all, the wisest, the strongest. No, you wouldn't like him at all."

"Answer the question!" Kerr managed, and held out the crucifix.

"*Sa!*" The thing crouched against the wall, face filled with hate, preparing to strike.

"Not the cross!" Eric shouted at Kerr. "Not yet!"

His words came too late. The thing leaped—flew—over their heads, and struck Kerr across the face as it passed. He fell. The thing landed on the far wall, hanging from its surface like a spider. Kerr struggled to his feet as it crawled across the wall, threatening them in words Kerr didn't recognize, but whose meaning was clear. Tom followed it in the sight of his revolver, but didn't fire. It would be useless against something like this.

"Last chance," Eric said, pacing the thing across the room toward the sealed window. "Answer my question, and your way back will not be painful. Who was the first through? Whose body did you corrupt first?"

The thing spat at them; viscous fluid bubbled on the floor. "You will know soon enough!"

"Then leave this place! We cast you out! Now!"

Something—some force—whipped past Kerr's head like a miniature hurricane. It slammed into the thing and threw it against the boarded-up window. The thin wood exploded outward with the impact, and the thing fell out onto the street.

"Come on! Hurry!" Eric shouted.

They ran outside to find the thing writhing in the dirt outside the store, its screams echoing up and down the street. Kerr saw Liz standing off to one side, her hand covering her mouth. The thing's skin turned black and cracked like the skin of an overripe melon, then sizzled and suddenly burst into flames. An oily smoke from the burning body fouled the air.

The flames died quickly, leaving behind only a black smear where the body had been a minute earlier. Behind them, Will was vomiting. Despite his concern, Kerr did not look toward him, knowing that would be all it would take for him to lose control as well.

Eric allowed them fifteen minutes' rest after the assault. He hated to spare the time, but he knew that it was necessary for every-one. Even knowing what to expect, he had been seriously shaken by what they had encountered, though he didn't dare let them see the true depth of his unease. They sat on the curbside, passing back and forth a plastic container of water they'd found inside, still sealed, replenishing what they had lost through sweat and fear.

Kerr was first to break the silence. "Twenty years," he said. "Twenty years I've been in the priesthood, and in all that time I never gave much thought to the question of demons. We were told possession was more the jurisdiction of the psychol-ogist than the priest. And yet there were always a few who were taken aside to learn the rites of exorcism. I never thought much of it; we all have to have our specialties, right? Demons were an idea, but now, actually to see one . . ." His voice trailed off.

"I guess I owe you an apology, Eric," Tom said after a moment.

"Forget it," Eric said, thinking that before this day was out, Tom might yet have reason to retract his apology. He'd sensed from the thing that it had come through very recently. Since they gained more strength the longer they stayed on this side of the gate, that meant that compared to the rest, this one was easy.

Even if everything went according to plan, there was no telling how many of them might die before the town was se-cured.

If they could secure it at all.

He went to Liz, who sat hunched against the building. Her eyes kept straying toward the dark stain on the asphalt. "How are you doing?"

"Okay," she said. He touched her shoulder. There was fear in her eyes, and incomprehension. But she was allowing none of it to come out where it might contaminate the others. He saw it, and he knew that she had let him see it.

He would get her out of here, he swore. Whatever might happen to him before this night was out, she would survive.

Eric waited a moment longer, then looked at the rest of them. They were ready now.

"Time to move on," he said.

8

Eric led them back to the general store, where they requisitioned three cans of spray paint (green, white, and red), thick candles (since flashlights were useless), and one hatchet and one ax apiece. They knew what the axes would be used for, but said nothing as they stuffed the items into the utility pouches they also took. There was one final stop back at the church, where Eric had no difficulty persuading each of them to take one of Kerr's pocket crucifixes. Kerr also took a vial of holy water, slipping it into his shirt.

They were as ready as they would ever be, Eric thought.

They moved down the street in a group. At each house and storefront, Eric paused, closed his eyes, and concentrated, trying to sense what was inside. Tom and the rest had by now accepted the fact that he was armed with his own special talents, though there were questioning looks, particularly from Liz, which he pretended not to see.

Empty houses got a brief spray of yellow paint; sleepers got a green; and where he felt a presence inside, red was applied. In case there was a chance to get the living out later, they would need the information immediately, with no allowance for faulty memories.

The first store they passed was a green, then two houses, a yellow and another green. They stopped in front of a two-story brick house, where Eric applied a splash of red to the door.

"This one's going to be hard," he said. "There's a couple of them inside." Worse yet, he knew, one of them was a two-nighter. "Same routine as before. Once inside, we've got to separate them. The crucifixes should be good for another five hours, until it gets dark, so make the most of them."

If Kerr had any response to a time limit on Christianity, he didn't mention it. At their nod, Eric tried the door. Locked.

"Allow me," Tom said, and kicked at the door. The first impact splintered wood, the second smashed the door wide open. Tom gave Eric a satisfied look. "This is still my town."

Like the rest, this house was dark inside, only faint traces of light slipping past the boarded-up windows. There were old chairs, a sofa that bent in the middle, doilies over everything. An old woman's house.

Eric took a step forward, the others close behind, then stopped abruptly. There was a shadow on the floor. "Something's here," he said. "A body."

He knelt down beside the body and lit a candle, content to take the risk. *They must know we're here by now anyway.*

"Mrs. Haggler," Will said, stooping down next to Eric. "Just a guess, but from the look on her face, I'd say it was a heart attack."

"Just as well," Eric said. "She died before they could use her." He held the candle down to her face, and shuddered at the horror he saw etched there.

They started away. "We can't just leave her like this," Kerr said.

"She'll keep," Eric said, surprised at his own bluntness. Despite the look of reproach he saw on Kerr's face, he knew they could not spare the time for last rites. He turned his attention outward, trying to get some sense of where within the house the things were. Softly, as though whispered into his ear from his brain, rather than the other way around, came the words *above* and *below.*

"One's in the basement; the other's upstairs."

The group tensed. "Okay," Tom said, "which first?"

"The basement." It felt right.

They found the stairs just off the kitchen and, lighting their candles, stepped slowly down into the basement. Eric led the way. Barely able to see, he stretched out his senses, trying to get a bearing on where the thing was, what to expect, what to—

The middle of the ninth step wasn't there.

Eric cried out as he fell through the gap in the stairs. He tried to get his feet beneath him, but only managed to twist awkwardly, falling on his side. The wind was knocked out of him, and for a moment the basement seemed to strobe out of existence.

Got to hang on, Eric thought. Distantly he heard the others yelling, heard something else snarling.

"Over here!" someone yelled. "Help!" It was Will. There were gunshots—two, then two more.

Eric struggled to his feet, coming around the base of the stairs to see Will on the floor, dazed. In the dim light of a single candle that burned on its side on the floor, he saw Kerr and Tom circling the thing, crucifixes held at arm's length. The thing snatched at them with one hand, shielding its face with the other. This one was virtually unrecognizable, so torn and distorted were its features.

That made it worse, not knowing who it had been.

Tom's foot nudged the candle.

"Look out!" Eric called, too late. The candle went out. The thing snarled and leaped.

"Down!" Eric shouted into the darkness. "Stay down!" He snatched the ax out of his pouch, held it out in front of him, senses screamingly alert. He was aware of the thing circling, all its attention on him. If it could take him out, that would be the end of it. He held his position, knowing it was watching him. He waited for it, trying to *feel* where it was. . . .

Left! It sprang. *There!*

Eric gripped the ax in both hands, and swung where he sensed the neck was. One shot; that was to be all he would ever get. He connected, felt tissue shear; felt the blade strike bone and continue, slashing muscle and fat and the hollow, rattling esophagus, and find open air at last.

The thing swayed for a moment, still upright. A sound gurgled from somewhere deep in its throat, and then it toppled. Eric waited until he sensed the presence inside the thing leave before he relaxed his grip on the ax. "Everyone all right?"

A cigarette lighter flicked on. Will. "Yeah, I think so."

"Tom? Father?" Eric called.

"Right here," Kerr said, and a candle glowed to life. Tom started toward the body. Eric put a hand on his chest. "You don't want to see it."

Tom glanced at the shadowed form. "Two down," he said, and grimly turned back toward the stairs. Eric felt a swell of admiration for the constable. Where Will and Kerr would do what was necessary, for Tom it had become a mission: protect his town. Like any good soldier, he was going to do his job, no matter what or who was thrown at him.

They headed back up to the first floor, signaled briefly to Liz, who was stationed outside, keeping watch, and continued up the stairs to the second floor. He didn't envy her position. At least they knew what to expect inside. Here, *they* were the hunters. But out there . . .

The thing was in the bedroom to the right of the stairs. It made no attempt to hide itself. Barely discernible, little more than a patch of darkness against the surrounding black, it sat in a chair beside a dresser. Waiting for them.

"Stay," it said. Its voice held the tone of superiority and command one takes with a dog or a slave. The same voice they had heard at the bait-and-tackle store.

They all spoke with the same voice, Eric realized.

He brought forward the candle to get a better look. The thing shrank back slightly but showed no fear. It was a woman.

"Judith Carlyle," Tom said, his voice mournful.

"Oh my God," Kerr said.

"Yes," it said, "*your god.*" Its voice dripped contempt. "Where is your god? Is he here? Or has the mad god gone on vacation for the past few millennia?" Its voice rose, became a child's recitation. "Where is God? God is everywhere."

"Last night—I heard you," Tom said. "The phone—"

"You heard all of us, and none of us." It looked at Kerr, its expression triumphant. "Unlike your god, we *are* everywhere."

Eric bit his lip, keeping the fear down deep, where he hoped the thing could not sense it. *This one is the two-nighter.*

"What do you want here?" Will asked. "Why are you doing this?"

"Ask the priest," it said, "after all, they started it. This is all his fault. He's not even a priest. Ask him what secrets he hasn't confessed, about—"

"Shut up!" Kerr shouted, holding out the crucifix.

The thing winced in obvious discomfort, then the shadow passed. "You will pay for that, priest," it hissed. It looked at Eric. "I offer you safe passage." No one spoke. "You are all free to go. Our servant will let you pass unmolested. You will die if you stay. Let us have this one place. It cannot be more important to you than your own lives."

"No deal," Eric said.

Its mouth lolling open, it looked toward the rest. "Does this one speak for you as well?" They nodded. "So you are prepared to die at the whim of one who is as alien to you as we are? He is not one of you." Its voice was a whisper, the words slipping into their ears like malign insects. "Ask yourselves if what he has done could be done by a normal man. Why trust him? He cares nothing for you. When he is finished, he will leave you to die in his place." It smiled at them horribly. "Do you accept my offer now?"

"Perhaps," Eric said, "if you tell us who came through first."

"The first shall be last, and the last shall be first . . . right, priest?" It turned back to Eric. "Do not think to lie to the prince of lies."

"You flatter yourself," Kerr said.

"I am just a humble servant to the true Prince, but I have my place."

"For the last time," Eric said, "who was the first?"

"What does it matter? When it comes your turn, it will make no difference. I may answer another question, though."

Eric considered this a moment, then panic hit. *Fool! It's stalling us!*

But why—

Then, from outside—a shot.

"Liz!" Eric shouted.

"On my way!" Tom raced out of the door and down the stairs.

The thing grinned at them. "And then there were four."

"Monster!" Kerr shouted. He pulled out the vial of holy water and threw it in the thing's face.

It screamed, and charged past Will and Kerr to the far window. Its face ran with pus and bleeding flesh. From outside came the sound of gunfire.

"You are dead men!" it screamed, then leaped through the barricaded window and plummeted down to the street below, bursting into flames as soon as the sunlight touched it.

Eric ran to follow Tom.

They reached the first floor. Tom stood just inside the front door, gun drawn. Liz crouched behind a chair.

"Sniper!" Tom said.

"Damn. It's Ray, it has to be."

"Yeah, that's what I figured too," Tom said reluctantly.

"I'm sorry," Liz said. "I didn't see him. All I heard was a shot from somewhere, and I ran inside."

"You did fine," Eric said.

"What now?" Will said. "He's got us pinned down in here."

Eric groaned inwardly. He had been a fool to allow himself and the rest to get into a prolonged conversation with one of the things. The creatures were fighting for time, working to get them into a vulnerable place. And now . . .

There was a way—maybe.

"Where is he?" Eric said.

"Up there." Tom pointed to the dome of the gazebo. Eric could barely make out a form lying there, flush against the roof.

But he could see the target, and that was the main thing.

"What's he using?"

"The same thing I am, standard police-issue .38 caliber. Good for hitting running targets. Why?"

"It'll help." Eric needed to visualize what he was doing. He closed his eyes and tried to concentrate on Ray, crouched on top of the gazebo; the revolver in his hand; the bullets in the chambers; the bullets heating up—

There was a *crack!* from outside, and a scream of pain.

"There he goes!" Tom yelled. Eric opened his eyes in time to see Ray, his arm dripping blood, slide down the gazebo, hit the ground hard, and head away from them.

"His gun must've misfired," Tom said, glancing curiously at Eric. "I don't think he'll be bothering us much anymore."

The headache back in force, Eric could only nod numbly. He glanced in Liz's direction. She, too, suspects I had something to do with that, he thought, saddened at the fear and awe he saw in her face. He was glad that Liz had not been upstairs when the thing had accused him of not being one of them. There were enough factors working against him without letting the creatures force a wedge between them. He had always been the different one, the outsider. He couldn't be that now. They couldn't afford it.

Worse still, they couldn't survive it.

TWENTY-NINE
THE CALL

By four o'clock, they were forced to rest at the Point Inn, once Eric had determined it was safe. Clearly, something had happened here during the night. The front door was broken, and there was glass all over the floor. But they were simply too exhausted to go on. Liz was grateful for the chance to get something to eat, regardless of how the food tasted, and to *sit* for five minutes. She took a seat on one of the counter stools, and put her hands on the countertop to try to stop them from trembling.

In the last two hours they had managed to dispatch only three more of the things. Strange, she thought, how fast they had come to think of the possessed bodies as *things*. Perhaps that was the only way they could deal with what they were doing. They weren't killing people, but destroying *things*.

Since the sniping attack, there had been no sign of Ray. He was still out there somewhere, possibly at the roadblock. There was no telling when or if he'd return, and the prospect troubled Liz almost as much as did the things themselves.

She closed her eyes. Since this morning, when she'd been found by Eric, everything had moved so fast. There was no way to keep up with it all. She saw the numb truth of this in the tired faces of the rest of their group. For the last hour they had been functioning on automatic, speaking only when necessary. Perhaps their thoughts were too hard for words; if one of them voiced the fears and doubts that surely they all felt, would they all just stop? Refuse to continue? She looked over at them, trying for a moment's eye contact, a sense of human companionship. But their thoughts were all turned inward, away from her.

She wanted to say something; she felt that somebody *should* say something. But nothing came to mind. The only thing she wanted was to sleep, to stop the ache in her bones and the weakness behind her knees where they had been locked to avoid trembling.

She looked to Eric, who stood by the window, peering out at the street through the slats in the venetian blinds. What was he thinking, she wondered. About their next step, whatever that was? She found it amazing how much he had changed. It was as though he had found a battery somewhere, and, once plugged into it, had become a light among them. And yet, at the same time, she had never seen him more distant, less communicative. She did not doubt him when he said that he would get them out of here, and that they would somehow restore the town; she sensed within him the power and the determination to accomplish the task. But she couldn't help wondering at his aloofness, and the nagging feeling that he was not telling them everything. She had seen him do things she would have thought impossible. Yet when pressed about it, he refused to explain.

Curious though she was, she was too tired to push the point. She took a small bite from a crescent roll she'd found beneath a plastic lid. It tasted stale, like everything else, but she forced herself to eat it, washing it down with water.

She wished that Eric would leave his post by the window and come to her. Nothing was moving outside, and she *needed* him. A word, a hug, anything would help. But he remained with his back to them, and she knew better than to ask for the comfort she so terribly wanted. This wasn't the time for displays of weakness.

But then, was it really so bad to want to go out with a hug still warm on her shoulders?

Will rubbed at his eyes, wishing vainly that he had some saline solution with him. But he couldn't even remember the last time he'd seen the stuff. For that matter, his memory of everything before he'd been found this morning seemed partitioned away behind a veil.

The more he thought about it, the more the saline solution became an icon in his mind. Because he couldn't have it, he could think of nothing else. Maybe he could talk the others into going by the pharmacy. If he could just have one bottle—

What the hell's the matter with you? he thought, dismayed at the triviality of his thoughts. Here they were, in the middle of a waking horror—and all he could think of was the comfort of his eyes?

Yes, damn it, it *was* all he could think of. The alternatives were too vast to consider. It was like trying to visualize a line stretching into infinity; soon the mind rebels and retreats to safer things. Better to think about his eyes than his life. In the latter lay the potential for despair.

And yet he was not quite willing to give in. They had, after all, eliminated six of the things, and so far they were all still alive. Perhaps there *was* some chance of survival, though each time he considered this, his thoughts came back to the staggering figure Eric had given them. Nearly three hundred more remained hidden throughout the Point. They couldn't possibly hope to destroy all of them before it got dark—and according to Eric, it was at night that their true strength would be revealed.

What's his plan? Will wondered. Eric had seen them through this much in one piece; perhaps he *did* know what he was doing—in an irritating, closemouthed sort of way.

Will thought he would feel better about a lot of things if he knew what their next step would be.

Father Kerr fought down a rush of emotions as he sat alone in one of the restaurant's booths. Above everything else, he was filled with a profound rage at what had happened to the Point. Things had moved so quickly that there had been little time for feeling, or for thinking things through; there had been time only for action and reaction. Now, though, as he let the reality of what had happened sink in, he was struck with a fury so deep that he trembled.

Judith Carlyle—he remembered her shy smile and her warmth. Dave Markle and the talking fish he said he'd once seen.

How could this have happened? How could a merciful God have *allowed* this to happen? He felt like Job, asking God to justify Himself. *Then the Lord answered Job out of the whirlwind, and said, Who is this that darkeneth counsel by words without knowledge?* But was it not part of human nature to ask questions, to seek reason where none seemed apparent? Job's humanity lay in his questioning mind, and the victory of God over Satan came because Job chose, deliberately, to do God's work.

More times than he could think of, he had been asked by Sam and others, "Why would a merciful god allow pain and suffering and the death of innocent children who don't have the facilities to understand what life, death, or sin is?" His answer was that however incomprehensible it seemed to mortals, it was still part of God's plan. So this, too, had to be toward a good end. Perhaps it would be through this that God would most clearly manifest Himself to the modern world.

Perhaps. But there certainly had to be an easier way.

There were other feelings rising up to confront him. He hated to admit it, but there was a kind of elation that came with fulfilling the offices of his church in this most physical of fashions. Most of his daily battles had more to do with plumbing than with the forces of Satan. He felt very much alive—and silently asked for forgiveness.

There was also a sense of relief. He no longer wondered what the cause of the odd events at the church had been. It was natural that there would be rumblings and movements within the building as the forces of good were awakened more fully in preparation for the coming battle. The secret room had been exposed in order to clear the spiritual air before the battle was joined. The crucifix moving, then finally appearing outside the church . . . it was a sign, the image of Christ Himself ready to go out and confront the darkness.

Finally, there were the fears that he knew he shared with the rest—fears of failure and inadequacy. He was a good priest—an *efficient* priest might be a more accurate description. There had been few challenges in his years of allegiance to the Church, most of them little more substantial than the occasional wistful—and quickly repressed—glance at a particularly buxom young woman. Was he ready for a confrontation such as this? Then again, would any amount of training ever prepare someone for the events he had witnessed in the last twelve hours?

He doubted it.

Tom fidgeted uncomfortably in his booth by the wall telephone. He knew he should eat something—who could tell when they might get another chance?—but he couldn't bring himself to do it.

From the start, they had all been kept busy, not allowed time to think. Maybe Eric intended it that way, and maybe that was the way the others wanted it, but it bothered him that so far they didn't have a concrete plan of action.

He corrected himself. That wasn't quite true. Eric apparently had a plan of some sort, but he wasn't about to let them in on it. They were, after all, too vulnerable. Hadn't the Almighty Eric Matthews said so, and didn't that automatically mean it was true?

It rankled him. Tom liked being in charge. He was *used* to being in charge, used to knowing how *A* would lead to *B* and eventually to *C*. But right now, only Eric knew what they would do next.

Eric. He looked across the counter to where Eric stood with his back to them in a gesture of—what? Isolation? Superiority? Disdain? Second-guessing him was maddening. So far, though, Eric had been right about nearly everything. Eric had overcome their disbelief and pulled them together, had twice saved Tom's life.

But there was much about Eric that still troubled him. Where had he been the previous night? Why was Eric's car the only one in the Point that still worked? How had he known what was going on? He'd said that he'd pieced it together from some Indian legends, but neither Tom nor anyone else had ever heard of them. And if Eric had known what was coming, why hadn't he taken action then, rather than waiting until now, when a full third of the town was gone?

But even supposing Eric had known, and had tried to approach him with this information, would it have done any good? Tom doubted it. Most likely, he would just have locked him up that much sooner. And all the questions wrapped up in *that* thought also bothered him. By detaining Eric, had he unwittingly helped bring about their present danger?

The only certain thing was that there was more to Eric than what he appeared to be. Hadn't one of the things said as much, that he was not one of them, that he was just using them?

No, Tom thought, catching himself. That was what *they* wanted him to think—and if they wanted him to think one way, then by God he'd go out of his way to think the opposite. Besides, Eric had exposed himself to danger just as much as the others had, possibly more. A man looking out for his own interests wouldn't do such a thing. And so far, he hadn't failed them. Unlike Ray.

Ray. Who would have thought that his own deputy, even against his will, could ever try to kill him?

Tom faced the inevitable facts. Eric was their only hope, at this stage, at least. There was simply no one else to turn to. But that didn't mean he would follow orders blindly. Sooner or later he *would* find out what all this was about!

Meanwhile, he wasn't about to let Eric out of his sight.

Eric looked out onto Walnut Street. In two hours the light would be dim enough for the demons to leave their places of refuge. And then . . .

He closed his eyes, afraid to let the others see the fear in them. As the day had darkened, so had his mood. The sense of confidence with which he'd begun this morning had long since evaporated. In its place there was only a sense of resignation. Part of it he could attribute to the oppressive air that hung over the Point, but the rest . . .

He knew that soon he would have to abandon the group and, after providing for their safety as best he could, strike out on his own. Where he had to go, they could not hope to follow. He wasn't sure himself what lay ahead; he knew only that he had to destroy the heart of the cave quickly and completely, with no guarantee that he would survive the effort.

Above all else, he hated the idea of leaving Liz behind. But at least she would be with the rest. He could only hope that, together, they could hold out long enough for him to do what was necessary before—

No. He would *not* think about that.

If everything they had done so far had its anticipated effect, then they had at least a chance of success. And their expeditions around the Point had confirmed his suspicions. Like Judith Carlyle and Dave Markle, when sunrise had come, the demons had taken up the first shelter available. He could feel them, feel the dread they emanated like static.

And from the moment he'd returned to the Point, that same sense of dread had come whenever he'd looked toward the caves, only magnified a hundredfold—which could only mean that a nest of them had taken shelter there. Individually, away from the power of the cave, the demons could be successfully confronted. But not even five others like himself could hope to take on so many of the things on their own territory.

He'd realized then that his only hope was to let them think that he and the rest were going to take them on one at a time, that they were unaware of the significance of the caves. Then, when night came, the things would leave the caves and swoop down into town to destroy the few obstacles to their plans.

And when they did, they would leave the caves unde-fended.

Unfortunately, that meant cutting it close. He had to stay in town, leading one attack after another, until the last possible moment. If he was lucky, they would not know what was hap-pening until it was too late. They were not omniscient. But they were not to be underestimated, either; the things would almost certainly detect an assault by his group on the caves, and at-tack before they got halfway there. Which was why he had to leave the rest behind. Not so much as bait, but as a further diversion. The demons would know roughly, but not exactly, where the group was. In time, though, they would be found. At that point their lives would be forfeit, as would his own—unless he could destroy the heart of the cave first.

Whatever *that* was. He didn't know what would happen when he destroyed it, either. He knew only that it had to be done, and done tonight.

He squinted through the blinds, to where the pale sun was dropping below the tops of the trees.

It was time to move, he decided, and turned to address the others—

As suddenly the telephone rang.

They were on their feet in an instant. The ringing filled not only the diner, but the streets outside. Every phone in the area, perhaps every phone in the Point, was ringing simulta-neously. The sound assaulted them.

"Well?" Tom asked. "You're in charge. What'll we do?"

"What do they want?" Liz asked.

"To talk," Eric said. "It's a good sign, in a way. They wouldn't try every phone in town if they knew where we were."

The telephones rang on.

"Do we answer it?" Will asked.

Then, as suddenly as it had started, the ringing stopped.

And an instant later, the building shuddered as a blast rocked the attic above them.

"Down!" Eric shouted, diving for the floor. *Stupid stupid stupid we stayed in one place too long they got a fix on us damn it all to hell*

Dishes flew in every direction, cutlery crashed against the walls.

The window blinds dropped and shut on their own.

Upstairs, something moved. They heard it scraping above their heads.

And the flies came.

Thousands of them. Millions. A living black cloud that filled the room. Buzzing into their ears, their mouths.

"Everybody out!" Eric yelled. "Now!"

Liz and Kerr, nearest the door, started toward it, when something exploded through the ceiling.

It fell to the floor, blocking their way to the door.

It rose up before them, nearly complete in its demonic evolution. The face was smoky, shimmering and distorted, barely recognizable as having once been human. Its limbs bent backward as well as forward, spiderlike. Skin flaked off its body in huge flaps.

Liz stood paralyzed before it, her mouth moving soundlessly, no longer seeming aware of the flies that now covered her.

It took a step toward her.

"No!" Will yelled. He jumped out from behind the booth and yanked her out of its way, putting himself between her and the thing.

The thing cocked its head at Will, its face twisted by a smile. "Very good," it whispered.

Then its hand shot out like a snake. It jabbed at Will's face so quickly it was almost a blur. Though it didn't seem to touch him, Will screamed.

"My eyes!" he cried, stumbling and falling. "I can't see!"

Kerr and Tom took a step toward it. It looked at them with anticipation. "Yes," it whispered, "come and play."

"Out of the way!" Eric called. "He's mine."

"He's mine," it mimicked.

Eric glanced at a box of silverware on the sink behind him—and it burst open. There was a flash behind his eyes as he reached out with his thoughts and hurled the knives at the thing in the doorway. They struck home, embedding themselves deep in its chest, arms, face, legs.

It didn't move, didn't seem even to notice. It only stared intently at him through slitted eyes—then looked at Liz. She grabbed at her throat, gasping for air.

The flesh around her throat pulsed, purpled, as though squeezed by an invisible hand.

"Leave her alone!" Eric said. "You want me, here I am! Come and get me!"

"Bastard!" Tom yelled at the thing. He pulled his revolver and emptied all six chambers into the thing's head and chest—to no effect.

Liz fell to the floor, struggling for air.

"Let her go!" Kerr shouted, and charged the thing, holding his cross in front of him.

It was all wrong, Eric thought distantly, as though observing the scene from somewhere outside. All their practice, their strategy, was useless, forgotten in the first counter-attack.

Without looking away from Liz, the thing slashed out, a backhand gesture that caught Kerr on the side of the head and slammed him against the wall, by the window—

The window!

The shades had dropped just before it crashed through the ceiling.

"Father!" Eric yelled. "The window! Open the blinds!"

Kerr fumbled for the drawstring, found it just as the thing turned and started toward him.

The venetian blind clattered up, and daylight filled the diner.

The thing screamed. The noise was horrible, an explosion of rage worse than all the rest. It staggered, drew back from the window—

But didn't die!

Liz stirred. The color was coming back to her face; she was breathing easier now. *It weakened him, but that's all!* Eric's heart fell. This had to be one of the first through, and now it was strong enough to tolerate the spare light that came in through the window.

It straightened, turned to them, its face seared and enraged.

Here we go!

It slammed a huge fist into the wall, and the building rocked, knocking them to the floor. The walls cracked around them. The miniature storm lamps on the tables bounced off, shattering—

Eric struggled to his knees. Storm lamps!

He grabbed one of them, pulled the top off, and threw it at the thing. The lamp shattered against it, kerosene dripping down its legs. Igniting his lighter, Eric leaped onto the counter and dove through the falling debris, landing a foot short of the thing. He thrust the flame into the pool of kerosene at its feet.

Flames rushed up the thing's legs, covering it like a living blanket of flame. The thing screamed again, and dove out through the window. It thrashed wildly, trying to put out the flames, its screams echoing off the storefronts. Then, finally, it collapsed and lay in the middle of the street, burning.

Tom snatched up a fire extinguisher from behind the counter and shot white foam over the blaze on the floor as Eric checked the hole in the ceiling, in case any others were on the way.

There were none. As he suspected, the wall between the diner's attic and the building next door had been broken down. A series of holes extended out and away, through at least four other buildings. He could see brief breaks of light through one of the holes. He'd been wrong about the purpose of the call; it had been a diversion, a way to cover up the noise while the demon who could tolerate momentary exposure to light slammed through one adjoining building to another, finally coming out right above them.

The things were getting desperate, and therefore dangerous.

Eric hurried to where Liz was huddled against Will, and looked at her throat. Deep, jagged bruises had been cut in the flesh, and she was breathing in great, wracking sobs. "It's all right," he said, "it's gone."

"It's *not* all right, damn it," she said, and turned away, though she did not leave him. He looked at Will, whose face was buried in his hands.

"Can't see," Will said numbly. Kerr stood by him, next to Tom, and muttered a prayer as Will rocked back and forth, in shock. "Oh God, I can't see. . . ."

They had just lost their first real battle.

The next defeat would be their last.

THIRTY

ST. BENEDICT'S

Eric held open the heavy front door of the church as Father Kerr helped Will inside, guiding the doctor to the last in the rows of pews. They had less than thirty minutes until sunset. Eric could afford a few more minutes to further convince the things he knew were watching that they were going to stay together, but no more than that.

"I'll check the rear doors," Tom said, heading away.

Liz glanced to where Will sat. "You're sure he'll be safe here?"

"It should be pretty safe," Eric said, "as safe as any place in the Point can be."

"Meaning not safe at all."

"They'll have to find us first," Kerr said. He handed Will a cup of water, then came toward them. "And then they'll have to come in here—and I don't think they'll be able to do that. Even the devil himself would think twice before violating God's own house."

"Don't count on it," Eric said. He didn't like the direction Kerr's mind was taking. "This isn't the Book of Revelations come to life, Father. There's no guarantee these things will respect anything, especially once it gets dark."

"We have hope, though."

"Yes, we have a chance, but only a chance. Overconfidence could end up killing all of us."

Kerr's face remained expressionless. "They will not enter here." He said it with the conviction of someone finally face to face with the reality of what his beliefs implied, and determined—perhaps inspired—to make a stand.

Eric saw no purpose in challenging Kerr any further. He turned to Liz. "You'll have to stay here until I get back, all right?"

"No. Father Kerr can take care of Will. Wherever you're going, I'm coming with you."

"Not a chance," he said. In his heart, he wanted anything but to leave her, but that was impossible now. "I need you here more than I need you where I'm going. It's too dangerous."

"And this isn't?" There was incomprehension in her voice.

"Not if you're well hidden." He looked to Kerr. "If—just if—those things find a way to break in, is there any place you can hide that they'll have a hard time entering?"

"A second line of defense?"

"Exactly."

Kerr thought about it for a moment. "Yes," he said slowly, "there is. But you'll have to wait here for a moment until I can get it ready."

Eric studied his face. There was something the priest wasn't telling him, but there wasn't time to deal with it. "All right," he said, "go to it."

With Kerr gone, there was only one thing left to do. Eric traced a hand along Liz's shoulder, felt her eyes on him, waiting for what he was going to say. He tried to find words that wouldn't ring hollow in his heart. *Be careful? You'll be okay?* How could he say either, when the first was beyond their control, and the second was laced with doubt? He wouldn't lie to her.

But Liz spoke first. "This isn't fair," she said. "Damn it, Eric, you can't just dump me here."

"Can, and will. I can't do what I have to if you're along, and I have to worry about both of us."

She stepped forward and held him. "If you leave, you're not coming back, I know it."

He held her close, but his thoughts were elsewhere, sensing the sun inching closer to the horizon. "Try and stop me," he said, and kissed her once, softly. "Now go help Father Kerr. He and Will are going to need you in the next few hours."

She nodded and, without another word, walked off in the same direction Kerr had taken.

Tom trotted back into the nave a moment later. "Rear doors are about as secure as they're ever going to be," he said.

"Good. Now until I get back—"

"Forget it. I'm coming with you."

"Damn it, Tom, I don't have time for this."

"And I don't have time for martyrs, either. You say you can do whatever the hell you have to do alone. Well, maybe that's true, and maybe not. You might need a backup. Never can tell."

"What's wrong with you?" Eric said. "Don't you understand what we're up against?"

"As much as I can, yes."

"Tom, I can't allow it."

"And how do you propose to stop me? If you drive away, I'll just follow on foot. Because in case you'd forgotten, I'm still the constable. Damn it, Eric, this is my town, and if there's anything to be done, I want to help."

Eric stopped. Tom was right. And there wasn't time to debate it any longer. "All right, all right. But on one condition— that no matter what happens, no matter what you think is happening, you have to do exactly as I tell you."

"Only if you tell me the whole story, no blanks."

"Agreed." If Tom was going to come along, he had a right to know the truth.

"I'll go tell the Father," Tom said. "Better get the car started."

"You've got exactly one minute," Eric said. He stepped out of St. Benedict's and into the street. The shadows were lengthening fast. He checked his watch.

Twenty minutes till sunset.

They were going to cut it awfully close.

THIRTY-ONE

THE POINT

"We'll need dynamite," Eric said, behind the wheel of the Datsun. He fought to keep the sputtering car going.

"I know a place," Tom said, "a construction shed not far from here."

He led Eric to the shed just off Lakewood Drive. He smashed out a window to gain entrance, took blasting caps, a half dozen sticks of dynamite, fuses, and a handful of road flares, and shoved them into separate canvas bags.

As they drove up the winding, dark roads that led toward the caves, Eric told as much of his story as they had time for. He talked about the nightmares, and the discovery that he could *sense* things. Tom had sufficient evidence of this not to need much convincing. His expression grew grave at Eric's description of Ray's attempt on his life, and the mention of Eric's visit to Sam's room and the cemetery.

Finally the car bucked and stopped, refusing to start again.

"Sundown," Eric said as the silence rushed in.

"So now what?"

Eric opened the door, taking one of the canvas bags. "We walk. Just as well, I suppose. There's less chance of running into any of them if we keep off the main roads."

Tom grabbed the other sack and climbed out. Together they pushed the Datsun off the road into a concealing stand of trees. "It's quite a walk," Tom said. "Will we have enough time?"

"I hope so," Eric said, and started walking. "But I don't think time is going to be our greatest worry."

"Then what is?"

Eric glanced back at him, unsure whether his grim look was readable in the growing dark. "Good question."

2

Kerr came down the hidden stairwell and entered the basement. Liz was huddled close to Will, holding a devotional candle in one hand, supporting the blind doctor with the other.

"It's ready," he said. "Follow me. You'd best hurry." Though there were no windows in the basement, he could feel night descending over the Point.

"This way," Liz said, and guided Will through the tangle of boxes, clothes, and folding chairs to the newly uncovered opening in the far wall.

At the top of the stairs, Kerr took one last look around the hidden room, then ushered them inside. Minutes earlier, he had found the skeletal remains crumpled on the floor again, as they had been originally, no longer sitting at the table. It was a good sign; the forces that opposed them apparently could not long maintain their potency within the church. It had taken Kerr only a few moments to return the figure to its original hiding place, then drape a few extra sheets over the bulk to obscure its shape. The room now seemed nothing more than a little-used storeroom—which, from this day forth, was all it would ever be.

He led them to the table, where he had set a bottle of water, two glasses, and a handful of candles. Only one of the candles was now burning, a cat's-tongue of flame that flickered through the cut glass. "The candles should last about an hour apiece," he said. "Normally we light these for the dead, but for now, they'll do to provide light for the living."

"They'll be just fine," Will said, trying to sound cheerful. "More than enough for my needs, anyway."

"Well, then," Kerr said, feeling awkward at what he was about to say, "I think we're set. I'll go downstairs and cover the entrance again. The two of you are to stay here until either Eric or I come for you."

Liz took his arm. "What do you mean? You're staying with us, aren't you?"

"This is my church," Kerr said. "To abandon my stewardship would mean betraying everything I believe. I don't think they'll dare to enter the church. But if they do . . ." He spread his palms, leaving the rest unsaid. "Please, Liz, don't ask me to hide from my obligations."

Her eyes met his and held. "At least be careful," she said.

"I will," he said, and continued toward the stairs.

"Oh, and Father?"

He stopped. "Yes?"

"I just wanted to say that I'm sorry about some of the teasing I did—kidding you, going along with Sam in giving you a hard time now and again—"

He waved away her concerns. "Forgiven." He smiled. "There, you see? I said that for you the confessional was always open, and now you've made good on my offer. What more can any priest ask for?"

He winked at her, then went back down the stairs. At the bottom, he pushed as many chairs, boxes, and piles of old clothes against the opening as he could find. He stepped back to survey his work and found it satisfactory. If you didn't know where to look, the opening would be all but invisible.

Good enough.

Kerr headed back upstairs, to the sacristy. He donned the vestments of his office, dressing as for Mass. The symbolism of his garments came home to him as never before, heightened by the awareness that this was as much the uniform of a soldier as military greens.

And now, like a weekend soldier pressed into regular duty, he was going to war. Perhaps it was naïve to hope for victory on the eve of battle, but victory was always a possibility. He would confront the things, and if a clear-cut victory was not destined to be his, he hoped—prayed—that he would have the faith at least to give Eric enough time to do what was necessary.

Though he knew that he would be sorely tested before the night was over, he looked forward to the imminent confrontation. He had always prided himself on being a reasoning, rational priest in a world where those terms were usually considered mutually exclusive. But even reason, in its way, was a trap, for there always would come a time when everything would come down to a question of faith. In a sense, it was a relief no longer to have to debate, to question. For the moment it was enough to act, and to believe.

He stepped into the interior of the church proper. The sky visible through the high windows was dark. Sunset had come at last. He went down the left-hand wall to the racks of candles set out for prayer offerings, lit them, then returned to the altar, genuflecting before approaching and lighting the altar candles that stood on either side of the crucifix. From his vantage point beside the chancel rail, it seemed that the church was filled with rows of stars, the candles flickering bravely in the oppressive dark.

There was nothing more to be done.

He knelt on the altar steps before the chancel rail, his eyes fixed on the light and shadows that played across the face of Christ, looking down at him, waiting with him.

When they came, they would find him praying.

3

Eric picked his way through the woods that led to Indian Lake. He moved slowly but steadily, concentrating on the task of putting one foot in front of another, for when he thought much beyond the next footstep, he came up blank. Once he and Tom reached the caves, what little he had planned in advance would come to an end, and then . . .

One foot in front of the other, he thought. Left, right, left, right, left—

(cold, so cold, want to go home, but they won't let me . . .)

Eric froze. The words strayed near the edge of his thoughts, resonating like the distant murmur of a conversation overheard through a wall. Distant, tenuous, and yet somehow familiar.

"Something wrong?" Tom whispered.

"I'm not sure." He concentrated on tracking the voice that moved across his mind with feather-touches. It had not been directed toward him; rather, it had found him by accident, like a powerful radio signal bleeding over into the neighboring frequencies.

(. . . so alone, they won't let me go, it shouldn't be cold, but it is, so very cold . . .)

Then it hit him. It was the same thought-voice he had heard yesterday morning, when he'd awakened to find Liz gone.

He closed his eyes, probing with his mind to try to touch the voice. He visualized the words, sent them out into the night. (I'm here, we can hear you, help you.)

The voice trembled, drew back in fear. (. . . no, you're one of those that hurt, that keep me in darkness, so cold, so alone . . . no, no more . . . let it be fire, let it be ice, but let me go, please let me go . . .)

(Where are you? We'll come as soon as we can.)

(. . . so cold, dark, dark hole in the ground, grave and not grave, not anything . . .)

Eric's concentration snapped. He became aware of Tom pulling at his arm, whispering urgently.

"Listen!"

He heard, not far off to the side, the sound of movement. A rushing of wings and a murmur of voices, coming fast.

"Down!" Eric said. They dove for the ground, hugging it as the sound grew louder. Instinctively, Eric clamped his eyes shut, burrowing mentally into the ground like a mole, going far away, not here, not here at all, blanking out his thoughts.

The noise grew louder. It was not just one sound, but a cacophony. There were footsteps and the rustle of things being dragged; distant hissings, and shrieking choruses; a noise like the padding of wolves' feet, a wind that rushed over them—

And the Eye.

He could feel it even through his skin, like the static crackle of heat lightning; he could sense it, even though his thoughts were as distant as he could push them. The image filled his mind—an image of an eye that searched everywhere, that searched for them, found only darkness, and continued its search, passing over them and probing farther on with unblinking thoroughness.

As it passed, there was the sound of something . . . *flying,* moving quickly on vast, leathery wings.

The first through, Eric thought.

Gradually the sound receded. When it was at a safe distance, Eric forced his head up. His head was ready to split from the effort of concealment. His eyes burned from the tightness of his lids, and his hands had been clenched so hard that red welts marked where his nails had cut his palms. Still, it was a small price to pay. They had not been discovered!

And yet his thoughts ran to the power of that terrible eye. He had managed to conceal them from that eye once; he doubted that he could do so a second time.

He knew then that there must not be a second time.

Tom lay little more than a foot away, his face pale and covered with perspiration even in the cool night. They waited silently for a moment, listening to the sound retreat, until they could be sure that the things had finally passed them, moving like a tide—away from them, and toward the center of town.

4

Liz poured a little water onto Will's handkerchief and dabbed lightly at his face, around his eyes. She couldn't help Eric—she was, in fact, trying hard not to think about him too much—but here she might be of some use. She held Will's face in her hands. It was sad, almost childlike, and vulnerable.

"Is there any pain?"

"Just a kind of numbness, like the front of my face was injected with Novocain." He shook his head. "The thing just . . . *touched* me." He ran a careful hand across his face. "No damage, I hope?"

"Let's see." She held the candle closer, and involuntarily gasped at what she saw. Where a little while earlier his eyes had been a bright blue, now a thick yellow film covered them. The film shimmered faintly in the candlelight.

He stiffened at her reaction. "What is it?"

"Nothing, really—"

"Damn it, Liz, this is no time to spare my feelings."

As clinically as possible, she described what she saw. He showed no reaction, but only nodded thoughtfully, as though discussing the condition of some other patient. But she could see his hands trembling on the table.

Damn, she thought, this is no place for an examination. Will needed trained medical help, there was nothing for them here. The room was septic, foul-smelling, full of dust and old boxes. More than that, the room *felt* bad. Liz kept expecting the flickering shadows cast by the candles to detach themselves from the wall and rush in upon them.

Let's not get carried away, she thought. Maybe later, when there's less at stake. Right now, Will didn't need a blubberer on his hands. He needed a nurse, and she was the nearest substitute they had.

She stroked his head. "I'm sure you'll be fine, as soon as we can get you some competent help."

"Don't kid yourself." He hugged his arms across his chest. It was getting cold. "I can't see a thing."

"Which is understandable. It's nearly pitch black in here."

"But there's some light, right?"

"Yes, a candle, but—"

"Hold it in front of me," he said. "I need to know if I can see anything, anything at all. Let's just give it one more try."

"If you're sure that's what you want . . ." Liz brought the candle around in front of Will's face, and moved it slowly from side to side.

"Anything?" she asked.

"Not yet."

The room grew a little cooler. Liz pulled her sweater closer around her shoulders. She moved the light to Will's left; he suddenly sat forward.

"Left?" he said.

"Correct."

His right. "Right?"

Her heart leaped. Perhaps there *was* hope!

Left. "Left."

Right. "Right."

She kept it toward his right side. "Right again." He was grinning broadly now. "Thought you could put one over on the old doc, eh?"

"Should've known better than to try."

Left. "Left."

Right. "Right."

"That's wonderful, Will!" she said, and put the candle down on the table.

"Left."

She stared at him. His eyes were moving back and forth, following—what?

"Right. Left. Left again! Now, Liz, I thought you could do better than that." His eyes continued to move back and forth, tracking—something, the glee on his face evident.

"Must be one of Kerr's prayer candles," Will said. "It casts a rather pleasant blue light."

The candle was encased in clear cut glass.

Liz felt a shiver race up her spine like a knife blade being traced along her vertebrae.

"Will, what do you see?" she asked, but her last word was swallowed up by a sudden sound that startled them both.

The sound of a tremendous hailstorm slamming into the church roof.

5

Father Kerr's head jerked up from the chancel rail at the noise. No, he realized, it was not hail at all. Rocks. Stones beyond counting were falling down onto the church.

Kerr rose, circling the nave as the volume grew. Now he could see small stones sliding down the stained glass windows, and jumped as a larger stone burst through the wheel window that was the church's frontispiece.

Then, abruptly, the hail stopped.

There was a knock at the church door.

Kerr took a deep breath. "Who is it?" he called. "Who's there?"

From beyond the door came the murmur of many voices— low, laughing, whispering—words that lingered just beyond his understanding. His skin crawled. How could he hear whispers that were on the other side of the door, when the door was at the opposite end of the church?

And then the whispers came from everywhere at once, from the windows above and beside him, behind the building itself. He caught a glimpse of something moving beyond one of the windows, but then it was gone before he could get a good look at it.

Kerr stood before the altar, his back braced against the chancel rail. "You cannot come in here," he shouted to the things outside. "This is a house of God!"

All at once, the whispering stopped. It was as though an ax had cut off the sound, leaving behind only a silence that roared in his ears.

Then: laughter. A wave of hideous, shrieking laughter erupted around him, deafening in its intensity. He pressed his hands to his ears, but the sound was undiminished, seeming to come from within his head as much as from without.

The laughter stopped.

And again, a knocking at the door. Soft, almost a scratching, like a dog asking to be let in.

"In the name of the Father, and of the Son, and of the Holy Spirit," Kerr shouted, dismayed at the tremor he heard in his voice, "you shall *not* be allowed here!" He gripped the railing to stop his hands from trembling. Where now was his anticipation for this encounter? Gone! It had been vain, foolish. And yet he was determined that he would let nothing happen to the two who had been left in his care. Nothing they could do to him would change that. Nothing!

The scratching stopped.

The door burst open.

A tremendous wind filled the church, whipping the curtains like flags in a hurricane. The candles he had so painstakingly lit were extinguished in an instant. The smell brought in by that wind—the smell of decay, of rot—was nearly more than he could stand, a foulness that coated the skin like an invisible mist, leaving it cold and clammy.

Kerr stood between the altar candles, the only two left burning, awaiting the inevitable assault. It did not come. Instead, there was a further darkening of the space around the door as they entered, moving slowly along the floor and up the walls toward the roof, spreading like a black pool of oil on concrete. He bit his lip until it bled, determined not to panic, not to run. They poured in, and though he could not see their forms or faces, sometimes they would look to him and their eyes would catch and throw back the light of the candles, hundreds of pairs of eyes burning a deep red.

They slid forward, across and above, filling first the back

pews and then the middle ones, an unholy congregation that moved with utter silence, as if waiting for him to speak. He caught himself at that. No, not waiting for him. Waiting for someone—or something—else.

He held his ground. If they wanted the satisfaction of seeing him run or plead, they were in for a disappointment. He would meet the stares of those burning eyes and, like them, wait.

6

"Almost there," Eric whispered. They stood just a few feet from the entrance to the caves. He pulled one of the flares from his sack, but would not light it until they were inside.

Tom laid his hand against a stone. "The rocks—they're nearly body temperature."

"I know. This is a place of considerable power. The heart is definitely somewhere inside." He cocked his head. "And so is someone else."

"One of them?"

"I don't think so. It doesn't have the feel of one of the creatures. As near as I can tell, the cave is clear, for the moment at least." He listened to the wind, rubbing his fingertips against each other as might a schoolteacher with chalk on his fingers.

Reading the caves. Sending in delicate tendrils of thought, feeling his way through the passages.

Finding trouble.

"As I thought," he said, more to himself than to Tom. "They've set up a ring of defenses. No telling what they are, or if any of them might bring the whole army of them down on us." He looked back at Tom. "You're sure you want to go on?"

"You have another suggestion?"

"Unfortunately, no. I can only tell you to be careful of anything we find inside—or think we find."

"Illusions?"

"Most likely. But there are real dangers as well."

"Can we tell the difference?"

A pause. "I can, I think. As for you . . ." He left the sentence unfinished.

Tom swallowed. "Let's go."

They moved inside.

The instant Tom stepped onto the cave floor, a solid wall of panic slammed into his mind. In the musty dark of the cave mouth, things moved and fluttered just at the corners of his eyes. Something huge and leathery bumped into his feet. There was the sound of great jaws opening and closing. The walls rushed in at him. Closing. No air. He grabbed his throat, his lungs working furiously. Couldn't breathe. No air, and all around him, *things*—

"No!" He dashed for the opening. Had to get out, get *out!*

"Tom!"

Something stopped him, prevented him from escaping. One of them, one of the things. He screamed, pulling at the hands that held him, smashing at it, *get away, get away.* Then it had him down, his arms pinned.

"Listen to me! It's me! Open your eyes!"

It was shrieking foulness into his ears, and he knew that if he looked into its eyes, he would die—horribly, in great and unending pain. He struggled to get free, but found his arms pinned to the ground as if held there by stone blocks. The thing . . .

"Tom! Fight it!"

The eyes, burning down at him, but not so alien now . . .

"That's it!"

He forced his eyes to focus, and found there not the thing he had seen earlier, but Eric, whose eyes were burning with a curious, cold fire, reaching down deep inside him.

Tom licked his lips. "What—" he said, and sat up. "There was a thing—"

"An illusion."

Shame hit him. "Not doing so great, am I?"

"You're doing just fine. You came out of it, that's the important thing." Eric released Tom's arms. It was then that Tom noticed for the first time that Eric seemed to have . . . grown somehow. Not bigger, but more *there,* as if he had lacked some part of himself until the moment they entered the cave.

Tom stood. Even now, when he looked away from Eric,

he could feel the panic nibbling at his brain. Only an act of will kept it at bay. "At least I think we know what happened to Sam."

"Yes." A moment's silence. "You ready?"

"I think so."

Eric stood. "Then let's get going."

7

Kerr did not have long to wait.

After only a few minutes, the black mass of figures at the rear of the church parted. He could not make out the last arrival clearly, but Kerr could feel the *power* of the thing as it moved down the aisle toward him.

It stopped a third of the distance away from the altar, close enough for its presence to permeate the air around him, but far enough to remain only a silhouette framed against the night. The glow of the altar candles stopped far short of the thing.

The altar! he thought, and hope stirred. *It doesn't dare come near the altar!*

From the shadows, only its eyes visible, the thing spoke. "Where is—the priest?" Its voice was a snarl that slipped as much into the mind as the ear, and in its wake was the sound of many voices.

Kerr cleared his throat. "I am here."

It spat, and where the brown spittle landed, it seared the floor. The thing spoke again, slowly, as if to a retarded child. "Where . . . is . . . the priest?"

And from the dark congregation came the whispered chorus: *Where . . . is . . . the priest? Where . . . is . . . the priest?*

"I told you—"

The thing faced him. It thrust one arm out—and all the windows on the left side of the church exploded inward. Needle-sharp shards of stained glass burst forth in a multicolored swarm. Kerr moved to protect his head with his arms. A piece of flying glass wedged itself in his arm.

"Ah!" he cried out, before he could stop himself.

Ah, the things echoed, hungry, pleased.

Then they were still. In the following silence, the thing spoke again. "You are weak. You are not a priest."

Kerr pulled the needle of glass from his arm, trying not to scream from the pain.

"No, not a priest at all," it said, and stepped closer. The terrible stench increased. "Where is the priest?"

And the dark chorus, over and over: *Where is the priest? Where is the priest? Where is the priest? . . .*

8

Liz sat at the wooden table, at an angle to Will. Since the hail sound had stopped, they had heard nothing more. She sat with arms crossed tightly, wishing she could run, shout, do anything but wait for others to act. She felt a stab of longing, wondering where Eric was, how he was faring. Will sat quietly beside her, staring straight ahead. From time to time he seemed to catch glimpses of a light that she couldn't see. A blue light, he'd said earlier.

Even now his eyes darted from side to side, tracking something. Then, abruptly, his gaze fixed at a point across the room, near some empty casks.

"Will?" she said, her voice a hoarse whisper. "What do you see?"

"I'm not sure. Is there—someone else in the room?"

A shiver crept up her spine. "No, of course not."

"Then who is he?" He pointed in the direction of the casks.

"I don't see anyone!"

"I do. Maybe it's just a function of the blindness, like an amputee still receiving impulses from a limb that's no longer there. Maybe I just want to see something, anything. But it looks so . . . real."

Liz closed her eyes. God, just get us out of here, she thought. When she opened her eyes, Will was still watching—something.

It was moving again.

9

When they were well within the cave mouth, Eric took out one of the flares and lit it. The flare cast a flickering, smoky glow through the passage they occupied, one that connected to the outer chamber. The passage extended out in either direction, each vanishing around a corner.

"Which way?" Tom asked.

Which way? Eric probed, unsure how much of what he sensed he could afford to trust. At least now that they had penetrated the first line of defense, the earlier panic had subsided. *Which way?* His impulse was to turn right, continue that way—

(. . . what do you want . . .)

Eric started at the voice that slipped into his thoughts, the voice that had been silent since the encounter in the woods.

(. . . you're going to bring them back, to hurt me, to put me in the cold place forever . . .)

(No! We're here to help, but you have to help us.)

(. . . can't . . . so tired, want to sleep, but they won't let me . . .)

(Then help us!)

A pause.

"Eric? What is it?"

"Ssh!" Eric said.

Finally: *(. . . where are you . . .)*

(At the first passage. Where are you?)

(. . . here . . .) Lunatic giggling at the edge of his mind.

(Which way?)

(. . . this way, to me . . .)

Eric felt an impulse to go left. The feeling was different from the first impulse, safer. From here on, it would be no difficult task to find the right path.

It was the uncertainty of what lay on that path that bothered him.

"This way," Eric said. He headed down the left-hand passage, following it around a corner. He held the flare aloft, moving forward as quickly as he could. Then he noticed that Tom was no longer beside him.

"Tom?"

"Eric?" The voice came from farther back in the passage. "Where are you?"

"Around the corner."

"What corner? All I see is a dead end!"

"Go to the end of the passage, close your eyes, and just turn right."

"If you say so."

A moment later: "Damn," Tom said from a distance. "I could've sworn there was a wall here a minute ago." Then he emerged from the darkness beside Eric.

"No matter," Eric said. He led the way down the passage, until he came upon an opening in the right-hand wall. Holding the flare out in front of him, he squeezed through, Tom following.

"Snakes!" Tom cried out.

The chamber, riddled with passages leading off in every direction, seemed filled with snakes. Most of them were small, but one huge serpent swayed before them, slitted eyes catching and reflecting the flare.

"There aren't that many snakes in all of Maine," Tom said firmly. "Not real."

The largest snake, easily the size of a man, moved away from the wall, gray-green scales scratching the rocky floor.

"Illusions," Tom said.

Eric blinked hard, trying to clear his eyes. He reached into the vibrant power within him, focused—and abruptly the tangle of smaller snakes vanished.

But the large one remained.

"Get back!" Eric yelled, and threw the flare in front of the serpent. It hissed and reared back.

Tom grabbed his revolver, fired three times. Two bullets found their target, throwing the serpent head over tail across the chamber.

It started to rise, swayed, then fell and did not move again.

"Jesus!" Tom muttered. His hands trembled as he removed the spent cartridges, and replaced them with fresh bullets from his belt. "Which way now?"

Eric scanned the passages, felt himself drawn toward the middle left entrance. "That way," he said.

10

Kerr watched as the things drew closer, until they ringed the front third of the church.

"False priest!" they chanted.

Kerr stood with his back to the chancel rail, determined not to retreat any farther. "It's Satan who is the king of lies, the deceiver."

The leader, the strongest, took another step forward. "Then tell me, *priest*—are you willing to die for your faith?"

"I wouldn't be the first."

"But are you *willing*?"

"I am willing to do that which God requires of me."

"Liar! You want martyrdom, you want to die so that you can sit at the right hand of your precious Christ."

"No!"

"Yes!" It was a prolonged hiss. "You *want* to die for your belief."

From another of the things, in the same voice, "You are no better than a suicide."

From another: "What does your God say about suicide?"

Kerr did not answer.

Softly, maliciously: "For suicide, you will burn in hell forever. Is that not your belief?"

Others joined in. "Is it?"

"Is it?"

No response.

"God is dead, priest," the leader said.

"Only a fool follows a dead god," said another.

Kerr straightened. "And only a greater fool fears a god that is supposed to be dead."

The thing looked past Kerr, to the crucifix. "Do you think I am frightened of your man on a tree?" It snarled, raised its arms—Kerr caught a glimpse of limbs that were only distantly human—and there was a crash from behind as one of the altar vases was knocked to the floor. Kerr spun in time to see the crucifix atop the altar totter, then rise into the air.

I won't move, I won't run, I won't abandon the others—

The crucifix rose higher, then moved forward, hovering ten feet above his head.

Something wet fell onto his face. He smeared it away with his hand. Blood. The crucified Christ was bleeding from wounds in its hands and feet, from the scourges, the crown of thorns—

"A false god, and a false church," the leader said.

"You found your Christ outside," another said. "Remember? Knocking on your door?"

From another: "It was not your Christ trying to get out."

Blood . . . everywhere.

"It was your Christ trying to get *in.*"

"False god," the things chanted, *"false church."*

Kerr did not move. To step back would be to admit fear; to step forward would only bring him closer to them. He closed his eyes, smelling the sharp scent of blood on his vestments. He raised his face heavenward in spite of the blood rain. "Our Father, who art in Heaven—"

"Hallowed be thy name," the thing finished for him.

"Blasphemy!" Kerr shouted.

"No," the thing said. "You are the blasphemer. You speak the lies." It stepped closer, its features clearer, hideous in their deformity. "Whom do you serve, priest?"

"God," Kerr whispered. "Our Lord Jesus Christ."

"Spawn of an idiot," it said, "you understand nothing! We were here long before your Christ crawled out from between a whore's legs. . . ."

And the others picked up the refrain. "Before the first Jew was ever born. Your words describe us—"

"But you do not name us."

"There is no Christ, no God."

"We take upon ourselves your words because they are convenient, they amuse us, and the fear they create serves us even better. You do our work for us. . . ."

"You help conceal our true nature. You are already working for us."

"In day you have some small advantage, but at night—"

"At night," the leader picked up, "at night *we* rule."

"Liar," Kerr said. "You know the truth, you know what you are—so does the rest of the world."

"And the truth will set them free?" Its voice was mocking in its false piety. "Then why has the truth not set *you* free? Why have not your symbols worked?" It leaned closer. "I give you

317

this last chance, false priest to a false god. Tell me where the others are, and you may yet live."

"No," Kerr said.

With a howl, the thing leaped upon the crucifix and ripped the head off the Christ and threw it across the nave.

Then it turned to Kerr. "You wish to be a martyr," it hissed. "Then so be it! Take the mark of your mad Messiah!"

Kerr screamed at the sudden tearing of his flesh. Gouts of blood seeped forth from the holes now piercing his palms. Blood spilled from his shoes, and he collapsed to one knee, his wounded feet no longer able to sustain his weight. Blood seeped down his forehead, into his eyes. He wore no crown of thorns, but the flesh circling his head was torn in a dozen places.

This isn't the way it was supposed to happen! His mind whirled through one agony after another. *My God, my God, why hast Thou forsaken me?* He caught himself. That was what the thing wanted, he thought, and through the pain, he managed, "Our Father . . ."

The thing leaned over him, its blackened, distended face only inches from his own. "Yes, my son," it said.

11

Tom stood at the end of another passage and squinted into the dark. Even the flare failed to cut through that pitch blackness, seeming to diminish into little more than a dull spark. He gradually realized that the flare was, indeed, dying out, long before it should have. It was as though the darkness were sucking the very life out of it.

"Better to let it go," Eric said, standing at the threshold of a large cavern. "It won't last more than a second in there anyway." He spoke absently, his head cocked to one side. He seemed to be listening to something beyond Tom's range of hearing. "The next entrance is straight ahead, through the cavern. We have to go in a direct line; any deviation and we'll never find our way out."

Eric took a tentative step into the cavern, and vanished almost instantly, passing into a darkness as solid as a wall.

After a moment he reappeared and removed his belt. "Take one end of this," he said, "and whatever happens, don't let go."

"Got it."

Once inside the cavern, Tom found himself in the middle of a darkness so complete, so oppressive, that he felt he was at the bottom of the ocean. When he breathed, it was with considerable effort; the air was thick, and no matter what he did, he couldn't seem to get enough of it into his lungs. Though Eric was only a few feet ahead, he could easily have been miles away. Their only connection, the only proof he wasn't alone in the cave, was the belt that drew him onward.

The ground was strewn with rocks and loose pebbles. He stumbled over one abrupt rise, and recovered quickly. He felt as if he were walking a ledge on a skyscraper, swaying from side to side with each vagrant wind.

They were not more than ten feet into the blackness when Eric cried out in pain and surprise.

"What—" Tom started, then felt it himself. Something sharp brushed his face in the darkness, then moved rapidly away with a strange, skittering noise. His grip on the belt loosened.

"What was that?"

"I don't know. Just don't stop, don't let go." Eric paused. "And whatever you do, don't look at them."

Thanks loads, Tom thought, and suppressed a shout as something with scales brushed against his leg. Out of the corner of his eye he glimpsed something—a brightness, like eyes—

Don't look! He forced his gaze downward, to where his feet were . . . somewhere. *One foot after another, left, right, left, right*— A sharp pain slashed up his right leg. He kicked wildly, connecting with a shape that withdrew quickly, making a high-pitched giggling noise.

"Damn," he muttered. He was limping now from the bite. How much farther did they have to go?

"Almost there," Eric said. "Just a few more—" His words were cut off by a muffled scream. Tom pulled forward on the rope, reached out to Eric—

One of the things was on Eric's face.

He could hear Eric wrestling with it, trying to get it loose. Tom grabbed at it, and something snapped rabidly at his hand. He jerked back as Eric shouted and flung the thing away from them. It landed not far away, with a scrabbling of claws on stone.

"You okay?" Tom asked.

"Yeah," Eric said, but his voice said otherwise. "Come on, we're nearly out."

They kept moving. Eric walked very deliberately through the darkness now, pausing at every other step, as though on a narrow, treacherous path. With that thought, Tom suddenly had the mental image of hundreds of twisted creatures ringing them on all sides, waiting with fast-fading patience for one of them to blunder off the path; and Eric, just ahead, as a center of bright power that even the servants of the cave didn't dare attack openly. But still waiting. Crouching—

"This way!" Eric said, and with a final rush as the creatures closed in, they entered a darkness that, though complete, was not quite so oppressive as the one they had just gone through. "We're past them. It's safe to use the flares, for a while." He lit one as he spoke.

"Jesus!" Tom said. In the light he could see that Eric's face was covered with scratches, long red streaks that worked up from his chin to his forehead. Fortunately, only a few of them had broken the skin to any depth.

Eric wiped a handkerchief across his face. It came away stained. "Damn it," he muttered. "I should've brought some water. We should wash out the cuts."

"Rabies?" Tom asked, examining his own wounds. The red welts were in the shape of wide, angular jaws.

"No," Eric said. "They weren't animals, exactly—more like allies of the cave. Not as powerful as the ones we're up against, but still dangerous. We can't afford to get careless."

They moved on toward the entrance to a narrow tunnel, barely wide enough for them to crawl through. It was the only opening they could see other than the one they'd come through—and Tom was in no mood to tempt whatever lived there again. Better to move forward.

Tom peered into the tunnel. It was just a foot or two wider than a man, and the floor was thick with a carpet of brown that edged up the sides toward the top.

He examined the brown coating more closely, and, with a gasp of shock and revulsion, realized what lined the tunnel.

Roaches. Thousands of them, in places piled at least two inches thick. They skittered over one another, antennae twitching. He could hear the sound of their feet climbing over each other, carapaces clicking.

"I can't do it," Tom said. He felt ashamed, but he simply could not bring himself to crawl through *that* for who knew how long. "I'd rather go back."

"I don't think we can," Eric said.

Tom felt trapped. Then a thought occurred to him: "Eric, are these things real?"

A pause, then, "No."

Tom stared hard at the roaches. They refused to disappear. But Eric had been correct so far. . . .

"All right," Tom said. "Give me the flare. I'll go first."

"You're sure?"

Tom took a deep breath, then crawled forward. At once there was a tremendous surge of activity among the roaches. They skittered over his arms and legs, dropping from the tunnel roof onto his head and neck, falling down the sides of his face.

Not real, not real, he kept repeating, sure that at any moment he was going to start shrieking like a child. Still, he kept moving, trying unsuccessfully to ignore the crunching beneath his palms and knees, the tickling of antennae in his ears. Tom crawled for what felt like hours until finally he emerged into a chamber only slightly larger than the one they had just left. He scrambled out of the tunnel, but still the roaches clung to him, falling only as he batted them away, tiny brown shells that hit the ground with a click before righting themselves and racing back into the tunnel.

"Pretty damn realistic illusion," he said, his knees threatening to give out. Eric clambered out of the tunnel and stood beside him, brushing off the roaches with frantic movements.

Peculiar, Tom thought. Why would Eric be batting at roaches if they weren't really there?

Answer: he wouldn't.

"Oh, shit," Tom muttered. "Oh, shit, shit, shit!" Now he was smashing them with redoubled vehemence, every inch of his skin crawling. A roach tumbled out of his hair. He ground it into the dirt with his heel. He knew he'd be feeling them in his clothes for months. "Why the hell didn't you tell me they were real?"

Eric barely looked up from his own efforts. "Would you really have wanted to know?"

Tom kept swatting. Eric was right, damn it, he was *always* right, it seemed. But that didn't make any difference.

"Forget it. But as soon as we get out of here . . ." He didn't know what to finish the threat with, but he was sure he'd find something. He stalked toward a boulder a few feet away. He had to sit down, if just for a second—

"Look out!" Eric yelled.

"What?" Tom turned in midstep, too late. The ground, which had appeared solid a second earlier, vanished beneath him.

He dropped down the side of a pit, fingernails digging into the dirt, scrabbling for a handhold. He slammed into the ground feet first. His right leg snapped. He screamed with the pain of it.

"Are you all right?" Eric called. The flare that Tom had dropped at the edge appeared in Eric's hand.

Tom squinted up at the flare, perhaps ten feet above him. It could just as well have been a mile. "I broke my goddamned leg." He tried to shift, to put the leg into a more comfortable position, but the slightest movement sent needles of pain through him. "You'll have to go on without me."

"Forget it," Eric said. The flare vanished, and for a moment Tom was thrust back into darkness. When Eric reappeared, the end of his belt was looped around his hand. "Grab hold," he said, and leaned into the pit as far as he could.

"You're out of your mind," Tom said. "I outweigh you by at least fifty pounds."

"Grab hold, damn it, before—"

Then Tom heard it. The ground beneath him was shifting slightly. Not like quicksand, but as if something were moving beneath it, digging its way to the surface.

Whatever it was, it was rising fast.

"Hurry!" Eric said.

Ignoring the pain that threatened to send his mind tottering into darkness, Tom grabbed the buckle with one hand, then the other. "Got it!"

"Hold on!" Eric shouted, then pulled. Tom felt himself suddenly yanked up and out like a sack of flour.

At the edge of the pit, Eric grabbed his shoulders and lifted him out. Tom glanced back, and for a moment he thought he glimpsed something silvery and soft appearing in the bottom of the pit, a wide, uneven mouth that worked wetly before it disappeared again beneath the soil.

He collapsed a few feet away, panting from the effort. "You're . . . stronger than you look."

Eric sat back on his haunches, breathing hard. Tom shifted, trying to shift his leg into a better position. Bone ground against bone. It was all he could do not to black out. He looked up, and his eyes met Eric's. They both knew what this meant. Though he was safe for now, there was no way that Tom could finish the rest of the trek.

"It's okay," Tom said. "I'll be fine. You just get going, all right? There's a lot more than either of us at stake here."

Eric looked into the bag of flares. "There's four left. I'll leave this one," he said of the one already lit, "and one more. I shouldn't need more than one each way to get where I have to go."

"Then get going already."

Eric hesitated. "I'll come back for you as soon as I'm finished."

"*Get out of here!*"

Reluctantly, Eric obeyed. In less than a minute he was visible as little more than a spot of red light in the night of the cave, and then he vanished altogether.

Tom cursed bitterly, suddenly realizing that he hadn't thought to give Eric his gun. Stupid, just plain stupid. Then his gaze returned to the pit, and he decided that it might be just as well. There was no way of telling if that thing at the bottom could climb.

It was not a comforting thought.

12

Liz started at the sound of a scream from somewhere inside the church—long, deep, horrible in its intensity. The thought that Kerr was in pain—if that was indeed he; the scream had been barely recognizable as human—was almost more than she could bear. But she couldn't leave Will behind, defenseless.

As it was, she worried about his sanity as much as her own. He continued to insist that he saw someone else in the room with them. And at moments she began to believe him. She had seen so much already. . . .

No, she thought, and backed away from the possibility. It *had* to be a hallucination. But she continued to watch with horrified fascination as Will's eyes followed something moving across the room. . . .

"Will?"

"Yes?" His voice was small in the room, only the left side of his face lit by the single candle.

Please, God, no more, she thought. "Is it—he—still here?"

"I can see him. I think he's trying to talk to me, but I can't hear him."

"What does he look like?"

"It's hard to tell." His voice was subdued. "Medium height. Dark hair. A flat nose. He's wearing a kind of greatcoat—I can't see much more than that. He keeps staring at something over here." He gestured toward his left.

"The candle?" Liz said.

"Maybe." He felt his way along the table, found the candle, and pulled it toward him. "Yes, it's the candle. He keeps staring at it. He looks tired, and—hungry." His head swiveled to one side. "He's going to the door now, crawling on his hands and knees."

Liz looked where he looked, but saw nothing.

Then: a scratching at the door.

"His fingers," Will said. "They're—bleeding."

13

Father Kerr reached up to touch his face, and found only soft, wet folds. His ribs scraped together agonizingly when he breathed. He took numb consolation from the fact that at least he wouldn't be breathing much longer.

The demon crouched near, looking at him with dispassionate interest. "Why do you do this to yourself?" it asked, its voice like dead leaves rustling along a sidewalk. "We know the others are near; we can smell your kind. We will find them. You can save us time, and save your life. We will let you go."

"Let you *go*," the dark chorus of things behind it chanted.

It crept back a step. "Or you will become like this," it said, and stepped back to allow him a glimpse of Ray, who stood by the wall, eyes blank, his bloody right hand wrapped in a shirt.

Kerr found the deputy through swollen eyes. "Ray . . . help me. Shoot . . . me." But Ray did not even acknowledge his existence.

"Ah, suicide again," the leader said with glee. "A mortal sin; oh no, no, we can't have that. We will attend to your passing. You will become one with us, like this." It pointed a claw to one of the things behind him. It separated from the rest and stepped out of the shadows.

"Dear God," Kerr said at the sight of what had once been Mrs. Graham. It looked down at him through alien eyes.

"You may have free passage; all you need do is tell us where—" Suddenly it stopped, rose, towering over Kerr like a great, shadowy bat, listening to . . . something. Then, suddenly, it howled. The sound shook the floor. Its face betrayed rage beyond anything Kerr could comprehend.

"*You!*" It grabbed Kerr by the collar, lifted him up within an inch of its face. Its eyes burned into him, its breath was foul. Then it threw him across the room. He landed hard by the altar stairs. Something in his back snapped. When he opened his eyes, he could dimly make out the thing as it flew past the horde of demons and out of the church.

When it was gone, the rest advanced toward him.

Please, God, Kerr thought as they closed in upon him like a black wave, *let all this not have been in vain.*

14

It knows, Eric thought, and the voice came again into his head.

(*. . . tried, I'm sorry . . . it feels my thoughts . . . it knows you're here. . . .*)

(*It's all right. I'm here now.*) Eric moved into the final chamber, his head pounding. As he'd suspected, the gate the demons had entered through was not far from where he'd left Tom, but it was better not to have brought the constable with him. If something went wrong here, Tom might still have a chance of surviving.

The cavern was round, flat in its middle, the roof curved down toward the floor. Stalactites dangled from the roof of the chamber like precariously balanced teeth, sharp and threatening. A backpack, a baseball bat, and several lengths of rope lay a few feet away from a thick stone slab in the chamber's center. Beside Eric's feet were a pistol and a knife coated with dried blood. At the far end of the cavern, one wall shimmered with a terrible glow that was impossible to look at directly. At least he wouldn't need his last flare.

He stepped toward the slab, pushing against the thick, resistant air. Every step forward cost him; he was nearly exhausted, the sense of pervasive evil so oppressive that he found it hard to concentrate. Ahead, a figure lay stretched out upon the cruel stone, his arms slashed. The body was withered, had in places even collapsed in upon itself, as if it had been devoured from the inside out. The cheeks were hollow, the hair drawn back, the feet curled inward—little more than a dried husk. He leaned over the figure, and saw in its face complete and utter despair.

Alive, and yet not alive, he thought. Dead, and yet not allowed to die. This, he realized, was the heart of the cave: one human soul, suspended between life and death, that kept the gate open. An unwilling conduit for the demons' entrance into this world.

(. . . please, hurry . . . let me go, let me sleep. . . .)

Sleep. It would be wonderful to sleep, Eric thought, to give in to the weariness, to go away and never return. He looked down at the plaintive eyes focused on something beyond what even he could see.

(. . . please . . .)

He could not help the man on the stone slab.

But he could at least bring peace—and with it, destroy the demons' sole connection to their source of power.

All he had to do was to push this one soul over the edge, tip the odds in favor of the death it craved so greatly.

Steeling himself against the agony that hammered at the back of his eyes, he hurried back to the discarded pistol and checked the chambers. Three shots left. He returned to the emaciated figure, and for a moment he thought its eyes flickered, found him, and gave wordless approval.

"I'm sorry," Eric said, and placed the muzzle of the gun against the figure's temple.

(. . . *please, hurry . . . do what you must . . . so cold . . . want to sleep. . . .)*

"Forgive me."

He pulled the trigger.

The first bullet sprayed bone and brain tissue across the slab. Beyond it, the gate flickered. Wild colors pulsed through it. He thought something moved on the other side, but refused to look more closely. Eric found he was crying.

The second bullet blew apart the rest of the head.

He hoped that would be enough. If not, he'd have to fire a third time, and he was not sure he could do so. But after a moment he felt the imprisoned soul rise up and out; he felt its presence in the room, and found in it no reproach for what he had done—only relief, and a sense of freedom.

Then, like a wisp of smoke in a brisk wind, it was gone.

The gate shimmered one last time, then subsided to a dull blue pulsation. It was still there, but without its link to this world it could no longer sustain the creatures that had come through during the last two days. Soon enough, they would begin to feel the consequences of their support being cut off.

The heart was dead.

Eric slumped wearily to his knees, head resting against the cold stone slab.

Distantly, through the pain and exhaustion, he thought of Liz and the rest, and hoped that he had been in time.

15

Kerr swam up from semiconsciousness at the first scream. It was not a sound that could have come from any human throat. He opened his swollen eyes. The church was lighter now, but the light was not coming from outside.

The screaming was coming from the things. First one, then the others cried out in agony. The features on their stolen faces ran, the husks no longer able to support the terrible forces within them. They beat at the walls and the floor, howling in fury—to no purpose.

One by one, they exploded into flame.

They did it, Kerr thought distantly. *Thank you, God.* The flame leaped from one of the things to another, roaring through the pews. The banners hanging from the ceiling burst into flame.

They were dying, but they were taking the church with them.

It was a small enough price to pay. At least now he could die with peace of mind. He lay back, ready to welcome the darkness that beckoned him.

Then, as from far away: *Liz! Will!*

He sat up, cursing his weakness. He couldn't let himself die, not yet. Liz and Will wouldn't know of the fire until it was on them, and by then it would be too late. He had promised that they would be safe; he couldn't abandon them.

He dragged himself up onto his knees, but the effort was too much, and he fell. The smoke was filling the room quickly now. He pushed his hands ahead of him and clawed at the carpeting, dragging himself on his stomach. One foot. Two. Lights were strobing behind his eyes. No, not yet, he thought. He couldn't give in, not—

A shadow fell over him.

One of the things, howling in its death agony, fell upon him, found him through eyes almost sealed by running, smoking flesh. "No," it whispered, "stay . . . with us."

Its hands clawed at Kerr's throat, and with its last remaining strength it threw him toward the inferno, toward the wall on the other side of the room—

No, Kerr thought futilely. *Not fair, not fair.*

The darkness came even before he slammed headfirst into the wall.

16

Tom looked up at the noise. It was a shrieking, lunatic wind that roared over his head, and its passing filled him with a dread that stilled his lungs.

It's coming for me, he thought.

But it paused only an instant, then went on, as though

he were of no importance. With a howl, it rushed into the deeper part of the caves.

Toward Eric.

In agony, Tom hobbled forward, following the sound.

17

Eric felt the creature's approach even before he heard it. Then the cry, "You *dare!*"

At the other end of the cavern, the demon-thing appeared, emerging from a dark cloud. Its eyes were huge, golden, slit down the center like a serpent's; its skin was blackened, its face elongated, its hands misshapen. Its outline was vague, and parts of it shifted in and out of focus as it struggled for stability in the absence of the gate's sustaining power.

The first one through.

The only one that was now able to stay in this world even with the destruction of the gate.

"You *dare* desecrate *my* church!" It pointed at the body on the slab. "You will take this one's place! Or find me another! Which will it be?"

Which will it be, indeed, Eric thought. He was tired, so tired. But even now, somewhere inside him, a flame burned, a last reserve of power that burned so brightly he feared losing himself in it.

Not yet, no, not yet.

He was still holding the pistol. It would be useless against the creature; but the final bullet was his last line of defense. The thing would not use him to reopen the gate.

The last bullet was for him.

But if he would die, then he would take the thing right to hell with him.

"No deal," he said.

So many screams! Liz pressed her hands to her ears. The scratching at the door was louder now. She couldn't just sit there, she thought, and started at a sudden sound from the bottom of the stairs.

Will heard it just as she did. "Someone's coming!" he said—and the scratching stopped.

"Ssh!" Liz ran to the doorway. Someone—or something—was removing the debris that camouflaged the stairwell entrance. In an instant, the opening was exposed. A light appeared at the bottom of the stairs.

"Father!"

Father Kerr ascended the stairs, immaculate in his vestments, holding a large white candle. "You must hurry," he said, but his voice was soft, oddly unworried.

Liz took Will by the arm, helped him up. "Where are we going?" he asked.

"Out!" she said. "Come on, we've got to hurry."

She guided him past Kerr to the stairs and started down. Behind them, Kerr lingered in the doorway. She heard him say something, speaking not to them, but to someone else. He then followed them down.

They were halfway to the bottom when they smelled the smoke.

"Fire!" Liz said. They stepped past the debris into the basement proper. It was filling with smoke.

Kerr moved ahead of them. "You must come this way, quickly."

"But what about the man upstairs?" Will asked.

"He didn't know he was dead," Kerr said. "He believed he was abandoned. He will find peace now."

They climbed quickly. Liz guided Will up the steps, wishing Kerr would slow down, give her a hand, but he was too far ahead, leading the way.

They entered the sacristy. Black, oily smoke poured into the room. "Stay low, where the air is better," Kerr said. "We'll go out the back way."

As they passed the doorway that led into the church, Liz glimpsed the blaze that roared through the body of the church. The fire danced up walls, leaped up draperies and along pews, and came together into a huge smoking pyre in the center of the church. She gasped as she saw that some of the things were still moving in the heart of the flame.

"Do not look at them," Kerr said. "Look only ahead."

She grasped Will tighter, guiding him away from the horror in the church.

"I could see them," Will said, looking back. "I saw—"

"Best not to talk about it," Kerr said. Liz marveled at how calm he seemed, how unruffled. There was something about his manner that helped to raise her spirits—that, and the implications of what she had seen: somehow, Eric and Tom had succeeded!

They climbed out into the cool night air, smoke roiling out behind them. As soon as they were a safe distance from the church, Liz let go of Will's arm. Her knees were no longer willing to support her, and she collapsed on the dewy grass.

"Thank you, Father," she said. "Father?"

Kerr was gone.

"Where did he go? Will?"

"I don't know," Will said. "He was here just a minute ago. I—" He paused. "Liz, I could see him. Why is it I can't see you, but I could see *him*?"

19

The thing flew at Eric across the chamber. What hit him was part wolf, part bat, part demon—a shifting, changing thing that snarled and cut. The impact knocked the revolver out of Eric's hands. It tumbled across the chamber, clattering to a stop by the entrance. The thing's flesh burned his hands as he seized it around the neck, trying to push it away. They struggled in the middle of the cavern, each momentarily unable to gain the advantage. Its face was barely an inch from his. Its huge canines snapped at him, its eyes burned with rage and a frightening intelligence.

Then, abruptly, it reached into his mind, dug into the soft tissue, chewing at what it found.

(no, get out of me, get out of me, getoutgetoutgetout!)

The flame within him fluttered, but held fast.

"Get *out!*" Eric shouted, and threw the thing back across the chamber. Its claw ripped a long gash along his arm. It landed on its feet and turned to him, snarling. He could see the triumph in its eyes at having drawn first blood.

It clawed at the floor of the cavern, and the ground exploded at Eric's feet, a geyser of rock and dirt. He jumped away, the flame within him feeding strength into his muscles. He dove behind the slab as rocks slammed into the wall above his head like mortar fire.

It was toying with him, confident in its superior abilities.

The thing reared back for another charge.

This is it, Eric thought.

The sound of a gunshot echoed just as it leaped at him. The thing howled, missed its mark, but landed unhurt, turning in its fury to the source of this interference.

Tom crouched in the entrance to the chamber, covered with dirt and scratches, both hands gripping his revolver. He fired again, but it moved too fast for him, too fast for anyone. The bullet hit the wall and ricocheted, knocking a stalactite from the chamber roof.

The roof. Eric looked up at the uneven rows of stalactites that dangled above them.

There was a way.

The risk was great, but if he didn't do something, they were both dead anyway.

In the second before the thing could spring again, Eric reached inside, found the flame that trembled within him, and fueled it with his own soul.

He let himself go, felt the dizzying explosion of power that rushed up within him.

Father, he thought.

And he was not alone.

Now, the voice whispered in his mind, the voice of calm power that added its own force to his own. *Strike!*

The sun burned within him then, and he became more than he was. Across the chamber, the thing sensed the change, and turned to him—too late to stop the light that filled his mind.

Eric threw his head back, his body shaking with the effort, and *screamed.* The chamber rocked with the sound, and more than the sound—a power, old and finally awake, that slammed into the roof of the chamber, knocking loose the stalactites. Instantly, the air was thick with spears of limestone. They rocketed toward the floor.

The thing saw them coming, too late. A long, sharp stone lanced through its chest, pinning it to the ground. It howled in agony, fighting to pull out the spear. Eric's sudden cry echoed the thing's. One of the smaller stalactites had pierced his side.

It hurts, Father, oh God, it hurts.

He felt the blackness that had come before returning now in strength. Part of him longed to give in, but another part, newly reborn, resisted. He felt that which he had released moving inside him, growing. Almost blind with pain, he pulled the bloody stone from his side and half crawled, half staggered the few feet to where the thing thrashed madly. It hissed at him as he raised the blood-coated stone above its throat, clawed frantically at the other stone that pinned it down, and finally threw it off with a shriek as Eric brought down the blade, a stone guillotine falling, a dark, decapitating death. . . .

They both screamed.

20

"Hey! What the hell happened?"

R.T. Williams rushed down the road toward Liz, his eyes fixed on the burning church. "I called the fire station, and the ambulance. Anybody hurt in there?"

Liz could see other people leaving their houses, rushing to investigate.

"I don't—" She stumbled over her words, not knowing where to begin or what to say—or not to say.

Will rose to his feet behind her. "She's in shock, R.T. We've got to get her to a warm place."

"Will needs a doctor himself," Liz said. "He's been hurt."

Behind them, the church burned with a terrible vengeance. "Was anybody in there?" R.T. asked.

"Nobody who can be saved now," Liz said, wondering, *Where's Eric?*

21

For a moment, Tom wasn't sure whether his eyes were open or closed. Then he began to make out stars. *So what the hell am I doing out in the cold, on my back?*

He tried to sit up; there was a terrible pain in his right leg. The last thing he remembered was seeing Eric fighting the thing in the cave. He remembered shooting at it, a darkness rushing toward him, and that was all. Except—he thought he remembered being carried bodily out of the cave, and looking up to see the face of someone he didn't recognize. An older man. With black hair.

But that wasn't possible.

Suddenly there was a rumbling beneath him. An explosion. Moments later, there was a second. The dynamite? he thought. Then someone raced out of the cave mouth and jumped down beside him just as a third explosion ripped through the cave mouth. Even from here, he could hear and feel tons of rocks falling, filling in the cave.

He turned to the figure who lay unmoving beside him. It was the old man again. But as he looked closer, the face blurred and became hard to look at. Tom rubbed at his eyes, and now he saw only Eric's face, quiet and at peace. Seeing things, he thought, and took Eric's wrist. He felt for a pulse and was relieved to find one. Eric was unconscious, but alive. Then he saw blood seeping out of Eric's side, staining the ground beneath him.

Tom fumbled in his utility sack for the last flare. He lit the red stick and waved it above his head, hoping that someone would see them.

"Don't you dare die on me," Tom said to the still figure beside him. "I won't let you." There was no response. "Damn you, this is my town!" He reached out to touch Eric, to reassure himself that he was still breathing.

"C'mon, somebody," he said, over and over. *"Hurry!"*

EPILOGUE

It was quiet. Nothing moved in the darkness that was, he realized, only another shade of light. In this place, day and night were one, and both were pleasant, warm, accepting. . . . He drifted through long corridors where people were discussing things that he knew were important, but that he couldn't quite understand. Then, though he resisted, he gradually found himself drifting back the way he had come, toward the other light, and though he wanted nothing more than to remain where he was, wrapped in the arms of this special night, he allowed himself to swim slowly up. . . .

"Welcome back."

Eric blinked. There was a gumminess in the corners of his eyes that hurt when he tried to focus. He went to rub them, and found his arms attached to long tubes.

"Here," Liz said, and touched the corners of his eyes with a moist cloth. It helped, and he finally found her, framed against a white wall. Daylight poured into the room from a window somewhere behind where he lay.

He licked his lips. "What day?" he asked. His voice was hoarse.

"Wednesday," Liz said, and pressed a gentle, restraining hand against his chest. "You've been out of it ever since they brought you in Saturday night." She stroked his hair. "You had us awfully worried there for a while. How do you feel?"

"Terrible," he said. Every inch of his body was sore; he was becoming steadily more aware of a sharp throbbing in his side. He moved his hand toward the spot, but Liz took his hand, held it in hers.

"Best to leave that alone for a while, until the stitches do their job. You had a hole big enough to park a car in, not to mention infection and some other complications I'll tell you about some other time. But none of the vital organs were damaged, so you should be pretty much clear unless there's a recurrence of the infection."

"What a . . . *cheery* bedside manner you have," he said.

"Is this any better?" she asked, and kissed him gently. "Does that hurt?"

"I'll let you know." He smiled at her, and even that seemed to require more effort than usual. He went to touch his face—

"Don't touch the bandages," she said, then picked up the telephone and dialed.

"Yes, Mommy."

She took a playful swipe at him, then pressed the receiver to her ear. "Tom? He's up. Okay." She replaced the phone.

"Tom," Eric said, memory flooding back. "How—"

"Tom's fine, in better shape than you are, as a matter of fact. He'll be here in a few minutes, probably with a doctor. We should get our stories straight before they get here. According to the reports Tom filed with the county sheriff's office, you two were poking around in the caves, trying to figure out what happened to Sam, when the whole thing collapsed. All you remember is the rocks falling. Got it?"

Eric nodded. It all seemed so far away, fragments from another life.

"As for the rest of it, well, this should fill in the gaps." Liz picked up a copy of the *North Cutler Journal* and handed it to him. "I'm afraid I still have a hard time talking about it."

"That's all right," Eric said. The article was circled in ink, though that wasn't necessary. With a pang, he recognized a photograph of St. Benedict's—or, rather, what remained of it. The article was datelined Monday, two days ago.

Dredmouth Point, ME—The worst fire in recent memory took place Saturday night in Dredmouth Point. According to police reports, over 300 residents were attending a Saturday evening Mass at St. Benedict's Catholic Church when a fire burst out in the main body of the church. The blaze quickly engulfed the entire structure, taking the lives of the 357 people trapped inside, including the parish priest, Father Duncan Kerr, and Deputy Constable Raymond Price, who is reported to have come to the aid of the victims.

It is estimated that due to the structure's age and composition, the fire spread far more rapidly than in a more modern building, cutting off the escape route of those within.

"It was terrible, just terrible," said Robert T. Williams, proprietor of a nearby store and one of the first to reach the scene. "I remember hearing an explosion, then the whole church blew. It was like the place was made of paper; it just went up fast. By the time we got there, the heat was so intense, you couldn't get within a hundred feet of the place." Fire trucks arriving on the scene were able only to confine the fire to the church itself, saving nearby homes and businesses.

"There's no reason right now to suspect arson," Constable Tom Crandall said, noting that the church had frequently experienced trouble with its electrical wiring in the past. An official statement concerning the cause of the fire is still forthcoming, but a spokesman for the investigative team indicated that, owing to the extent of the destruction, "we may never be able to pinpoint the exact cause."

The release of a complete list of the victims is pending identification of the bodies, said to be ongoing at this time, and notification of next of kin.

"It's a terrible, terrible tragedy," Crandall said, himself injured the same night while investigating a recent injury in the Indian Caves area. (See related story, page 7.) Crandall also recommended a posthumous commendation for Deputy Constable Raymond Price, who is reported to have been on the scene and "gave his life trying to get those people out of there," said Crandall.

Bishop Edward C. O'Leary, reached in Portland, was distressed at the tragedy, and urged prayer for the survivors.

Eric set down the newspaper. He'd read all he would ever want to about what had happened. He thought of the dinner with Father Kerr, and found to his frustration that he could not bring Kerr's face to mind.

"He refused to stay with Will and me in the room," she said. "He went out to confront those things. He bought all of us time. But, Eric, I swear to you, *he came to us.* He got us out of there before the whole place burned down. It was either him or—or a part of him. I know it sounds crazy, but—"

"I believe you," Eric said. The door opened. Tom entered in a wheelchair, his foot propped up in a cast, followed by a doctor.

"Well," the doctor said, "so we're up and around." He extended a hand. "I'm Doctor Alridge. You can call me Ben. How do you feel?"

"Okay," Eric said, as Alridge lifted his shirt and probed his chest with a stethoscope. Eric grimaced at the sight of the sutures sewn in a broad, jagged circle on his side, but said nothing. He was alive, and that was good enough.

Alridge thumped Eric's chest. "Sounds good," he said.

"He won't sound good for long if you keep hitting him in the chest like that," Tom said.

"Don't believe it when people tell you that doctors make the worst patients," Alridge said. "The police have it over us by light years. When he hasn't been racing around in that wheelchair like it was a mini—police car, he's been in here every day, looking in on you."

"Professional curiosity," Tom said.

"Yes, well, that professional curiosity of yours is going to lead to a relapse." He looked back at Eric. "Your friend here got bit by some animal while the two of you were waiting for help. Ended up with a pretty powerful infection. To top it off, he's refusing to accept rabies vaccinations."

"Don't need 'em," Tom said. "I have that on the very best authority."

"We'll see," Alridge said, picking up the chart that dangled over the foot of Eric's bed. "You're pretty lucky yourself. Coming around even faster than we could have hoped, given the injuries."

"How long until I can get out?"

"Maybe the end of the week. Now that the observation period is over, the constable can probably leave tomorrow, provided he doesn't overexert himself."

"Rely on it," Tom said.

"Well," Alridge said, "I've got a few more calls to make. I'll be by to chat in more detail in about an hour. See you then."

As soon as the door closed, Eric turned to Tom. "What about Sam? And Will? How are they?"

"Well enough," Tom said. "Sam came out of the coma about the same time the cave went up. He was pretty upset about losing his find, but now that the place is solid rock, even he's willing to admit defeat. As for Will," he added, "the ophthalmologists can't find any physical damage. Liz says she saw a film on his eyes, but it disappeared by the time the docs got a look at it—so naturally they don't believe it.

"They think it's psychological, something to do with seeing the church and everyone in it go up in flames, and not being able to do anything about it." Tom frowned. "Naturally, we couldn't tell them everything that really happened, or they'd have us all under the microscope. But they say he's seeing a little more now than he did yesterday, so there's a chance that he'll regain some, maybe even most, of his sight."

"A little trauma goes a long way," Liz said. "That's the official reason for why everyone left in town is a day behind the rest of the world. Every psychologist in the state has been down here talking to people, trying to figure out how trauma over a tragedy could make everyone lose a day."

Tom sighed. "All those experts, all that work, and I don't think they'll ever figure out what happened. At times, I think it all must've been just some bad dream, a nightmare to end all nightmares. But then I look down at this thing," he said, gesturing at the cast on his leg, "and I know that it was all true—God help us. At least it's over now."

"Is it over, Eric? Finally?" Liz asked.

"I think so," Eric said, as the drowsiness returned. "I do think so."

Then he lay back and let the warm, healing darkness drift back behind his eyes.

2

When they released him from Cutler Memorial Hospital, Eric took the long way back to the Point. He drove the old Datsun down the sun-strewn Cutler roads to the cemetery at the edge of town.

He stood before his father's headstone. From it he felt

only peace, only silence. He shared that peace. The nightmares were gone at last.

He was free now. But he no longer felt lost, rootless. He had seen too much for that—and felt that he was still linked with the world he had discovered.

Which was part of why he knew he had to return, to see his father just once more. To say thanks.

And good-bye.

3

Eric Matthews pulled the Datsun over beside the road leading away from Dredmouth Point and onto the highway. He had considered continuing on into town, but there was no need. He had done that which he had been summoned to do. And, judging from Liz's story, he suspected that now there would always be someone watching over the town in his absence.

Besides, he had always hated good-byes; the world was too finite for them. He would always know where to find them all, Tom, Will, and the rest, when and if he ever needed them. Telephone numbers and addresses were no longer relevant.

He would just know.

He felt a delicate finger tracing a line down his neck. "Where to now?"

He turned to Liz, sitting beside him. The rear seat was filled with her bags. The book—her *novel*, he corrected himself—was packed away separately in the trunk. Priorities, Liz had explained.

Where to?

"West," he said, and started the car. "Maybe Seattle."

It felt *right*, somehow.